CJ Butler

THE JAPSON CLUB

The Japson Club
Copyright © 2017 CJ Butler

All rights reserved. No part of this publication may be reproduced, stored on a retrieval system, or transmitted, in any form or by any means, without the prior permission in writing of the author and publisher, nor be otherwise circulated in any form of binding or cover other than that in which it is published and without a similar condition including this condition being imposed on the subsequent publisher.

All characters and events in this publication, other than those clearly in the public domain, are fictitious and any resemblance to real persons living or dead, is purely coincidental.

www.cjbutler.net

Tellwell Talent
www.tellwell.ca

ISBN
978-1-77370-277-3 (Paperback)
978-1-77370-278-0 (eBook)

In loving memory of Tom

And with thanks to my friends:

Julia
(Developmental Editor and my
own personal Francesca)

Susie
(Who so generously shared
the wonderful Tom)

And to my Editor, Bridget, who
helped make this story sing.

PROLOGUE

The lashing of the rain came as a constant metallic roar on the roof. The gusting wind howled in the surrounding trees and forced the vehicle sideways. Her heart hammered throughout her entire being and her stomach constricted ever tighter with her rising panic, as she finally neared the end of what felt like an interminable and desperate race to the finish. Emerging from the black of the country lane, the lights of the village were an inebriated blur, smeared by the wipers which couldn't keep up with the blinding haze of gushing water. Pulling up, she threw open her door, feeling the cold deluge instantly soaking through her jacket, beating on her scalp and running down her collar. Her feet were immediately sodden in the cascade of water which bypassed the overburdened drains and streamed turbulently down the road. Throwing the door shut she ran, barely able to see, up the pathway to the main door of the church, desperate to get to him first.

The church was dark and the door stood ominously ajar. Wiping at her eyes, and hearing her breathing loud and ragged she pushed it open far enough for her to enter as subtly as she could. The interior was menacingly black and she crouched for a moment, listening and waiting for her eyes to adjust. There was no sound; just the weather howling outside. The faintest light became visible, seeping from one of the ante-rooms at the far end of the church. She crept along the aisle and towards the light, stopping at the opening to the corridor, listening intently.

A line of something with a sheen like ink crept across the floor, reflecting the dim light leaking through the door which was open a crack at the end of the corridor. Creeping forward inch by inch, like a prey animal about to be set upon from any direction, she forced herself towards it. Her hand shook uncontrollably and dread rose in her gut as she reached to push open the door. Then she saw. He was there, among the hanging robes, lying next to the body of a colossal man sprawled face-down, in a rapidly spreading pool of his own blood. All sounds deadened as she rushed towards him, gasping and feeling adrenalin flash through her body. Blood was matting his hair and splattered across his face, and in slow motion his eyes opened, meeting hers.

"Anna," he whispered.

NEW ARRIVALS

7 months earlier…

"Heading down now. Meet me for a conference tonight?"
So he was back again already. The hubbub of the sunlit coffee shop receded into the background as she read the words glowing so shamelessly on the screen of her phone. The apparent innocence of the request veiled his real meaning. The tips of her fingers hovered over her lips to hide her reflexive smile as she remembered the heat and the play in his eyes, the last time they had been together.
Suddenly conscious of a beckoning wave from her colleague, she wrenched her mind back to her imminent client meeting and thrust her phone in her bag. The complication of his return would have to wait until later.

• • • • • •

The engine of the Land Rover idled as Anna came to a halt at the end of the driveway and put her head out of the window, savouring the sweet evening air and gazing at the beauty around her.
"Wow, loving this!" she breathed.

The sun slid lower, creating golden drama in the tree tops high above the driveway which swept round a gentle bend, banked on either side by mature rhododendrons. The enormous blooms hung heavily, luminous in the evening light against the backdrop of dark, glossy green leaves. Stately iron gates framed the entrance and stood open invitingly while still portraying a hint of austerity. The extravagant 'R' wrought into the ironwork asserted the old-world ego of the Rosemount estate, fully established and comfortable in its rightful place on the English landscape. The grandeur of the place had struck a resounding note during her first visit in the broad light of day, and now, in the still of the summer evening, it exuded a magical and even more exclusive flavour.

Stepping from the office into the warmth of the evening, Pete Southington stretched his tall upright frame, and sighed contentedly as he cast his eyes over the beautiful Sussex Downs as they rose, softly enveloping the scene; the perfect backdrop, hazy in the evening light.

"Pete; remember we have to go in 45 minutes," prompted Penelope as she passed him, seeing her husband sliding comfortably into a reverie.

"I know. I'm expecting our latest arrival any minute so we should be in good time," he replied as he checked his watch. It was his favourite time of day. The sunset glinted off the crystals sporadically distributed through the pebbles in the turning circle, and cast a resplendent glow on the fine old buildings.

"Ah, as if on cue," he said to himself, as a Land Rover pulling a horse trailer rolled into the yard.

Tom, Anna's spirited ex-steeplechaser thoroughbred, snorted and stamped, frustrated by his confinement inside the trailer. He knew he was somewhere new; the air was full of other horses and unfamiliar earth. Anna stepped from the Land Rover, appreciating the wholesome crunch of the stones beneath her boots, and the evensong of a blackbird which rung out pure and clear from the dignified old trees.

"Evening! It's been a while since we met, Anna," said Pete, appearing next to her with his hand extended, appreciating her smile she turned to meet him. She immediately recalled his attractiveness from their first encounter, three months previously. His receding fair hair was close cropped under his flat cap and his sparkling blue eyes were set in a strong square-jawed, good-looking face which broke into a broad smile. "We finally came through with a stable for you!" he said as he led her round the end of a row of stables to where a large stall was ready and waiting. The perfect woodwork of the stables met the pale well-swept concrete cleanly the entire stretch of the block. Everything carried an air of quality. It was a far cry from the scruffy facility she had just driven from, which had been Tom's lodging for the months since she had bought him.

"This place is immaculate!" Anna marvelled.

"Ha! I get on the cases of messy people," he said jovially, briefly reacquainting himself with Anna's striking appearance; her arresting, somewhat aristocratic features and slender body. She flicked her lustrous dark hair which hung long down her back as she gazed around her. "Repeat offenders find anything they leave out gets chucked!" continued Pete with a good-natured laugh. "I like military order and cleanliness round the yard."

"Noted!" said Anna, taking that as her friendly warning to conform to Rosemount standards. She had never boarded at such an exclusive yard and was anxious to measure up, feeling a little out of place. Pete smiled as he led her round to the paddock allotted for Tom. She had a nice way about her; he sensed a definite hint of smart humour beneath her polite exterior.

Their final stop was the tack room, which was possibly the most luxurious Anna had ever seen. Benches ran the perimeter of the room and everything was clad in pale wood which gave the feel of a Swedish sauna. It was warm and there was a suggestion of balsam on the air and Anna felt again the slight status anxiety, as though she and Tom had been promoted and given the key to the executive lounge too soon.

"This one is yours," said Pete, indicating a large locker. "Huh, that's quite some breakage," he commented, distracted by the one thing out of order in the room. A stylishly scarred polo mallet hung from the handle of one of the lockers, having obviously seen its last game; the bamboo of the shaft was split and splintered. It looked aesthetically aged and heroic and Anna guessed it was the only kind of mess allowed. Pete looked swiftly at his watch. "As long as you're sure you don't need a hand, I need to dash. Give us a call if you need anything; numbers are in the information pinned outside your stable."

The yard was peaceful, with no sign of anyone else. Tom willingly sprang from the trailer, alert and with head held impossibly high. He wheeled in circles for a moment, towering athletically over Anna before she could assert some authority and walk him round to his paddock, pleased no-one was there to judge her momentary incompetence. After a moment of amusement, watching Tom as he bucked and charged in his new field, she hurried to stow her supplies and equipment, conscious of daylight slipping away. The sun had set and the alluring stillness of night descended on everything still glowing with the warmth of the day. She inhaled the scented, silken air deeply. Then hooves sounded on the driveway and the dim shape of a horse and rider rounded the bend. The horse was an impressive hunter type, around 17 hands, and walked at the enthusiastic click of one ready for his supper. The rider appeared to glance in her direction momentarily before they continued round to the stables.

It was on her final run to the tack room, laden with an assortment of Tom's blankets and pausing to retrieve a wayward leg strap that was trailing round her ankle, that a voice came from the dark.
  "Help you with that?"
  She turned to see the same rider who had ridden by earlier.
  "Yes, thank you," she said, unable to discern much of him due to the rapidly darkening evening and the heap of blankets obscuring her view. He took the bulky pile from her and strode ahead towards the tack room.

Once inside Anna saw him clearly, his good looks striking her immediately; close cut dark hair framed rich brown eyes and serenely handsome features. His build was robust - that of a man who spent his time hauling horses and hay bales around, rather than playing in the gym. He looked dapper and masculine in his country attire, the collar of a pale shirt with small checks peeking from a lightweight Barbour jacket. Anna usually made fun of this kind of dress sense whenever her friends adopted it for fashion purposes, but this guy wore it well with an unconscious ease which made it natural and unpretentious.

"I'm Anna."

"Damien," he responded simply, not looking at her and shrugging off his jacket, tossing it on one of the benches. She felt struck dumb by this new stranger and couldn't think of anything to ask, though felt an immediate frisson of interest.

"You were riding late," she commented with the only thing which came to mind.

"Yep. Time got away," he responded shortly as he turned and hung up the bridle he had been carrying.

She studied the back of him, noting how well-groomed he was; the neat perfection of his hair shaved close at the nape of his bronzed neck and the evident quality and excellent fit of his clothes, hanging well from him. It was unusual to meet a man so well turned out. Even the scuffs of dust on his breeches appeared stylish and intentionally placed. He seemed unconscious of her, completely uninterested. Abruptly she became aware of her worn jeans and tee-shirt, scruffy from a full day on horse duty, and felt an intense need for a shower or at least a hairbrush; the exclusivity of Rosemount drew a well-bred, well-heeled crowd and she was plainly not making the grade.

The absence of conversation was palpable, but her mind was blank and the silence stretched out. Feeling uncomfortable, Anna busied herself piling the folded fleece blankets she had brought with her into the top of her locker. Suddenly aware of his glance at her, she turned her eyes to him and forced a question:

"So how far did you go this evening?"

"About ten miles. My horse needs to get fit," he said with a slight shrug before falling yet again into silence.

"It seems very quiet here tonight," she said, feeling slightly exasperated and trying a final time to be conversational.

"Sunday night," he commented matter-of-factly, rubbing a smudge off his saddle. "And the bar's not open."

"I bet it's popular," she commented.

"Yeah; given the polo crowd and the hunt. You know horse people and their drunken debauchery," he said, with a faint wry smile which warmed his features appealingly.

"True," she answered, but at the same time wondering what kind of debauchery to expect. Maybe the unorthodox mix of hunters rubbing shoulders with the polo set created some interesting evenings at the bar.

"You know it," said Damien, looking at her steadily for a moment. Then he picked up his jacket, grabbed his keys from the table, and was gone.

Anna was alone again. What a bizarre exchange. Hardly anything had been said and there was the sense of floundering in the protracted silence which had enveloped the whole meeting, out of her depth and decidedly out of his league. His abruptness had shut her down and it seemed strange that he even bothered to help her. Regardless; she felt pleased with the new place she had found. A new life chapter had opened, and with it a feeling of unpredictability and excitement.

The hard light of day washed everything brightly that Monday morning. Dominik gave a sigh as a line of red brake lights shone in the narrow lane ahead. He leaned out of the side window to see what the holdup was. Would he ever get there? He looked at his watch; he had been on the road for well over eight hours. The darkness which had shrouded the lonely moors at the start of his journey had given way to the quiet glimmering dawn and the solitary pleasure of witnessing the sun emerge burning over the land. Then full daylight brought the population explosion on the roads. Everyone and their dog was out – as his wife would say - and they were all in his way.

"C'mon, c'mon!" he muttered he watched a car pulling a caravan tentatively negotiate the entrance to a campsite, crawling at snail's pace. A horn sounded up ahead; obviously another frustrated driver. He took a long breath, filling his lungs with the soft Sussex air, the earthy tones mingling with the scent of the enormous oaks shadowing the road. He was minutes away now. He just had to get through the last couple of miles. Finally the road began to clear and the V8 engine of his imported pickup truck gave a throaty roar as he stepped on the power once again.

The sun shone with bright intensity across the main yard. A blackbird pulled busily at a worm in the lush grass, and a large ginger cat paused lazily from his washing; deciding it was too far away to be worth the effort he went back to pre-nap wind-down. A stable hand whistled as he mucked out one of the empty stalls, and horses grazed in the fields beyond as Pete strode smiling to greet the latest newcomer. Two new people in as many days, and this one he was particularly keen to welcome: a fellow polo player and a good one at that, to join Rosemount's swelling polo ranks. Behind the big black pickup truck was a long cattle-style trailer, and inside it a closely packed row of six horses whose hind ends could be seen beginning to shuffle, sensing they had arrived at their destination. Though accustomed to long journeys packed in together, they always welcomed the point of unloading and the chance to run free.

"Dominik!" said Pete, extending his hand to the rugged-faced individual who climbed from the truck. "Welcome to Rosemount! Good to see you. Great to have another polo player here! How was the journey?"

"Okay," replied the newcomer, who stood just under six feet tall and spoke with an American accent. "Man, the traffic here always kills me though! There's just so much of it, and when you think you've got ten minutes to go, you're still crawling along forty minutes later and have to stop for gas again."

"Tell me about it," sympathised Pete, as Dominik rolled his broad shoulders under his rumpled shirt, and stretched his neck, shaking off the hours on the road. "It took me over two hours to get a couple of horses over to Plumpton the other day. Still, we've got your stables and paddock ready. Want to follow me round?"

"Sure." Dominik stepped back towards his truck, enjoying the freshness of the light breeze before climbing into the still heat of the cab once again, as Pete started off across the yard.

"So, is your wife moving down here?" Pete asked as he and Dominik leaned on the fence, watching the freshly unloaded polo horses roll and play in their new paddock.

"No. She's got a busy job and she hates the South. I got a contract down here for six months, and with all the polo happening in this area I wasn't going to leave the horses at home," said Dominik, watching his grey trotting high tailed in a circle round the rest of them.

"Only six months?"

"Ya, well that's what they say. These things usually go longer."

"Yes, invariably! I recall a six month contract of mine that turned into a directorship!" said Pete.

"Really?" laughed Dominik, regarding Pete's confident face and easy smile. "But you're out of it all now?"

"Yes, I had enough of it. Can't be doing with that life anymore," said Pete, taking a deep contented breath as he thought of the day he had inherited the rambling grandeur of Rosemount. The place had soon got under his skin and prompted retirement from the city well before he hit fifty. "There was no time for horses or anything else. What's life for? Plus, look at this place!" he continued, gesturing at the rolling fields which shone with the colours of the summer grasses bowing gently in the soft breeze, and the South Downs rising gracefully behind. "You just can't top it, especially when the sun's shining. You want to check out the field?"

"Sure!" answered Dominik enthusiastically, liking the man even more. The polo field was why he was there, and they strode off leaving his horses frolicking and racing.

Although Rosemount played host to the usual mix of equestrian activity, Dominik had been attracted by Pete's enthusiasm for polo and the club he was growing which was as yet free of the formality and enormous fees usually associated with the regal sport. Not one to do things by halves, Pete had put in a full-size polo field which drew an expanding group of enthusiastic players enjoying regular games and practice sessions. It seemed to Dominik the ideal place and an easy environment for getting in on the action of the latter part of the season.

"It's a great pitch!" exclaimed Dominik approvingly, taking in the vibrant green of the short grass, shining in the sunlight.

"Yes, it's looking good right now. We've got some of the chaps from Cowdray Park over for a friendly this Friday evening. You free to join?" asked Pete, looking sideways at Dominik.

"Am I ever! What time?"

"First chukka at six and we'll play until the light gets too low. There will be quite a few of us, so we'll alternate players."

There was absolutely no way Dominik would be going home at the weekend; there were now too many reasons to stay put. Summer was wearing on and the remaining days of the polo season were numbered. His wife would have to overcome her dislike of travelling south and visit him if she wanted to see him.

"We'll have a barbeque afterwards. It'll be a good evening I reckon," continued Pete, brushing his knuckles across the stubble on his jaw and tipping his head back, feeling the sun on his face. "Weather's supposed to be fine."

DAILY GRIND

Anna paused at the exit of Canary Wharf tube station in the stark bright light of the early morning, attempting to rally her senses. The massive glass and metal towers of Docklands rose around her, obdurate and sterile places of business, and the week stretched ahead of her like an interminable route march. Last week she had been absent from the vast, hectic city in one of her favourite places: the island of Tresco. Her grandmother had lived there for many years until her death, in a tiny whitewashed cottage which the family had retained as a holiday home, and to which Anna was a frequent visitor. To her, the island was a tangible slice of paradise. The atmosphere retained a whole charge of its own; where feathering surf rushed onto pristine beaches and pounded against the rocks, rending the air with a raw energy. There she felt intensely and thoroughly alive.

Back in the city, dissatisfaction gnawed at her and she felt uncharacteristically cynical as she unwillingly trudged to work. In the crushing crowds of her faceless counterparts on their mindless Monday commute, the exhausting scene of London came like a rude sledgehammer. She shook herself; she needed to snap out of her mood. Her London career financed a good life, and it was just yesterday that she had moved Tom to his new home. Rosemount beckoned her that very evening.

The glass and granite of the lobby sparkled at Anna as she passed through the slowly revolving doors of her building, and the reality of her corporate existence drew her back in. At the long counter, aesthetically flanked with enormous scented lilies, three impeccable receptionists worked fast to check in visiting suits. Riding up to her floor, she regarded herself in the mirrored walls of the elevator, reflected to infinity. She sighed, thinking of the constant Tresco sun which had left its golden glow on her fair skin. Straightening up, she ran her fingers through her long hair which looked almost black in the dim light, and stared directly into her reflected dark blue eyes, silently issuing a swift pep talk to bolster her attitude. She would work swiftly, have a productive day, and leave in good time for her first foray onto the South Downs with Tom that evening; Rosemount was going to be the arena for the simple enjoyment she had been craving. The doors slid open on the business floor, brightly illuminated by the sunlight flooding through the glass walls, and Anna briskly made her way to her desk.

Anna's productivity was foiled in the first hour by an enigmatic piece of paperwork which she was discussing with one of her colleagues when Greg, a tiresome office presence, arrived on the scene.
"Right. Stop. Slow down. I'll tell you what we're going to do about this," he barked, ripping the paper from her hand and waddling like an overweight duck to the nearest chair. He threw his pear-shaped frame into it, his manner aspiring to authoritative intellect and effortless command of the situation. He stretched one arm up to place a small pudgy hand behind his head of thick silver hair, revealing a sweat patch at the armpit of his shirt. His right ankle rested on the opposite knee and his grey suit leg rose to reveal a white hairless calf bulging above his grey sock.
Anna shook her head, amazed at how stereotypical he seemed; a true institutionalised product of the public sector. As far as she could tell he had survived against the odds, side-stepping through departments, ineffective, over-compensated and working the system for maximum self-profit. Anna watched his small wet piggy eyes blinking behind

square brown framed spectacles reminiscent of those issued by the National Health Service years ago. His brow crumpled in puzzlement as he encountered the problem on the paperwork.

"Well, it means..." he broke off. "What *does* this mean?"

Anna simply looked at him, leaving him to consider the point in question. She had already established it fell under his jurisdiction and had no intention of hand-holding him through his own issue.

"Well they're supposed to state the date, time and materials here, as on the order they received," he whined.

Remaining silent, Anna tipped her head expressively, wondering whether he would ever bring any wisdom or sophisticated thought to the table.

"They've messed up. What am I supposed to do?" he flapped uselessly.

"I understand you are the procurement agent in this department," she retorted cynically, "And therefore the logical action would be to pick up the phone and discuss it with them."

"I think you should do it," he instructed, pointing the paperwork at her. "I have so much to do. I've got impact assessments building up, estimates, orders, and I still have to get sign off on a pile of completions. You see, there are so many hoops to jump through," he griped, gesturing flaccidly with one unnaturally tiny hand.

"Admittedly if I called them it would be resolved faster," said Anna pointedly, "But the fact remains that this falls under your role, hence in the category of your problem." She knew she was being distinctly unhelpful, but could feel her irritation rising. She was not in the mood that day to deal with his constant shirking.

"Well, I delegate it to you, as I certainly can't spare any time," he said, with an annoying grimace.

Why did he always assume seniority when it most definitely did not exist? The fact remained that she was the project manager there and knew far better than to rise to his divisive taunting. Refusing to be drawn any further into the discussion she walked round to her chair and sat down dismissively.

"Nope. You manage to find time to continually read the paper, go on walk-about round the building, and take a full lunch break. Perhaps you need to look creatively at your day to find a way of crow-barring your job into it," she said, deadpan, as she studied her next email.

Greg's mouth twisted into a small smile, perversely enjoying her blunt irritation. He regarded her high-cheekboned profile for a moment. Immaculate in her smart business dress which hugged her svelte figure she was straight from the pages of a glossy magazine, and by far the most mesmerising woman in his orbit. Heaving himself up, he sighed.

"Alright, keep your hair on." He stood for a moment, studying the sheet at arm's length, and then ambled away muttering.

Anna threw a final glance at his retreating figure. She needed a move from her current assignment, away from Greg and all the personalities like him. The place was full of overpaid, unimpressive men, all with learned helplessness whenever it came to solving issues. She huffed, dissatisfied. Why wasn't she better at dealing with him? Why wasn't she assigned to a higher profile position? Maybe it was her? She sighed. Negativity was stalking her that day. Reminding herself to take deep cleansing breaths, she refocused on her goal of leaving the office. She turned her gaze to the sunshine bouncing off the reflective mass of water in the docks beyond the tinted windows. It was a beautiful day, promising a perfect sunset at Rosemount.

Striding down the platform to board her early evening train, Anna felt uplifted; she could hardly wait to get to Rosemount once again. She found herself thinking of the previous evening and the awkward interchange with Damien. She knew nothing about him, having been bereft of any conversation in his presence, but he seemed strangely fascinating. She had been gauche, and should have handled their meeting better. Then again why did it matter? She was there for the simple pleasure of riding, and didn't need to focus on relating to anyone who made things difficult. Neither the Gregs nor the Damiens of the world would flatten her spirits or distract her from the fun she intended to have.

That was what she had determined the year would be about after all; fun. It had been nine months since Anna had split from her long-term boyfriend, with whom she had suffered for far too long. It had seemed like a giant step, and all too frightening, but the last straw had been the discovery of his lies. Then any affection she had for him evaporated and she was unable to bear his presence a moment longer.

She had found a functional apartment in which to decompress and moved out, finding that the welcome absence of his constant criticism and manipulation allowed her to breathe freely once again. However it was not long before a dark anger set in, as she recounted his arrogance and narcissism, and she was as furious with herself as she was with him; disgusted at her own weakness, wondering why she had allowed him to treat her so.

She was thankful when the ferocious anger subsided, and a quiet depressed acceptance took its place. She avoided her friends and spent her evenings alone, going to bed ludicrously early, wondering if freedom was going to get better. After a few months of apathy, cycling mechanically through work and sleep, she began to emerge from her self-imposed cocoon and made the snap decision to move out of the city, and buy herself a horse. She had always loved riding; it made her feel free, and cheered her from the blackest of moods. In fact it was the only hobby which had remained a constant throughout all the ups and downs of her life.

The shake-up changed the very rhythm of her daily existence, and hope began to dawn on her horizon. In her new-found liberation she had vowed to spend at least a year focussing on herself; she had to discover who she was once more and avoid any relationships with the opposite sex which would distract her. She was content to be an island, enjoying her new regime away from oppression. And right now, the exclusivity of Rosemount was full of undiscovered promise.

A NEW FRIEND

The glowing farewell of the sunset glimmered along the ridge, and Anna sighed contentedly, patting Tom, who seemed to be enjoying the view as much as she was. Suddenly he turned his head sharply to the left and pricked up his ears; then Anna heard the thud of hooves, lots of hooves. Into view came one rider and six horses. Tom shifted uneasily, and Anna tightened the reins, knowing Tom's racehorse tendencies to leap to full speed and protect what he considered his rightful place: leading the pack.

Dominik sat astride his grey, his five other horses all around him on long lead ropes.

"Hey! Gorgeous evening!" he greeted her, with easy friendliness.

"It really is," agreed Anna, noting his American accent. Then casting her eye over his menagerie she remarked, "That's a whole lot of horses!"

"Yeah well, they're polo horses. They exercise well in a group," he replied, looking at them as they clustered together obediently. Then he turned to watch the rapidly descending fireball of sun. "I love this place".

"You must be at Rosemount," said Anna, thinking she recognised a couple of the horses from the paddock next to Tom's.

"Yeah," said Dominik, rubbing his face. "I just got there."

"Me too. I'm Anna."

"Dominik." Then with an affirmative nod he added, "Dom; call me Dom." He looked back over the hazy valley with the fire of sunset on his face. "It's a good place. The people seem cool and Pete's got a great polo field."

"There's a game on Friday evening isn't there?" asked Anna, remembering the sign on the tack room notice board. "Are you playing?"

"Ya. You gonna be there?"

"Definitely. Watching polo on a summers evening sounds like a place I want to be!"

"You play?" he asked.

"I've had a couple of lessons and played some practice chukkas," said Anna.

"Hey, if you want to stick and ball with me, you're welcome," said Dom amiably, his eyes swiftly taking in Anna's slim body and long legs in tight denim jodhpurs. "It'd help me exercise my horses."

"I'd like that. Don't expect much talent though! I haven't played at all in the last year," Anna answered with a smile. She doubted she would prove a challenging stick and ball partner, but she needed to get out of her comfort zone and this man was promisingly friendly.

It was a pleasant ride back to the yard. Dom seemed a relaxed and cheerful type. He had a rugged masculine look, with an easy smile and exuberant laugh. He was animated and youthfully boisterous with a natural irreverent humour. Anna liked him immediately. She guessed he was around forty. He rode without a helmet, his short wavy hair blowing in the light evening breeze, as he sat back casually in the saddle. An old pair of polo jeans, more brown than white, clung to his athletic legs, and a faded Sarasota Polo Club tee-shirt was stretched across his reasonably broad shoulders. She found out he was originally from New York but met his wife, a Brit, whilst working in Manchester and he'd never gone back to live in the States. He told Anna they had a farm near Edinburgh but he had moved south for a contract in London.

"And is your wife here too?" Anna asked.

"No, she's got horses at home and her job is up there," he answered. "I do a lot of short-term contracts so we can't uproot every time. Plus she hates the crowds down here, so I am going to be back and forth a bit. Well, I'm supposed to be," he added in an equivocal tone.

It was another quiet night at Rosemount as Anna strolled across the front driveway to her Land Rover savouring the rich scent of the foliage on the evening air. Dom drove past her on his way out and waved from his truck like a familiar and long-established friend, shouting to her to stick and ball with him on Thursday evening, before accelerating away. Silence then descended punctuated only by a blackbird, singing out uninterrupted, and Anna gunned the engine and headed home.

The tiny cottage still felt like a holiday home. So entirely different from Anna's London apartment, it stood in a row of equally diminutive and charming properties which bordered the churchyard. She hadn't gone in search of a house adjoining a graveyard but the owner and curate, an old university housemate called Mateus, needed a renter while he was away ministering in the US. It was sheer coincidence that the village lay just a mile from Rosemount and, knowing she would be moving Tom there, she had leapt at the chance, feeling the universe had come together for her.

Mateus was truly different to everyone else she knew. He had studied theology at university, and had not really been a part of the regular student rowdiness and shenanigans, but given their mutual propensity for deep thinking they had formed a friendship which happily picked up from where they left off anytime they met. Not seeing eye-to-eye spiritually made their discussions challenging and often comical as they were forced, exasperated, to agree to differ.

Anna loved her rural surroundings and quaint cottage. Situated in the old part of the village, it was a world away from the impersonal crowds of the featureless suburb she had left behind. The village was small and picturesque with a green where cricket matches were played on fine evenings, and the local pub, The George and Dragon, conveniently facing it. An assortment of cottages and houses, uneven and twisted with age, lined the short high street, and the church at the north end was perched on the low rise of an ancient Saxon burial mound. Newer houses had been added, swelling the village population and bringing the useful addition of a couple of convenience stores, but its quintessential character remained.

Anna parked next to the small wooden gate opening onto the churchyard and walked up the sloping brick pathway, lined with yew trees, to the cottage. The frontage (for there was no garden to speak of) consisted of some bushy lavender plants which perfumed the air wonderfully, as did the honeysuckle climbing up the substantial oak post which supported a small canopy over the heavy oak front door. She loved the air of antiquity which surrounded the place. Casting her gaze round the peaceful churchyard with the quiet fields beyond, Anna smiled contentedly to herself before opening the front door and going inside. If she could just get out of her current work assignment and on to something more interesting, life could be perfect.

The Docklands air felt unusually bracing as Anna exited the tube station early the following morning. She took a deep breath of the breeze which carried a coastal scent, reminding her again of Tresco. She paused in the sunshine, tilting her face skyward. It seemed almost deserted; a pleasant anomaly, thought Anna as she walked along the waterside path to her office building. Two cormorants dived and resurfaced, the water running off their close feathers in crystal globules. She smiled inwardly, recognizing the difference from her outlook of the previous morning.

Sadly her buoyancy began to dwindle as she sat in front of her laptop contemplating some of the emails sent late the day before. What made people revert so readily to childish tit-for-tat, copying in the rest of the known universe? Why didn't they try picking up the phone and having an adult conversation instead? The emailed antagonism, indelible and unretractable, was all part of the culture where glory hunters shamelessly threw their colleagues under the proverbial bus with murderous intent.

It was a place for egos to fester and swell, then beat their chests and fight. The daily struggles and resistance must have kept productivity at about fifty percent of what it could be.

"Don't these jerks realise how bad they look?" sighed Anna as she scanned the back-biting for any actions which would fall to her.

"Talking to yourself?" chirped Francesca, grinning over the partition at Anna.

Anna smiled back. Francesca was a consultant from the same firm as Anna, and a valuable ally in maintaining sanity. Both of them had been brought in for a supposedly swift three-month assignment, which had turned into almost a year, and they were jaded with the ceaseless drone of the environment.

"Hey Fran. Just wondering what on earth I am doing here," sighed Anna. "I think I'm going to have to look for an alternative placement. This place is a catwalk for pin-striped child egos to strut their stuff and achieve nothing."

"Tell us what you think!" Francesca laughed, looking down at Anna as she dejectedly pressed her forehead against her palms. "I must say you have a wonderfully contemptuous way with words!"

Francesca had a deliberate and well enunciated way of speaking, which made her amusing to listen to. She was always glamorous and immaculately dressed from a continuously renewing wardrobe, testament to her enthusiastic and frequent retail therapy excursions.

"They're a bunch of idiots with all the commercial nous of a gaggle of school kids; you know that. You just need a change from this place. There are some short-term contracts coming up for New York," Francesca suggested, twirling her finger absently through her long auburn hair.

"Are there?" pondered Anna, considering the idea. Then thinking of Rosemount and Tom, she dismissed the thought. She'd just moved him there and had the rest of summer and autumn to get in some great riding and maybe some low-level eventing. But Fran was right; she needed change, it was what kept her fresh and the main reason she worked as a consultant.

"I think we've both been in the office long enough to deserve a coffee break," Francesca said. She slid her large black sunglasses on and grabbed her Burberry bag in one hand and Anna's sleeve with the other. Grinning, and feeling a bit like a skiving student, Anna scampered towards the door.

THE ROSEMOUNT CROWD

"Get your shoulders back!" commanded David Stockton, the resident instructor at Rosemount.

The sun streamed in through the open end of the covered arena, lighting the millions of dust particles which were drifting through the air, kicked up by the big grey mare dutifully lapping the circuit at a steady trot. Her rider was a stringy long-legged, fifty-something woman called Pamela, with forced blonde hair and an excess of make-up which revealed rather than disguised her age. Small beads of sweat covered her forehead from her physical exertion.

"Better. Now try it again one more time!" called David, his rich voice carrying the length of the arena. Puffing slightly, Pamela changed the rein and circled her mare midway down the arena.

"Okay. Good, we'll call that a day's work," said David, his words music to Pamela's ears. She slowed the mare to a walk and let her stretch her neck long. "Not bad. Any questions?" asked David, as she brought the grey towards him at his standpoint in the middle of the arena.

"Phew!" she exclaimed with a smile. "No, that was good, but exhausting as usual."

"Just get her in here a few times before our next session and do that again and you'll find we can take some paces forward in your training," said David authoritatively, hoping she heard his sternness. If she got fitter and committed to her riding they could stop replaying the same lesson time and time again. But she was one of a number of kept women who had their 'pets' at Rosemount; they weren't really there for the challenge, more for simply passing the time.

Pamela thought David was fantastic. He was an accomplished equestrian from a strict traditional background, and he pushed all his clients, not putting up with excuses. He wore crisp beige breeches and long leather boots with spurs. Pamela slid her eyes over him appreciating the man-in-spurs look and considering how his breeches would look thrown on her bedroom chair. She felt as if she was melting, both under the intense gaze of David's dark piercing eyes and from the body heat she had produced over the intense forty minutes they had been schooling.

"Okay. Go turn her out. I'll be in the office later if you want to pre-book the next session," said David briskly.

Pamela guided her mare towards the open end of the arena and David watched her go with a slight smirk. He knew he could have her anytime he wanted. The woman was putty in his hands. However now for a more tempting prospect; he turned towards the other end of the arena where Chantelle was entering with her black thoroughbred mare. Chantelle was tall, blonde, busty, all of twenty, and came complete with Daddy issues, an easy in for a forty-year-old authority figure and opportunist like David.

Upstairs in the observation gallery above the arena, Kevin, Rosemount's full-time yard worker, was taking a break gulping a black coffee. He stared fixedly through the window at Chantelle as she stepped onto the mounting block. Kevin was twenty-four, a long haired, guitar-playing wily urchin, always scouting the yard for attractive female clientele. Blindly ignorant of the fact that neither his manner nor his scrofulous unshaven appearance was likely to market well to the Rosemount residents, his vast over-confidence spurred his dogged persistence.

"You could park a motorbike down there," he leered as Pete came in, his eyes glued to Chantelle's cleavage as they watched her mount her horse.

"Hmm, some outfit for a riding lesson," observed Pete. "Have you finished the stalls?"

"Just a few to go," said Kevin, not tearing his gaze from where it was rooted.

"Well, get them done. I want you to help me with the fencing," ordered Pete, tweaking the sleeve of Kevin's shirt, keen to move him away from his excuse for slacking.

Kevin wandered off whistling, wondering if he had a chance at nailing Chantelle before David got his hands on her. He had every chance – David was way too old. Pete, still at the observation window, caught David's eye down in the arena, and they exchanged a grin as they appreciated Chantelle's ample bust swelling provocatively from the minute top she was squeezed into, as she urged her mare into a trot.

Thursday was another fine evening and Anna, mounted on one of Dom's polo horses, which seemed unnaturally small in comparison to Tom, was hammering down the polo field at full pelt after a ball which Dom had just pounded past her.

"Back it!" he yelled from behind her as he circled away on his grey.

With barely a moment to think about it, Anna raised her mallet in front of her and swung backwards. To her amazement the head of her mallet connected powerfully with the ball, which arced away behind her. Elation was immediately usurped by alarm as her well-trained mount turned as though on rails to follow the ball. An involuntary gasp escaped her as she held on tightly to avoid being dumped on the ground.

"You're pretty good at this for someone who hasn't played much," congratulated Dom as he cantered up to her.

Anna smiled, despite her pounding heart. She had been concerned about re-learning the co-ordination required for one-handed riding while juggling double reins and the mallet, not to mention actually hitting the ball. However, once thrown into the game, her concerns were forgotten as she rode and struck instinctively.

"I had forgotten how addictive this game is!" she said. "I found it just came back to me."

"Oi!" came a voice from the sidelines. It was Pete, standing with hands on hips, looking at his pitch. "You two are going to do a divot walk afterwards. It may only be a friendly but I want these guys back, so the pitch can't look like the Somme when they show up tomorrow!"

"Sorry, Pete! We're done!" Dom turned back to Anna grinning, and said, "Better get this pitch stamped down before we lose the light."

Anna chuckled. Dom had said they would work at walk and trot but that lasted a couple of minutes before Anna had shown him she was bolder and better than he thought; then they were cantering, passing the ball and hooking each other's mallets, laughing and shouting in mock protestation.

They dismounted and walked the horses off the field, removed the leg wraps and tack and hosed them down swiftly. It was a warm evening and the horses steamed in the pink-gold evening sunshine.

After a good twenty minutes of diligent field stomping and repairs, with much banter and laughter, Anna and Dom headed up to the yard again.

"Hey, want a beer?" asked Dom with a mischievous grin.

"Definitely!" she agreed.

The bar was clean and stylish with long windows overlooking the polo field, and a couple of big architectural plants in enormous clay pots. There was an assortment of furniture which seemed to work well together; a rust coloured sofa against one wall, wicker chairs near the window, and some elderly winged leather chairs. The furnishings and the high vaulted ceiling, along with a colonial-looking fan revolving slowly, gave it the feel of a British club. A pair of French doors stood open leading out to a terrace and deck where Pete was cleaning a large barbeque on wheels.

"Hey Pete, can I get a couple of beers?" asked Dom cheerfully, sticking his head out.

"Sure," said Pete, stepping inside and walking to the bar. "Did you two make my field spotless again? I'll be checking first thing and beers are on you tomorrow if not!"

Anna smiled. It was as though they had all known each other for a long while, though she had only met Dom on the Tuesday night and hadn't seen Pete since he'd greeted her on the first evening. Anna guessed it was due to Dom's unabashed, easy humour which seemed to dissolve initial shyness or inhibitions. She noticed her own customary guardedness had gone and she liked it.

"It's like we were never there," she contributed. Pete tipped his head expressively and smiled.

"Didn't know you were a polo player too, Anna. Perhaps I'll get out there too one evening for some practice chukkas. It's nice to have a female player here too. Right, what do you want? I've got Kronenbourg and Spitfire on tap at the moment and lots of different bottles in the fridge."

Sitting on the deck with a cold beer, watching the evening light disappear, made Anna feel as if she was on holiday. The brick wall of the building was still warm from a full day in the sun and radiated its glimmer on them as they sat chatting. A few other riders joined them as they finished with their horses for the evening. One, a particularly brash and entertaining character named Olivia, a strikingly tall and well-built horsey type with a cropped bob of glossy brown curls, bright red lipstick and scarlet nail polish, shouted with unrestrained laughter as she sat on the edge of the deck in a masculine pose, one foot up, smoking a cigarette. She told Anna she worked in media sales in the city, a stereotype Anna thought she fit like a glove.

Pete's wife Penelope joined the group for a while. She was a petite and attractive lady with a ready smile, dressed in a casual yet sophisticated style with her pink striped shirt collar up and a soft sweater tied around her shoulders. Her blonde hair was loosely pinned up emphasising her diminutive features, and she had a gentle, kind way about her with a hushed cultured voice.

Anna learnt a few more names and faces, including a fellow thoroughbred owner called Suzanah, Zanah for short, who had been at the yard for about a year. She had an expressive face framed by brightly peroxided hair which (with her somewhat unorthodox attire) gave her an off-the-wall look. She appeared to have ridden in a glittery tee-shirt and showy white tasselled full chaps belted at the waist. She lay at full stretch on the boards of the deck propped on one elbow, elucidating about her horse's difficulty with the flying change, gesturing with a beer bottle. She and Olivia appeared close, arguing good-naturedly together. Zanah asked Anna if she'd like to ride out on Saturday.

"There's a fantastic flat where you can go, well, *flat out*. A lot of jockeys exercise there," she said. "I can take you up there at the weekend if you like."

Anna readily agreed. Tom would love it. So would she, as long as he didn't get too competitive with Zanah's younger ex-racer; though she had a hunch Tom would easily out-pace the competition, given his breeding and the sheer speed he had demonstrated time and time again.

Anna's musings on the social pitfalls of owning an overachieving horse were interrupted by a sudden rise in the conversation and laughter from Olivia as she leant towards Penelope.

"OMG Penelope, did you see Chantelle today?"

"No," said Penelope questioningly, with a smile. She knew Chantelle was a laughing stock amongst the other female riders at the yard, given her appearance and unfriendly manner.

Olivia grinned and shifted forward in her chair, and holding her hands out in front of her chest mimed a large pair of breasts bobbing. "She was barely, and I mean *barely* in the tiniest top you have ever seen!" she guffawed. "Kevin was following her around with his tongue hanging out and his eyes on stalks. She looked ridiculous! It was like something you'd see in a porno!"

"Who? This girl I have to meet!" laughed Dom.

"Oh, you'll know her when you see her," said Olivia matter-of-factly. "She's our yard bint."

Penelope's face rumpled slightly in sympathy for Chantelle. "I actually feel a little sorry for her. She's a pretty girl who doesn't need to dress like that for attention. She will get herself into trouble. I think she must have been damaged by men in the past."

"Can't be much in her past, darling," chuckled Pete. "She's hardly twenty-one years old is she?"

"Oh yes, I'd say some definite issues there," Olivia added, nodding.

"She needs to mix with the other girls here more," continued Penelope.

"Well, she's unresponsive to women," asserted Zanah, waving her beer. "I was here with my friend Daniel the other evening and she hung around him all the time I was riding in the arena and the moment I dismounted and went to join them she disappeared! Honestly she has a problem; it's like a pathological need to be the honey pot."

"Honey pots frequently get taken by bears!" laughed Olivia.

Penelope grimaced. "Well, I hope for her sake that she makes a few female friends."

"What? Or one of our resident bears might..." started Pete, stopping at a chiding "Pete!" from Penelope. "Sorry Penel. You're too nice, you know that?" he chuckled.

Anna smiled to herself as she drove home later that evening. She felt part of a crowd for the first time in years, and everyone seemed eager to enjoy themselves. It was the antithesis of her last yard where bickering was the predominant theme. Still, Anna knew that everywhere had its demons, and Rosemount's would appear sooner or later. She parked up next to the church, wondering how they might show themselves. Rosemount was to be her sanctuary; it would get her through however much time was left on her loathsome work contract, and feed her new mission of self-discovery. Politics she could do without.

POLO NIGHT

"Are you coming for drinks at Brodie's this evening?" Francesca asked Anna as they walked to the meeting room on Friday afternoon.

"No, I'm out of here asap for a polo match at Rosemount," answered Anna, checking her phone and wondering if she would get back in time.

"I'm going to have to check this place out with you. I didn't realise it was so posh," said Francesca, raising her eyebrows. Anna gave her a quizzical look.

"Oh, do come on Anna! Polo's posh and everyone knows it!"

"Come with me if you want," laughed Anna.

"Another time, I'd love to. I'm heading out of town early tomorrow and I'll be very late back tonight if I travel all the way out to your place in the sticks!" They reached the glass door of the meeting room and Anna pushed it open.

"Anna. Bang on time. Take the hot seat," said the programme manager, Andrew Mansfield, indicating the chair at the opposite end of the table. He had a shaven head, rounded face and a heavy short neck which protruded from the collar of his tie-less shirt. His features always struck Anna as being like those of a baby; wide, innocent eyes and a small rosebud mouth, but there was absolutely nothing cute and vulnerable about Andrew. Frighteningly direct and insistent, with a hair-trigger temper, he was far more akin to a dangerous dog gnawing on a bone. He took no prisoners and did not subscribe to any HR theories of morality regarding dignity at work or politically correct language. There were no excuses for those not meeting their milestones. Victims would squirm as their failings were publicly laid bare, before being struck down with whatever killer blow he cared to inflict. He was not a man to discuss the merits of the soft-side of management, and Anna had learnt to keep her discussion and reporting entirely secular in his presence.

The project team who had gone before gathered their paperwork, gratefully accepting Anna's arrival as their cue for dismissal.

"Don't worry, Anna; it's Friday afternoon and he's in a good mood," said Ken, another project manager, as he moved past her.

"Yeah? Don't you bloody believe it," said Andrew with a lopsided smile, "If you slip that schedule any more then I won't be in such a fantastic mood next week!" Ken pulled a face and left with a grin.

The meeting went well. Thankfully Anna had no major issues or anomalies to deal with; it was more a plod through high level progress and explanation of some re-shuffling in the schedule, and Andrew's micro-management tendencies did not surface. It helped that Anna had prepped thoroughly. If ducks were not lined up in a smart row and explanations were not completely water-tight, a project manager would be put through the wringer and leave one of Andrew's meetings with the overwhelming need to hit the bar.

Andrew watched Anna as she carefully explained the changes made, running the tip of her pen delicately along the Gantt chart. She looked professional and angelic all at once, with a hint of attitude; neatly pinned dark hair, flawless skin and full lips, and a stylish shirt that wasn't quite corporate. She was tantalizing and slightly mysterious, and Andrew enjoyed her presence far more than he cared to admit. He snapped his attention to the project once more as she turned her mesmerising eyes to him, and immediately forced an automatic question at her to deflect his own thoughts.

"You two out this evening?" he asked Anna and Francesca once they had finished.

"I am. Anna's not condescending to join us as she has some polo match to attend," said Francesca airily.

"Oh polo. Jolly good!" mocked Andrew in a fake upper crust accent. Anna grinned at the table, and closed her folder.

"No doubt there will be champagne afterwards!" said Francesca, picking up the thread.

"Rather!" brayed Andrew, getting up from his chair and slamming his notebook shut.

"Hey, what can I say? We move in different circles," Anna smirked, to the jeers of the other two. Then she checked the time once more, and seeing it was later than she thought, dashed back to her desk. There were a couple of things to get done before she could leave.

She was late. The office had kept her for too long and she had missed the train she had intended to catch. She was now racing to make the start of the match as she bounded up the staircase in her cottage, peeling off her shirt and skirt. She pulled on dark blue jeans and a crisp white shirt. Running a brush through her hair in front of the mirror, she studied herself – Did she look a bit tired and gaunt? And maybe her jeans were too shabby? She stopped, debating a change of clothes. From the hallway, the reassuring tick of her grandmother's clock quieted her fears. She took a deep breath and nodded. She looked absolutely fine. Who the hell did she need to impress anyway? She knew that voice of doubt; it was all that was left of Adam, her critical ex, and he was long gone.

The yard was busy. There were two long horse trailers with a row of polo horses tied along the length of each, with tails braided and taped. Anna felt a little sorry for them as they stood quietly with no fuss or impatience, looking somewhat naked with their manes shaved and their tails bound up so tightly. Polo players hustled to and fro carrying tack, punctuating the rush with shouts of laughter and banter, sporting and heroic in their team colours, white jeans and rugged polo boots. They too, it seemed, were running late. Anna filled her lungs with warm evening air vibrant with the scent of grass and countryside. Rosemount was a far better place to be than drinking in London, talking work.

"Hey Anna! Over here!" shouted Olivia as Anna walked onto the terrace outside the bar. "I've got a great spot for you!"

She had obviously arrived first and had commandeered the best place on the deck with a perfect view of the polo field, organizing the seating to her taste. She was lazing with one leg hanging over the arm of her chair and a beer bottle in her hand, alongside a number of others who Anna hadn't met.

Dom was mounted up and cantering in easy circles on his grey. Anna thought he looked good, wearing a classic polo helmet, clean white jeans and a polo shirt in the burgundy colours of Rosemount, sporting the number 3. Pete was also warming up on an athletic-looking bay mare. Anna had never seen him ride, and he looked comfortable and competent as he rose in his stirrups rhythmically with his horse's canter, his mallet hanging at his side.

"You got here in the nick of time," said Olivia to Anna. Then turning to the others she introduced them all swiftly, indicating each as she went with the neck of her bottle. "This is Jemima, Nicolette, Paul, Jess and Andrew." They smiled or waved a hand at Anna as they were introduced, except Andrew, who turned startling blue eyes toward her, and studied her for a moment with a glimmer of a smile.

"Don't worry about trying to remember all those names," said Paul accommodatingly as he leaned forward, interrupting Andrew's line of vision and releasing Anna. "We'll reintroduce ourselves later."

"Game's a' starting!" announced Olivia energetically, sitting forward.

It was a high-spirited and noisy match. The players switched in and out through the chukkas, reappearing on different horses. Play was swift and dauntless, and Anna was amazed at the skill on the pitch. Some of the players were exceptional and kept the ball close to them, fluidly playing it both sides of their horse as they extricated it from the opposition and rapidly surged away, covering the full length of the pitch to score and bringing forth whoops and cheers from their team mates and the increasing crowd on the deck. Some of the ride-offs were aggressive and had the watchers exclaiming. Anna marvelled at the attitude of the polo horses, fearlessly streaming after each other in close formation, slamming one another hard in some of the clashes. They seemed generally unperturbed by the rough and tumble, with only moments of occasional restrained panic and flattened ears as they were utilised (quite against the rules, she was sure) as the rider's weapon. She grinned as she heard Dom yell indignantly as he was almost knocked from his mount after taking a blow from one of the opponent's horses.

As the light dimmed play was halted and the horses came off the field, necks relaxed and long, compact bodies soaked with sweat. Relieved to have their tails pulled loose from their bindings, they used them to swat at the evening insects which were intent on biting them. Leg wraps and tack were stripped off rapidly and cool water hosed over every steaming form.

When the spent horses were tied at the trailers once again, shiny as sea lions from their dousing and contentedly munching at hay nets, the players hit the bar. They arrived with forceful presence, exchanging high volume joshing and good humoured mockery. All were sportingly tousled, shirts grubby, hair sweat-soaked and ruffled from being encased in polo helmets.

"Anna!" shouted Dom, putting his arm round her shoulders and taking her beer, gulping it down like a thirsty dog. "Did you see me?"

Anna raised her eyebrows at his familiarity and laughed. "Fantastic goal! I can't believe you got your seat back in the second chukka; you were so almost off! I seriously thought you were heading for the floor!"

"Yeah!" he shouted raising his voice and grabbing at the sleeve of a tall young green-eyed blond man who appeared to Anna the stereotypical Etonian. "After that totally illegal foul!"

"You had it coming after crossing my line!" smiled the accused, in a marvellously rich and plummy voice.

"When? When did I cross your line?" shouted Dom incredulously, his American accent ringing out against the backdrop of Queen's English.

"When I blew the whistle on you," contributed the referee, who had just joined the group.

"Oh, yeah…maybe," grinned Dom with feigned sheepishness.

"Beers?" said Pete from the other side of the bar, looking equally as sweaty as everyone else.

"I'm Hugo," said Dom's blond assailant, leaning towards Anna and grinning at Dom. "Can I get you a beer, since this crass American unashamedly robbed you of yours?"

"Oi, she's my student! I can steal her beer!" insisted Dom, pointing a finger at Hugo. "And what do you mean 'crass American'?! I spice up your cucumber-sandwich-nibbling-Pimms-drinking sedate scenery!"

And so the ribbing continued.

The dark had fully set in and the visiting players began leaving to load their horses back on the trailers. Anna was enjoying a flirtatious farewell with Hugo, who had gravitated to her throughout the evening. He touched her arm and smiled as he breathed words close to her ear. Suddenly feeling watched she looked up, and to her surprise met the eyes of Damien for an instant before he snapped them away. He disappeared through the door to the terrace, leaving her feeling curiously self-conscious.

"You should come to one of our matches. We're only about twenty minutes away," Hugo was saying as he kissed her on both cheeks. "We can stick and ball and I'll teach you some moves to knock Dom off."

Anna smiled, fairly sure she would never see Hugo again, but his attention had been fun. As he headed out she turned to join the Rosemount residents on the deck, only to meet the astonishing blue eyes which had arrested her earlier then evening; Andrew was standing at the other end of the bar looking straight at her, with a smile on his face.

"I was wondering if you needed extricating, but you seem to know what you're doing. You had your fun before sending him packing," he remarked.

Anna was taken aback. Damien had come as a surprise, but he was a shock. Had he been watching her? He was presumptuous, considering they had not spoken before.

"I do know what I'm doing," she returned, with a shrug.

"I can see that," said Andrew, passing round the back of the bar and retrieving a beer from the fridge. Seeing Anna's questioning look, he said; "Would you like one? Don't worry; I'm a kind of business partner to Pete."

"How so?"

"I arrange a lot of the sponsorship and funding for Rosemount events. I'm here a lot. We're bound to get to know each other." Then he looked over at the door to the terrace, as Penelope appeared, calling to him.

"Oh Andrew, as you're there, would you grab a bottle of the Bollinger from the other fridge?"

"Bollinger, no less," he remarked to Anna with a grin. "I'm sure I'll see you out there," he said, leaving the bar, tearing at the foil round the cork as he went.

Anna watched him go. He seemed young to be a business partner of Pete's. There was something about him. He seemed so sure of himself. It wasn't even that he was that good looking; the piercing blue eyes were certainly notable but his bronzed face and sandy hair were not stereotypically handsome. Perhaps it was sheer force of personality. Whatever it was, it arrested her attention.

Outside, the terrace was illuminated romantically by candles flickering in lanterns on the tables and along the rail which surrounded the upper level of the deck.

"There she is! Come to join the home team now there're no enemies left to fraternise with?" called Olivia from where she was sitting at a large round table on the deck. With her were Dom, Zanah, Pete, and also Damien, their faces illuminated in wavering gold light from the candles which threw everything around into soft relief. Smiling demurely, Anna sank into a seat next to Olivia.

She raised her beer bottle to her lips and paused before taking a sip to say, "Just circulating. Helping Pete with hospitality."

"Thanks Anna," said Pete deadpan, raising his glass to her and then curling the corners of his mouth in a smile.

"So is Hugo going to fly you to the Rolex in his helicopter?" asked Olivia with an exaggerated refined accent.

"He has a helicopter?" asked Anna.

"I don't know," Olivia grinned. "But he looks like he should, and I think you should find out!"

"Unlikely," said Anna with an ironic smile before switching to Dom and Zanah's conversation, removing herself from Olivia's uncomfortable spotlight.

Again she became conscious of being watched and turned her head to meet Damien's gaze. His dark eyes were only just visible in the fluttering light from the candles, but they were unmistakeably focussed on her, almost drinking her in. And through the darkness he maintained contact for a definite and tangible moment. It was electric.

Later as Anna walked up the yew-lined pathway to her front door, she thought of Damien. What was going on there? In the ten awkward minutes of stilted conversation with him on her first evening at Rosemount, he had seemed uninterested and taciturn. But there was undeniable drama as their eyes met over the table that evening; time had paused for a moment and just the two of them existed in a silent space. Anna smiled at her own fancifulness as she put the key in the lock. It was definitely time for bed.

DAMIEN

The sun was high and bright in the sky and invisible skylarks overhead twittered in the bracing air of the ridge. Anna was up in the stirrups, flying on Tom's amazing stride; it was like riding a swift mountain stream. The smoothness of his gallop always blew her mind. She knew any onlooker would see the huge powerful movement of his long legs and athletic body with its well-sprung rib cage working in poetic motion, and would hear hooves thundering over the turf. But from her vantage point in the very eye of the storm, that magical point where there was an almost eerie absence of turbulence, all she heard was the wind in her ears.

Reaching the end of the flat where the ground began sloping downhill, Anna eased Tom back to an easy canter before slowing to a halt. He stretched his neck and snorted, shaking his head and licking his lips in self-satisfaction as Zanah arrived on the back of her horse, Charlie.

"Woah! That's a lot of fun!" shouted Anna exuberantly, wiping at the tears brought forth by the wind and sheer velocity.

"Fantastic, isn't it!" Zanah agreed. "It's great to have someone to gallop it with who is in Charlie's league! I came up here with Olivia the other week and was waiting for ages for her hunter to catch us. I can't believe Tom's pace," she went on. "He's mega fast for an older boy. Competitive monkey isn't he? Those flying bucks he started out with looked difficult to sit!"

"I'm kind of used to his caprioling. Probably explains why I got him so cheap," said Anna, patting Tom's neck. Tom had started the race in strong competitive style, and she was secretly relieved to have remained on board after the bucks he had put in. "Where to now?"

"If you're up for more of a ride then we can head down the hill and through the forest and circle back to the yard that way," suggested Zanah.

Anna gratefully took in the view which spread ahead of them, rolling and open. The shadows of clouds raced transparently over the airy expanse of land which seemed to breathe back at them. The soft curves and muted tones of the country spread for uninterrupted miles before them, on and on, all the way to the coast. Anna felt she belonged there as she took a deep breath of the bracing current as it flowed through her and over the landscape.

As they rode down the slope to the forest path they heard a shout to their right and saw two horses on the bridle path. Both were immaculately groomed powerful bay hunters.

"Oi jockeys!" shouted Olivia from her seat astride one of the horses. "You two were going like smoke!"

They waved and guided Tom and Charlie over towards the others. With a quickening sensation spreading rapidly throughout her chest, Anna realised the other rider was Damien. They exchanged a brief glance as they all fell in together on the bridle path. Zanah took to the front with Olivia, and Damien rode next to Anna. He sat comfortably, riding one-handed with his other hand relaxed on his leg. He looked completely at home, perfectly matched with his tall muscular mount.

"You were really shifting!" went on Olivia. "Either of you ever clocked yourselves?"

"Funny you should say that," said Anna, remembering she was wearing her GPS watch from running to the stables that morning, having taken a taxi home the night before. Clicking through the stats, she found their top speed. "39.9 miles an hour!" she exclaimed. "Not bad, Tom!" she said patting him again, as Zanah whooped.

"Really?" said Damien, sounding impressed. Anna felt proud, gratified by his reaction.

The bridleway turned into the forest and led them downhill. It was noticeably cooler under the dense cover of the trees, and the air oozed earthiness after the clean blow on the ridge. Anna loved the smell of the forest; the pine aroma wafting from the evergreens was fresh and fragrant. Olivia and Zanah chatted most of the time but Damien and Anna rode in a comfortable silence. It seemed that he was much like her and preferred to ride in quiet and appreciate the scenery. Or was it that they had nothing to say to each other? Olivia suggested they pick up the pace a notch, to which they all agreed and set off at an energetic trot as the bridleway turned, leading back uphill.

"I guess you're not riding in the eventer training session tomorrow, Damien?" asked Olivia when they slowed to a walk again.

"No, I'm working tomorrow for the next few days," he answered.

"What do you do?" asked Anna, curious as to his strange shift patterns.

He reached forward, removing a twig from his horse's mane and answered without looking at her, "I'm a pilot."

"Who do you work for?" asked Anna.

"Virgin Atlantic."

"He never shows up in his uniform, though!" Olivia added, turning in her saddle. "I mean, what's the point of knowing a pilot if you never get to see him in his uniform?"

Damien gave a kind of half-scowl and looked away.

"Don't worry, he's always this aloof!" laughed Olivia. Looking mischievously at Damien again she said, "I'd have much preferred to see the RAF uniform, though. That would definitely do it if you're ever to have a chance with me!"

Damien raised an eyebrow but made no response. Anna imagined that he would indeed look fantastic in any uniform but sensed he simply wasn't to be drawn into Olivia's teasing, so she remained quiet. So he was ex-military. It made sense. She had a couple of colleagues who were out of the army and they both had a certain quiet poise and serious outlook, not talking extensively and exhaustively round a point like so many corporate clones. Instead they tended to use a few concise well-chosen words to get something achieved or communicated. She felt more approval for Damien, even if conversation was proving challenging.

As they neared the yard she had the sense of time slipping away and with it her opportunity to speak to him. She could feel her insides urging her to say something but her mind was blank. Finally she looked at him, admiring his handsome profile, realising that she had not actually looked at his face much, having been too shy to meet his eye for long. The faintest of smiles glimmered at the edges of his mouth and he turned to meet her gaze.

"Want to ride out on Friday evening?" he asked simply.

She smiled and answered just as simply, "Yes."

"You look different," said Francesca, fixing Anna with a probing stare.

They were taking a break from the stifling environment of the office, having lunch outside at a waterfront restaurant near Canary Wharf, the Tower climbing into the sky above them, glinting in the midday sun. A light breeze stirred the enormous parasol over their table as Anna looked down at herself and back at Francesca.

"Don't give me that. There's something," insisted Francesca, craning her neck forward to look into Anna's eyes. Anna felt decidedly self-conscious and spread her hands out questioningly, not sure what Francesca was after. "You've got a secret," said Francesca conclusively, removing her sunglasses and propping them on top of her thick and immaculate hair so she could eyeball her friend. "What is it?"

Anna felt tension creep in. Francesca was doing that thing she did; reading her. Now the questioning would begin. Francesca was a professional people-watcher, well-schooled in psychology, body language, neuro-linguistic programming; and she was a mind reader where Anna was concerned.

"Come on, spill! We are not going anywhere until you have shared!" Francesca pressed.

"What? Why do you think I've got a *secret*?" asked Anna, using her fingers to put inverted commas round her last word. Francesca narrowed her eyes and cocked her head, thinking for a moment, as though compiling her mental evidence file. Anna winced, knowing the look and awaiting the inevitable barrage of difficult-to-answer questions.

"Who is he?" Francesca accused.

"He? He who?" asked Anna, stalling for time, astounded once again at Francesca's psychic ability. Damien had been dominating her thoughts that morning; his wonderfully masculine profile, as she had seen it when they rode side by side on Saturday, at the forefront of her mind.

Francesca rolled her eyes. "Oh for goodness sake, Anna! Whoever you were thinking of this morning when you were smiling into space and zoning out in the team meeting!"

Anna struggled with a response, not thinking as fast as she would have liked. "I was thinking of an amazing gallop I had on Tom on Saturday!" she answered in an elated tone, triumphant at deflecting Francesca. "We got to over 39 miles an hour," she added, feeling the detail would add strength to her case.

"Right," said Francesca matter-of-factly, undeterred. "And who were you riding with?"

"My friend, Zanah."

"And?"

"And no-one."

"Yeah right! Anna, no-one drifts off into space with that dreamy look on their face because they had a nice hack out in the country with their four-legged friend," said Francesca with palpable frustration.

"Regardless of how fast you went!" she added quickly, seeing Anna's look of protestation.

Anna reverted to child, slumping forward on her elbows and giving Francesca a sulky look. "Did it ever occur to you that I'm not ready to share?"

"Now we're getting somewhere," said Francesca in her interrogator's voice. "Anna, you never want to share. You're one of those who goes through life holding all your cards to your chest, a complete enigma, shutting everyone out and so no-one understands you!"

Anna thought for a moment. She had never really thought of herself as an enigma to others, though Francesca's description felt like a truth. "Huh. Is that what I seem like?" she mused.

"Yes. It makes people think you're stuck-up or feel you're untouchable. It's why I didn't like you when we first met! Now, tell me who he is, who has you swerving off course in this anti-man year you imposed on yourself."

"You didn't like me?" asked Anna, aghast.

"Focus, Anna! That's not what we're talking about. Now who is he?"

"You won't know him," Anna said, still stalling, and slightly shaken from Francesca's brutally honest admission.

"I don't care."

There was no-where else to go with the deflection tactics, and Anna took a breath, feeling she had reached a cul-de-sac. "Okay. He's a guy at the stables I have moved to." Her words came dragging like a confession.

"And?"

"Well, I met him on the first evening. He helped me unload some of my stuff..."

"Yes, yes," cut in Francesca impatiently. "What happened?"

"Nothing. Nothing's *happened*," said Anna, bewildered. After all, nothing had actually happened. They'd had a conversation, met eyes a few times and ridden together in almost complete silence and agreed to ride out on Friday – the thought of which gave Anna excited butterflies.

"Right there! You just smiled again!" exclaimed Francesca, pointing an accusatory finger at Anna's mouth. "*Something* has happened. I've not seen you like this."

Anna sighed, seeing she was going to have to share more. She started again with the first night and told Francesca about meeting Damien for the first time, and her tongue-tied state. Reluctantly, and feeling embarrassed, she told her about meeting his eyes so intensely on the night of the polo match. And she finished with the almost silent ride smattered with abrupt conversation, and the fact they agreed to meet on Friday. It sounded like nothing now she recounted it. Was she so removed from men that simple things felt like a big deal, like she was an inexperienced teenager again? No, she hadn't been banished to a nunnery; she had lots of male friends and colleagues and the energy never felt like it did with Damien. Nevertheless, what had taken place between her and Damien sounded commonplace in her account, didn't it? So why did her feelings burn within her as she thought of him?

Francesca sat back in her seat and smiled at Anna. "Sounds a bit like you have found a male you, and have immediately fallen in love with him," she diagnosed.

Anna made an indignant sound and looked sideways, folding her arms. "No! That's ridiculous! It's not *love!*" she spluttered, enunciating the last word like it was alien to her, with the resistance of a schoolchild repulsed and embarrassed by the same suggestion.

"Oh, really? Staring into each other's eyes through the crowd, shyness, inability to speak, and on top of all that you're drifting off into reveries," said Francesca, raising her eyebrows and smiling knowledgeably. "Sounds like love to me. Sounds like love at first sight to me."

"Impossible! You're reading way too much into it." Anna frowned again, but was unable to ignore the delighted tingling spreading through her at the thought of meeting with him on Friday. Maybe she was in denial.

Francesca's eyes sparkled affectionately at Anna. "Not to mention the fact you are off your food!" she crowed triumphantly, nodding at Anna's over-populated plate. "See, it can be good to share. Right, now let's get back to the pin-striped monkeys," she said decisively, signalling to the waiter for the bill, and sliding her sunglasses down over her eyes once again. With a sigh Anna remembered it was the project review meeting with senior management, where they would drudge through three hours of variance reports and earned value analysis for every project on the network.

"Hey, at least you've got a date to look forward to tomorrow evening!" Francesca teased.

"It's not a date!" Anna protested uselessly.

"Yeah right, it's just two people exercising their horses!" laughed Francesca as she paid the bill.

It was Friday evening. The rhythmic grooming of Tom's shiny bay coat had begun to soothe the intense fluttering in Anna's stomach. It had been a breakneck dash from work to make the train on time, and now she was nervous. What on earth would she and Damien talk about? Maybe it would be an uncomfortably silent ride punctuated only by sporadic, meaningless exchanges. She exhaled deeply and deliberately, trying to expel her uneasiness and restore calm. At that moment Penelope stopped to chat, and her grounding friendliness came as a welcome distraction. As Anna lifted Tom's saddle onto his back, Penelope called to Chantelle, who was passing.

"Oh Chantelle, would you please put in the office book when your farrier is coming? I need to make sure Kevin is there to get your horse in."

"I just put it in," said Chantelle, taking a step towards them and stopping. She had shoulder-length champagne blonde hair and a doll-like button-nosed face which, though attractive, was marred by an expression of tense mistrust and wariness, like a foreign soldier in enemy territory. Olivia's mockery of Chantelle rang though Anna's head, as she registered the blatantly augmented breasts spilling over the electric pink top.

"Thank you. Are you having a lesson this evening?" Penelope smiled, adopting an encouraging questioning style, a little like trying to get a child to open up.

"Yes, but David's over-running with Pamela. She fell off," said Chantelle, shortly, with derision in her voice. Then she moved off without another word.

"Goodness me," said Anna, smiling at the ground, understanding the opinions she had heard the other evening.

"Yes," Penelope sighed, evidently wise to Anna's thoughts. "I do worry. I really hope she won't be handed about like a plaything amongst the men here. There are a few predators amongst them, regardless of marriage I'm afraid," she went on, raising her eyebrows meaningfully. Then, seeing Pamela leaving the arena, she excused herself.

Anna watched her leave. She seemed so caring, almost motherly, probably seeing Chantelle in the right light; with sympathy, rather than demeaning her as everyone else did (though she herself couldn't find much compassion for Chantelle's type). In her experience, women like that did nothing for other women, and were so ravenous for attention they had few qualms about intruding on established relationships. Her cynical reverie was interrupted by Damien as he rounded the corner leading his horse, Barnabas.

"Ready?" he asked with a quick smile.

"Yes," said Anna, leading Tom to the mounting block. Her chat with Penelope had diffused a lot of the tension she had been holding inside. Keen to maintain her sense of ease, she grinned across in Chantelle's direction, watching her mince across the yard towards the arena and guessing she must get more out of her lessons with an imposing male instructor than merely improvement of her riding skills.

"I just met Chantelle," she said to Damien.

Swinging his leg over Barnabas and planting himself on the saddle he followed her gaze with a grim smile and said matter-of-factly, "Yes, not long before she gets banged in the tack room by someone, probably Kevin, she's that easy."

Anna smiled. She had deflected Kevin's attentions a couple of times herself, recognising him as a young, dumb opportunist on the prowl.

"Who's that?" asked another male voice.

"James!" said Damien in greeting, shaking the hand of the newcomer from the top of his horse. "What brings you here?"

"I'm meeting Pete and Andrew to get the first hunt bash booked in," he said, looking distractedly after Chantelle as she disappeared in the arena door. "Is that the new totty? Too cheap for you, Damien?"

"Yep, but not for you," grinned Damien.

"I like 'em obvious like that," leered James.

Anna frowned slightly; she knew how a lot of men talked, and she didn't enjoy listening to it. It was the sort of derogatory attitude that made her feel like equality had never come to the world, and that men just pretended to it in the presence of women.

"She's a microwave meal; fully labelled, just unwrap, heat internally, devour and discard!" went on James, grinning broadly and unashamedly up at Damien. Anna recoiled at the violence and disrespect, wrapped as it was in cheap, clumsy humour.

"James, there is a lady present," disciplined Damien, nodding at Anna.

"Whoops, sorry!" said James, smiling light-heartedly at Anna, leaving her confused as to whether to maintain her repulsion and anger or shrug off his offensiveness as simple obnoxious male jocularity. Then he peered past them and immediately began to stride away, saying quickly, "I see Pete. I'll catch you again soon."

Anna was pleased to be going in the opposite direction to James and it must have showed because Damien gave her a sideways look as they rode towards the gate.

"Typical hunting bloke. You know, crass and crude," he said in brief explanation, and left it at that.

It felt to Anna as they rode from Rosemount almost like they were sneaking off together like two teenagers. Ahead of her, Damien sat relaxed and nonchalant on the dark bay Barnabas, and she found herself unable to take her eyes off him as he led them down bridleways that

Anna hadn't ridden on before. As the path widened to a farm track she moved alongside him, though having no idea what to say.

"Good week?" asked Damien, looking at her.

Anna was surprised; thinking he didn't do small talk. She certainly didn't feel that her working week had been pleasurable, so she responded by talking about the people she had met at Rosemount. She was taken aback when he asked her what she did for a living, though she didn't know why. He was perhaps more normal and less aloof and mysterious than first impressions suggested. She felt he was listening to her intently, turning his gaze to her now and then, his eyes dramatically still. She couldn't meet them for long without feeling like she was blushing. He wore the slightest of smiles at the corners of his mouth, which warmed his expression and made him even more alluring.

"Ever hunted?" Damien asked as they neared the end of the track.

"No," replied Anna, not sure what she could add to that, as she abhorred the thought of fox hunting.

"This is one of the routes the hunt often takes," he said, leaning sideways to open a gate for them, pushing it wide so they could both trot through before it swung shut again. They were now in a large open field which rose uphill. "There's a good hedge to jump up there," said Damien, gesturing to the top of the hill where the perimeter hedge could be seen against the skyline. "Want to jump it with me?"

"What?" exclaimed Anna, feeling nervous.

"It's not as bad as it looks from down here, and it flattens out up there. There's good ground. He'll be fine, he looks like a capable jumper," he said nodding at Tom.

"*He'll* be fine, yes!" said Anna, knowing Tom was a highly accomplished and athletic jumper. His breeding line was distinguished; he took his genes from a leading sire of jumpers. No, it was her own lack of talent and confidence in the jumping department that bothered her. But then again, she didn't want to come off as a wimp in Damien's eyes. She knew Tom's expertise had got them over a number of obstacles; even from a poor line with little run-up, he would sort out his own stride and bound like a stag. All she had to do was hold on. Steeling herself, she resolved to be brave and let Tom do the work.

Taking a deep breath and looking up the hill she said; "Ok, let's go for it."

"Good girl!" Damien said, impressed. He had only half meant for her to take him up on it. He loved the adrenalin burst of a challenge during a ride out but hadn't thought she would agree to join in. He shortened his rein and kicked his horse on, surging into a forceful canter.

Anna held Tom for a moment, wanting Damien to lead the way and jump first. She watched Barnabas, gauging his speed. He was a big, well-muscled horse of far larger build than Tom and moved athletically but at a far slower pace than Tom would take the hill. Tom, frustrated at being prevented from competing, began side stepping and wheeling, his back rounding. Anna, knowing the fight would only become dangerous, gave him his head and urged him forward. Tom sprang joyfully into the air, bucked, and then dived forwards, exploding to pursuit speed. Anna gasped, but kept her seat and put her legs hard against his sides as he powered up the hill after Damien and Barnabas. She saw Damien up in his stirrups as he took off, and Tom pricked his ears eagerly, seeing what they were about to do and expressing his excitement at the worthwhile obstacle. Anna's heart was in her mouth and she hung on grimly as they reached the hedge, which now looked like a solid ten foot wall. She left it all to Tom who stepped up to the job as happily as ever, altering his stride effortlessly before launching them both into orbit. They blasted upwards, clearing the top with ease. Anna looked down onto the wide straggly mass of small dense leaves and brambles which wound their way through the twiggy branches, and all seemed quiet for a split second. Then they were tilting into descent and Anna braced against the stirrups for landing. They met the earth once again on the other side, the air expelling from Anna's lungs in a short gasp. Tom was beside himself with joy and flung his head down between his front legs, emitting a squeak, before flooring his accelerator to maximum and covering the ground towards his quarry with devastating velocity. Anna's whole body was flooded with adrenalin by the time they passed Damien and Barnabas with the eye-watering speed of an F16 taking a Lancaster bomber.

Her heart banged in her chest and fire raged through her nervous system as she finally brought them to a halt. Tom's nostrils flared and he licked his lips and snorted. Anna felt intense love for him right then, feeling the bond between them strengthen a notch as it always seemed to when they rose to a challenge together and came out breathing the other side.

"That horse of yours can certainly go, can't he!" exclaimed Damien as he drew close alongside her.

"He can!" laughed Anna, rubbing Tom's neck.

"He cleared that hedge with a foot to spare," Damien nodded.

"I thought he must have done. It felt like I was aboard a rocket ship!" laughed Anna, the glorious feeling of achievement and grateful relief intermingling with the adrenalin. "I've never jumped so big." Her hands shook and she blew out a breath as she willed herself calm again. Damien looked at her with a smile.

"Look at you shaking. You're glad you did it now aren't you?" he said, reaching out to catch her hand.

Anna's breath caught in her throat for a moment, the simple touch of his hand an electrifying thrill, rushing through all the other chaotic sensations.

"Yes," she answered, embarrassed at her trembling hand, and her deep blush. The touch and heat of his masterful grip enfolded her completely, intoxicatingly, and she didn't want him to let go.

He looked seriously into her eyes for a moment then smiled and squeezed her hand as though willing her calm, before breaking the contact. Then he nodded ahead to where the lambent orange sun was sliding downwards, illuminating the sleepy valley below.

"Shame to waste a romantic sunset," he smiled.

They basked in the magical evening glow together. Maybe Damien felt the same way about her as she did about him – he must do. In a moment he turned and met her eyes again, and she was drowning in the depths of his dark stare.

The sensation of Damien's touch still tingled as they rode from the pathway and into the forest, where the trees rose thickly, wrapping them in shadow. Anna floated along on Tom in a charged silence. Everything seemed exquisitely beautiful in the earthy atmosphere. The wood anemones glowed on top of lush green leaves which covered the dark forest floor like a massive glossy carpet. Shafts of golden light from the very last of the sun glowed on the stout tree trunks, throwing their rough bark into angular relief. Emerging into view at the end of the forest path she could see the rolling fields, soft and perfect in the evening light, the longer grasses flowing back and forth in the gentle breeze like waves in the sea.

Damien too seemed disinclined to commentate needlessly on the natural beauty as they plodded towards the light. A sudden snapping of branches followed by a scuttling and sliding, causing both horses to jump in unison, shook them from their collective reverie. As the two horses pranced sideways, a stag jumped from the bank into the middle of the path. He stood regal and magnificent for a moment, framed by the surrounding trees and backlit by the golden evening glow as he regarded them. They were close enough to see his nostrils twitch and the gleam of his wary eyes. They all remained frozen for a moment, and then as swift as his arrival, the stag was gone, disappearing rapidly into the trees the other side of the path. Damien and Anna turned to look at each other in mutual wonderment, Damien shaking his head in disbelief. Then they urged their newly alert mounts forward once again.

The sun had gone and they covered the last half mile in the rapidly descending dim of the evening.
    They chatted as they entered the gates of Rosemount once again, reaching the grounded everyday topic of irritating workplace stereotypes, a topic prompted by Anna's colourful description of Greg, whom she had dealt with extensively that day. Damien looked amused as she recounted her testing transactions with him, and retaliated with his own run-ins with a know-it-all co-pilot, making her laugh. He seemed

as normal as she was as he opened up and it felt good to get to know him a little.

"Want to get a drink?" asked Damien, dismounting.

"Sure," Anna agreed with a smile.

Happiness bubbled within her as she watched Tom rolling in his field, flailing his long legs in the air. Damien materialised next to her, chuckling as he observed Tom vigorously scrubbing between his ears on a tuft of grass, before heaving himself from the ground for a full body shake. He looked back at them both and then took off energetically, bucking and expelling gas emphatically, causing the other inhabitants of his field to throw their heads and join the chase.

"I think he'd get a lot out of a day's hunting," smiled Damien, obviously enjoying Tom's antics.

"Probably," agreed Anna. "But he gets pretty competitive and can be hard to handle. I understand fly-bucking your way past the huntsman is a no-no on the hunt field." Damien slid his elbow along the fence rail until the bare flesh of their arms touched. Anna could feel the heat of him against the cool of her own skin.

"That is true. Perhaps we can introduce him gradually." It felt like they were a couple, leaning there on the rail together, with Damien involving himself in helping with Tom.

"I think you're overdue a drink after your acrobatics this evening," he said grinning, putting his hand on her shoulder momentarily as they moved away from the fence and sending an electric shiver though her. It was almost like he felt her internal reaction, as he met her eyes for a moment with an expression she couldn't place; perhaps it was surprise, intense and freighted with meaning.

She felt on top of the planet as they walked into the bar together. There were a number of people in, enjoying a Friday evening drink, and they were greeted by Olivia, Penelope and Pete who were chatting at the bar.

"My goodness, you two really pushed the evening light," exclaimed Penelope. "Did you have a good ride?"

"Yes. It's such a lovely evening," Anna enthused.

"Anna cleared Lofter's hedge by over a foot," Damien told them.

"Did you really?" exclaimed Olivia. "Blimey Anna, that's a mighty jump! Particularly at the moment while it's in full summer fling. What possessed you?"

Anna grinned at Damien, who comically averted his eyes from her accusatory glance. "It did feel rather like a mountain! I'm not sure Damien was all that honest about the size of it before I jumped it!"

"You'd never have done it if I did tell you," said Damien, his mouth twitching mischievously and a twinkle in his eyes.

"Oh by the way, Damien, Caroline called," said Pete, almost apologetically. "She said she couldn't get you on your mobile, and to remind you of dinner plans this evening."

"Shit," said Damien, looking at his watch and scowling.

"She sounded a bit cross apparently," added Penelope with a cautionary smile.

"Yeah, she's often cross," said Damien shortly, pulling his phone from his pocket and walking to the back of the room. Anna could feel her eyebrows rising in dismay; who was Caroline? Not a girlfriend, surely? Please let her be his sister!

"That's his wife. She's a bit scary!" confirmed Olivia, leaning confidentially towards Anna.

Verification came like a crossbow bolt to Anna. He was married? How could he possibly be married? She reeled, feeling like the room was turning and there was no air to breathe.

"Between you and me I am sure he's a bit of a player," went on Olivia, in a discreet tone. Then, misreading Anna's look, she asserted, "Oh come on, look at him!" She jerked her head in Damien's direction, clearly referring to his good looks. "And he's off for days at a time camped out with a load of trolley dollies in exotic places. Bet he has a blast!"

"Oh," managed Anna in a small voice, Olivia's brutal assumptions landing terminally on her misguided euphoria. "He didn't seem like that."

"Not here very much, though I think he's had the occasional drunken fondle at the odd hunt ball."

Unable to listen to any more, Anna slid off her bar stool and pulled on her sweater. Had she been played? She usually knew if someone was trying it on. What an idiot she was. The evening had felt so real.

"Whoops, I've got to go too," she said, pulling out her phone and feigning a time check. Uttering a quick goodbye she opened the door and stepped into the evening air once again.

Walking swiftly to her Land Rover, she swore under her breath as she struggled to find her key. Coming across it in her other pocket she grumpily hit the unlock button, and reached for the door handle.

"Anna?" Damien's voice came quietly from behind her. She spun round, having no idea he had followed her.

"I had a really good ride out with you this evening." He looked at her with apology.

She widened her eyes in disbelief, struggling with her raging emotions. There was nothing she could say. She had been so happy, so wrapped up in him, and then found herself plummeting in confusion onto cold concrete disappointment.

"I thought..." she broke off and looked at the ground, floundering. "I er... Yes, it *was* a spectacular ride."

"I'll see you tomorrow. I'll be here in the morning," he said hesitantly, searching her face with troubled eyes.

Anna shrugged and sighed. "Ok, whatever..." and then unable to finish any kind of coherent sentence, she shrugged again and pulled open her door.

Damien walked back across the yard to his car hollow, gutted, and angry at his wife. What a crappy way to end the evening. His wife had effortlessly destroyed his rare feeling of well-being, and now there was dinner with two of the most tiresome people he knew. He screwed his eyes shut and swore as he revved the engine.

Anna angrily wiped away a hot tear as she drove fast down the country road to the church. What a gut-wrenchingly depressing turn of events. How did she not know he was married? Where was his wife anyway? She'd never heard or seen anything of her. How was it that he had seemed so into her as far back as the polo night, if he was married? Maybe he just wanted a fling? Did she come across as the fling type? Confused and increasingly angry, she parked, and ran up the path to her house.

Why was she so upset? Nothing had happened. Not really. Was she just being a silly girl about everything, over-thinking and over-feeling? But who was she kidding? The feelings were raw and intense; undeniably something had gone on. He must have felt it. The way he looked at her; his eyes had been so deep. Maybe he *didn't* feel the same. Maybe she misread him completely and it was just fun for him. What if she looked a complete simpleton? A smitten sixteen-year-old? And now he was probably bemused at her petulant exit or worse still, laughing at her. She couldn't face him tomorrow or anytime soon. She went to the kitchen and poured a large glass of wine to try and numb herself into some kind of restfulness, but her tumultuous thoughts continued to roll around and around. Feeling angry at herself and impossibly confused, with repetitive questions clamouring inside her head, she stomped upstairs for a shower and then climbed into bed.

OPPORTUNITY

The sun filtered through Anna's pale cotton curtains with friendly morning light. Her phone chimed from her bedside table for the second time, alerting her to another incoming message. She groaned and rolled over to look at it.

Both messages were from Francesca; the first asking her how her date/ride had gone, followed up by the second 10 minutes later, demanding: 'Well?!' Anna sat up and rubbed her eyes. It was 6:47am.

"Who texts this early?" she grumbled in irritation. It had been a night of fitful, restless sleep.

She gulped some water from the glass on her bedside table and headed over to the window to pull back the curtains. The churchyard looked quaint and pretty in the early morning sun. Anna leaned against the low window frame, thinking over the events of the evening before as she stared out over the silent residents of the churchyard, under their slabs of stone. The mental turmoil of the night before had receded to grumpiness. Damien's face drifted across her mind, his features illuminated by golden sunset, and she felt a pang of depression. She frowned at her own moodiness and confusion, and forced herself to decisiveness. She would not talk to Damien that day. Plainly she needed to let her thoughts settle. Plus she must reassume her dignity, so she wouldn't come off as a fool with a crush.

"Let's go," she said to herself aloud. And without showering or breakfasting, she pulled on breeches and a shabby tee-shirt, grabbed her keys and left for the yard. She would take Tom out for an early morning burn and leave again before anyone else showed up.

Anna was up on the Downs before 8 o'clock. The morning smelt fresh and the dew sparkled on the long grass. There was a chill on the air which had the hairs on her arms standing up. Tom was surprised at the unusually early start but jogged along with an enthusiastic racehorse gait, his ears pricked and shoulders working as they powered up the slope. Remembering her way from last weekend's ride with Zanah, Anna found the jockeys' favourite flat at the top. The scenery rolled out in endless miles before them. Distant hooves thundered on the turf and Tom's ears pricked as four jockeys streaked along together in a close pack on long-legged thoroughbreds in the fresh bright light. All were poised over their saddles, stirrups impossibly short, keenly staring along the necks of their mounts. Anna, thankful that they were sufficiently far off to not invoke Tom's competitive instincts, turned in the opposite direction, and asked him up into canter. With no extra encouragement, he kicked into gallop and flattened out into his racing dash, bringing a smile to her face and a surge through her soul. This was why she rode; never mind how dour her mindset, Tom always cheered her up, infusing her with a sense of freedom. It was the energy she thrived on. They cantered down the slope to the forest path and trotted through the woods. After about half a mile in trot Anna slowed them to a walk, anxious Tom should get a break; but as soon as the next rise came he was gnashing at the bit again, so they cantered up the next hill and along a broad bridle path which ran alongside a field of Jersey cows who watched them in quiet cud-chewing calm.

As soon as the rhythm of movement slowed, her mind ceased its focus on her own physical demands and busied itself with relentlessly turning over the events of the preceding evening. Every detail: looking down at the huge Lofter's hedge from Tom's back, the touch of Damien's hand, the sunset illuminating his handsome features, the ethereal appearance of the stag, the bounding feelings of happiness. Her jaw tightened as her too-reliable memory brutally reawakened her feelings of disappointment and foolishness. Angry at herself for her oversensitivity and delusional preoccupation with the events of the night before, she increased the pace again. She pointed Tom at the fallen trunk of a dead tree which he bounded over with fervour, temporarily unseating her and creating welcome hair-raising distraction.

It was just before 9 o'clock when Anna trotted through the back meadows of Rosemount on an exuberant and sweaty Tom. She scanned the yard for signs of life, eager to avoid everyone. With a jolt, she saw the low-slung BMW roadster which she recognised as Damien's, parked alongside her Land Rover. He was early! She hurried, seeing Barnabas gone from his field. He must have ridden out. If she was quick she might get done before he returned. Her thoughts were not straight, nowhere near. She leapt off Tom's back and un-tacked quickly. He steamed cinematically in the sunshine and rubbed his face on her back as she up hung his bridle. Quickly she hosed him down and squeegeed the excess moisture from his shining conker-coloured coat, the water running hot from his flanks. She left him to munch on a small feed while she ran to put his tack away, scanning the yard again for Damien. He wasn't there. It seemed strange he was early too; maybe he wanted to see her? She shook her head, trying to physically dislodge the thought, annoyed with her repetitious obsessing.

Anna affectionately rubbed Tom's forehead as she walked him to his field, thanking him for their energetic jaunt. He hung his head low and snorted as he walked into the field, and stamped the ground, sniffing, before lowering himself to roll in the dust.

Anna crossed the churchyard, morosely satisfied to have got away unaccosted, turning her attention to the rest of the day. She had to busy herself. Making a decision, she pulled out her phone to finally text Francesca back.

"Terrible," she keyed, and went inside to make a cup of tea.

Barnabas was sweat-soaked and steaming as he trotted into the yard. Foam hung from his mouth and he stamped and rubbed his head on his foreleg as Damien jumped from his back. Looking over to where he'd seen Anna's Land Rover earlier, Damien exhaled heavily.

"Damn it," he said under his breath, seeing it gone.

"Oh my word, he's worked hard!" exclaimed Penelope, approaching across the sweeping gravel turning circle.

"Hmm? Oh yeah," said Damien distractedly. "Have you seen Anna?"

"I saw her turning Tom out just after nine. She must have been out very early," Penelope answered, wondering what had Damien looking so out of sorts. Damien excused himself and led Barnabas over to Tom's field. Tom had the look of a sun-dried otter, the water having crisped areas of his coat, and there were patches of dark soil flaking from his rump where he had rolled.

Damien sighed. He had seen them on the flat tearing up the turf with their devastating grace, but he had been too far away down in the valley. He'd ridden like a man possessed to catch them but had no chance. He wasn't even entirely sure why. The abruptness with which his evening with Anna had come to an end felt depressing and had him rattled. He couldn't remember a better ride out with another person, and the closeness had felt warm and beguiling, contrasting starkly with getting home. The sudden halt to the enjoyment at his wife's behest and then returning to her agitation at his lateness, followed by an enforced dinner date with two uninspiring people, had rendered him mentally absent the whole evening. He had Anna stuck in his mind; her big dark blue eyes and shy smile in the evening light had bewitched him. He frowned.

What was he doing? It felt bad: awkward and disjointed; and it felt like it was his fault.

Not two minutes after sending her text, Anna's phone was ringing, Francesca's name emblazoned on the screen.

"You don't waste time," said Anna, answering the call.

"You can't put me off for hours and then send me a one-word cliff-hanger!" complained Francesca indignantly.

"You texted me before seven in the morning! What are you? Part of the dawn chorus?" jibed Anna, feeling better for talking to her friend.

"I was up early! Please Anna, no deflections!" begged Francesca. "What happened on your damned date?"

Anna sighed, hardly knowing where to start. "Are you free today? I kind of need to get out of here."

"Yes! Mike's away and I think you should come over here! Stay for the night! We can have dinner, wine...lots of wine!" Francesca enthused excitedly.

"Ok, I'll come to you. We'll talk then. I'll tell all," promised Anna, feeling catharsis might be the only way to halt the ceaseless replay.

The quartz counter top sparkled brilliantly under the theatrical spotlights in Francesca's converted warehouse apartment. The old brickwork walls faced off in architectural juxtaposition with the extreme structural modernity of glass and steel landings and stairways suspended in the old shell of the building. Anna threw her gaze around the room, appreciating the clean-lined luxury for a moment, as she meditatively swirled the white burgundy in her decadently oversized wine glass. Francesca sat across from her, eyes wide and intent as she absorbed every detail of her friend's account of the preceding evening.

"See, I just don't know, I'm probably over-reacting. Nothing actually happened! I probably completely misread him and now I feel like a bit of an idiot because leaving like that would have made me look like a pathetic, smitten little girl!" Anna sighed, stopping herself from continuing with her confused tirade.

"No honey, you're not an idiot!" protested Francesca. "It sounds like the most romantic first date I have ever heard about in real life, and there is no way you can deny something big went on! Feelings like that always communicate, and it took both of you to create an atmosphere like that. You can't spend gooey time staring into each other's eyes, holding hands, without *knowing* there is something going on! Sounds like love to me."

Anna moved uncomfortably, still feeling disquiet at Francesca's repeated assertion of 'love'. "He only held my hand because he saw it was shaking," she protested half-heartedly.

"No, he held your hand," insisted Francesca as she topped up their glasses. "Trouble is, he's married and you can't mess with that. That is exactly why it ended the way it did; you both had an amazing time out there in la-la land together away from everyone else, riding in this magical evening sunset, but then you got back to reality and he remembered he's married."

"Yes, and that's where it stops," said Anna firmly.

"Hmm. He's a bit of a sod for not having told you."

"It never came up," said Anna with a shrug. "We never really talked before last night, and what was he going to say? Prefix the ride with 'by the way, I'm married'?"

"No, but he might have mentioned his wife in conversation, so as to share the reality of his situation!" protested Francesca. "But of course, that would have ruined his marvellous romantic date!"

Anna was tired, too tired to continue the fruitless circling. It all came back to the same undesirable conclusion; she had to forget about it and move on. Feeling as though she had been through the emotional mill and back, she gratefully dropped into the big soft guest bed, under an enormous fluffy duvet, and slept like the dead.

Monday's early start had Anna grumpy again as she hurried down the platform at Victoria Station to the tube. It was the monthly meeting at her head office, starting at 8am, which always seemed like a wrench at the beginning of the week.

"Right, 'Other Business'," read Tess, the Area Manager, from the minutes, knocking on the boardroom table with her pen, and jolting Anna from her abstraction. Staring into her coffee, she wondered how long it would take to get over the few hours of Friday night which had her so disturbed. Obviously her months of living alone had turned her into a drama queen when it came to men.

"Martin, do you want to do yours first?" Tess continued, looking over her glasses at Martin Davidson, a Senior Partner, and a pleasant-faced individual with steel-grey hair and an aura of effortless calm and capability.

"Sure. As you all know we have the New York metro project going on, and Tony's been out there handling things. But we hit on a few snags during the enabling works, and in the interests of avoiding a delay we need an extra pair of hands on deck right now for a couple of weeks to get things done and help with the inevitable increase in paperwork. I was wondering if either Marcus or Anna might have capacity and inclination to take that on?"

Francesca looked in Anna's direction and saw she was already holding her pen up with a purposeful expression on her face. "I'll do that," she volunteered. "My projects are very manageable right now; no dramas."

"Oh, thank you, Anna," said Martin, pleased at the swiftness of an eager taker.

Smiling over at Marcus, Tess removed her glasses, folding the arms, and said wryly, "You've got to be quick when you want an opportunity round here. How does that work with Anna's post?" directing her latter comment at Martin.

"Actually very well," he replied, considering his list. "Anna's work is winding down and we have both Gemma and Francesca there to cover if need be."

"Great; thank you, Anna. We'll work out the details off-line after the meeting. That's going to happen fast, so you'll need to hand over today," said Tess. "That's high profile for us in New York, and any slip is definitely undesirable, particularly with the press all over it as they have been."

"Only two weeks?" questioned Anna.

"Yes, thereabouts," said Martin. "We're carrying the cost in this instance, so we'll bite the bullet and Tony thinks about two weeks of an extra PM's time will have them back on track."

Anna felt pumped. Two weeks was short, but never-the-less an opportunity to get noticed and elevated to higher profile work. Given the terminal boredom and frustration of her current assignment, a challenge under the spotlight would be the shake-up she needed. Undeniably though, her primary reason for volunteering had been the fact that New York offered two full weeks of time and space to clear her head properly of Damien.

Either way, the whirlwind of departure preparations swept away the black mood which had so gloomily engulfed her day. She was rushing along on a new wave, one which would turn her life on end for a couple of weeks. It was just what she needed, with impeccable timing.

She strode the Victoria Station concourse for the 2pm train. She would visit Rosemount to make arrangements for Tom during her absence and then pack and get some rest. Her flight from Heathrow was early the next morning.

NEW YORK

Anna loved travelling alone. It gave her a soaring feeling of independence and freedom. Fired up with enthusiasm, she hardly felt the effects of her 4am start as she settled into her seat on the plane and pulled out her briefing documents. The change in routine and her sense of adventure bolstered her with reserve energy, and she was determined to be ready to hit the ground at sprint on her arrival in New York. At that moment, she didn't care if there was no day off, or even sleep, for the whole two weeks; this was her opportunity to shine. She would get noticed and release herself from the drone-like existence she had been enduring, feeling ignored, utilised simply as a reliable cash cow for her employer.

'Second Avenue Subway: TBM Launch Box Construction,' read the front of the brief in Anna's hands. It was New York's biggest transit project and was currently the proud feather in the cap of her organisation, which had been brought in for a critical phase due to their extensive rail infrastructure and excavation experience. She would join the team just as they hit a major milestone and began excavating the area for the tunnel boring machine; it would all be in the glaring public spotlight.

Suddenly distracted by the red tail fins of the Virgin fleet lined up at their terminal, she craned to look out the window as her plane taxied to the runway. Damien sprang to her thoughts once more, but she caught herself, urging him away. She reset and focussed on what was actually important for her future, not some schoolgirl dalliance. Excellent performance was her only option and she would work day and night to make her mark.

Eight hours later and over thirteen hours since getting out of her bed, Anna strode purposefully from baggage reclaim into the arrivals hall at JFK.

"Anna!"

Looking around in surprise at hearing her name, she saw Tony detach himself from the crowd. Quite unexpectedly he had come to meet her, and he reached for her hand, shaking it warmly. She had always liked him; they shared an appreciation of one anothers' talents and she found him inspiring to work with. He was an executive director within their consultancy and was posted in New York for the duration of the project phase, managing the team. He appeared relaxed, shirt open at the neck and sleeves rolled up. His young face, tanned from the intense sun which dependably bathed the city, creased into a smile.

"I bet you're tired," he said, looking at his watch. "If it's midday here, you were on an early flight!"

"Yes, tired. But I want to get going asap."

"Always the go-getter! We'll drop your stuff at the hotel and then grab some lunch so you can at least re-charge."

New York was loud. Despite being expected of a city, loudness seemed a specific trait of the place, in comparison to other cities Anna had visited in the world. It was also notably vertical, the buildings rising massively all around, dwarfing them as they walked along the streets. London's Square Mile didn't come close to the kind of ambition that packed in so much and so many bodies into such a small area. It was also hot and constantly on the go. Anna guessed the height of the place trapped all the heat and sound at street level, where the inhabitants simply co-existed with these elements, and never slept. It was an interesting and surprising place, and made her impromptu trip and task there feel even more like a blast of new white noise to her senses. Her hotel was a short walk from the construction site office and it seemed her whole life for the next two weeks was concentrated into a small geographical space which catered to her every requirement.

By the end of the first day her energy levels crashed dramatically and that night she slept long and soundly. She woke refreshed early the next morning, ready to charge head-on into her commitment of tireless long hours.

Once at work, surrounded by American accents, she was initially poignantly aware of being a foreigner. However, it didn't matter; the team play on site was in stark comparison to the attitudes and back-biting of the London office from which she had just come. Everyone was direct and focused, driven towards their common goal, and Anna marvelled at the effect it had on her. Suddenly she loved her work and was filled with confidence and momentum.

Immersion in the incessant pace of the day kept Anna occupied, but in the evening, parted from her team and also without Rosemount and Tom, she found herself restless.

On Thursday night, staring out of her hotel window, watching the traffic move across the intersection on the street down below, and feeling like a child confined to her bedroom, a thought occurred to her. She had a friend nearby; Mateus's church was about an hour outside of the city. She immediately picked up her phone and texted him; perhaps she might meet up with him at the weekend?

"I'm in town too! Would you care to meet for dinner?" said the swift response as it flashed up on her phone.

As she walked along the street towards the little Upper West Side bistro which Mateus had suggested, she thought back to when she had last seen him. He had been visiting England, and she recalled how they had shared lunch in the local pub while arguing good-naturedly about the existence of God and destiny in life. Her last memory of him was as he handed over the keys to the cottage and hugged her goodbye.

The bistro was busy and the small tables were pleasantly mismatched and crammed in. The decor was bold, strong colours and old French advertisements and artwork depicting Parisian street scenes adorned the walls. And there was Mateus, always prompt, already seated and beckoning her over with a smile, projecting his usual warmth, even across the restaurant. He was tall and slim with a young supple face and broad smile. His skin was tanned and his deep brown eyes were framed by his thick dark blond hair. He got out of his seat and put his arms round her and she hugged him back.

"So good to see you Anna. How have you been?" he beamed. As ever he emitted a pure feeling, lacking agenda or criticism; however something about him had changed, as if recent experience had matured him. Despite his retaining his youthful looks, his eyes somehow seemed more thoughtful and serious.

* * * * * * *

A steady rain was falling at Rosemount and the skies were grey. Undeterred, the horses continued to graze in their fields, including Tom, whose coat was muddy from rolling and darkened from the soaking. Vibrant green had leapt forth once again, rejuvenated after the considerable period without rain. There were fresh hoof prints in the yard from a group of riders who had defied the elements and hacked out regardless of the miserable outlook. First to the bar was Olivia who perched on a stool, scraping her bedraggled hair back into a perky little pony tail.

"Ugh! Bloody awful out there. I'm soaked to my underwear!" she complained to Penelope, who was behind the bar that evening.

"I know! Isn't it dire," sympathized Penelope.

"Have you seen Anna?" asked Olivia, switching subjects.

"Yes, well I saw her on Monday. She was here in the afternoon to say she'd just been called away to New York," nodded Penelope as she opened a beer bottle and passed it to Dom, who had just appeared and nodded wordlessly at the cooler.

"Really? Why? I was wondering where my stick and ball partner had gone," he said, taking a swig as Zanah and Damien joined them.

"Work. It sounded like a good opportunity suddenly cropped up," responded Penelope.

"Did she say anything about it to you on Friday, Damien?" Olivia asked, as Damien shrugged off his wet jacket, slinging it indifferently on a bar stool. He shook his head, and reached for the beer Penelope handed him. "I don't even know what she does," continued Olivia.

"She's a project manager," Zanah contributed. "I think she said she's been working in rail."

"She's a bit of a dark horse, just taking off like that," laughed Olivia. "Almost as bad as you, Damien. She's not gone for good, has she?"

"No, she guessed about two weeks," answered Penelope.

"She didn't even message me," said Olivia, looking at her phone.

"You're not everyone's mother!" laughed Zanah. "I'm just off to wash the horse muck off my hands; should I text you?" she grinned, digging Olivia in the ribs.

"You should. Get in the habit. I like to be in the loop!" joked Olivia deadpan.

"You're such a control freak!" Zanah threw over her shoulder as she disappeared.

● ● ● ● ● ●

After a pleasant dinner Anna and Mateus strolled back through Central Park in the direction of Anna's hotel.

"Forgive me Anna," said Mateus in his considerate and slightly old-fashioned way, "But you don't seem all yourself." He looked at her and added, "I don't mean to pry, but it feels like you need to talk."

Anna sighed, looking at him in acknowledgement. He was so perceptive. Even the brash novelty of her new environment and frenetic days couldn't conceal her unusually pensive demeanour from him.

Mateus smiled and said, "I've nowhere to be and I'm your friend."

Anna turned to look at him appreciatively; he had such a genuine peace about him and an honest caring which she trusted and felt safe with. Any time they met they always seemed to pick up as though no time had elapsed since last seeing one another. But it seemed weird to share a relationship issue with a male friend, at least one who was not gay. Mateus, however, was different, and though embarrassed about her feelings, she ran through a conservative version of what had happened and her recent confusion over Damien. She ridiculed herself openly at the fact it was nagging at her now.

"I don't want this. You know what I went through with Adam and I swore to myself I would take a year to be alone. I don't want the complication. I just want things back to how they were a week ago when I was happy at my new stables, having fun, playing polo and having a laugh with new friends. And I especially don't want to feel like this about someone who's married!"

Mateus looked thoughtful and remained quiet, as if giving her space to reflect on her own words.

"I need this gone from my head. I have more important stuff to focus on. It's ridiculous! We weren't in a relationship!" she ranted.

"It sounds like you were," said Mateus steadily. Anna looked at him uncertainly and he smiled at her. "We build fortresses of denial round ourselves these days to protect our egos. Interaction between people, though subtle, can have a profound impact. But we deny those subtleties when it suits us to do so because we can, because vibrations like that are easily dismissed as fanciful or over-sensitive." Anna regarded him. They had never spoken of relationships before, and his words had sense and truth. "A lot of people have parameters for what a relationship must be; be it sex or a certain amount of time spent together, or meeting the parents or any other criteria they assign to the word 'relationship'. But relationships don't have to be that physically obvious; they can amount to an energy that exists between people, which can be just as powerful."

"And deniable," said Anna, thoughtfully, assuming Damien – if he felt anything about the evening – would deny the intensity of that

Friday evening. Had he felt it too? She might never know. It could be completely one-sided.

"Denial is a useful tool when a relationship is inappropriate, or one has second thoughts," continued Mateus in an almost cynical tone, as if reading her mind.

She noticed that he didn't lecture her on the sanctity of marriage. There was no judgement apparent in his demeanour.

"It wasn't a relationship," she insisted, more for herself.

"Fair enough," he said reasonably. "But regardless of what you feel it was, the premise is the same. It's something you have to move on from, and the best way is to just accept it and let it go. Don't judge."

Anna pondered as she carried on walking. By the time she returned to England, she would have re-established her bubble, and removed Damien from it. She looked at the ground, knitting her brow, knowing that she was fooling herself.

"I'm here for a few days yet. Would you like to meet up again?" he asked, looking up into the trees above them.

"Definitely!" Anna agreed, with a smile. "And thank you, I get more clarity from talking to you than anyone else I know!"

He smiled humbly, and looked thoughtful. "Come with me to church on Sunday morning, then we'll do breakfast."

"Church?" said Anna uncertainly.

"Church?" mimicked Mateus, with mock horror, squeezing Anna's arm playfully.

She laughed, feeling like they were back at university.

"Come on, come with me!" Mateus urged. "The pastor's a really dynamic speaker. I think you'll be surprised."

Friday and Saturday were both working days, and the hours flew by in a blur of frantic action. The team worked like it was possessed; the reputation of everyone relied on meeting their deadline, and the atmosphere was feverish under the perform-or-die media spotlight. Anna barely slept, and when she did, her dreams had her at her desk in the light of her laptop or running on the construction site, surrounded by noise and hunted by time. It was a world away from the boredom she knew back in London. On Saturday night, milestone achieved, they celebrated at last, victorious and running on nothing but adrenalin.

"Disaster averted!" said Tony, as the group clashed glasses over the table in an underground jazz bar. The project was back on track, and they would begin excavation sharp on Monday morning as planned. The feeling of camaraderie was palpable and Anna felt genuine affection for every one of the people round the table. That was what work was supposed to be about; that feeling of purpose and being a part of something genuinely impacting real time and real things. They would party until late that evening then crash for Sunday before hitting site early on Monday. Challenge, play, rest. It was what life was all about; certainly all that Anna wanted.

Back in her hotel room that night, she felt disconnected from her people, like a component separated from its machine. For the first time in her life, she thought she understood those who married their jobs and worked all hours; it was where they drew their strength. But it seemed sad, and maybe a little dangerous, to rely so exclusively on one area of life for all one's happiness and meaning.

Sunday brought about her church date with Mateus, and feeling fuzzy-headed, she hauled herself from her bed. Why had she agreed to go to church? It certainly wasn't her choice of pastime, and particularly not while she was still breathing alcohol. The last time Anna went to church she was part of a Brownie pack. It had been a freezing Remembrance Day, and they had stood in a windy cemetery, watching various dignitaries step up one by one to the grey stone memorial to lay a wreath. Then they had marched as a group to the old church in the village and sat in the deathly cold pews, desperate to warm up. Time had stretched until the hands on her Minnie Mouse watch looked like they were actually crawling backwards; it had seemed like a thousand years listening to the meaningless drone of the vicar high up in his stone pulpit. They had knelt on rough embroidered hassocks, with the cold draught whistling at floor level numbing knees and feet, and Anna had prayed for home time.

Ever since then, religion had been completely irrelevant to her life; it simply did not enter her mind. She had gone through a period of outright atheism, with scathing disbelief in any notion of a deity; it could not be more than a childish fancy, unsophisticated, tribal and antiquated, to suppose there could be some invisible force or entity. Her life continued its course mostly under her command, with all its ups and downs. She had become distant from her family, her parents having separated when she was a child and become involved in their new partners and new children, seemingly uninterested in her. Relationships and friends too, came and went, all on their own agendas and courses of life.

Anna wasn't sorry for herself; she simply accepted the transience of things and people, and was fiercely self-reliant. After all, one had to be, when no-one could be relied upon.

She sighed inwardly at her train of thought as she walked along. Francesca would tell her she was cynical, and the cause of her own isolation. She could see her smiling at her, telling her she would do better to share. But what was to be gained? Building strong bonds and sharing one's innermost thoughts seemed pointless, sometimes even folly, given the flightiness of people and their ever-changing motivations.

Mateus was waiting at the steps to the church. She managed an uncertain half-smile as they met, the internal monologue and twenty-year-old memories still lingering disagreeably.

"Morning, Anna!" he said, grinning at her expression and putting his arm round her shoulders in a big-brotherly manner. "Come on, you! No church, no breakfast!"

The gothic architecture of the church was grandiose, both inside and out. Though magnificent it did nothing for Anna's comfort levels. It seemed formal and foreign, and somewhere she wasn't really supposed to be. She felt self-conscious; like everyone would know she was a non-believer and had no place there, a barely legal alien in both New York and church.

Mateus led the way and they sat down, Anna looking about doubtfully. A woman sitting on the other side of Anna smiled kindly at them and said a cheery good morning. Upon hearing their accents she immediately launched into an enthusiastic account of a trip she had taken to England in 1981, her vision of the country making Anna and Mateus smile given the changes and the burst of population there had been in the decades since. But the everyday conversation helped Anna's mood, and by the time the service began, her prey-animal jitters had subsided.

There were a couple of hymns, which Anna stood through, not having the first clue as to the words. Mateus made no remark, but she leant close to him and justified herself, "It's not 'Jerusalem'; that's the only hymn I know." Mateus simply nodded and smiled.

As they took their seats again, Anna looked around her at the other people; some seemed happy, others serious, some wore earnest expressions, some clasped Bibles. Surveying the diverse mix of young, old, male, female, smart and unkempt, she was struck by a strange feeling; she could feel a lump in her throat and goose bumps on her arms. It felt like she was going to cry. She frowned. What was this weird tidal wave of emotion from nowhere? It was overwhelming and she looked down and took a breath, tensing her jaw, bewildered. The next moment thankfully saw the arrival of the guest speaker, a pastor from another church in Vermont. His appearance distracted her. He was young and vibrant, a bit like Mateus. He wore a casual shirt and jeans, and ambled to and fro as he poured his heart into his animated sermon. He was speaking about freedom in life – something Anna was a big fan of. He used normal slangy language, and spoke with a passion which lit him up charismatically. Anna had never seen a member of the clergy in this light. Where were the robes and the endless references to Matthew, John, Luke and the other bloke, chapter whatever verse wherever?

She sat transfixed as she listened intently, thinking it was more like a lecture on life empowerment and living well than a sermon. When he mentioned God for the first time, he did so with such passion and intimacy that Anna, in her admiration for his engagement and sheer projection of personality, did not squirm uncomfortably. She continued to drink in his words, sitting forward as he declaimed about internal frustration and difficulty in doing the right thing.

"This isn't new!" he insisted. "We have always struggled; humans have always struggled to do the right thing! I mentioned this guy earlier, the apostle Paul yeah, and in Romans, check out what he says – don't worry about your Bibles, I've got it up here on the screen," gesturing with his thumb to a giant projection screen behind him. "– Romans 7:15-16, here's what he says…and just imagine his frustration ok, he's frustrated with himself, he's really going off on one! He says; 'I do not understand what I do. For what I want to do I do not do, but what I hate, I do. And if I do what I do not want to do, I agree that the law is good.'"

He reiterated the verse for clarity and then bounded on. "And the law he mentions there could be any law. Could be Bible law, your country's law, or maybe your own internal law, what you think is right and wrong. Why do we do it? I mean, you can forget about laws imposed on you by your wife, husband, mother-in-law…" He laid into the last words with a comical weariness, drawing laughter from the congregation. "I'm talking about what *you* think is right. And what you think is right, you often disregard! You contravene it! You blunder on and do the wrong thing, all the while knowing it's wrong! And then how does it make us feel? Once the initial pleasure – as it's usually our greed for something, right? The money, the triumph, the last word in the argument, the woman, the man, the cake?"

He paused as more laughter rippled through the vast interior of the church. "– so once this initial pleasure in doing the wrong thing subsides, how do we feel? Empty? Hollow? Disappointed? Embarrassed? Sad? Whatever it is, it's not good, right? So why? Why do we do this? Our friend Paul is making the point that in order to live in freedom and happiness, we need rules; we need them to stop us doing these stupid things we are inclined to do!"

"Well?" asked Mateus as they jogged down the steps into the fresh air again.

"Amazing. I was blown away," Anna admitted. "Who knew the clergy had quietly updated themselves and there were young, startlingly attractive vicars wondering around out there delivering far better emphatic speeches than any politician or company director?"

"Perhaps you might allow God and the church into your life a little after all?" he said, looking along the street for a good spot for breakfast.

"Well, perhaps if I had known about this transformation I might have considered it a while ago," said Anna. "But still, I am not convinced by all the God stuff. I like the teaching, it's totally sound and he put it across so it actually applied to life, but bring God into it all and that's where you're losing me."

"What have you got against God?" asked Mateus, opening a door to a café and standing aside for Anna. They paused as they found their seats and opened their menus.

"Well, I just have a belief problem that there's this bearded bloke up there who is apparently omnipotent but doesn't seem to do much with it," she shrugged, studying her menu.

"Bearded bloke, Anna? Really?"

"Well okay, that was a childish illustration probably forced on me years ago," admitted Anna, feeling the feebleness of what she was saying. "But I just can't make that leap of faith that there is this God – the fact He's referred to as a He for a start."

"You don't like He? Would you prefer She?"

"No, neither. If there's a god, surely we're not talking about a person – that would be totally implausible. It can't be a human. It's got to be more like an all-encompassing force, a force that penetrates everything and everyone?"

Mateus nodded seriously.

"Therefore," Anna continued, "using the word He is all wrong for me. It feels odd. God is a genderless thing, maybe not a thing or an it...," she pondered, thinking aloud, "but an unquantifiable entity of some kind."

"Maybe you're worrying about semantics," suggested Mateus. "It almost sounds like you're creating a barrier to entry." Anna noted his deft utilisation of business jargon; he was smart and knew how to talk. "If that's what you're worrying about – what is the best term of address – I'd ask you, for your own sake, to disregard that obstacle for the time being and just let God into your life. You'll work the rest out in time. Every step of faith is met with an answer."

"Faith," grunted Anna, as she slumped back in her seat, putting her hands round the mug of coffee the waitress had just poured. Her brain felt addled. Faith in anything had never worked for her.

"Have you got anything to do today?" Mateus asked her.

"Not a thing, apart from be in bed mega early for a dawn start on site," said Anna, thinking of all the equipment which had been arriving on site over the last two days for the start of excavation.

"Come with me, then. I'm having a picnic in the park with my friends on the course. They're a good crowd of people, it'll be fun."

Anna was reluctant. She'd had enough God talk for the day already and was worried she'd be grilled by a whole platoon of vicars if she went along.

"Don't worry," smiled Mateus, seeming to know yet again what was on her mind. "I made Cornish pasties! They're going to blow my American friends away!"

Anna relaxed and laughed. Mateus had always been enthusiastic about Cornish pasties, as far back as university. He'd once tried to make double-ended pasties, with the main course in one end and the dessert in the other end, but it had been a disaster: meat peas and potato awash with raspberry jam and custard, all wrapped in puff pastry.

Mateus's friends were a truly warm and genuine group. There was a mix of all ages, and far from interrogating Anna, they were remarkably easy to be around. There was a feeling of care and respect for one another she wasn't accustomed to. That habitual underlying air of judgement or ridicule, which seemed so common in daily life, was simply absent. Their characters surprised her, not conforming to her perception of clerics on a conference. She accepted Mateus as not fitting the mould but was taken aback that there were a number of cool types. One, a lady called Sheila whom she chatted with for some time, was vibrant and bubbly, and looked like a stereotypical inhabitant of Woodstock in her bright mix of colours and hair braided round her head like a crown. She told Anna animatedly of a retreat she had been to, where in two weeks of complete silence she underwent dramatic self-realisation, pain and transformation.

"…I remember the first day the silence really made an impression. That was the day I looked in the mirror and saw someone different in my eyes. Silence can be frightening at first, and you can find yourself not liking some of the motivations and thoughts you have…"

Anna listened to her, fascinated. To think a woman like this, who seemed so wholly good, could be disturbed by her own motivations… What on earth would Sheila make of the muddle inside of Anna's head? Then she did an unusual thing; she opened up and told Sheila about her own experience on Tresco, and the sense of awe she had felt. Sheila attended closely, her smiling eyes seeming to read Anna's thoughts and identify exactly with her.

"It's awesome to feel God's power in those moments," she commented, tipping her head back and looking up through the leaves of the enormous tree they were sitting under. "It's that connection we all yearn for, in the lonesomeness of the duality of this life."

Her words resonated with Anna, as she thought of the sense of belonging she had felt with her new team, and the jarring loneliness of the quiet evenings. Then she considered the happy ease and profound connection she had felt in solitude on the Tresco beach. It had been deep and real, but she couldn't get her head round it being the presence of God; although it did seem strangely connected, or coincidental, to being there with Mateus in New York.

She spent the whole afternoon with the group, relaxing and enjoying the company of people outside of work for the first time in a week. Conversation was easy and sometimes humorous, but without the harder edge of sarcasm, profanity and sexual innuendo which so frequently figured in interchanges at Rosemount.

She wondered how the people she was with would function in the world which was normal to her. Would they consider it to be loosely governed by a set of poor morals? Maybe they would be right. Maybe most people in the world lived thoughtlessly and badly, creating much of their own and other people's misery without even realising? She contemplated how thoughtless she was in her communicating; sometimes ungenerous in her assessments and even wilfully misunderstanding people like Greg. She rarely paused to consider what trials others could be going through which might cause their antagonistic behaviour. If nothing else, she was resolved to try and be more mindful of her thoughts and actions. That would surely be an admirable takeaway from her strange day.

"You're going to be ok, Anna," said Mateus as they neared Anna's hotel, which he insisted on walking her to.

"Yes. I'll be fine," she smiled. He had obviously come to a conclusion within himself about her. "I'm pretty self-sufficient."

Fleetingly, Mateus looked sad. "Don't be lonely, Anna. Remember you're not alone. I'll pray for you."

He smiled into her eyes for a moment. The warmth he exuded made Anna feel the same emotion she felt that morning in the church: a lump rising in her throat and her eyes growing hot. What was it? Was she so unaccustomed to the warm feeling of genuine love?

"Thank you," said Anna, looking at the ground for a moment. She felt awkward again. It had been a most unusual day.

Mateus looked at her slightly mischievously. "Remember that the god you don't believe in does not exist," he enunciated, slowly and somewhat cryptically. "But that strength you find in yourself, that power you have that drives you, what you felt in Tresco; that's God." He hugged her goodbye. Then he smiled and, turning to go, promised, "I'll call you when I'm over at Christmas." He walked away waving over his shoulder.

Anna had watched him go. As she walked the corridor to her room, she repeated his words in her head, trying to make sense of them. The god you don't believe in does not exist. What a thing to leave her with. Did he do it deliberately? Of course he did; she saw the look on his face! He knew how introspective she was.

She closed the door of her room and stood motionless with her back against it, thinking. The whole of the last month seemed to have been one intense lesson, transforming who she was and how she thought. Things appeared to happen each day which were accelerating the pace at which she was changing herself and her outlook on life.

Kicking off her shoes, she poured herself a glass of wine and threw herself down on the bed, staring thoughtfully out of the window. Then she reached for the drawer in the bedside table and found just what she expected: a Bible. Thumbing to and fro for a while, she eventually found Romans, and turning her eyes to the ceiling for a moment she scanned her memory. Verse 7...something?

Carefully parting the crinkly pages, she saw the words again, under verse 7:15. Then she noticed, amused, that a bookmark had been marking the page. She could almost see Mateus laughing at this coincidence, which of course he would insist was no coincidence.

'I do not understand what I do. For what I want to do I do not do, but what I hate, I do. And if I do what I do not want to do, I agree that the law is good...,' she read.

"Self-control by my own government," she pondered aloud.

As she reached to turn out the bedside lamp that night, she thought of Mateus; his expression as he had said that he'd pray for her. It gave her a curious and pleasant feeling of protection.

THE RETURN HOME

Penelope was perched on the edge of the sofa at a low table in the bar area, studying the accounts with her bookkeeper, Annetta.

"Here are the invoices for the feed for that month," she said, handing over her paperwork, looking over the thin silver rims of her reading glasses which were perched halfway down her nose.

Annetta looked them over swiftly and slotted them into her file. "We're seeing more return on the polo side of the business this season," she remarked, turning her attention to revenue.

"Yes, not bad. Considering Pete really just put the field in so he could stick and ball with some friends," answered Penelope, glancing out at Kevin as he cruised the length of the polo field with the finishing mower, sitting back in the tractor seat, languidly puffing on a cigarette.

"I'm not happy with the records on the funding Andrew puts in," complained Annetta.

As she was speaking, David walked into the bar, followed by Chantelle and her only female friend, a slim, sulky-looking girl called Nicole. Chantelle was wearing bright pink jodhpurs and one of her customary plunging necklines, with the word 'Trashy' scrawled across the front.

Her feet were bare and she wore pink glitter nail polish and a silver ring on her right little toe.

"Have you got the book?" David asked Penelope, walking over to where she and Annetta were sitting. "I need to put the girls' lessons in for next week."

"Hello darling," said Annetta in a deliberate and meaningful tone as she looked at David, and then threw a glance of undisguised disapproval at Chantelle.

Annetta was David's wife, and a horsewoman herself. She was severe and judgemental, hard on anyone who failed to meet her exacting standards – which Chantelle had no hope of reaching. Aside from any other considerations, riding gear in non-standard colours was a no-no, but throw in wanton little tee-shirts and toe rings, and her opinion of the offender nosedived irreparably toward contempt. David gave her a quick smile, knowing what she was thinking.

"Don't even go there," he smirked, taking the book from Penelope.

Annetta watched him go, with stern eyes.

She was the money behind their particular outfit. Having for years made her living in the professional services environment, she struck out alone in business after the collapse of her employer, when the Big Five became the Big Four. She was doing very nicely and she wanted David to match her status by setting up his own equestrian establishment. While he made a reasonable income from his private clients and from judging dressage, he was essentially just a yard manager and instructor, one who spent far too much time basking in the admiration of his assorted female clientele. The arrival of unsubtle, barefoot girls on his scene, following him around like stray dogs, would doubtless result in distracted stalling on his part. He wasn't stupid enough to actually do anything, but he certainly enjoyed his associations too much, and Annetta despised him for it.

"We could really do with less of her type here at Rosemount," she said, her eyes on Chantelle.

Penelope, not one to speak badly of anyone, gave a small shrug and spread her hands helplessly. "Throw her out!" snorted Annetta, turning grumpily back to the accounts.

At the bar Chantelle and David's fingers touched for a long moment as she passed him the money she owed for her lesson. He cleared his throat and circled her next appointment in the book.

"Okay, Friday, same time," he said briskly, then met her eyes for a second and turned to go. Fantasizing about Chantelle laying on her back in the middle of the riding arena was his current go-to, and the image raged through him as he strode from the bar.

It was close to lunchtime when the review was completed, and Penelope sat back, happy to turn her eyes away from the figures at last.

"Hey hey hey!" said Pete heartily, appearing with Andrew, and rubbing Penelope's shoulder affectionately.

Their arrival lifted the atmosphere, and Penelope smiled at him. "You look like the bearer of good news!"

"Absolutely! Guess who's booked yet another polo game in two weeks with some high goalers visiting from Argentina *and also* the hunt kick-off do as well!" he boasted.

"Good work!" congratulated Penelope.

"I'll say! They're playing at Guards and Hurlingham, so it's a big score for us!" Seeing her questioning look, he added; "Thank Andrew. He seemed to have some influence there."

Penelope looked around the room doubtfully. "I'd better get this place spruced up a bit."

"And just how does Andrew pull in these favours?" demanded Annetta. Andrew bothered her. His irrepressible confidence and carefree attitude were irritating; moreover his financial arrangements were a mystery, and he seemed to take perverse pleasure in evading her every demand.

"You leave the contacts to me, Annetta," Andrew responded in a self-satisfied tone.

"No, Penel, it's fine!" said Pete, responding to her concern and looking at the ceiling and around the room. "Plus we're running a horsey establishment here, and let's face it, the associated alcohol consumption tends to prevent critical attention to the décor!"

"There's a smudge there," said Damien, pointing at the wall with a grin at Pete, having heard the end of the conversation as he approached.

"I thought you were going out?" said Pete, smiling back.

"Yes, I'm just stalling. Chantelle's looking for a riding buddy and it's not going to be me."

"There you go!" said Annetta in triumph. "She's actually a pain to have around!"

Penelope turned with weary amusement to Pete and Damien, who were looking perplexed. "Annetta doesn't approve of Chantelle's presence here."

"Damn right I don't! You should get rid of her sort, Pete."

"Oh I don't know," shrugged Pete. "She doesn't say much to anyone, and therefore doesn't upset anyone, she's quiet, she keeps her area clean, she pays... well, *her father* pays on time," he went on, correcting himself. "Isn't he a hunting friend of yours, Annetta?"

"Yes, he's decent so I've no idea why his daughter is such a tramp. But she lends nothing to the image of the place, turning up looking like she's going to her night job," sneered Annetta bitchily.

"Is this your problem with non-classic riding apparel?" jibed Pete, winking at Damien.

"You know my opinion on that, but it's more the fact that this place is a better class of yard. It's not the place for the barefoot gyppo look, and the runaway knockers staring blatantly over her pointless top! She looks like a hooker for god's sake!" asserted Annetta, getting shriller. Pete and Damien snorted with laughter.

"I'll talk to her about the shoes," said Pete solemnly, lips twitching.

"I'm serious, Pete!" protested Annetta.

"Okay, Damien, will you address the – what was it? – the runaway knockers with her when you ride out?" winked Pete, unable to leave it alone. Damien was looking out the window and, seeing the yard empty, moved towards the door.

"I suggest you leave that one for Annetta; she'll handle it – or should I say *them* – admirably," he said with cheery irony as he left.

· · · · · ·

The week had been a flurry of hectic action. Anna had been on site at 5am on Monday, and had worked late into the evenings. Sunday's spiritual pondering had slipped into the background as her familiar peer group surrounded her once again, and life seemed more straightforward for it. The week had started as planned, with the major milestone of breaking ground. In the midst of the din, as the huge excavator made its inaugural slice into the concrete, Anna had looked upwards at the cobalt sky, so different from the skies of England, imagining how the scene looked from above. The intense focus of man and machine over one tiny spot on the planet and the dogged toil which had preceded seemed excessive, simply to arrive at the apparently straightforward point of making a hole in the ground.

The two weeks had filled Anna with gratification, and she was wiser, braver and more capable for the experience. Her own drive and resourcefulness had surprised her, and she realised that the tedium and dreariness of the role back in London had sapped her self-esteem. The work and the office environment had been an oppressive weight addling her mind, making her lose faith in herself and her abilities; it was like drowning. Here in New York everything was clear and obvious. Though not easy, the path was distinct. She confided in Tony as they sat in a coffee shop taking a rare break.

"Now I've been here I can't bear the thought of going back. It's like being demoted from president to drain cleaner."

"Make sure you talk to Martin when you get back. Get them to move you. Let's face it, you've proven yourself as a project manager, a runner, a field engineer, and an accountant, while you've been here!" laughed

Tony, as he counted off on his fingers the roles she had covered in her frenetic days. "I've worked on the grotty boring stuff too, you know, amongst those personalities you talk about: the charisma-bypass club! You are getting some fantastic experience in that environment, and now you definitely know where you do and don't thrive. It won't last forever. I often think that all the experiences, all the pain we go through, is for a reason, building us for the next challenge. Nothing's wasted."

He sounded like Mateus talking of destiny. What a huge couple of weeks it had been. Life had changed again.

It was a little before 8pm on Wednesday when Anna boarded her flight home. The sun was low over the city, the architecture stacked along the hazy orange skyline like building blocks. Suddenly she felt tired. The pace had been incessant, but they had combated any delay and were on site and on schedule. Her self-assurance had returned. The achievement had bolstered her and she was ready for the impact it would have on her career. The roar of frantic thoughts about Damien had thankfully subsided and she felt calm about seeing him again, fortified from her time away and ready to press the reset button on their relationship, or whatever it was.

* * * * * * *

Dom had chipped off early and was strolling across the yard at four o'clock, enjoying the afternoon sunshine, as Pete called to him:

"Chukkas are on this evening! We've got a full house. Keith's coming over with Anthony and Benson and also Paul's back with his son Lucias. Add you and me, and we've got...oh, one too few," he broke off. Then they both heard a vehicle rounding the bend in the driveway and turned to see who it was.

"Well, what do you know?" exclaimed Dom, waving at Anna. She smiled at them both through the open window of her Land Rover as she pulled alongside. "Anna, you're back! And just in time! Ready to play some chukkas this evening? We need another player."

"You need another player who plays as badly as me?" joked Anna.

"Any player! Any player and you are her! Besides, we need a woman on the field to chase!" laughed Dom boisterously.

Anna grinned and pulled away to park up. She had flown all night, landing just that morning, and was intending to visit Tom and then get an early night. But seeing the others lifted her, making her feel energetic. A game of polo would be a way to hit the social scene of the yard again with a bang. She was a young achiever so what was a bit of jet-lag?

"How was the Big Apple?" asked Pete as she strode over to them. As she chatted to Pete, an unfamiliar car drove in the gate and Dom waved and called out.

"You're early! Obviously the London traffic isn't as bad as you make out."

The female driver had shoulder-length brown hair and a good-natured smile, and Anna guessed this must be his wife. How long had it been since they had seen each other? Dom had been playing polo most weekends and hadn't been home as far as she knew, so presumably his wife had finally given in and travelled to him.

The game had been going for thirty minutes and the sun was low. Anna had been feeling out of her depth on the field. The others were all far superior polo players and she had not had much of a look-in on play, but at last she had the ball. Their horses were tired and everyone was beginning to wind down as the light slithered away. Her strike was powerful, and her horse, apparently pleased to finally be part of play, kicked off at an enthusiastic pace in pursuit of her strike. This provoked a second wind in the others and there were shouts behind Anna as they squeezed the last action they could from their weary mounts.

The chill of the evening had begun creeping in and the purity of bird song rang across the yard as Damien got out of his car. Shouts from the polo field drew his eye and he slowed, double-taking, as he realised one of the riders was Anna. He had got used to her absence and hadn't even noticed her Land Rover parked in the yard. He drifted off course towards the deck, stopping for a moment to watch keenly as she rose out of her stirrups, looking over her shoulder for the ball.

Out on the field, Anna urged her mount into a gallop as the ball raced past her from Pete's strike.

"Go, Anna, go!" Dom yelled behind her.

She sensed Lucias, a tall and enormously confident 22-year-old with wavy chestnut hair protruding from his bright red polo helmet, surging in to ride her off. The air was knocked from her as his horse crashed into hers. She put her leg hard against the side of her mare, urging her to fight and lean into the onslaught to defend her line. She stood in her stirrups, leaning into the attack.

Lucias laughed rakishly, "Yeah baby!" he shouted.

"Oi! Foul!" yelled Dom. "And dammit Anna, circle! Where's the ball?"

Anna, realizing play had degraded way beyond any rules, shoulder-barged Lucias before circling sharply away to rejoin the line behind Dom. He swung and missed the ball. "Shit! Anna!"

"I'm there!" shouted Anna, totally focused and swooping down on the ball to strike it perfectly. It flew, and she raced after it like a hare, hearing Dom exclaiming in admiration:

"Anna, you witch!"

They thundered down the field in a pack, everyone with renewed vigour. Sensing Lucias and his fast, thuggish horse breathing down her neck once again, she raised her mallet, praying he wouldn't hook her, and swung again. The ball rocketed through the goal, much to her elation and that of her team. What a re-entry to the UK!

"Chukka!" called Pete's voice through the hubbub, bringing an end to the game. "*Definitely* chukka! I can't see anymore!" It was almost dark and they all slowed to a walk, shook their feet from the stirrups and jumped from their steaming horses. Lucias shouted exuberantly, high-fiving Anna, then shaking her hand. Anna loved the handshake at the end of the match; it sealed the good-humoured rough-and-tumble camaraderie on the field.

"Beer!" commanded Dom, clapping Anna on the shoulder and turning her in the direction of the bar. The polo horses were resting in their stalls under their coolers, dozily munching hay, and Anna could feel the inevitable weariness of her 32 waking hours kicking in.

"Argh! I should really go," she exclaimed. "I'm back in London early tomorrow and I feel like I'm still on Eastern Time."

"You're staying for one!" stated Dom, pulling her along with him. Anna grinned and gave in. He hustled her into the bar where the rest of the players were already sinking cold bottles of beer. "Two more, Pete!" said Dom, marching Anna to the bar.

"Where did you find this one?" asked Lucias, his slightly gritty voice resonant, looking Anna up and down and addressing Dom.

"At the top of the Downs riding a big-ass thoroughbred," answered Dom. "Looked like she could use some team sport in her life!" The guys roared jocularly in unison.

"I'm going, if you're going to carry on like this," said Anna in mock reproof as Dom thrust a beer into her hand.

"Glad you're back, Anna. What were you up to anyway? You just disappeared!"

Anna explained her precipitous absence and found herself animatedly talking about her project work. New York had certainly given her a new enthusiasm for what she did, and she was surprised as they all listened to her, seemingly fascinated. Dom had a nostalgic knowledge of the streets in which she had existed for the past two weeks, and was full of all kinds of questions.

"Hey, Pete's lined up a great game for the weekend after next" said Dom, having exhausted the topic of New York, and moving onto his favourite subject of polo. "There're a couple of seriously high goalers from Argentina coming. I need you to groom for me on the day."

"As long as there are workplace rights and perks," she said with a grin as she finished her beer. "Now I really have to go." Everyone wished her goodnight, and she pulled the bar door closed behind her and headed off for a final check on Tom.

As she walked from Tom's field through the dewy grass in the chill night air, she saw a figure leading a horse silhouetted at the arena door, backlit from the lights inside. As they drew closer, she felt a little leap in her chest as she saw it was Damien. She hadn't bargained on seeing him so soon. Taking a deep breath she continued walking purposefully.

"Hi," he said as they neared one another. He sounded muted, almost shy.

"Hi," she returned, feeling a small surge of nervous energy run through her as she looked at him.

"Good game?" he enquired.

"Yes. I didn't really mean to get involved," said Anna, trying to answer him as normally as possible. "I just landed this morning and I'm shattered."

"Yeah, west to east hurts more than the journey out," he agreed. She realised he must have found out where she went. She took a breath, trying to think of something else to say. Barnabas threw his head and tugged at the end of the reins which Damien was holding loosely. Damien turned and flicked at the reins and issued a brief low warning at him. Then he turned his eyes back to Anna, and once again she felt like she was drowning.

"Listen, I wanted to talk to you before you left," he started, "I enjoyed riding out with you," he paused awkwardly. "It was a good time."

Anna shifted, processing his inconclusive statement, restraining the urge to question him. She was over the tumultuous emotions now.

"It was a really good evening," she answered, not really knowing if she sounded wooden, or whether he heard any meaning in her words. What did it matter? It was irrelevant now.

Damien remained silent for a moment and then seemed to shake his head infinitesimally before pulling himself together. "Maybe we can ride out sometime soon when I get back?" he suggested. Then as if sensing the inappropriateness of it he added, "I don't ride out much with other people. Too many of them incessantly ramble on about nothing, spoiling the quiet. It's nice be with someone who shuts up like me."

Anna smiled, identifying with him. "I'd like that," she said, forcing herself to begin moving away, and not labour the moment. After all, they were just yard acquaintances now.

THE MATCH

Floating on the ripples in the docks, seagulls busily pruned their immaculate feathers, and the naked glare of the morning sun glinted off the water, penetrating the boardroom windows. Anna sat straight in one of the chairs round the large rectangular meeting table, gripping her pen, watching the latest drama play out. She wasn't ready for confrontational theatre, feeling disconnected and suspended between time zones. Images of her adventure in New York were dominating her mind, and she felt like a confused bird that had just been snatched from the air and crammed in a cage.

"I don't really give a flyer why it happened! I just want to know how the bloody hell we're going to get this project back on track!" shouted Andrew Mansfield, throwing his seat back and putting his hands behind his head so his armpits commanded the room.

Anna and Francesca exchanged glances. The sight of this man exhibiting such baldly obvious lead-chimp behaviour was giving them the giggles. His shirt was unbuttoned sufficiently to reveal a tasteless flurry of curly chest hair, and he rocked back on his seat, legs splayed, parking his crotch at table top level. Others round the table, particularly the few women, were all now exchanging suppressed smiles. Exhibitions of alpha male churlishness were not uncommon from Andrew and were astounding to watch. Did he think he was impressing authority on his minions? Did he not realise how laughable he was? No; he would blunder on in his favourite spot of limelight and see his tirade through to its grand finale, beating it to exhaustion. Two of the other male attendees kicked their seats back, adopting counter stances, causing Anna to shoot a wide-eyed look of disbelief in Francesca and Gemma's direction.

A message appeared on Anna's phone; "David Attenborough approaching with film crew!" read Francesca's sharp quip. Anna bit her lip hard, looking down to control her laughter.

"I mean, what the fuck? The whole thing just reeks of total and utter incompetence," Andrew snarled, now leaning forward across the table, jaw jutting and stare ferocious. "I am simply unable to fathom how we got from where we were last month to the bottom of the fucking shit-smelling pit we are in with this!" he threw at the wide-eyed project manager directly opposite. "Don't even bother!" shot Andrew, flattening the project manager's effort to speak, and contemptuously tore the project schedule in half. He pointed an aggressive finger, indicating his two senior planners who determinedly avoided eye contact, "Work with these two to get this shit sorted out!"

Anna's mind was made up; she had to leave. She would put a call out to Martin Davidson straight after her release from the room, and plead for a move to a new assignment. Enough was enough. Though Andrew liked Anna, and she was never likely to encounter this kind of public flame-grilling which the other poor soul was enduring, she couldn't rest on her laurels like a pet of the Gestapo. New York had opened her eyes. She thought of Tony on site under the dazzling sunlight, watching the excavator ploughing on with its unerring work. Soon the launch box would be formed and ready for the next stage. She wanted to be there involved with that, not grappling with bureaucracy and egos under the flail of a volatile dictator.

She dashed from the office just before noon, desperate to breathe some real air and free herself from the building for a moment before the next meeting. She pulled out her phone and called Martin's number but on getting his voicemail she hung up, frustrated. It wasn't the time for voice messages; given her mood she would end up garbling disjointedly and dementedly. She threw her phone back in her bag and marched across the road to a small row of shops where there was a Starbucks. She hoped Francesca might be there for some after-meeting catharsis.

"You really move with purpose," said a voice from behind her.

She looked over her shoulder, surprised, and saw Andrew from Rosemount. As with the last time they had spoken, his remark had her on the back foot and she was unsure how to respond.

"You look frustrated," he continued, over-familiar as usual.

"Well, yes, I guess I am," said Anna, unwillingly.

"What's up?" he asked straightforwardly – impertinently, Anna felt.

"Nothing I have time or inclination to go into right now," she said shortly.

"Suit yourself," he said good-naturedly. "The annoyance decreases if you work for yourself."

"I'll bear that in mind," she returned, cynically. "What are you doing here anyway?" she asked, turning the queries back on him.

"Oh, I just bought a small apartment building near here to reno."

"That can't be cheap round here," she said, surprised. His age struck her once more; he seemed too young to be buying apartment buildings.

"It's an investment. Should make a killing on rental, and then I'll sell it as the market comes back up," he responded with a cryptic smile. "Must dash. See you soon." And abruptly he was gone, striding away in the opposite direction.

Anna was taken aback. What was it about him? He seemed to put energy into observing her, and gain some voyeuristic pleasure from it, before making a precipitous exit. And he did it in such a cool easy-going manner.

It was busy in Starbucks, with the tables all claimed by people in business dress. She looked around at the lunch meetings in progress, the grey suits, the laptops, and the phones to numerous ears. A woman in a pinstriped skirt and bold red shirt, texting furiously, punctuated the otherwise dull palette of black and grey attire, but there was no Francesca. Anna ordered a latte and was waiting at the counter when a familiar face entered her peripheral vision. It took a moment to place but then she realised it was Dom, looking utterly different in a suit. She only ever saw him in polo gear, and he looked odd in such unfamiliar apparel, his rugged face perhaps handsome. He wore no tie, and had his shirt open at the neck and his jacket over his arm.

"Dom!" she said, moving to his side.

"Hey, Anna," he said in surprise, speaking more quietly than normal. His whole demeanour was subdued and controlled, in marked contrast to his customary exuberance. "You work round here?"

"Yes, just across the road," she answered. "You're not based here, are you?"

"No," he said, looking at his watch, then over his shoulder, "Just here for a meeting." His accent seemed more obvious away from the yard, and suddenly he was an American businessman in London. It was strange how environments altered people.

Anna's coffee arrived on the counter and she picked it up to go. She looked at him as he collected two coffees, wondering if he was going her way. He seemed distracted as he walked to the door with her. They stepped out onto the street and Anna looked towards her building.

"Well, I've got to dash. I'll see you at the yard later no doubt."

"Sure. Want to stick and ball tomorrow evening?" he asked, seeming to regain a modicum of his usual tone.

"You bet," she answered with a smile, and crossed the street. As she passed through the revolving glass door she saw him for a moment turning this way and that, as though gaining his bearings, and then he was gone from her sight as the pretentious granite grandeur of the lobby enveloped her once again.

He had seemed so different. She wondered whether work changed everyone so drastically. Did she also get the blinkered corporate look Dom seemed to have? Maybe she had caught him at a bad moment, under pressure of time. His habitual openness was missing and he had seemed a muted version of his usual self.

Having lacked horse time in New York, Anna was at Rosemount every evening, riding out to enjoy the sunsets and soaking up the thrill of racing Zanah along the flats. There was also the usual repartee on the polo field with Dom who, out of London, was back to his normal self. He had been coaching her with purpose, and her polo prowess was coming on in leaps and bounds. Damien was notably absent, which she decided was a good thing, feeling on reflection that it was better if they had little to do with one another.

Dom's wife Karen had stayed since the night of Anna's return from the States. She was a keen horse rider herself, and seemed (as Anna got to know her a little) calm and sensible; the yin to Dom's yang, she supposed.

"We to and fro around the country a lot, and sometimes Europe too," Karen explained to Anna. "Dom's always on contracts and has been for years. They can be pretty much anywhere. I've travelled to all kinds of places to visit him. He takes time out to play polo most summers, so he's home then and we get a normal life for a while."

Though it had obviously not been so much the case that summer, thought Anna; rather than dashing home periodically, he had been at Rosemount for the whole back end of the season.

On the day of the much-anticipated polo match with the Argentineans, Anna arrived at the yard early. She wanted to enjoy the morning out with Tom before getting caught up in the hard work of grooming for Dom. She had no doubts he'd be demanding. As she walked across the yard, Damien drove up. She waved at him and purposefully continued to the tack room. She had Tom tacked up and ready to go quickly, and was mounting up when Damien rode round the corner on Barnabas.

Anna was surprised, knowing he must have worked fast to be ready to go at the same time.

"Want to ride out together?" he asked, apparently relaxed.

"Sure," conceded Anna. She figured it was better that they did not deliberately avoid one another, and instead put their relationship on a normal footing. Though it had never really been normal, had it?

They ambled out through the back field on a long rein, basking in the bright morning sun, and in almost comfortable quiet.

After a climb up some bridleways Anna had not ridden on before, they rounded a bend and Anna could see in the distance the ridge where she took Tom to gallop.

"I saw you galloping over there from here, before you left," said Damien.

Anna was struck by that statement. She remembered her lone frantic early morning ride, fighting the mental turmoil. Had he been out looking for her? She looked across at him.

He smiled and added, "And there was absolutely no catching you."

Anna couldn't answer, but looked down at the pommel of her saddle. Her thoughts were spiking into chaos again. He'd been trying to catch up? Why? And why was he mentioning it at all? Had the ride on the Friday evening struck as strong a chord with him as it had with her? His expression seemed oddly intense. She looked back at him, confused.

"I had no idea," was all she could say. Now she was slipping again, that hopeless, overpowering swell of feeling for him welling within her.

He shrugged slightly, and then they rode on in silence once again.

The flat of the gallop spread out before them and a light breeze stirred the downland grasses.

"Let's race," said Damien with a grin.

Anna looked at him doubtfully and raised her eyebrows, throwing her glance from one horse to the other.

He laughed. "I know Barney doesn't stand a chance."

"Well, okay. If that's what you want," agreed Anna with a smile.

Then before she had prepared herself, Damien gave her a swift playful glance and booted Barnabas into action. Tom, instantly alert to a challenge, flattened his ears, bunny hopped and surged forwards.

They drew level and immediately pulled past Damien and Barnabas. Tom, excited by his quick victory, bucked and then leapt forward, loosening Anna's seat, and just as she steadied herself back in the stirrups, he bucked twice more in quick succession. The movement seemed huge, and Anna felt herself leave the security of her saddle and fly forwards. Suddenly level with Tom's face, still with the reins in her hand, she realised she was at the point of no return.

Remarkably, she landed on her feet, only tripping when she hit the ground as velocity took her down. Tom stopped abruptly and ran round her looking genuinely startled. Anna veered from anger to embarrassment, and took a strong breath, commanding herself to remain cool. Tom stepped towards her, his nose outstretched towards her face as if checking her.

Damien trotted up, looking concerned.

"You okay?" he asked, to which Anna nodded and exhaled audibly. "He's a bit of a so-and-so when he gets fired up isn't he?" he commented, looking at Tom, who was now standing quietly with his ears relaxed and hanging out to each side, looking more like a donkey considering a nap than an overwrought steeplechaser.

"Yeah. There's a reason for his short career," said Anna rather breathlessly, moving to Tom's side to remount. She hated mounting from the ground; Tom seemed too tall and her stirrup too high to reach, and the shakes were setting in. She was thankful she managed to remount fluidly and without a struggle.

She took a moment and filled her lungs with the downy grass-scented breeze, quickly clamping her shaking hands to the pommel to still them. Damien was studying her, and moved closer. Close enough that Anna felt she could sense his warmth and energy, sending a shiver through her.

"I had a grey a few years ago," he recalled. "Barking mad. He used to do something similar when we were riding close to the hounds and I discovered by sheer reflex one day, just as he was about to unload me, that a bloody hard slap on the neck with my whip would make him think."

Anna smiled, her supercharged system gradually calming. Their horses were standing close and her knee was a breath off touching his leg. She breathed deeply in and out, then looked up to meet his eyes, finding uncommon warmth glimmering back at her. It was no good. Her denial was useless. Something within her just responded to him. He was like no-one else.

"Hey Anna!" shouted Dom as she and Damien clattered into the yard. "Time to get down here and do some *real* horse stuff!"

"I'm not your servant! You haven't even offered to pay me!" she fired back at him.

"You'll get beer and like it! Now get down here! Leg wraps need starting!" he shouted, pointing at her.

Anna shook her head and took her feet from the stirrups, stretching her ankles. Damien looked after Dom and then at her questioningly.

"I'm grooming for him this afternoon," she explained. "There's a match Pete laid on with the other club and Dom's het up because there're some high goalers to compete with."

"I might hang around for a while," said Damien.

"Have you played before?" she asked, dismounting and running up her stirrups.

"No, but I'm happy to watch the odd match," he answered, following suit. "You okay? Not strained anything after that fall?"

"I don't think so. I'm lucky. He's unloaded me several times and I usually bounce or land on my feet." She smiled, and then seeing a horse transport pulling in up the driveway, she took Tom's reins. "Better dash."

The afternoon was hot and Anna was glad to get a break. She had put leg wraps on six horses, braided tails and helped Dom tack up in record time. He was mounted on his grey, warming up on the field and Anna stood in the shade under a huge chestnut tree swigging water from a bottle, watching the players.

The two high goal Argentineans were instantly recognizable; apart from their ridiculously stereotypical chiselled dark good looks, their positions in the saddle were easy and natural, and their swings graceful, fluid and immaculate with a balance that set them so obviously apart. Once the match was underway, she marvelled at the superiority of their play. One of them bounced the ball continually on his mallet head for half the length of the field, then on nearing the goal, he flicked the ball upwards effortlessly, took a full swing and cracked it at lightning speed through the goal.

"No way!" Anna exclaimed to herself.

"Not bad, eh?" said Olivia as she stepped up beside Anna, handing her another bottle of water. Damien was with her and leant against the tree trunk watching the match with an indifferent eye.

"What do you think of those foxes they brought with them?" leered Olivia, her eyes fixed on the backside of one of the Argentineans. Anna surveyed her with amusement. "Oh come on, Anna! Are you immune? There is no way any woman in her right mind would kick one of them out of bed...or both of them!" she guffawed.

Anna said nothing. She felt uncomfortable passing comment with Damien there, although she knew she was being foolishly sensitive.

There was something else, though; since her time in New York with Mateus she had felt a greater internal pressure to be a better person. She noticed a difference in herself; she had been thinking more favourably of people, and consciously strove to use positive language. Openly lusting after men had never been a natural behaviour for her, private as she was in her thoughts, but now it seemed even more improper. Wondering what on earth Mateus had done to her, she remained silent.

"What are you, a nun?!" badgered Olivia.

Anna laughed and conceded, "Yeah, they're pretty chiselled." She casually leant back against the tree trunk, and evaded eye contact with either Olivia or Damien.

"I don't get you, Anna. You're young, gorgeous, unattached...yet you seem totally resistant to getting it on with *any* guy, and you have a troop of them following you around!" Olivia's tone was outraged, with a hint of envy.

Anna laughed sceptically, gratified yet embarrassed. She felt acutely aware of Damien as he leant next to her, further round the immense trunk of the sycamore.

"I was unaware of a *troop of guys* following me around!! What do you mean? You're obviously in the realms of fantasy."

"Well, Dom obviously has a thing for you, never mind how relaxed he plays it. Lucias certainly likes to get physical with you. Then there was Hugo, the rich helicopter-owning, blond Adonis. And I guess you haven't even noticed Andrew Japson's attentions?"

Anna laughed again; this was getting sillier by the minute. Then, abruptly realising the time, she pushed away from the tree and started back to Dom's polo horses who were waiting patiently in the shade of the stables.

She called over her shoulder as she moved off, "Sorry, gotta go! They're going to call chukka any minute!" She was delighted to have a genuine excuse for physically removing herself from the spotlight.

"This isn't over! I haven't finished!" shouted Olivia behind her.

Anna flashed another smile over her shoulder and broke into a run, wanting to have Dom's next horse ready at the call of chukka.

What on earth was Olivia on about, though? She was of no serious interest to anyone on Olivia's list, and where on earth did Andrew's name spring from? Surely the brief and frustrating exchanges with him had been unwitnessed, and why would he report them? Andrew appeared to cruise through life seeking amusement for himself, and Anna had reluctantly served that purpose a few times.

Approaching the horses, Anna shifted her thoughts back to the job on hand. Dom's face had been serious when he mounted up earlier and she could see he had switched to a higher competitive gear that day. It made him rather intimidating, and she did not want to be late with his next horse.

She quickly folded up the braided tail of his bay mare and taped it neatly, then led her out towards the pitch for a warm-up walk and trot. Four minutes later chukka was called and Dom cantered over, his face set.

"Girth tight?" he asked quickly. She nodded.

He pulled up hard and jumped deftly straight from the back of his grey to the bay mare. Anna raised her eyebrows, not having seen him use the manoeuvre before.

"Good, huh?" he said with a wink, and with that he was off at a canter, leaving his grey abandoned.

Anna looked at the bedraggled horse and gathered the reins. He was puffing, his nostrils flared, showing pink. He was utterly spent, his coat soaked and smudged with foaming sweat.

"My God!" exclaimed Anna, appalled. "You poor thing! Let's go get you cool."

"What's wrong?" asked Damien, who was waiting for her at Dom's stable area.

She looked up, troubled. "This poor horse!" she said, quickly pulling his tail from its taping and rushing to remove the leg wraps. "This match is supposed to be a friendly!"

"Bloody hell," exclaimed Damien, swiftly removing the saddle and other tack. "They really don't spare them in polo, do they?" he added with disapproval.

Anna threw aside the leg wraps and bathed the poor grey with a cool sponge, concentrating on the main arteries, eager to get his temperature down but scared to douse him with the hose; it was too extreme and would send the poor beast into arrest. The sun beat down incessantly and there was no breeze, and the water ran from the horse instantly hot.

"I've never seen a horse worked this hard before, even in polo," she said frowning, her hand on the grey, willing his rapid breath to slow.

"I'd say Dom's a bit fired up today," remarked Damien seriously, nodding towards the pitch where Dom was thundering along in the middle of the pack, staring fixedly, obsessively, straight ahead. "He's riding outside of his horse's fitness."

He paused and moved closer. "Maybe hunting doesn't look so bad now?" His arm was almost touching hers, tanned and masculine. She glanced up into his dark eyes which seemed to reflect the light sparkling from everything around.

"It's not the exertion of hunting that bothers me; more the plight of the pursued," she said, smoothing more cool water along the horse's neck. Then remembering Oscar Wilde's words on the subject, she added, "The plight of the uneatable."

"Making me the unspeakable," said Damien quietly, drawing closer still, tilting his head and looking down into her eyes with a smile.

She caught her breath; delighting in his level of culture.

"Perhaps," she said, melting into his gaze. Then with enormous effort she forced herself to turn away, patting the hot grey horse who thankfully was regulating his breathing. "I'd better walk him a bit," she said, determinedly refocusing.

Anna felt grumpy and upset as she prepared Dom's other horses for him over the course of the afternoon, feeling like she was lining up lambs to the slaughter. By the end of what had proven to be a tough and sweltering day she was jaded and well and truly ready to finish as she cooled the last horse down. Dom had been distant, slinging the reins of his horse to her as he left the field following the final chukka, and joining his team mates and opposition for high volume, testosterone-charged post-match banter.

Anna dumped Dom's tack in its place in the tack room, feeling used.

"What, you're not cleaning that?" said Olivia mischievously, appearing at the door holding a beer out to Anna.

Anna opened her mouth, about to issue a profanity, but clamped it shut again, then with a primness which Olivia evidently found comical, uttered a simple and clearly articulated, "Definitely not."

"I've never seen you annoyed, Anna, but you look thoroughly and absolutely pissed off to the back teeth."

Anna grunted and took a long grateful swig of beer, relishing the extreme coldness of it. Resurfacing from the bottle, she looked at Olivia seriously and said hotly:

"I feel taken for granted, and a bit stupid for doing all this. I should have dragged his arrogant backside over and told him to deal with his own horses, who I am happy to say are still alive after his insane pace out there."

"True," agreed Olivia. "But right now you need to come outside and get a load of this. We have half-naked South Americans!" she announced dramatically, her inflection rising. Then she grabbed Anna's arm and dragged her out the door. "Come on, I'm determined to make some kind of dent in your crystalline purity!"

"I've got to admire your perseverance," Anna said matter-of-factly, as she followed Olivia.

"Most definitely thoroughbred!" said Olivia, nudging Anna and nodding at the assembled players gathered on the deck in the warm afternoon sun.

As she had promised, most of them had stripped to the waist, including the handsome Argentinean visitors. Their bodies were the kind of tanned well-muscled forms commonly photographed for men's fitness magazines or teen pin ups, but rarely seen in real life. Olivia turned and projected a broad and feisty grin at Anna, then dragged her towards the deck.

"Anna!" called Pete, coming out from the side door of the bar. "I have been instructed to furnish you with beer!"

Anna smiled and downed the last of her previous bottle before taking the fresh new one, which was aesthetically beaded with condensation.

"Enjoy the match?" asked Lucias, swiftly pulling a fresh polo shirt on over his own surprisingly well-developed torso and then clashing his beer bottle against hers.

"What I saw of it, yes. I was grooming for Dom so I missed quite a bit," she said.

"Ah ha, this is the good-looking groom," said one of the beautifully formed Argentineans. "Anna, yes?" he said, stepping forward and shaking her hand. "I'm Fernando." His voice had a beautiful exotic lilt to it, with a perfect mix of youth and man. He was clearly well versed at, and enjoyed, talking to women. His hair was fairly long and waved like an advertisement for shampoo, and he flashed an easy disarming smile at her. "I was asking my team mate, Hugo here, about you, and he says you're wasted on Dom!"

Anna smiled back at him, feeling spot-lit but flattered he had noticed her. "I would have to agree with you," she answered, trying to keep her eyes on his face, suddenly acutely conscious of his half-nakedness. He was built with the perfection and artistic license of an action figure.

"Put some clothes on, you oaf," said Hugo, tossing a clean polo shirt at Fernando.

"Sorry," said Fernando, "I'm in a state of undress. It's freakishly hot for England."

He pulled the polo shirt over his head and emerging looking like a catalogue model. The movement diverted attention away from his amazing physique toward his immaculately chiselled face, his eyes dancing with light and fiery with passion. Anna didn't think she had ever seen such a perfect example of male beauty. How was it that some human beings grew into such pleasing examples of the species, whilst others (thinking of many round her office) developed barrel waistlines, double chins and jowls? Perhaps it was about passion in life, or maybe it was simply down to a collection of beautiful genes.

Anna's mood lifted dramatically as she enjoyed the lingering warm afternoon in the company of the ardent and beautiful. Fernando advised her on her polo swing, insisting on flirtatious physical coaching. He stood close behind her, breathing soft words into her ear while moving her arm through the perfect trajectory and guiding her hips to follow, prompting roars of bawdy mirth from Anna's friends.

Finally Olivia, unable to stand another second of being left out, threw herself forward shouting, "Me! Me now! You've got to fix my swing too!" sending Anna and Fernando staggering in different directions, as she lurched into them flapping one long arm in a clumsy mock swing.

More and more members of Rosemount, in addition to the crowd who had shown up to watch the match, came to join the throng as the sun melted away. The smells of the barbeque and the flickering of the lanterns on the deck pervaded the still air of the beautiful late summer evening.

As she was chatting to Zanah, Anna spotted Damien crossing the deck towards a group of people she had never seen before. He handed the glass of wine he was carrying to a blonde-haired woman who looked strangely familiar, but Anna couldn't place her. She guessed this must be his elusive wife. Their group looked like a crowd at an aristocratic garden party, the women in heels, wearing dresses and hats, and the men in slacks and shirts. Fighting her own internal curiosity, Anna tried not to look in their direction. She knew that nothing was ever going to happen between her and Damien, despite their apparent affinity. Still, she felt a burning unpleasant sensation in her gut, a covetous interest which appalled her.

"Snotty crowd, that lot," came the now unmistakeable commentary of Andrew. He was standing against the railing, watching her over the brim of his whisky glass.

"Why is it I never see you until you pipe up with one of your remarks?" asked Anna, the beer she had consumed prompting reckless honesty. He smiled then and looked down for a moment before fixing his sharp blue eyes on her once again.

"I find you interesting, Anna."

"I just wish I saw you coming," she complained, but slightly taken aback.

"You seem to think more than a lot of the people here. You're smart, I can see that. And you're much too good for all the people whose attention you seem to have."

What on earth could he mean? She couldn't think what to say.

She must have given him a quizzical look because he went on, "And you know you do. You don't say it, or maybe even admit it to yourself. But you know it. Maybe it's that lack of self-assurance that makes it all the more powerful..." He tailed off, as though considering that idea.

Anna was floundering. She couldn't respond. Anything she said, he'd shoot down. He'd certainly dismiss any claims of ignorance. Perhaps she did know people noticed her? She'd always assumed she got the same or less attention than other people, but he was echoing Olivia's words, and it made her uncomfortable. What difference did it make anyway? Didn't men frivolously send their attentions in any direction they found attractive, in a mud-at-the-wall type of way? It didn't mean they'd actually do anything about it.

Andrew chuckled quietly. "I can feel you trying to retort."

"Stop analysing me," said Anna abruptly, deciding that not entering into debate would be her best defence. He smiled. "What makes you assume they're snotty, anyway?" she asked, nodding at Damien's group.

"They always show up to events like this, like Lord and Lady Muck, the lot of them. They arrive and usually order two magnums of Bollinger, straight off the bat, and then they commandeer an area where everyone can admire them, in their impenetrable hoity toity circle, with their enormous hats and elevated plummy voices, and won't associate with anyone outside the group. It's all for show of course, and their need to be admired is so obvious it's laughable."

Anna considered them. Perhaps he was right. His words seemed to ring true with the vibe they emanated. Did Damien fit that assessment, though?

As though reading her mind, Andrew continued, "Damien's been shipped into the group by his wife. He's not quite one of them, but I think he'd like to be."

Anna was silent. Was that true? If it were, it felt like a rather un-admirable chink in Damien's perfect armour. At that moment Andrew's phone rang. He put it to his ear.

"Hi," he said briefly, then listened for only a moment before saying, "I'm coming." He put down his glass, smiled at her, and left.

Anna watched him go, the thoughts he'd set in motion rolling round her head. Once again, he had left her hanging.

"Ugh, I'm beat," said Dom, appearing next to Anna. Taking Andrew's place, he leaned against the rail of the deck. "It was so humid out there and play was fast."

Anna decided against chiding him for the stress he put on his horses, not feeling it was the time. "You get a competitive face on in a match like that," she said instead.

"Yeah. I've got to get better. Maybe I need a season in Florida," he said, rubbing his face wearily. "You want to come too and groom?"

At that moment Anna felt eyes on her, and was surprised to see both Damien and his wife looking at her for a second before averting their eyes. She dismissed it and looked at Dom again.

"Grooming for you was a little more than I bargained for."

Dom gave a small burnt-out laugh. "You'd be amazed what fun I am," he sighed, finishing his beer and turning his face to the sky, closing his eyes. Then he hung his head again.

He seemed more than weary; distracted or depressed, maybe. She wasn't sure what it was, but he was not his customary buoyant self.

Dom did not seem to be able to climb from the doldrums all evening, even in the presence of their usual lively group, finally excusing himself just before 10pm to check on his horses and turn them out for the night. Anna too felt like the evening was done and went to say goodnight to Olivia and Zanah. It was time to get a cab home. She saw Damien leaving with his wife, without bidding any farewells. Aside from that moment while she was talking to Dom, he hadn't looked in her direction all night.

Zanah, who had not been drinking, offered to drive Anna and Olivia home and went to fetch her battered jeep. Anna ran to collect her bag from the Land Rover and on her way back across the yard saw Dom walking from the tack room with an armful of blankets.

"Hey Dom," she called, "Everything okay?"

"Yeah," he said with an element of defensiveness in his voice.

"Do you need a hand?" she asked, frowning at the heap of blankets.

117

"Oh, no... Thanks. I'm just moving these to the trailer," he said, continuing on his way.

"Anna! Are you out there in the dark?" called Zanah from the jeep.

Anna ran over, looking back at Dom's outline retreating round the corner, wondering why he was doing chores so late. She shrugged and jumped into the front seat, chuckling as she observed Olivia slumped and snoring across the entire back seat.

STRANGE HAPPENINGS

A breeze was getting up as Anna walked up the churchyard path to her cottage. She could see faint light in the church. It seemed rather late for anyone to be there, but she didn't think much of it. The quarter hour chimed from the bell tower, but feeling increasingly woozy from her alcohol consumption that evening, she had no idea whether it was quarter past ten or quarter past eleven.

As she neared a small wooden door, presumably an exit from one of the back rooms of the church, she heard voices from inside. Then there was a loud exclamation, which caused her to stop and listen. What has she heard? Her head felt thicker with every passing minute. She was just about to continue when she heard, this time unmistakeably:

"No! I don't want to be involved! I won't be!"

The man's voice came from behind the door, as though he were directly the other side of it. Anna sidled closer to the great stone wall next to the door.

"Oh, look at you and your selective morals," came another voice, in mockery. "When you think of the repercussions of the other money, is this really much different?"

"Yes!" came the indignant protest, the man's voice rising. "And if you can't see that, you're lost!"

"What? Even more than I already was?" sneered the other voice.

"I'm out. I'm done," insisted the first voice.

"Oh, are you?" came the response, laden with incredulous, cynical derision. The tone made Anna's skin crawl. It sounded so callous, so evil. "You really think you can just walk out of here, now?"

There was silence for a moment.

"I won't say anything. I just can't be involved."

There was laughter; frightening laughter. Anna felt a knot in her stomach. The danger seemed palpable. What on earth was going on in the church, on the other side of that door?

"And I bet you want to draw your share, now?"

"No. I just want out," came the gruff response. There was a hint of uneasiness, as if the speaker sensed the situation was past repair, that getting out was not an option.

"And what would you do if you were me?" Now the tone was sinister, poised on the edge of grim conclusion.

There was silence again. Anna could feel the hair rising on the back of her neck. The wind blew, rustling the tree branches and the large flat leaves on the shrubs round the small doorway.

What was that?

For a moment she fancied she heard a scuffle and a thud. The wind subsided for a moment and there was quiet.

Suddenly resolved, she stepped up to the door and tried the handle. It was locked. She hurried to the front door of the church. The wind gusted in her face, as though urging her to stop, but she didn't Now she was running, and as she reached the dark porch at the main church door, her heart was hammering in her ears.

She paused as the blackness of the porch checked her. What was she thinking? Was she insane? What if there was some maniac or killer in there? She hesitated for a moment, her hand on the wrought iron handle, debating with herself; then, making a sub-conscious decision, she pushed open the door.

The church was empty and quiet. A small lamp near the altar was the only light. There were flowers on the altar, oddly cheerful. She hesitated again, and listened. There was nothing. Taking a determined breath, she walked down the aisle. Suddenly the curtain which hung across the opening to the anteroom corridor was pulled open from the other side, causing her to stop in her tracks, her heart almost leaping from her chest. There was no time to hide.

"Anna?" said Andrew Japson, in surprise. "What are you doing here?"

"I might ask you the same thing," she muttered suspiciously, checking her exit to the main door.

"Me; I've just dropped some stuff off to the vicar for an event he has tomorrow after the service".

His assertion sounded absurd. What on earth did he have to do with the church, and why would he be here (regardless of duty) at such a late hour? She could feel the expression of disbelief cross her face.

Andrew must have read her loud and clear because he continued, "He's a friend of mine. I help out here from time to time."

"Huh? You didn't strike me as the religious type," said Anna, her cynicism evident despite herself.

"I'm not," confirmed Andrew with a shrug, his usual offhandedness showing itself. "Anyway, it's late. I've got to take the keys back to him before he gets to bed."

"There's no one else here?" questioned Anna, raising her eyebrows.

"Why? Should there be?" he asked, looking around.

"I heard people," said Anna, forthrightly. Her expression was challenging.

"Well, you shouldn't have done. I'm the last here," he said, moving to the altar lamp and switching it off.

Anna was not prepared for the sudden insecurity of darkness. It closed around her threateningly and alarm rang through her again. Had Andrew been distracting her while someone sneaked up in the shadows, preparing to attack? She snapped her head round towards the main door, then darted up the aisle, colliding with the door and fumbling desperately for the handle. Finding it, she wrenched at the door and rushed through it into the dim porch.

Andrew stepped out, looking at her as he pulled the door closed.

"What's the matter? Are you okay? You're getting *me* spooked, and I don't spook easy."

She stood still and alert, feeling safer with the fresh air of the night blowing into the open-fronted porch.

"Hey?" he questioned, standing in front of her and touching her shoulder. "Are you okay?"

She looked at him, not knowing what to say. He was too calm. Maybe he wasn't involved? But he must be. Perhaps he was just the doorman; a passive onlooker.

She stared at him, wondering, and then stepped outside, looking down the path which ran past the side door she had stood beside minutes before. It was still closed, and there was no sign of anyone else. No voices, no vehicles. Nothing, except the breath of the wind.

Andrew stepped up to her again, and followed her gaze along the dark pathway. He put his hands on her shoulders, squaring her to him, and searched her eyes with his own. His fair hair ruffled in the moonlight and she suddenly became aware of how tall he was; she hadn't realised. He stood at over six feet, and now she looked at him, he appeared powerful, with broad shoulders. He could easily overpower her if he wanted to. Her head was swimming again. "Seriously, Anna?" he was saying, "Are you okay?"

"Erm, ya. I guess..."

"You had a long day in the sun. Maybe you got sunstroke?" he suggested, looking at her with what appeared to be concern.

"Maybe." Maybe she had. The beer didn't help, of course, nor the two shots of tequila Olivia had bullied her into. It didn't explain what she knew she had heard, but there was no evidence of anything having happened.

"What are you doing here anyway?" he asked.

"I live here," she said reluctantly, immediately acutely aware of the lack of wisdom in her admission. Regardless of how he might appear at that moment, he had been involved somehow in what she heard.

"Here?" he asked, looking around the churchyard.

"Not under one of the stones in a sarcophagus, you understand," she responded with dry, flat humour. There was a pause. "Okay, I'm going," she announced conclusively, but not moving.

"Okay." There was the merest suggestion of a smile at the corners of his mouth, as he took his hands from her shoulders.

"I want you to go first," she asserted.

"Why?"

"Let's just say I am having a trust issue," she answered, scanning him.

"Me?" he exclaimed.

"Uh huh," she responded, her eyes not leaving his face. Then he chuckled.

"Well, okay Anna. I'll leave you to find your way. I'm just worried you'll stumble across something else that's going to freak you out," he said smiling and backing away from her, his eyes fixed on hers. Then he stopped for a moment, holding her gaze a second longer before turning and leaving on a nonchalant stride.

Anna watched him go, not moving for a full minute after he had disappeared. Then, feeling the wind gust against her one more time, she turned and ran to her door.

"What's that noise?" asked Penelope. It was just after 5 o'clock on Sunday morning and something had woken her. It seemed too early for anyone to be arriving at the yard, but maybe there was someone heading out to a competition.

"I don't hear anything," said Pete, sleepily, not moving on his side of the bed.

Outside in the yard Dom's truck was parked up near his stables, connected to his trailer with ramp lowered, ready for loading. His horses stood quietly in a line outside the stables. Some wore travel bandages, and Dom was working alone at a swift pace, wrapping the legs of the remaining horses, his face set with purpose.

Anna was up early. Sleep had been elusive and fitful when it came; obscure images and feelings circling, spectre-like, in her disjointed dreams. She had stood alone in the church once again staring at the altar with its vase of strangely cheerful flowers. Shouts echoed around the stone vaulted ceiling, and the scene spun around her, and then the mocking cruel voice penetrated her senses, resounding painfully: "Did you really think you could just walk out of here?"

Then she was outside the little side door once again. This time it opened. The wind was howling, and the violence of the gale followed her through the door. Her vision was blurred, and she saw the vestments flapping in the wind; vestments spattered with blood. Then she was running through the dark church, desperate to escape, Andrew Japson leaping over pews in pursuit. Then he was holding her shoulders and looking at her. Reflected in his eyes she could see the altar flowers, dried and dead.

Awake again in the reality of the bright morning light streaming through her curtains, she doubted her recollections. While knowing something strange had happened, she didn't trust herself. The adrenalin and the alcohol had created a fog, and now, crushed under the bizarre horror of her sleeping fiction, her memories drifted out of her grasp. It felt like the whole thing was the wild working of a freakish lucid dream.

Realising she needed to ground herself, she decided to run to the yard to retrieve her Land Rover. Running always instilled a rhythm through her, and the faster she ran, the less her mind spiralled.

It was 7:45am as she jogged round the bend between the huge rhododendron hedges, and she was surprised to see Pete standing in the middle of the turning circle looking puzzled.

"Morning Pete. Everything okay?" she asked, jogging over to him. His troubled look didn't seem to fit him, given his usual spritely air.

"Not really. I'm not sure what's happened, but Dom's gone," he answered, frowning at a piece of paper he had just removed from the envelope in his hand.

"Gone? What, gone with his horses? Gone for good?" exclaimed Anna disbelievingly.

"It seems so, yes. Penelope said she heard something early this morning. I found his horses gone on my morning check. He hadn't mentioned going to a match anywhere. I just found this pinned to the door of one of his stables."

He looked up as he heard Penelope walking over. "Dom's gone," he said, holding out the letter and envelope to her.

"Gone?" she exclaimed, looking baffled. Her eyes scanned the letter.

"Does he say why?" asked Anna, flabbergasted. Had he really just packed everything up and gone without a word? "He did seem in a peculiar mood last night. And I saw him carrying blankets to his trailer."

"His locker was left wide open and empty in the tack room. All his tack, everything, has gone. He's simply cleared out and left," Pete said in bewilderment.

"But why? What happened? I don't get it!" exclaimed Anna, helplessly. "He hasn't given any reason at all in his letter?"

"No," said Penelope. "He just says thank you and he has to leave. And he's paid what he owes," she said, pulling a cheque from the envelope.

Anna was dumbfounded; she felt lost. He had seemed strange and defensive the night before, but she couldn't think of anything that had happened or been said which explained his bizarre and sudden exit. She felt bruised; hadn't they been friends? Why didn't he say anything? She realised she had never got his number so she couldn't call or even message him. But would he respond anyway?

She suddenly felt all too conscious of the passage of people through life; the transience of individuals and humankind in general, all occupied with their own agendas, one minute best friends the next evaporated into the ether. Was there anyone to rely upon or trust?

Anna's thoughts consumed her all day, bouncing between what might have happened in the church the night before and Dom's unexplained departure. She couldn't settle on anything, and there were no answers.

The week wore on in much the same way, with the Rosemount residents gossiping and questioning, but in the absence of facts all they could do was speculate. Dom did not re-appear and didn't respond to anyone who attempted to contact him. There was no news; just silence.

Anna tried to distract herself, but it was impossible. Damien, given his absence, was obviously working, Olivia and Zanah talked only of Dom, and Dom - who Anna now realised had been a greater source of fun and friendship than she had appreciated - was of course a ghost.

Another person who made no appearance that week was Andrew. Their odd conversations had a raw truth and familiarity to them, and despite the fact he was obviously mixed up in something sinister, she felt confident enough to challenge him.

However, any questions she formulated for him began to sound more and more far-fetched. Either way, she knew his defence would confuse and confound her, and she would come off sounding unhinged, like a drunk who had spooked herself in the dark. Nevertheless, and knowing she might never find any answers, she resolved to watch him, whenever he re-appeared.

On Friday evening after a torturous week of work, Anna arrived at the yard to take Tom out, to clear the debris of the previous few days from her head. Despite the light drizzle that was pitter-pattering softly on the foliage, she was determined to go out for a fast ride. She had her route planned in her head and she was keen for a blast of cool breeze on the flats at the top.

As she headed towards the tack room for her saddle, she saw Damien bringing Barnabas in from the field. Having not seen him all week, she hoped she could be ready to leave at the same time. As she dashed from the tack room she came face to face in with a woman she recognised. Though not having got a good look at her the other evening, she knew this was Damien's wife.

"Hi. Have you seen Damien?" the woman asked, sounding slightly exasperated. "I've walked round the entire yard but I can't find him."

"I just saw him bringing his horse in," answered Anna, taking her in swiftly. She had the well-heeled look of one born into money. She was immaculately groomed, and wore pearls round her neck which seemed oddly too old for her. Her face was attractive but slightly long and horsey, framed by blonde hair perfectly styled in a sharp bob. Her eyes were clear and green, perhaps a little cold, and looked questioningly at Anna.

"Really? How did I miss him? I don't even know which stable is his," she was saying.

Suddenly concerned that she appeared to be staring dumbly, Anna introduced herself hastily and offered to show her round to Damien's stable.

"I'm Caroline, his wife," added the woman, seemingly as an afterthought as she walked next to Anna. Anna had the feeling she had seen or met her somewhere else, besides spotting her on the night of the polo party. Then as Caroline looked at her phone which buzzed in her hand, she remembered her from the coffee shop the other day – the distinctive red shirt in the sea of grey.

It seemed too trivial to mention, so instead she asked, "Are you a rider too?"

"Yes. I event and show jump," she answered, in a tone which suggested she did something a little more highbrow than other disciplines.

"Where do you keep your horse?" asked Anna, wondering why husband and wife weren't boarding at the same yard.

"I keep my horses over at my instructor's yard about 10 miles away," she said in a lofty tone. Then glancing at Anna she asked, "Do you hunt?"

"No. I hack, do the odd competition, play a bit of polo," said Anna, summarising her varied experience briefly, feeling sure Caroline would be unimpressed.

"Polo? It looks fun, but I never tried it. It often seems to be played by a pack of men who can't ride."

"It's just totally different," said Anna in a laid-back tone, thinking of what Dom's reaction might have been to Caroline's casually thrown insult.

They rounded the corner to see Damien grooming Barnabas. Anna noticed Chantelle leaning in a provocative manner against the stable door, attempting to engage him in conversation, and wondered what Caroline would make of her.

"Good lord, who's that slut?" sneered Caroline, eyeing Chantelle, who was wearing cut-off diamante-studded denim shorts, so abbreviated they allowed her buttocks to peek out, and a tiny white sequined vest top rising to reveal a piercing in her St-Tropez'd belly. Anna couldn't help but laugh aloud at Caroline's bare-faced loathing.

"That's Chantelle," she answered. "I've never seen her conservatively dressed! And she only ever talks to the men in the yard."

"Oh, one of those," said Caroline, a cool grim smile settling across her face.

Damien looked up as they drew close, a fleeting expression of surprise or discomfort crossing his features.

"Hello, darling," said Caroline purposefully, watching Chantelle with hard eyes as she slunk away in the manner of a whipped dog.

Anna decided it was time to excuse herself and said politely, "It was nice to meet you, Caroline," and then turned and walked to Tom's stable.

"Yes, you too," said Caroline absently, after her.

Anna noted Chantelle drifting into the office where David was, in search of her next fix of male attention no doubt. Why, she wondered, did Chantelle do it? Her behaviour appeared ingrained and automatic; compulsively cutting herself off from women and being parasitic around men, amorally indifferent to their marital status. Surely it resulted in a life of constant rejection and loneliness, punctuated by presumably degrading sex inevitably followed by shunning and denial? Whether or not that was true, she certainly didn't come across as particularly happy.

Still, who was she to criticise? She seemed to have a crush on a married man who made fleeting guest appearances in her own life, hypnotising her, charging her with sensual fervour and then disappearing, leaving her alone and disconsolate. What, she asked herself, was the attraction with unhappiness?

She looked up from her gloomy reverie to see Penelope walking in her direction. She waved and looked like she was just about to say something, when they were both alarmed by a car arriving at pace.

"My goodness, it's Karen!" exclaimed Penelope, as the car came to a halt next to them, drawing in its wake a cloud of dust from the gravel turning circle. The door opened and Karen climbed from the car looking bedraggled, her face stricken.

"Karen! What brings you here? What's wrong?" exclaimed Penelope, rushing round to her.

"I can't find Dominik! Where is he?" cried Karen, her voice cracking with emotion.

"What? You mean he hasn't contacted you?" asked Penelope, aghast.

"No! What's happened? I can't find him. He hasn't answered my calls or emails. He was supposed to be coming home yesterday evening to visit but I haven't been able to reach him!"

"I'm so sorry, but he left here without explanation on Sunday. I had no idea that he wouldn't have told you! What about his apartment; have you been there yet?" Penelope asked urgently.

"He's not there. It's all locked up and it looks like he's gone from there!" Karen choked, suppressing a sob.

"Oh Karen, come up to the house!" said Penelope firmly, seeing that Karen was visibly weakening as she clung to her car door, tears running down her face. She closed the car door and ushered her up the private driveway to the house, leaving the car abandoned where Karen had haphazardly parked.

Anna stood desolate, feeling hollow shock vibrating through her. What was Dom doing? How could he just run away like that – not just from her and the others at the yard, but from his own wife? It was like he'd hit the quit button on his life and all the people in it.

Walking slowly, she pondered. He took his horses, though, so polo and that part of his life was apparently still figuring in his mind. Someone must have seen him, surely; he must have had somewhere to take all those horses. Maybe he was having a mid-life crisis or an affair... or both? But that didn't seem to fit; he usually seemed so at ease, and he never brought anyone else to the yard with him, or mentioned any woman besides his wife.

No answers came, and she tacked up quietly and rode out alone, feeling a poignant despair with the man who had previously made her feel so buoyant.

The next few weeks saw a change in the weather. The mornings took on the unmistakably crisp feel of autumn. Anna loved riding at that time of year in the early chill, revelling in the golden sunshine that lit the colourful trees and the rolling land. Back in the village there was the faint suggestion of wood smoke on the air, and the old-fashioned streetlamps were flicking on earlier than before. The small leaded windows of the cottages glowed as interior lights spilled their cosy glimmer outside.

The polo residents of the yard enjoyed their last match and a few practice sessions before the pitch, given the increasing rainfall of the season, became too soft. Throughout the colder months any practice would be in the arena, and most players chose to simply abandon the sport until the return of the fine weather.

Anna joined a few indoors stick and ball sessions at invites from Lucias and Pete, riding a neat little roan who was Pete's old faithful. But she missed Dom. Despite the fact weeks had passed, somehow the place was empty without his loud mouthed incorrigible banter. Even Lucias's spirited humour and mischievous, overly physical tactics to tackle the ball away from Anna couldn't compensate. Dom had taken her under his wing and trained her with effortless authority, disguised by his distinctive clowning; nobody could take his place.

In London, she purposefully threw herself into work with new zeal, boosted by the accolades she received from her New York success. Martin had urged her to see out her current assignment given that government budget cuts would see cancellation of many projects; consultants and contractors would be the first people out, leaving the permanent staff to manage the surviving projects. Then Anna would be free to take on new challenges.

But while career take-off was imminent, her previously thriving personal life was stalling. It felt like she could not have both. Moreover, with Dom gone from the scene, and her hopeless feelings for Damien continuing to plague her, pleasures seemed diminished.

The hunt season had started and was to kick off officially that weekend with the opening meet. More and more riders were schooling and exercising their horses in readiness, bringing a change of atmosphere to Rosemount. The coloured shirts of casually swaggering polo players, sporting jeans stuffed into brown buckled boots, were replaced by structured hacking jackets, close fitting jodhpurs and classic, elegant black hunter-top boots. Anna hadn't seen Damien much and when she did see him their schedules didn't meet, and he would be riding out with the unfamiliar faces of the swelling hunt crowd.

"Anna!" called Olivia on the Friday evening, as Anna climbed into her Land Rover. "While you might not be hunting, you're coming to the hunt kick-off do, right?" she urged, "It's always fun!"

Anna agreed, thinking she had better do something on Saturday night or she'd revert to Miss Havisham mode: lonely, reading a book in dismal solitude, and wondering where her life had gone.

It was frustrating; try as she might to distract herself, Damien entered her thoughts frequently and she wanted him gone and her independence and freewheeling attitude to return. Yes, she had to go out and have a good time.

When she arrived on Saturday morning Anna found the yard was fuller than she had seen it before. Enormous hunters with their manes braided, coats clipped and hooves oiled, stood high-headed sensing the anticipation. Riders had ditched their rat-catchers for formal hunt coats, and were immaculately finished in cream breeches and tall boots with spurs. Everyone was on time and mounting up to ride to the meet together. The mood was good and laughter rang out on the autumn air.

Anna crossed the yard at a casual pace on her way to fetch Tom. She was in no rush and would see the hunters on their way before leaving with him. She wanted no involvement with the hunt for fear of Tom's inevitable antics should he be caught up in the crowd.

As she rounded the corner, Damien rode up on a freshly clipped and braided Barnabas, who looked gigantic that morning in his fired-up state. He pranced sideways and tossed his immense head as Damien halted him alongside Anna. He looked different himself; smarter in his formal hunt garb than in his customary Barbour.

"Hello, stranger," he said with a smile.

"I haven't seen you for a while," remarked Anna, patting Barnabas's neck.

"No, I've been working a lot. I like to try and pick up as much work as I can, do some tours, in the run-up to hunt season; then I can work less and ride as many of the midweek hunts as I can."

"It's busy. I haven't even met a lot of these people," said Anna, looking across at the gathered riders.

"No, and I'm not sure how some of them will survive the day. They've just shown up, polished their horses who are fat on a summer of doing little, and expect them to keep up. There'll be some injuries today," he said matter-of-factly. "Opening meet is always madness; a hundred people or more."

"Yep. Not the place for me and Tom," said Anna, feeling left out and wishing she was going with him.

"I'd think not, given what he did racing Barney and me," said Damien dryly. "You going this evening?"

"Probably," replied Anna, playing it cool.

"You should," he said, looking down at her.

A shout came from the front yard to ride out and the sound of a herd of hooves clattered forth. "Gotta go," said Damien, as Barnabas eagerly stepped into trot to catch the group, and then he was gone.

Anna stomped on round to Tom's stable, annoyed at the way Damien had removed himself from the scene so suddenly and unceremoniously.

'What do you want? A goodbye kiss?' jeered the voice in her head. 'That'd be nice,' she admitted silently, and then rolled her eyes in derision. Great, now she was talking to herself. She definitely needed to get out this evening.

Taking a deep breath and willing the voices inside to cease their jabber, she went to fetch Tom. Did everyone else have the internal chat going on or was she alone, paddling in the shallows of insanity?

HUNT BALL

Anna really didn't feel like going out that evening.

She and Tom had explored the Downs for a few hours after the hunt had left, and by the time she got home and had had dinner she was more in the mood for flopping on the sofa and vegetating in front of the television. Sinking down further on the cushions, she felt increasingly apathetic. Seriously, what was the point in going out?

Her phone chimed its text alert. Knowing it would be a call to action she resolutely ignored it for a full minute, before reaching for it unwillingly.

"Where are you?" demanded Olivia's message forthrightly, winking on the screen.

Anna groaned, feeling less inclined than ever to get off the sofa. Maybe she should just ignore it. Maybe she should just go to bed and be done with it; she would probably feel less dour in the morning.

"Still at home," she typed, stalling for time.

"Don't make me come get you!" said the immediate response.

Anna gave the tiniest of dejected smiles. At least she had a friend looking out for her. It had seemed friends were a bit sparse recently; she had spent too much time working late and riding alone.

"Dress code?" she texted, as she hauled herself up.

"Sexy!" came the inevitable response, followed by, "I'm in a dress, so you have to be!"

Anna raised her eyebrows. She had never seen Olivia in a dress and imagined, given her height and powerful build, that she would look quite startling.

Anna stalked into the bar in her trusty black cocktail dress. She had spent a while unenthusiastically pondering her options, and it came out as the best bet, classy yet sexy in an understated way. She wasn't out for attention but it would hopefully keep Olivia from driving her home to find something else to wear.

The pulse of the music hit her as she opened the door. The place was rammed and the area assigned as a dance floor was full. As she arrived at the bar she noticed that the person next to her, drumming her fingers and looking impatient, was Caroline.

"Hi, Caroline," she said, forcing a cheerful tone.

"Oh, hi. Anna, right?" said Caroline, apparently dredging Anna's name from her memory bank.

"Competed today?" asked Anna, slightly narked that Caroline appeared to have forgotten who she was.

"Ya! I did fab. I just won in my class at Hickstead today!" Caroline gushed, suddenly animated.

"Wow, congratulations," said Anna, feeling underwhelmed.

"Did you hunt today?"

"No. I'm not a hunter," Anna reminded her. She had obviously retained nothing of their previous conversation.

"Oh yes. You're into polo," said Caroline dismissively, and then without waiting for a response continued, "The opening meet is always horrendous anyway. Too busy and lots of fresh horses with riders on board who can't hold them for toffee. They had a couple of people taken away in ambulances today."

"Really?" exclaimed Anna, relieved she hadn't been tempted to take Tom along. "Damien said he thought there'd be some falls."

"Well, he was right," Caroline said, collecting a bottle of Bollinger and an ice bucket from the barman. Then she turned and left.

Anna sighed, with an inward smile at the unceremonious exit; she was just like her husband. Then she remembered Andrew Japson's comment: 'Bollinger for the group'. How right he was. She grinned to herself, and then wondered if she'd see Andrew that evening; she hadn't seen him since the night at the church. Surely he would be at an event like this?

Seeing the number of people waiting at the bar, Anna decided instead to go in search of familiar faces.

"Anna!" called Lucias. "Why didn't you hunt that beast of yours today?" Lucias was now immersed in the hunt season. Having turned his polo horses out for the winter, he was enjoying bounding around on his 17-hand dun warmblood in the thick of the hunt field.

Before she could respond, his eyes widened as he looked over her shoulder and he uttered, "Crikey! Target incoming!" as Chantelle slipped by. She wore a sequined dress which was almost too short to qualify as such, and the usual plunging neckline was even more extreme that evening, reaching almost to her navel, her jutting breasts threatening to spill out altogether. Anna felt embarrassed looking at her.

Lucias put his tongue out once she'd passed and leered, "Definitely falsies, but someone obviously wants to get laid this evening!" and then he was off, hot on Chantelle's ridiculously high heels. Anna shook her head and smiled at Lucias's honest lechery, it was distasteful, but really, could she blame him?

"There she is! Classy chic," exclaimed Olivia, appearing beside Anna, looking her up and down. She wore a bright red dress which matched her customary red lipstick and nails; a bold and incandescent giant.

"You haven't got a drink! Come! We have a bottle of quaffable champers on the go over here," she commanded, pointing to a table where Zanah was sitting, wearing an outlandish short dress covered in fluffy feathers. She was sipping from a champagne flute and surveying the scene with bleary-eyed interest. Anna smiled at her obvious tipsiness and followed Olivia.

Suddenly feeling watched, she turned, and across the sea of people met Damien's eyes for a moment. He was immaculately turned out in black tie which accentuated his smooth good looks.

"You've seen Damien? He's as sleek as a wet otter this evening," leered Olivia, following Anna's gaze. Without further acknowledgement, he turned back to his group. Anna shrugged. Why did he bother?

"Good day on the hunt field?" she asked Zanah as she arrived at the table.

"Oohh yeah!" Zanah enthused. "My boy beat everyone!"

"Yes, that was a problem by the way" said Olivia leaning forward, holding up a disciplinary finger. "It's not the races. Never pass the bloody Huntsman!"

"I didn't!" protested Zanah.

"You were going to! Honestly, you promised not to embarrass me; I'll put you on a leash next time!" Olivia warned her.

"Okay, I'll behave," said Zanah, faking submission and pouting ostentatiously.

"Seriously, you'll get yourself thrown off the field. We're going over the rules properly before I take you again."

Anna cast her eye round the room while Olivia continued with her reprimand.

It looked like everyone was there that night, and they all looked so different. The transformation that formal dress effected, on people one was accustomed to seeing in breeches and a riding hat, was astonishing. Some people pulled it off well and others looked like they had been shoe-horned into their outfit against their will. She noted that Pete and Penelope looked wonderful; the honourable hosts, well-dressed and comfortable with it, circulating the room together.

Her attention was brought back to their table as Lucias appeared, his collar open and bow tie undone, calmly helping himself to the last of their champagne and immediately halting the argument between Zanah and Olivia.

"Oi! Does everyone need to be reminded of proper behaviour today?" complained Olivia. Zanah ogled him.

"Hmmm mmm, you pull that outfit off rather well!"

Lucias bit his lip and nudged up against her.

Finding her glass empty, Anna left the group to their chaffing and headed to the bar. It was still manically busy, the two barmen working at a frenetic pace which was impressive to watch.

Ahead of her there was a raucous group of men crowded together yelling at each other, so Anna perched on an empty bar stool and surveyed them while she waited. She recognised one of the men as James, the lewd character she had met briefly on the evening of her first ride out with Damien. He was leaning on the bar talking over his shoulder to a man she had never seen before – and Damien, who immediately locked eyes with her.

"Damien! So you're back from shagging trolley dollies!" James was shouting. "Want a drink?"

"Yeah, I'll have another of these," said Damien, nodding at the barman.

James grabbed Damien's glass and sniffed it. "What expensive shit are you drinking this evening?"

"It's brandy and Benedictine," said Michael, from behind the bar, diverting him.

Damien skirted the bar and to her surprise grabbed Anna's hand, pulling her from the bar stool and into the darkest corner of the dance floor.

Holding hands, they turned slowly around one another. He looked her straight in the eyes, regarding her steadily. Anna said nothing, still annoyed with him but intensely aware of her pulse beating against his hands. It had been a long time since they had been this close.

"I'm not the kind of chap people like James make me out to be, you know," he said.

139

Anna huffed in irritation. "I don't see what difference it makes. Or why you care what my impression of you is."

She was weary of the off-and-on of their strange relationship. Was he just trying to get her into bed?

He frowned. "Of course I care what you think. You seem out of sorts."

"I am. I'm fed up," she confessed. "The fun seems to have stopped recently."

"Maybe you just need something new. Come with me tomorrow," he urged. "I'm taking Barney over to the farm to see the hounds. Let's see how Tom does."

Without waiting for an answer, he gathered her to him briefly, sending a rush through her, then pulled her from the dance floor.

At the bar, which was noticeably quieter, he reached for his drink.

"Get that down you!" he commanded.

Anna smiled in spite of her mood and took the glass. Looking him in the eye, she took a sip. It was very smooth, the richness of the brandy mingling with an almost herbal taste she didn't recognise.

"That's really good," she said with a grin.

"Finish it," he told her, putting up his hand to Michael for two more.

"You're liking these," smiled Michael, appearing like magic with refills.

"Can't believe I never had one before," answered Damien, raising his glass to Michael.

Anna looked at him appreciatively. He had lifted her mood and restored that effervescent sparkle she always felt when she was with him, and he'd done it in an instant. Any anger she had felt towards him was gone, evaporated without trace.

Caroline appeared next to them at the bar and ordered another bottle of Bollinger from Michael. Without acknowledging Anna, she glared at Damien and said, "I trust you're going to grace the group with your presence rather than propping up the bar all evening?"

He said nothing but looked quickly at Anna, then turned and left, moving in the direction of his friends. Caroline wordlessly collected the bottle of champagne and followed him.

Anna stifled an indignant noise, her mood crashing and burning instantly.

Who was she kidding? He had no regard for her; he was just trying it on. She looked down at her drink on the bar, the character of the wood enhanced through the golden colour of the spirits. Sighing, she downed it and pushed the glass back across the bar. Damien was an energy she seemed to feed and depend on, but he wasn't constant, and whenever he left she fell flat on her face. She hated her vulnerability. She was stronger and better than that.

"Here," said Michael's comforting voice, as he slid a flute of champagne across the bar to her.

"Thanks," she said, surprised.

"He likes you," he said, almost as if he sensed she needed confirmation.

Anna had no idea what to say, so simply gave him a self-conscious half-smile. A well-seasoned barman could be one of the most worldly and clairvoyant of people. Their anonymous aspect unnoticed by the carelessly inebriated fools in their pathetic life drama of the moment.

"Stick to the champagne. It's a happier drink than spirits," he said knowingly. Then he moved away to serve someone else, leaving Anna feeling strangely cared-for.

She looked across at Damien and Caroline, involved in their group. He didn't look over.

She sighed, exasperated. He was so totally inscrutable, she simply couldn't read him. He and Caroline seemed like a couple who carelessly crashed through other peoples' lives. One minute heeding them, making them feel significant, the next, failing to recognise them even as an entity; retreating to their privileged inner circle in their elite, nebulous group.

She took her champagne and went in search of Zanah and Olivia again. She saw them through the window, outside on the deck clutching cigarettes. It was cold, but the brandy and Benedictine had started to swirl round her system and she felt the fresh air would do her good.

"How are the smokers?" she asked as she arrived on the deck next to them.

"We're all good here!" said Zanah happily, the feathers on her unusual dress rippling in the light.

"We had to come outside as Zanah's world started to spin!" laughed Olivia.

"I know the feeling," said Anna, leaning against the rail.

"I didn't think you'd had much," said Olivia, taking a final drag on her cigarette and flicking the glowing butt into the ashtray.

"I hadn't but then I got persuaded to down some shots at the bar and they're kicking in now."

"About time someone tried to loosen you up! Lucias, was it? He looks good tonight, at least Zanah thinks so!" She took a breath. "Well, I need to catch up on the drinking and I hear from Jess that Chantelle has outdone herself this evening. She sounded so appalled I just have to see her," said Olivia, heading for the door.

"Yes, she looks like she should be dancing in a cage at a Soho club," said Anna dryly. Then she looked at Zanah. "Lucias?"

"He looks good tonight, and did you see his physique on the big polo match day?"

Anna smiled, deciding against telling Zanah that Lucias was pursuing Chantelle that night.

"Are you ready to go back in?"

"No, I feel swirly. I want to stay out for a while. Let's go for a walk."

"It's going to have to be a quick walk. Its freezing out here!" said Anna.

"Let's go and say hi to our horses," suggested Zanah, stepping off the deck and into the dark. Anna followed, treading carefully to avoid her heels sinking into the soft ground.

The moon emerged fitfully from the scudding clouds and bathed the yard in pale hazy light, creating dark shadows and a moody ambience. The breeze chilled them as it channelled between the buildings, and made them creak and unseen things rattle and scutter.

"What's that noise?" hissed Zanah, stopping dead.

"Are you trying to scare me?" asked Anna, her nerves leaping involuntarily.

"No, I can hear something," Zanah whispered, creeping forwards.

Then Anna heard it too, coming from one of the stables nearby. Hardly knowing why they were being so furtive, Anna walked quietly behind Zanah along the row. Then they heard gasping followed by a masculine grunt. Zanah crept forwards and looked though the nearest stable door, which was ajar.

"Oh my god!" she mouthed at Anna, grabbing her arm and pulling her forward to see.

Almost immediately Anna pulled back, but it was too late; the image had already burned itself onto her brain.

In the corner of the stable, lit dimly by the moon shining through the window, they could see the back of a man, jacket hanging loose and belt trailing. Long naked legs were wrapped tightly around his waist, and a sequined scrap of nothing glinted in the shadows. He was thrusting roughly, grunting, as the gasps grew louder and louder.

Anna felt sick.

The scene was bestial and disgusting, with an undertone of shoddy violence. Chantelle had fulfilled her sad purpose and was being illicitly seen to by a lust-fuelled whoever against a brick wall.

She backed away hastily then turned and walked away, embarrassed at her unwilling voyeurism which somehow made the whole scene that much cheaper.

Zanah caught up, exclaiming breathlessly, "I can't believe I just saw that. It was kind of vile, don't you think?"

"Yes! Totally vile! I really did not need to see that!" Anna agreed, trying to erase the mental image. "Who was that with her anyway?" she asked uncomfortably, wondering if it was Lucias.

"I think it was David; you know, the riding instructor?"

"No way!" hissed Anna. "I saw him here earlier with his wife!"

"So she's there at the party whilst he's nailing Chantelle in a stable hardly a hundred feet away!" exclaimed Zanah, sounding stoked on the sheer nerve and scandal of it.

"You're not going to go in there and tell people, are you?" asked Anna, horrified, her hand on Zanah's arm as they stood on the deck once again.

"What? How can I not? There's no way we're keeping this to ourselves!" Zanah objected, jumping up and down, her dress feathers quivering in the night air.

"And what if his wife hears? She's in there! How would you feel if the whole room was talking about your worthless bastard of a husband, who was seeing to the yard whore when he was supposed to be with you at the party?" demanded Anna, surprised at her own strength of feeling. "Imagine her humiliation! She probably should find out, but not like that."

The door next to them opened and Olivia stepped out looking suspicious, closely followed by Damien.

"What's going on?" she hissed at them, evidently sensing scandal.

Anna looked at Zanah, willing her silence, knowing Olivia's appetite for melodrama.

"I want to tell!" insisted Zanah, bouncing on the spot in front of Anna. Anna felt like they were small children up to no good, their parents demanding to know what they'd been up to.

"What? Oh, now I have to know!" urged Olivia, moving closer.

Damien closed the bar door and joined them, his curiosity obviously piqued.

"Come on, spill!" Olivia insisted.

Zanah looked at Anna then turned deliberately and dramatically to her new audience. "We just went for a wander and you'll never guess!

We saw Chantelle and David in a stable fucking each others' brains out!" The last few words emphasised for maximum effect and rising to a squawk, made Anna squirm.

"No way! You actually caught them at it?" exclaimed Olivia. "David? The instructor, David? David whose *wife* I was talking to just ten minutes ago?"

"We can't know for sure it was him," interjected Anna.

Olivia turned to her, wide-eyed and questioning.

"We only saw the back of him," she explained reluctantly. "And we didn't *catch* them, so to speak; they had no idea we were there."

Damien looked at Anna, the corners of his mouth slightly upturned. She drew closer to him, obscurely reassured, as Zanah leapt into more breathless details.

"You look appalled, Anna," he said quietly, smiling more now.

"I am a bit. It was a pretty grim scene," she confessed.

"Do I need to buy you another fortifying drink?" he asked, touching her arm.

"Well, the last ones knocked me sideways, and when I looked back you were gone," she complained.

"Share mine out here, then. I'm not going anywhere," he said, handing her his drink. Then he removed his jacket and put it round her, immediately enfolding her in the scent and heat of his body. "You're looking bloody hot tonight, but you feel a tad chilly."

"Thank you. You look pretty sleek yourself," she answered, taking care not to meet his eyes. Then silence settled on them and she felt the same old sense of being struck dumb.

After a moment she diverted to the happenings of the day. "I heard there were some injuries out there today."

"Yes, just as I thought. Pamela fell and I think she broke her leg and another guy smashed his collarbone when he took Lofter's, that hedge you jumped with me back in summer."

"Seems a long time ago," remarked Anna, smiling as she remembered.

"Yes it does," he said, meeting her eyes.

There it was again; that feeling of intense connection. No matter how hard she tried to resist him, nothing seemed to change. She was doomed.

The door opened behind them and Annetta looked out and scanned the deck.

"Are you okay, Annetta?" asked Olivia.

"I'm looking for David. He's been gone for ages," she said, looking frustrated and troubled at the same time.

Zanah and Anna exchanged brief glances, and Olivia looked at them then back at Annetta. "Sorry, we've not seen him out here on the deck," she said accurately.

"Let him know I'm looking for him if you see him, will you?" said Annetta, and she shut the door again.

They all exchanged awkward glances.

"I guess we're more certain it was him, then," said Zanah, looking at them flatly.

Anna sighed, feeling the uncomfortable burden of unshared knowledge.

"Yes, but Annetta can't find out here. And definitely not now," stated Olivia decisively. "Come on, children!" she said, opening the door. "Once more unto the breach, dear friends."

A noise behind them alerted them to another presence and they all turned.

It was David, stepping up onto the deck and heading for the door. He was looking down as he fastened a button on his jacket; Anna cringed.

She felt Damien's hand on her back and looked up at his face. He was stern, eyes fixed on David.

"Evening, David," he said crisply. "Bit of a cold night for a stroll."

David lifted his eyes briefly and said shortly, "Yeah, 'tis a bit," before passing through the open door.

Anna did not sleep well that night. The alcohol she had consumed, coupled with disturbing images of Chantelle and David pressed together into the dark corner of the stable, effectively banished quality slumber. Her dreams were mixed and fitful, running at exhausting speed. Larger-than-life images, obscure but looming threateningly, pressed close; and then were impossibly far away before rushing at her again. And Damien's face drifted repeatedly before her, his mesmerising eyes drinking her in.

HORSE AND HOUNDS

She woke early on Sunday and immediately downed two pints of water, a handful of vitamins and a painkiller.

Hangovers were rare for Anna. Brandy and champagne were not her usual choice, and their effect did not sit comfortably.

She stared out at the churchyard, its surface finely veiled in ice which sparkled on the long grass in the pale morning sun, and thought of Damien's face as she had seen it the night before, tense and unyielding as he spoke to David. She realised she was more hooked on him than ever.

She had to do something about it. He was married, and she abhorred wanton unfaithfulness, the more so since the evening before had revived bitter memories and old anger. Aside from Adam and his treachery, there was her family, torn apart by her father's infatuated wandering. She had been a child then, but the hurt still lingered and she would not repeat his folly.

As she was brooding, a group of people caught her eye, walking up the church path. On impulse she went to the door, stepped into her shoes and grabbed her jacket and keys.

Outside the morning smelled fresh and the merry peal of the church bells filled the air, as she walked purposefully down the path to join the rest of the congregation. The notice board caught her eye; 'Vicar: The Reverend Joshua Kramer,' she read, and passing through the heavy arched door of the church, the same door she had used several weeks before in the dead of night, she felt momentarily uncertain. Then, pushing the memories away, she stepped inside.

The cold mineral essence of the stone walls and the earthy smell of the wooden pews, mingled to create that distinct aroma which welcomes visitors at an old church. She slid into a pew near the back, recalling the self-conscious discomfort she had felt in the church in New York. Allowing her gaze to sweep upwards with the vaulted stonework, she felt the change in herself; a few months ago it wouldn't have occurred to her to visit a church.

She imagined Mateus' amusement at her sitting in the very church he used to preside over. What was happening to her? He had certainly instigated a change of sorts, but was it really an undeniable pull to religion, or was it all in her head? After all, she had a lot on her plate; there was the frustration of work, Dom's inexplicable disappearance, the frightening night she met Andrew in the church, and of course her struggle with Damien. He was the very reason she was there that morning. Perhaps she was just feeling desperate, unable to talk to anyone but needing some kind of help.

She looked at the sad-eyed saints portrayed in the stained-glass windows and at the body of Christ hanging limply and forlornly on its cross, and felt the same unmistakable and inexplicable surge of emotion, the lump in her throat and her eyes welling, that she had felt in New York. She swallowed and looked down, willing herself to get it together. What was wrong with her? Maybe she was losing it.

The vicar began his introductory address. His face was kind and he smiled as he spoke, and although he lacked the dynamism of the pastor in New York she felt an instant liking for him. Apparently in his late fifties, his curly receding hair closely cut, glasses perched on his nose, he looked more like a librarian or an Oxford don than a man of God. The cords he wore, accompanied by a thick woollen sweater, reinforced the impression of scholarliness, and only the obligatory dog collar revealed his calling. He was well spoken, his delivery precise, and as he talked he gestured economically, his body language measured and decisive. She listened thoughtfully, with a sense of descending calm, her entire being seeming to take a long deep breath.

She felt calm and refreshed as she left the church, and it was time to go to the stables and take Tom out. She stuffed her riding clothes into a backpack, then donned her running gear and set off at an easy pace, still feeling a dull ache in the front of her head. The hill up to Rosemount was a long pull and she fought the urge to stop and walk, leaning to the incline determinedly and ignoring the bite of stitch in her side.

"You don't give up, do you?" said a familiar voice from a car which had drawn level with her.

It was Damien.

"Want a ride?"

Anna laughed and conceded, doubling over for a moment and exhaling with a whoosh. Then she took off her backpack and climbed in next to him.

The interior was low and dark, all black leather and brushed aluminium. She was aware of his eyes on her, appreciatively assessing her body in its tight running outfit.

He drove fast and fluidly. Anna tried to tear her eyes from him and face front.

Thinking quickly, she asked, "How was your head this morning?"

"Not fantastic," he said, staring ahead as he took a bend in the road at speed. "But I've definitely had worse. I think sharing a couple of drinks might have slowed me down a bit. How about you?"

"I think my head was worse than it would have been, having shared some drinks I wouldn't normally have had," replied Anna, deadpan, raising one eyebrow.

He smiled across at her briefly. "Still want to take that competitive horse of yours out with me today?"

"Sure," said Anna as nonchalantly as she could, sitting back in the seat. "But I thought you'd be giving Barney the day off after hunting?"

"We're not going far today, and he didn't work that hard yesterday. There was too much stop and start and too many people," he answered with a shrug.

"Is anyone one else coming?"

"You're kidding, right?" he chuckled. "We'll be the only two there. Did you see how trashed Olivia and Zanah were at the end of the night? And pretty much everyone else. They won't surface until midday."

Anna laughed. "How long have you been up, then?"

"Ages. I might not have felt much like breakfast, but I got up, walked the dog, went to church, picked my car up, flew to the store and now I'm here," he said smugly.

Anna felt herself do a double-take. Was he serious? *Church*?

"Church? You're a churchgoer?" asked Anna, almost choking on her words in astonishment.

He looked self-conscious, as if expecting ridicule.

"Yes, well, not diligently and devoutly every week." He went quiet for a moment and cast a look across at her. "It's kind of a new thing for me. Only the last six months or so. I er...had a friend die in Afghanistan. Roadside bomb. Gave me pause, you know?"

"Sorry to hear that," said Anna. "You're not alone. I went too."

"You were in church this morning too?" he asked in surprise.

"Yes. It's a *very* new thing for me," she said, looking out the front as they pulled into the yard.

Anna was pleased with Tom. Having flared his nostrils a few times and put his head low to the ground to observe the hounds as they moved around him, he obviously decided they were nothing to be concerned about.

"We may get him hunting yet!" said Damien as they trotted the length of the field together. "Now let's turn, stick close and canter back. Keep it controlled."

Loping along on Tom next to Damien, Anna felt supremely happy. She still felt resistance to joining the hunt, but if it meant that she got to be with him she could overcome it.

Damien seemed to read her mind. "You know it's all trail hunting now, don't you?"

"Then what are the hunt protesters on about?" asked Anna with a disbelieving smile.

He looked back at her with a glimmer of dark amusement. "Okay, so maybe not everyone's legal."

Was he? Probably not, she guessed. Almost immediately she realised her distaste for hunting, or any resolve that had taken her to church that morning, was irrelevant. None of it mattered; she was hopelessly lost in him.

They were out for a long time and rode for miles, mostly in friendly silence. Such conversations as they had were short, and every now and then they exchanged fleeting glances. Neither of them seemed to want to go back to the yard, but the light was dropping and they had to pick up their pace to make it back before dark. Reaching an open field, they broke into a canter. This time Tom wanted to race and plunged forward and then bucked. Anna gripped hard, refusing to come off; another tumble in front of Damien would be downright embarrassing. Remembering his tip, she brought her whip down against Tom's neck just as he popped into another buck, and to her amazement he paused, apparently confused.

"Now shorten your rein and kick on!" urged Damien.

They galloped the length of the field neck-and-neck. Much to Anna's surprise Tom rose to the challenge and carried it through. He simply pulled hard against her contact and powered along, somewhat indignant but unprotesting.

"There you go! Pretty good," said Damien as they dropped to a walk.

"Yes! I remembered your trick!" Anna said, elated. "I can't believe it worked so well! I was on my way to ending up in a ditch in the dark," she laughed.

"Not such a bad place to be. I'd come for you," he said, turning in his saddle and winking at her.

Anna felt herself blush as she grinned mischievously, unable to hide her feelings. He looked at her intensely and then turned to face front and they rode back in silence, Anna bursting with happiness, her brain teeming with images of lying in a ditch with him in the dark, drowning in his beautiful eyes.

There were no other cars in the yard and it was almost dark. The thud of their riding boots on the concrete and the ringing of girth buckles sang out in the evening stillness as they carried their tack. It had been a long and wonderful day, a day of having Damien all to herself.

"Are you working much this week?" she asked him as she put her saddle away, thinking of her own start back to routine the following day.

"Yes, tomorrow until Wednesday then a long one from Friday through to the next Wednesday," he replied as he washed his horse's bit in the sink.

Dammit! He was away for a week and half?

He turned and looked at her for a moment, then asked, "You want to keep working on Tom? Get him hunt fit? You'll have a better horse if you do."

"Sure. But I'd rather hunt when you're there," said Anna, smiling shyly.

He put his hand on her shoulder as they walked from the tack room, squeezing it briefly. "Just get out there and work him, and work him at speed with some others. You're ready anyway. When I get back…"

She could hardly wait.

GOSSIP

Anna had lost all focus, her eyes drifting to the window to watch a pair of cormorants diving out in the dark waters of the docks. They disappeared for what seemed like minutes at a time, re-emerging with water running in viscous rivulets from their inky black feathers, throwing their heads back to swallow impossibly large fish.

She was conscious of Patrick, her assistant project manager, shuffling through the paperwork in front of them and she shook herself to attention. She was next up in front of Andrew. Budget cut backs had massacred most of the projects of the department. Teams already working on site were forced to demobilise; construction crews, plant and equipment, all brought grinding to a halt, and millions of pounds of budget spent on design, coming to nothing. For Anna it spelled the start of a new epoch but she felt sorry for the cantankerous programme manager. Despite the violence of his management style, he had sweated blood getting the department structured and staffed to deliver, and now everything was crashing down around him. He looked at Anna expectantly.

"When will you have the last one closed out?"

"We've got a couple of stakeholder comms to do and I'm awaiting the sponsor's final sign-off on the cancellation and close-out of the last three now"

"And that bunch of jerks will take their time as usual," he grunted, despondently. He was a shell of his former self; his whole ego had rested on his departmental sovereignty and now his kingdom lay in ruins.

She went back to her desk and collected her jacket, eager to get some air.

It had been nearly two weeks since her day with Damien, and Anna hadn't seen him since. Probably for the best. She had felt far too close to him on that Sunday, and enforced time apart had reinstated some sanity. She had been exercising Tom as much as possible and had gone out in a large group on an organised hack over the weekend and found him increasingly manageable. She had also surprised herself by attending Sunday morning service, partly due to the peace it prompted in her and also because she now knew Damien went to church. It seemed to link them in some way.

Outside, the day was bright and cold, and Anna walked briskly as she left the building. As she crossed the street she thought she saw a familiar figure further down the road. Something about the gait struck her; could it be Dom?

She stopped and strained to see but the man was disappearing into the crowd. Not wanting to lose him, she sped up. Arriving at the square she looked about, searching, but whoever it was had been swallowed up in the hordes of people.

She stood watching the fountain for a while, mesmerised by the flow of water, thinking of Dom. Where had he gone and what was he up to? He probably wasn't even in London anymore.

Suddenly aware of someone next to her, she turned her head as Francesca grabbed her arm.

"Good, I'm glad I caught you! Let's celebrate our forthcoming departure with hot chocolate with masses of cream!" she said, dragging Anna towards a coffee shop.

"Honestly, honey, I wish you'd go get a date with someone who's actually available," complained Francesca, sucking whipped cream from her spoon.

"I'm not ready," sighed Anna. She knew she was on course for heartbreak at some point, it was like an execution with no set date, but she wasn't ready to break it off. "While he's on my mind the way he is, I can't get interested in anyone else."

"You just need time," agreed Francesca, with a nod.

"I thought about taking an assignment abroad," Anna confessed. "It felt wrong, though. It seemed too drastic."

"Well, yes! You don't need to cut off limbs!" laughed Francesca. "Think; you love Rosemount and your lifestyle here. You need to move on from him, and things will be easier. Your feelings and obsessing have got you trapped. Let me set you up. I know a guy who'd fit with you well."

As she was speaking Anna's phone rang, Martin Davidson's name showing on the screen. Anna grinned mischievously at Francesca, knowing she was off the hook for the moment.

"No!" commanded Francesca, pointing at Anna.

"Saved by the bell!" laughed Anna, getting up and walking from the noisy shop to take the call.

"Anna," came Martin's voice, "Come in and see me this afternoon. It's the time you've been waiting for; we've got to discuss your next move."

He was obviously smiling at the other end of the line, knowing Anna was itching to move on. She wanted to hop up and down on the spot like a child just told she was going to Disneyland.

"Yes!" she enthused. "Do you want me there now?"

"I'm here all afternoon. Come over when you can."

Returning to the yard on Saturday afternoon after a lone ride, enjoying the earthy autumnal scents and scenery, Anna was feeling good. On Friday she had packed the few things she had in the office and left its bureaucracy and cartoon characters behind forever. Up next was a short-term project within the Secret Intelligence Service. Just like that, her months of trudging in mediocrity were done and she was flying to the underworld glamour of the strangely well-known and obvious, yet sinister building on the banks of the Thames.

The hunters were back, un-tacking and washing their muddied mounts down as she rode into the busy yard, which was vibrant with the energy they had brought with them.

Zanah walked by with her saddle and called cheerily, "Pub this evening, Anna?"

"Sure! Where?" asked Anna, jumping down from Tom's back.

"The George and Dragon after we've all finished up here," Zanah replied.

Anna looked round the yard to see whose cars were there and picked out Damien's BMW, feeling a rush of excitement and wondering if he would be going too. She was now desperate to see him.

The tack room was warm and quiet as Anna put her tack back in its place before sitting down on one of the wooden benches to take her riding boots off. As she unzipped the first boot she heard footfalls and murmuring out in the corridor. One of the voices was Chantelle's and there was another female voice which Anna assumed must belong to Nicole.

"No way! Is he really?" Nicole was exclaiming.

"Yes. He totally said so," replied Chantelle in more hushed tones.

"He's leaving her?" came Nicole's voice again, incredulous.

"Yes. He hates her," insisted Chantelle simply.

Anna gaped, guessing they could only be talking of David. The scene in the stable had been discussed endlessly but no-one had seen anything since, apart from one weekday evening when Olivia had walked into the feed room and found them stepping away from one another. No-one wanted to tip off Annetta, and the gossip was dying down; a nine days' wonder. Anna shook her head. Now Chantelle really thought he was going to leave his wife for her? The poor, stupid girl.

"When did you see him last?" hissed Nicole.

"Last night. He came round to mine."

"Weren't your parents there? Do they know?" asked Nicole.

"No, they're away."

"How old is he anyway?"

"He's forty, I think," answered Chantelle.

"Forty? Kind of old! I've never been with anyone that old!" said Nicole with a short laugh.

Anna smiled at their youthful naivety, wondering what age she had been when forty no longer seemed old.

Nicole continued in an excited schoolgirl whisper, "Is he good?"

"He's amazing. We were at it all night! We did it on my parents' bedroom floor and in the middle of the dining table!" came Chantelle's breathless answer. Nicole uttered a gasp and they both giggled.

Anna took a long grim breath. This was bad. This was very bad. Chantelle was young, naive and selfish – an affair with a married man twice her age was just another thrill. What did she care who got hurt, or how it ended? But David, with a wife, and supposedly a modicum of sense, was another matter. What was he thinking?

Chantelle and Nicole stopped sniggering abruptly and moved off as another set of footsteps became audible in the corridor. Anna hastily removed her other boot, feeling a little underhand having listened so intently. Zanah came in with a lead rope and threw it in her locker.

"Almost ready?" she asked.

"Yes," said Anna, then realised her reaction to what she had heard must be showing on her face because Zanah looked at her closely and asked in a suspicious tone:

"What's with you?"

"Nothing. Tell you later," replied Anna, putting her riding boots away and stepping into her yard boots.

Perhaps they were going to have to break the news to Annetta. Regardless of what David was going to do, he was carrying on with Chantelle and a number of people knew. It was their duty to tell Annetta, wasn't it? Or should they confront David instead? Anna shuddered;

either would be hideously awkward and embarrassing. One the other hand, perhaps it wasn't any of their business and they should just leave it to run its course.

She couldn't decide; it was hopeless. She needed to talk to the others and see what they thought.

The street lamps and house lights of the village glowed in the almost-dark of the evening as Anna parked her Land Rover at the church. As she got out, she saw Andrew Japson emerging from the church gate and walking in the opposite direction along the street. She hadn't seen him since the strange night in the churchyard. How odd to see him now. She wondered why he was there.

The pub was a short walk from her cottage, so she strolled contentedly alongside the graveyard wall, inhaling the crisp evening air. She could smell wood smoke as she neared the pub, and as she passed its low windows she saw the open fire roaring in the inglenook fireplace. Next to it were Zanah and Olivia, having claimed the best table in the house.

The George and Dragon was a low squat building with cosy low-ceilinged rooms and the usual complement of shining copper kettles, antique warming pans, horse brasses and hunting artwork in ornate frames. In the main bar, the exposed oak beams overhead were scarred from years of abuse and woodworm, and above the bar itself twinkling fairy lights twined around hop branches. It was warm, welcoming, and deliciously antiquated, and Anna loved it, especially in the winter.

She bowed her head as she passed under the low door frame and headed to the bar. Olivia and Zanah were sitting opposite one another deep in discussion while Damien stood at the bar, chatting to the landlord.

"Damien's buying if you're quick enough," said Olivia, looking up. "Then get your hiney over here and tell us whatever it is you have to tell us!" she commanded.

Anna smiled and headed over to Damien. Acting as casually as she could, she put a hand on his shoulder. Still talking, Damien put his arm round her briefly and gave her a friendly squeeze.

"Hi. It's been a while," he said, turning to her. "What do you want?"

"What's good, Jack?" asked Anna.

"I just got the Winter Meltdown on tap," said the landlord, smiling at her. "It's good!"

"It is good," confirmed Damien, taking a swig from his glass.

"Go on then, I'll join in!" said Anna, enthusiastically.

"Good girl!" said Damien, impressed. "I didn't think girls did bitter."

"There you go, Anna," said Jack, topping up the pint he'd just pulled and setting the foaming glass on the bar. "How's the job?"

"Fantastic – I just quit the rail projects on Friday and I'm lining up a new gig," replied Anna, taking a sip of her beer.

"Good stuff. In London, still?" asked Jack.

Anna nodded. She became aware that Damien was watching her intently.

"Where are you going?" asked Jack, leaning against the bar.

"Well, if all works out, I've got a bit of work for MI6 – but I actually can't talk about it," Anna added hastily.

"You can tell me but you'd have to kill me, right?" smiled Jack.

"I'd have to kill both of you," she affirmed, grinning.

Jack laughed and turned away to greet a group of new customers. Damien leant towards Anna and smiled confidentially.

"I'd love to have you try," he whispered, then picked up the drinks on the bar for the others. Anna followed, trying not to laugh.

"It's about time!" exclaimed Olivia. "A girl could die of thirst round here! And since when have you two been so friendly?"

Anna summoned up an uncomprehending expression, and saw Damien too looking at her blankly.

"I've been riding out with you for years and you've never greeted me with a hug!" she fired at him accusingly. He looked amused and drank from his glass.

"Anna's sweeter than you," he said in a considering tone, taking a seat at the table. Anna glowed, taking the remaining seat and looking into his eyes for split second. Olivia eyed them both sharply.

"Come on! What was it you were going to tell us? Your expression was a picture!" said Zanah, apparently blithely unaware of the tension. She tugged at Anna's sleeve impatiently.

"I bet it's the Chantelle and David melodrama. Zanah said she saw Chantelle scampering off furtively as she was going to the tack room," said Olivia. "And I heard Annetta whinging to Penelope about David – apparently he's out a lot," she finished, labouring the last words.

"Sounds like it's more than just that one night," said Zanah.

"Bound to be. He knows where the cookie jar is now," said Damien dryly.

"You're right," said Anna. "From what Chantelle said this evening, it definitely is. She seems to think he's actually going to leave Annetta for her."

"What?!" exclaimed Olivia and Zanah in unison. Damien just shook his head, and Anna relayed what she'd heard.

"Stupid girl!" said Olivia. "He'll never leave Annetta. He'd be really dim to do that."

"That was my reaction," said Anna.

"The trouble is, we all know about this but Annetta's still in the dark. I feel like she should know but there's no way I want to tell her!" said Zanah. "Can you imagine her reaction? She's scary at the best of times! How would she react to us saying, 'Hey Annetta, we saw your husband screwing Chantelle's brains out against a wall a few weeks ago and apparently they've been at it ever since and we're just telling you about this now!'"

"Not tempting," agreed Olivia. "Mind you, Chantelle's so indiscreet she'll end up blowing his cover on her own. That'll be the next thing on the Rosemount soap opera, and it'll be worth seeing."

They bounced the topic around inconclusively for a while before drifting away from it, progressing to talk of the day's hunt. Anna felt left out and looked at the table, only half-listening to their enthusiastic account. Only when Damien interjected did she pay much attention, smiling at his sometimes caustic wit directed at Olivia, and absorbing the sound of his voice.

Olivia and Zanah wanted to get supper at the pub and Anna, having no-where else to be, decided to join them. Damien got up to leave, saying he was working early the next day. He threw on his jacket and touched Anna's shoulder as he passed.

"You want to take Tom out for another drill?" he asked softly.

"Sure, when are you around?" asked Anna, sitting back from the table and turning towards him.

"How about Thursday? Can you get away early and we can do a quick evening jaunt before it's dark?"

Anna considered for a moment and nodded. Given her week at head office waiting for the next assignment, it was a good time to skip out early one day.

"I'll be at the yard around half past two. Get my number from Olivia. Let me know if you can't make it," he said, then turned and left.

"You going to get Tom hunting?" asked Olivia.

"That'll be fun if we all go together!" Zanah enthused.

Olivia ignored Zanah's comment and said suspiciously, tilting her head towards the door, "He's obviously into you. I've never seen him make such an effort before."

Anna summoned up an innocent expression and shrugged. She sensed a barrage of questions coming her way over supper.

FIRST HUNT

Anna leant against Tom's stable door, watching him lick the last of his supper from the feed bowl. It had been a long day at head office, working on the MI6 assignment, and Tom was relaxing company.

She considered the assignment. Although it was short, much of it was relatively new territory so she would be learning fast and developing her skills – all to the good for her career prospects. Admittedly she would be learning about internal administrative and management processes, which didn't exactly fill her with glee, but it couldn't harm to broaden her experience; and there was the bonus that her co-worker, Phil, was entertaining even if he was a nerd.

She shifted against the door as she contemplated the change in her fortunes, and a chilly gust of wind whipped across her face, bringing her abruptly back to the present. She zipped her collar up; it was time she went home and fixed herself some dinner.

As she rounded the corner near the office and bar she almost collided with Chantelle, who ignored her and stormed off in the opposite direction looking like a stroppy teenager. Anna spotted Annetta and David in the office together and guessed Chantelle was suffering from jealousy.

She grinned to herself, wondering how long David would play Chantelle along as his convenient sideshow, and get away with it – because that was surely all he had in mind.

There seemed no shortage of drama going on: Chantelle and David, Dom's unsolved disappearance – and if she didn't get a grip on herself she too would be a major talking point. She shook herself; best not to think about that. But the horse world did seem to encourage scandal; for some reason it brought out people's appetites for thrill, adrenalin – and each other. Perhaps, she mused, it was because relationships were tight and incestuous, and that, coupled with the sheer physicality of riding itself, brought out impulses that in a less pressurised setting would never come to the boil. It was just a matter of time before Chantelle and David's affair erupted publicly, with repercussions she didn't like to contemplate. That wouldn't happen to her, though; definitely not. Confounding as her situation was, there was no way she was going to allow anything to happen between her and Damien. He was married and she was just suffering a stupid crush. It would pass.

The quiet week at work meant that it was easy to leave early on Thursday. Sitting on the train as it clattered across the bridge over the Thames, Anna turned her gaze from the crumbling chimneys of Battersea Power Station to her phone.

Damien's number was up on the screen. She hadn't used it. She looked at it, wondering if she should text him. No. He said contact if you *can't* make it. She'd look desperate if she texted to say she was on her way.

It heightened her anxiety, being in possession of his number. She almost wished he hadn't given it to her. Maybe if she used it she'd set off a sequence which would take them down a road of no return. After all, they seemed to be getting closer all the time and text contact would provide a secret hotline; a private one-to-one, its facelessness making suggestive flirtation so much easier. Then they'd be embroiled in the oh-so-predictable, stereotypical drama where the wife discovers suspicious texts from a girl at the stables on her husband's phone. Anna shuddered at the thought. They were safer as they were.

She sighed and rolled her eyes. Was she over-thinking it? Probably he didn't feel the same way and was just enjoying a bit of careless flirting. She grimaced at herself. The politics of the thing were messing with her brain. She threw her phone in her bag and pulled out her book. She had to take her mind off him before there was a cranial systems crash.

Anna looked doubtfully at the sky where the clouds had gathered and were scudding along. The light would not last long that afternoon. As she rode round to meet Damien in the front yard, Penelope appeared on her chestnut hunter.

"Oh, are you going out now?" she asked them.

"Yes. Want to join us?" he replied casually. Anna felt herself willing Penelope to say no, but to her disappointment Penelope agreed.

"Tom needs more of a challenge," said Damien, looking at Anna. He went on to tell Penelope about their project with Tom, while Anna rode behind scolding herself for her childishness.

It was a fast ride, and they took the wider bridleways and open spaces working at pace together. The rain started as they were heading back downhill towards Rosemount.

"I think you should give him a try at the weekend," said Penelope, looking at Tom's ears as they relaxed outwards in a satisfied fashion.

Anna nodded, but nevertheless felt a little nervous. It was all very well working with two considerate riders, but on Saturday it would be a horde of galloping others. She was silent for a moment as she inwardly lectured herself about being brave and seizing the day. She would look weak if she put it off now.

"It'll be a fun one this Saturday!" added Penelope.

"Not necessarily," said Damien, "But probably more up Anna's street."

Anna looked at him quizzically.

"Yes, it will be fun," said Penelope firmly, looking at Damien with maternal amusement. Turning to Anna, she explained, "We're hunting the clean boot on Saturday, meaning we're hunting runners. I don't think the die-hard hunters like Damien approve! The chap who leads the local running club apparently challenged our huntsman one night in the pub!"

"Bet he's regretting it now," said Damien, flicking his whip at an overhanging branch.

"Why?" asked Penelope.

"Oh, come on! A drunken challenge and suddenly he's training to do five or six hours of running in the cold across claggy ploughed fields. It'll be miserable for them and boring for us."

Anna grinned but didn't say anything.

"I believe they switch the runners at points. Honestly Damien, you are being a misery about this," laughed Penelope.

Damien gave her a begrudging grin and kept quiet.

Back in the tack room Damien took off his wet jacket and looked across at Anna as she put her saddle away.

"You'll do fine on Saturday," he said shortly.

"Thanks, coach," Anna responded, annoyed with herself for feeling apprehensive.

"He responds well to the neck slap. You won't be riding in the front field, and if he gets too much, you can take him home," said Damien simply.

Anna gave him a flat smile. "Yes, I know."

He moved to her side and nudged her. "The girl who jumped Lofter's hedge on our first ride out can tackle this," he said with a wink. "I'll see you bright and early on Saturday. Half nine to ride out," he said over his shoulder as he left.

Anna stood thinking for a moment, realising she would have to dig out her smart jacket and white breeches, clean her boots and tack, and braid Tom's mane.

"What a faff!" she groaned, closing her locker. Hacking out was easy, all one had to do was saddle up and go; no need for the hours of prettying-up which went hand-in-hand with organised events. She hoped it would be worth it.

Nervous anticipation nagged at Anna as she finished the final braid in Tom's mane on Saturday morning. She just wanted to get on and get going. Taking a deep breath, she did up the buttons on her jacket. The butterflies would subside soon enough; they'd better do.

Grabbing the reins, she walked Tom to the mounting block and hopped on his back quickly as he fidgeted. He was particularly alert, his head high and long ears pricked straight up. The shout to ride out came as she rode into the front yard and Olivia fell in next to her.

"There you are! Welcome to addiction! You'll have a cracking day. There'll be no turning back after this," she promised.

Anna gave her a brief smile, hoping she was right.

Ten minutes later they arrived at the meet and Anna shortened her rein as Tom danced excitedly on the spot, having clocked the multitude of horse trailers, riders and foot followers milling around in the field.

"Get that down you!" said Olivia, handing Anna a stirrup cup.

"Thanks," said Anna, downing what turned out to be cherry brandy. She felt the warmth of it in her throat, spreading through her chest.

Damien rode over and smiled at her from the back of Barnabas who was pacing excitedly. His hunt whip was coiled neatly at his side and he took a swig from a hip flask then handed it to her.

"Looks like you need another one," he said.

It seemed early to be hitting the spirits but she dutifully took a gulp.

"Thanks. I'm probably going to fall at the first obstacle or burst into flames if I drink any more."

"Nonsense! One has to be drunk enough to bounce with bravado!" boomed another rider who had appeared next to them on an enormous freckled horse. He looked to be in his early fifties, with steel grey hair and a well-structured face. His riding hat appeared to be an antique; no chin strap and so thin as to afford little protection if he were to bounce, with or without bravado. In his scarlet coat he was the quintessential hunter.

"Alright, Simeon?" said Damien. "Haven't seen you for a while."

"I've been working. Case just went on and on," shrugged Simeon.

"Lawyer," said Damien, leaning towards Anna and gesturing towards Simeon with his whip. "This is Anna," he said, introducing her.

"Not seen you before," smiled Simeon.

"No, it's her virgin voyage," answered Damien for Anna, his eyes on her. Anna smiled.

"Excellent. I hope you have a good day. Must get off now," said Simeon, looking at his watch.

He moved away, raising his hand in a friendly gesture.

It all seemed so civilised. How was it these people enjoyed hunting an animal to exhaustion? Anna shook her head to halt the train of thought, knowing that next she would be questioning herself for being there.

"Looks like we're off soon," Damien commented. "I'm up front, but you stick with Olivia. Drinks tonight. You can tell me how much fun you had." He flashed a smile and rode away.

Anna's tension subsided once she was up in her stirrups at an easy canter with Olivia and Zanah, with Paul and Jess riding behind. There was a feeling of camaraderie riding in a tight pack, and Tom pounded along steadily. Anna's quadriceps were on fire when Olivia called for the group to slow, and she gratefully sat into trot.

"Steady, everyone!" Olivia warned as they came to the top of a steep hill. They poured down it like possessed lemmings, and Anna gasped as Tom followed the others, bounding into an eager canter which had her heart in her mouth as she braced against the stirrups.

The heat of pursuit left no room for timidity, and as she heard the distinctive blast of the horn and excited baying of the hounds, she urged Tom to a gallop.

"Watch it, Anna! Ditch coming!" shouted Paul as he dashed along with her.

"Fucking hell! Slow down, you two!" yelled Olivia as Anna and Paul raced headlong into the wet mud approaching the stream, sticky black mud and murky water flying from their horses' hooves. Paul's horse leapt over the stream and Tom flattened his ears and charged through the water, sending it arching about them. Anna held him fast, blinking muddy water from her eyes and praying he wouldn't buck.

"Tiger trap!" called Paul, gesturing with his whip. "One at a time."

"Me first!" she insisted, feeling Tom rounding his back.

He leapt for the jump early, Anna exclaiming and gripping his mane as he exploded from the ground six feet ahead of the obstacle. She heard Paul shout behind her, and hunched low over Tom's neck, narrowly missing the low hanging branches overhead.

Landing the other side, Tom flattened into a gallop and Anna planted herself into the saddle, hauling on her outside rein, knowing she had to regain control or she would be overtaking the huntsman and trampling hounds. She caught sight of Damien and Barnabas up ahead on the hill tearing after the group of runners, who were now checking over their shoulders and pumping hard to escape the snarling hounds who were bearing down on them.

"Are you okay?" called Paul, as he caught up with her.

Anna nodded, still hanging on to Tom, her biceps burning.

"Bloody hell!" he continued. "He jumped huge! I thought he'd have your head off when he took the tiger trap; he cleared it with three feet to spare! Can't believe his pace!"

Anna was too breathless to respond immediately, her legs shaking as she clung to Tom.

"Sit deep," urged Paul.

Finally they slowed to a walk and Anna breathed once again.

"Where are the others?" she asked him.

"Far behind!" laughed Paul. "Olivia will have words with us later! But fuck it, let's move up the field now we're here. We're almost on the runners!"

The light was beginning to fade as they jogged along a wide track and Anna suddenly realised they must have been going for hours.

"We're getting close to the end," said Paul. "Let's take it up a gear for now and then we'll cool off for the last mile or so."

They surged forward together across the shoulder of a broad rolling field, falling into single file for the next track. Anna held Tom firmly as they cantered, narrowing her eyes against the mud flying at her from the hooves of Paul's horse in front.

As they burst out of the woods, a long straight track down the side of a vast field beckoned. Paul looked at her mischievously, checking for Olivia over his shoulder.

"Okay, maybe one more race?"

Anna laughed and called out, "Go on Tom, have at it!" Attentive to her shout, he slipped again into his fluid sixth gear.

Paul exclaimed and pushed his big hunter along to match her for a moment before Tom lengthened his stride, sweeping away from them. Nearing the woods, she reined back and Tom relaxed into walk, finally tired, his head low at the end of his long neck, as Paul re-joined them.

"I can't race you!" laughed Paul. "It's no good for my ego, or his," he added, patting his horse. "Blimey! Look at us!"

Anna looked down at herself for the first time and giggled as she saw the results of their headlong charge through the stream; she was splattered in muck from head to toe, and she could feel the mud on her face already starting to crack as it dried.

They walked on a loose rein home, peeling off on a familiar bridleway and clattering heroically into the yard late in the afternoon.

Still pumped full of adrenalin, Anna leapt from the saddle and rubbed Tom's head affectionately. His coat was soaked with sweat and mud and she quickly removed his tack and washed him. He steamed and shook himself vigorously with a grunt, and she loved him even more.

THE ATTACK

The bar was buzzing with hunting talk, and Zanah, Paul and Olivia cheered and raised their drinks at Anna as she strode up to them beaming.

"Bravo, Anna! First hunt!" shouted Olivia, handing her a bottle of Becks. "And nary a fall nor mortal injury!"

"You totally showered me when you took off with Paul through the water! Look!" Zanah laughed, standing in front of Anna and gesturing at her hunt coat.

"I was saving the reprimand for later, but since you've started…" began Olivia.

"Oh, give over!" cut in Paul. "It's her first hunt! Don't be such a kill-joy!"

They were still in animated conversation when Damien joined them. He squeezed in next to Olivia, smiling as he watched Anna and Zanah gesticulating excitedly.

"So, did we catch the runners?" Olivia asked him.

"Yes, right at the eleventh hour. We got them," he answered, still watching Anna.

"You've really taken her under your wing," commented Olivia probingly, following his gaze.

Damien looked at her questioningly.

"I've never seen you look after anyone before. I thought you hated babysitting," she said.

He shrugged and made no response.

"Oi oi!" shouted James raucously, suddenly appearing and clapping Damien on the shoulder.

"What on earth are you doing here?" asked Damien.

"A few of us decided to drink here this evening. The Hare and Hounds has some function going on so we thought we'd bring the party to Rosemount!" said James, leaning over the bar in search of a server. "Alright darling!" he shouted to the female bartender. "I'll have a pint of Spitfire when you're ready."

He turned and nodded at Olivia. "Seen anything of Vince recently?" Vince was a member of the hunt; Olivia had an on-off relationship with him, which tended to start on drunken evenings then last for a few weeks at a time. At 6'5", he was a comfortable height for Olivia, and was sufficiently rowdy to counter her boisterousness.

"Not for a while. His horse had an op on his right fore and has been on box rest" she said, downing the last of her gin and tonic.

"So you're not bunking together at the moment?" said James with a lewd grin.

"And what about you and that girl Jennifer?" demanded Olivia, rounding on him. "Last thing I heard, her father was throwing you off the property and threatening to get a restraining order against you!"

"The whole thing got totally blown out of proportion," insisted James breezily.

"Well, you probably should have known better than to date a 17-year-old," commented Damien.

"I heard you fled the premises with a Doberman Pinscher's teeth at your arse," laughed Olivia.

"Yeah. That did happen," agreed James, grinning. Then he picked up his beer which had just arrived and downed half of it in seconds.

Olivia shook her head at James and moved over to where Zanah and Anna were talking with Paul, Jess and Lucias. James followed her with his eyes, his gaze coming to a rest on Anna.

"That your bit of extracurricular activity?" he asked Damien, nodding at her.

Damien smiled. "Why would you think that?"

"Just seen you together a few times. Seemed to be something between you. Wouldn't blame you either," he said, looking at Damien nonchalantly. He turned back to Anna again. "Well, if you're not doing her then I might later," he leered.

Damien's eyes grew serious for a moment, and then he turned and followed James's gaze, leaning one elbow against the bar.

"I have a strong feeling that you're not her type."

"Challenge accepted," said James, knocking his glass against Damien's, not taking his eyes from Anna.

"I couldn't believe that hill!" Zanah exclaimed. "I nearly went over Charlie's head!"

"You want to keep that pert butt in the saddle then, don't you," said James as he sidled into the space between Zanah and Anna.

Zanah looked at James witheringly, while Anna eyed him suspiciously. She had formed a pronounced dislike for him, which he was strongly reinforcing by the moment.

"Evening, Anna," he said, grinning at her mischievously.

"Good evening to you," she articulated carefully. She narrowed her eyes sceptically, sensing foul play.

"Did you have a good day? I heard it was your first hunt?" he continued undeterred, ignoring the amused looks from the rest of the group.

"It was good, thanks," answered Anna, increasingly dubious. Why was he talking to her?

"I doubt you know but it's the tradition to consummate your first hunt," said James with meaning, pressing his fingertips together earnestly. There were snorts of laughter from the others.

"Consummate your first hunt?" repeated Anna slowly with a harder edge settling into her voice. There were a couple of sniggers, Anna's friends knowing that she was not a willing target for James's asinine wit. Undaunted he bungled on.

"Yeah; as in to have it off with an already inaugurated hunt member."

"I see," said Anna, matter-of-factly. "And am I to understand you are putting forward your own services as a viable option?" She saw Damien, who had moved alongside, smile. Zanah chuckled.

"If you want to put it that way..." said James, eying her, now sensing shut down.

"Hmm, no thanks. I'm sure if that's the tradition I'll source a better alternative," said Anna, raising her eyebrows.

Olivia snorted with laughter and added, "Why would she pick you, James, while there are dogs in the street?" Laughter rang out raucously and James looked around at them all, swore roundly, and strode off waving his finger over his shoulder.

"This is not over!" he called.

Damien leaned towards Anna and warned, "He means it, you know. He'll be back later to pester you."

"Wonderful," said Anna sarcastically, noticing James watching her from his new vantage point at the other end of the bar, as he launched himself into the jocularity of the group he had arrived with.

"Don't worry. I am sure Damien will protect you!" laughed Olivia suggestively.

Seeing irritation in Damien's eyes as he turned them on Olivia, Anna said hastily, "I was going to rely on you for that, Olivia! I sense he's the kind to be far more annoyed if it's a woman who delivers the put down."

"Well, well, Anna; you're now a hunter," came a familiar voice from next to her. Anna turned to face Andrew.

"I haven't seen you in a while," she remarked.

"No, I've been occupied elsewhere." He looked, unusually for him, somewhat tired.

"Have you been working long hours?" she asked him, looking at the faint circles beneath his eyes.

"You could say that," he said, with a laugh which seemed to indicate a private joke.

"You don't seem your effervescent self."

"No. I've been dealing..." He tailed off for a moment as though seeking the right words. "I've been dealing with some shit."

"Nothing you'd care to share?" she ventured, already knowing the response.

"Nothing I *can* share," he returned enigmatically.

Anna looked at him searchingly. Questions about the night at the church jostled to be asked, but it seemed too public. At the time it had sounded like someone was in real trouble. If it was real and he was there at the scene, what he was involved in was deeply unpleasant. Curiosity gnawed at her.

"Really? You'd be surprised at the secrets I am entrusted with," she prompted him.

"I'm sure. But some things you're safer not knowing," he answered, meeting her eyes.

A little chill ran through Anna. There wasn't a hint of his normal casual demeanour. His eyes were different; deadly serious.

"What's wrong?" she urged. Why was he talking like this? She must have been right that something was badly amiss, and this was surely a call for help on his part – whether he realised it or not.

He looked away for a moment, appearing to check himself, and when he looked back he had re-established a partial smile, masking whatever lay behind. Then he sighed.

"I've got to see Pete," he said, his tone switching to businesslike.

Reverting to his customary overfamiliarity, he remarked, "You look good in your hunt gear, Anna. I kinda like the mud splatters too," he added, winking mischievously as he moved off.

He was impossible. However, she felt a pang of concern for him. His usual cool had been shaken by something and he was hiding it. He was a loner whose business was a mystery, but it seemed sinister, and the solemnity in his eyes had scared her.

She looked outside at the dense blackness of the fully descended night. The next day she had arranged to spend with Francesca in London, and it was time to go home. Heading to her Land Rover, she passed someone sitting on the wall, smoking.

"Hey, Anna!" he called. Anna realised with a flutter of concern that it was James, who she had managed to evade for the remainder of the evening.

"Goodnight," she said, speeding up.

"Oh no, no, no!" he said, jumping up and following her with a drunken swagger. "We never did finish."

"We did as far as I was concerned," she returned as casually as possible. A mental alarm was ringing and an inner voice told her to get away from him. She walked faster. She sensed him close and a spasm of shock rattled through her as she felt his hand on her arm. Suddenly acutely aware of her vulnerability on her own in the dark with him, she squared her shoulders and turned to meet his eyes with an admonishing glare.

"Don't touch me," she warned. Surely he wasn't seriously going to try anything; that would be crazy. But an insistent alert continued in her gut.

"Oh, come on, I'm harmless! And you're in denial," he said, breathing potent spirits and the reek of cigarette breath in her face.

"You're drunk and I am going," stated Anna clearly. Then she turned around again and swiftly unlocked her door. Her hand was on the door handle when she felt him again. She couldn't quite believe what was happening and felt a deep lurch of primal fear. He twisted her round and pinned himself against her, pressing her against her door, with a predatory smile. His hands grasped at her wrists, holding her fast, and he bent his face to hers. Anna reacted instinctively, bringing her knee up sharply, and pushing him forcefully as he crumpled forward.

"Shit!" he groaned. "That was uncalled for!" Then, recovering far more quickly than Anna expected, he stepped towards her again. Anna's eyes widened in horror and her body flooded with adrenalin, ready to fight. The scene slowed to a surreal frame-by-frame as James lunged towards her, throwing her against the Land Rover again, this time with purposeful and terrifyingly mindless violence.

Suddenly there was another person there, tall, robust and protective. He stepped like a shield in front of Anna and pushed James away roughly, overpowering him without effort and sending him tumbling backwards to an awkward collision with the ground.

"What the hell are you doing?" Damien shouted angrily.

James scrambled back to his feet looking indignant and aggressive, like a hunting dog pulled from its prey. "Where the fuck did you spring from?" he shouted, stepping up threateningly.

"Don't you dare come at me!" warned Damien. "Just go, James. Walk away!"

James stood rigidly, glaring for a long moment, but then seemed to return to his senses, knowing he didn't stand a chance against Damien. Still staring, he touched the heel of his hand to a scratch on his face from his fall and then turned and melted away into the darkness.

Damien watched him out of sight, not moving. Anna was shaking and she released her breath and clenched her fists, holding them against Damien's back and willing herself to be still and calm. He turned to her and caught her hands in his.

"Are you okay? Did he hurt you?" he asked urgently.

"No," she struggled to say, feeling her breath coming quickly. He touched her chin and turned her face up to his, eyes full of concern.

"What happened?"

"He followed me. I didn't think he'd actually try anything, but..." Stifling a sob, she stopped. "He threw me against my car and he er..." She broke off, her teeth chattering as the shock of being attacked set in. "Thank God you were there."

He wrapped his arms round her and held her close. "You're okay," he whispered.

He seemed like her guardian angel, and she buried her head against him and clung to him for what seemed a long time as she willed herself calm. They remained in silence, with only the breeze in the trees and Anna's own breathing in her ears. She could feel Damien's heartbeat slowing from its previous thunder. He felt solid and powerful.

"Can I drive you home?" he asked, his voice rumbling against her ear.

"Thank you, but no. I'm okay. I'm so glad you were here. I just want to go home now." She stepped back and looked up at him. She loved him even more now, but she felt compelled to be tough and recover herself. Nothing had happened and she was okay.

He looked at her doubtfully. "Are you sure?"

"Yes. I'm fine."

He pulled her to him again and said, "Make sure you drive carefully. Do me a favour and text me when you get back."

Watching the lights of the Land Rover disappear round the bend in the driveway, Damien stood alone in the dark yard. Then he turned, his face set, and marched purposefully back to where the light of the bar spilled out onto the driveway. He glanced in the windows, but continued round onto the grass and stood motionless, listening.

"What's up, Damien?" asked Zanah from the deck, where she was smoking a cigarette, her feet dangling from the edge.

"Have you seen James?"

"Yes, he went into the undergrowth over there. I think he's spewing. He looked wasted. Olivia went to see if she could find him," Zanah went on.

Footsteps came from behind and Paul appeared at Damien's side.

"You alright, mate? I thought I heard a shout."

"Yeah. Come with me, will you?" said Damien, heading in the direction Zanah had indicated. Paul followed immediately, and Zanah, sensing drama, jumped off the deck, throwing her stub into the grass.

"James! Are you okay? What're you doing?" called Olivia, blindly stepping through the brambles. There was a groan from further into the trees.

"Nothing. Just leave me alone," came the subdued answer.

"I can't leave you in here, drunk on your own. It's too cold to fall asleep and spend the night out here!" she insisted, stopping to strain her eyes through the blackness.

"Olivia!" Damien bellowed through the darkness from somewhere behind her at the edge of the woods.

"Over here!"

"Is he there?"

"Yes, well, somewhere here. I can't actually find him," she said as Damien's shape appeared next to her in the gloom.

"James!" shouted Damien. There was no response.

"I wonder if he's passed out?" wondered Olivia. "He just told me to leave him alone."

"No, he just doesn't want to see me," said Damien grimly.

"Why? What happened?"

Damien didn't respond as he stepped forward through the undergrowth, pushing aside low branches.

Paul followed with Olivia, shrugging at her repeated question, this time directed at him. They heard a scrambling in the undergrowth and James's voice came angrily, "Just bloody well leave me alone!"

"No, you don't get that luxury now. You're lucky I didn't take you down!"

Olivia and Paul exchanged glances.

There was a crashing noise and the sound of breaking sticks and brambles tearing against something, and then James scrambled clumsily from the woods with Damien close behind.

James stumbled from the brush past Zanah, and continued towards the yard.

"What are you doing?" she asked, catching up with him as the others came from the woods.

"Nothing. Going home," said James shortly, fumbling for his keys.

"You're not driving!" gaped Zanah.

"No, he's not!" said Olivia firmly, running a few paces and snatching his keys. James stopped and turned on her.

"Olivia, just give them to me!"

"You're not driving. Don't want anyone else hurt tonight, do we?" said Damien pointedly, stepping to Olivia's side, his eyes dangerous.

"Such a fucking hero, aren't you," snapped James.

"What's happened?" asked Olivia, exasperated, looking back and forth between them.

"I don't want to do this now," said James, turning away looking defeated and weary.

"Yeah, come on mate. I'll give you a ride home," said Paul, putting his hand on James's shoulder and ushering him to the front yard. James, numbly obedient, wordlessly walked alongside him. Olivia handed James's keys to Paul and watched them leave. Once they were out of earshot she turned and looked questioningly at Damien.

"Well?" she demanded. He pulled his stare from James's retreating form, sighed and turned to go.

"Oh no you don't! What happened?" she demanded, reaching for his sleeve.

Damien turned back and looked at her, spreading his hands. "What? He's had too much to drink."

"Yes, he often has too much to drink. But you don't go searching the woods for him. What happened?" she demanded.

"And Paul said he heard you shout. Did you have a fight? What did you mean about no-one else getting hurt?" put in Zanah.

Olivia looked at Zanah and back at Damien. He sighed again and looked down.

"He attacked Anna," he said, the words coming unwillingly.

"What?" Olivia exclaimed, astounded. "No way! What happened? Is she okay? Where is she?" The questions tumbled from her and she looked swiftly around as though searching for Anna.

"She's okay. She went home," he responded.

"What? You let her drive herself home?"

Damien exhaled and closed his eyes for a second, not speaking.

"What happened, anyway?" demanded Olivia.

"James followed her to her car and tried it on."

"No?! What did he do?" she asked breathlessly. Zanah looked on silently, mouth open, eyes wide and unblinking.

"He was holding her against her car when I got there."

"What?!" cried Zanah, agog. "Seriously? I can't believe it! He's never done anything like that before, has he? Sure he's a total wanker, but I thought he was essentially harmless!"

"So did I. But something got him fired up tonight," said Damien, looking at the floor. Just then his phone buzzed and he pulled it from his pocket, looking at the illuminated screen. "She's home safe," he reported.

"Good!" said Olivia with a sigh. Then she looked at him again, hungry for details. "So what did you do when you saw what was happening?"

"What do you think I did? I sent him packing."

"Did you hit him?"

Damien looked up at the sky, wanting escape from the inquisition.

"Come on! Did you hit him?" harried Olivia.

"I pushed him over!" he shot at her, exasperated.

"Paul said he heard you shout," added Zanah.

"I just got him to back off. He looked mad. I thought he was going to come at me," said Damien, stepping backwards, ready to turn and leave.

"Hang on. How did you come to be there anyway?" queried Olivia, looking across the yard to the dark corner where she knew Anna's Land Rover had been parked. "I mean, thank goodness, but how come you were out there?"

He shrugged and started walking to his car. "I went to check on Barney and luckily I just happened to walk back at the right moment," he said over his shoulder.

Olivia, realising she wouldn't get anything else out of him, watched him leave.

"How very convenient," she said under her breath.

That night Anna tossed and turned in the kind of half sleep of illness, and her dreams flashed vividly at her, veering sickeningly between the horrible realities of the evening and charged, frightening nightmares. She was running but barely moving, gasping for air, then she was holding tight to someone in the dark. It was Damien, his eyes were on hers and his finger came to her lips, willing her silent. In the next moment she was paralyzed against the cold metal of her car, James pressed against her smiling grotesquely, his hand round her throat. She was losing consciousness and felt herself fall, crashing to the ground, the stone cold and hard to the side of her head. She screamed, her eyes flying open upon the face of Andrew Japson, horribly inert, his body lifeless and grey…

Gasping, she sat up in bed, reaching for her glass of water and willing an end to the horror.

The next day was Sunday and Anna woke early, groggy from her lack of sleep. Her immediate urge was to go to Rosemount and see if Damien was there, but instead she walked to the church and joined the congregation just as the vicar began his sermon. She sat in a deadened trance, hardly present, with images of the night before whirling through her mind.

One word penetrated, jolting her from her daze: 'forgive'. The vicar had chosen that morning to discuss forgiveness. Inwardly, Anna grunted derisively. What a topic. Some things wouldn't be forgiven, at least not quickly, in fact not ever. Nevertheless it struck her as another freakish coincidence in subject matter, remembering the relevance of the sermon in New York and the conveniently placed bookmark in the hotel Bible. They were just stacking up, challenging her. Was it just her searching for meaning? Probably the message was relevant to everyone…but surely not with the same excruciating timing?

The vicar continued eloquently, speaking of the peace brought about through setting oneself free of grudges and hatred. Anna remembered Mateus talking of the importance of letting go of anger, too. But her experience of the previous night figured far too large in her mind to even consider forgiveness.

The vicar's eyes seemed to rest right on her as he concluded; "I want to quote Martin Luther King if I may. He said: 'Darkness cannot drive out darkness; only light can do that. Hate cannot drive out hate; only love can do that.'"

He paused, letting the resonance of the words settle on the congregation. Then he urged, "Now let's pray and even if you're not feeling ready to forgive someone, just allow them to pass through your mind as you think of forgiveness."

Anna was torn between contempt at the suggestion and recognition of the wisdom of it. She knew her obsessive nature would have her endlessly wandering back and forth over the horror of the night before. She was already beginning to feel the burden of all-consuming anger. Maybe a complete, enforced change of thinking was the only way to be free of the dark negativity. So she grudgingly acquiesced, bowed her head and allowed James to pass through her thoughts as she meditated on forgiveness.

Walking back along the pathway to her cottage once the service was over, she felt angry. What was the point of being forgiving? James would never change and he deserved no forgiveness. She should have him charged. She felt foolish for thinking otherwise. Then she thought of Damien, her guardian angel, and how he had appeared from nowhere in her defence. She shuddered at the thought of being there alone without help, and what James might have done. Thank God for Damien.

As she was hunting for her door key, she suddenly remembered she was supposed to be going to visit Francesca that day, and pulled a face. She didn't feel like seeing anyone at all, apart from Damien, but she wasn't going to cancel on her friend at the last moment. She opened the door and hurried upstairs to change.

Her phone chimed the arrival of a text from Olivia, asking if she was okay.

Anna was worried. Why was she asking? It wasn't like Damien to spread news around, so something must have happened.

She would have to avoid Rosemount for the day. If Olivia knew what James had done, she would be ambushed the moment she arrived and forced to relive the entire horrible experience again and again. She definitely wasn't ready for that. She would get on the next train to London and stay over at Francesca's. But what had happened after she left?

Quelling her own curiosity, she texted back quickly in the affirmative, and then dug out her overnight bag and began stuffing in work clothes.

Sitting on the train Anna forced her thoughts away from James.

Pushed to the back of her mind by the attack was the drama surrounding Andrew, which had intensified last night. Again, his behaviour was mysterious and unexplained. He seemed to want to say something but checked himself, and reverted to his self-assured air, but it wasn't real. She sighed; she couldn't guess what was happening there, and it didn't feel safe to ask anyone. There seemed to be so many things which should not be spoken of – and that included her vengeful feelings towards James.

And then there was Damien, who definitely could not be spoken of. Her ardour towards him was now almost overpowering. She had to keep a lid on her feelings; there was nowhere for them to go. So, what with him, and Andrew, and now James, she had to hold everything in, telling no one, and it was exhausting.

That made her think of Mateus, and how he had urged her to not be alone. She realised, casting her mind back over her past, that she was often alone. She rarely shared her feelings because in her experience other people were either not trustworthy or not interested; it had proven safer to err on the side of self-reliance, so secrecy had become a natural default position. People were free with impulsive advice, but they had their own agendas; moreover, they didn't have to cope with the consequences of acting upon it. Coming from a perspective which was not her own, such advice tended to be misguided – all too often, it was toxic.

Yes, she had to avoid everyone at Rosemount for now.

GOOD AND EVIL

It was Wednesday before Anna spoke to anyone at Rosemount. Self-imposed solitary confinement had enabled her to dodge anyone who might bombard her with questions or sympathy, and as her own internal raging subsided, a level of normality returned. The emotional bruising of Saturday night had receded to a manageable yet uncomfortable bundle of thoughts which she grudgingly accepted for the time being.

She had been exercising Tom in the arena for three quarters of an hour, keen to keep his fitness up, when she realised David was watching her, leaning relaxed against the entrance gate.

"He moves well," commented David pleasantly, his voice sonorous and attractive.

"Yes, he's a good lad," agreed Anna, dismounting and running up her stirrups.

David strolled over and ran his palm gently over Tom's nose. "Yes, he's a good personality. You can see it in his face," he remarked.

Anna smiled. It was true; Tom's face shone with his very essence – certainly to her. However, it was unusual for another person, particularly a reputedly strict male riding instructor, to register it. She liked his respect and gentleness with Tom and was surprised at his amiability, having built him up in her mind as a callous scoundrel. She had expected a colder, harder character.

"Did I see you hunt him at the weekend?" he asked.

"Yes. It was our first one and he did really well."

"I thought it was him I saw. He was certainly jumping exuberantly," grinned David, rubbing Tom's ears. "He's got good bone. Know anything about his bloodline?"

"Yes, his sire is Supreme Leader," answered Anna, thinking fondly of the Weatherbys passport Tom had come to her with, testament to his purebred racing status and lofty ancestry.

"Really?" he said, obviously impressed. "A lot of good jumpers came from him. Perhaps you should come to one of the clinics after Christmas. I'm doing a cross-country class which might help you calm his leap a little. He'll be a better hunter for it."

"I might do that," said Anna.

With the drama of Saturday evening, the hunt had taken a back seat in her thoughts. She had enjoyed the day immensely. It seemed to bring a whole new purpose to riding, and had lit her with the impulse to improve her skills. Tom was too fantastic to rest on his laurels and plod along hacking for the rest of his life.

"You're here a bit late, aren't you?" she asked. "Have you got a late lesson?"

"No, I've finished. I just saw the lights on and came to turn them off. I didn't realise you were in here."

"Well, I'm done now," said Anna, warming to his down-to-earth manner, and taking him in. She could see why so many of his female clients liked him. His attitude and his good looks, plus the riding garb which sat so well on him; he had a certain something. But why Chantelle? Or maybe there were many more, and Chantelle was just one of them.

"I'll talk to you about the clinic nearer the time," she said.

"Do that," he smiled.

Anna walked Tom out, wondering how it was that so many men projected an attractive, even admirable, image, but were entirely different underneath. It was like biting into an apple, green, firm and apparently perfect, only to find the core rotten and crawling with insects. David, she thought as he tied Tom outside his stable, was an excellent example. Then there was Dom – whatever had happened there. And Andrew; who on earth could fathom what he was into? And of course there were the suggestions she had heard about Damien; that he was a careless womaniser, insensate and disregarding of others.

"There you are! I've been looking for you!" said Olivia, breaking into Anna's thoughts abruptly.

"Here I am," Anna said, looking up from picking out one of Tom's hooves under the lights of the stable row.

"I was worried about you," said Olivia. "I haven't seen since you disappeared on Saturday night."

"I guess our paths just didn't cross," said Anna casually, knowing what was coming. "I've been here."

"How are you?" asked Olivia in a confidential tone, stepping close to Anna as she put Tom's hoof down and straightened up.

"Fine. I'm fine."

"Damien said James had you up against the car!" she whispered, despite there being no one else in sight. Anna looked at the ground.

"Yeah, well, thankfully it was okay… and I managed to knee him in the bollocks for it," she added, trying to lighten the conversation, not wanting the horrible images to start up again.

"You did? Well done. I've wanted to do that for a long time," Olivia remarked with a small smile. Then her face turned grave. "It sounded serious though, Anna. He was deranged. I never thought he'd do anything like that. And it's lucky Damien was there."

Anna agreed silently, remembering his shielding force and being in his arms.

"I thought he was going to kill him when they were in the woods!" Olivia continued.

"What? What happened?" asked Anna, suddenly alarmed. Having avoided everyone for a few days, wrapped up in her own turmoil, she had forgotten her worries about the aftermath. If Damien had confronted James, Olivia would be doubly suspicious that she and Damien had something going on.

Olivia told Anna about the scene in the woods and how Damien had ploughed in to bring James back out. Anna's eyes widened.

"Yes!" continued Olivia, feeding off Anna's expression of horror. "I couldn't actually see but I seriously thought he was going to beat the shit out of James! He said, er what did he say...?"

She broke off, trying to formulate her words.

"Yeah, James was yelling and Damien shouted, 'You're lucky I didn't take you down!'" she relayed, attempting to imitate Damien's masculine tones. "He came off pretty sexy now I come to think of it, taking command like that!" She gave a titillated grin but then turned penetrating eyes on Anna again. "Seriously though, you're okay? He didn't, well, touch you, did he?"

Anna grimaced. "No more than holding me against the car," she said swallowing, remembering James's body pressed grimly against hers and her rising panic.

"But what was Damien doing there?" mused Olivia, still looking at Anna.

"He just came out of nowhere. I have no idea where he came from, but I'm glad he did," said Anna, diverting her eyes and putting her hoof pick back in her grooming kit. Olivia moved round in front of her again.

"You were bloody lucky, Anna. You were parked right in the darkest, furthest corner, I remember. I don't know how he saw you."

Anna shifted. She had no answer. She hadn't thought much about that aspect.

"It just seems he's there for you rather frequently and conveniently," continued Olivia, probingly.

"What?!" exclaimed Anna, not liking where Olivia was going with the conversation. "When else has this happened? What are you getting at? I'm just glad someone was there," she insisted defensively. "Why all the analysis?"

"Sorry! Don't get stroppy. It's just interesting. He's singled you out and seems unusually attentive. He's not like that. He's a real law unto himself; he just turns up and does his own thing, only sociable when it suits him, never tells anyone anything. I had to bully what happened out of him - he was going to leave without a word! We had to force him to tell us why he had dragged James out of the woods."

Despite her disquiet at Olivia's relentless probing, Anna felt a warm glow. She was special to Damien after all. Their fleeting conversations and moments of electrifying physical connection must have meant something to him too. And then on Saturday night he'd obviously gone to find James, but then had to stand up to Olivia's characteristically brutal interrogation. She felt the wall of evidence she had built up against Damien, proving that he cared nothing for her, crumbling away.

"Still with me, Anna?" Olivia was asking, waving her hand.

"I...er, yes. I don't know what to say," she stuttered. "He's just a quiet type I guess?"

"Yeah! That makes you peas in a pod!" snorted Olivia. She sighed and looked at Anna. "C'mon, let's get a glass of wine. I want to talk to you about the hunt on Saturday."

For all of that week and the next Anna saw nothing of Damien. She guessed he was hunting midweek but he wasn't there at the weekend or on any evening that she was at the yard. She ached to see him again. Why was he so elusive?

Determined to stop thinking about him, she threw herself into her work. The extensive security clearance procedure for their assignment had taken longer than expected, but as soon as it came through they hit the project in force, working long days to keep to schedule. The lonely evenings were more of a problem, lending themselves as they did to introspection and fevered imaginings, but thankfully the Christmas season brought the usual round of obligatory functions. Sipping inferior Malbec while joining in the corporate camaraderie, Anna could at least temporarily keep her thoughts at bay.

One genuine distraction was the novelty of walking into the wonderfully distinctive and enigmatic SIS building at Vauxhall Cross. Its blockwork and dark green glass stepped up in uniform symmetry as it sat solidly on the banks of the Thames, its shape reminiscent of a Mayan temple. It had always drawn Anna's eye in the past, veiled as it was in intrigue, but she never thought she would have reason to go inside. Now she did, and didn't feel she could ever tire of the feeling of being one of the elite. Being admitted to the building was the stuff of spy novels, recognised as she was by retinal scan by the single-minded emotionless guardian technology, gatekeeper to the inner sanctum.

"Are you hunting this Saturday, Anna? Olivia now says she has to work, and I need a buddy!" said Zanah on Thursday evening, as they worked side by side grooming their horses.

Anna assented as she brushed Tom down. She had been planning to anyhow.

"Can't miss the last hunt before Christmas," said David as he walked by, obviously overhearing them. "Would you like to ride with me? I'll help you with his jump, Anna."

"That would be great," she agreed, surprised.

"See you Saturday then," he said as he walked off.

Zanah stepped close to Anna. "No way! When did you two get talking?" she asked in a low voice.

"The other evening when I was using the arena."

"He seems so nice! It's hard to imagine him mercilessly banging Chantelle on her parents' dining table!" laughed Zanah.

Anna wrinkled her nose in distaste and nodded in agreement, watching him disappear round the corner. Just as he was out of sight they heard his voice again, this time directed at an unseen person.

"Hi there, James. Haven't seen you in a while. How are you?"

Anna froze and looked at Zanah.

"James? The James we don't want to see?" hissed Zanah. "You can go if you like and I can stay with Tom."

"No," said Anna firmly and quietly. "I'm not running from him. He's the one who should be ashamed."

As she spoke, James rounded the corner and looked straight at her. Her stomach felt cold and she busied herself with throwing Tom's blanket over his back. James paused for a moment but then approached them, looking apprehensive.

"Anna?" he said quietly as he drew near.

Anna could hardly believe he was actually addressing her and hesitantly turned towards him, conflicting emotions warring within her. He was out of riding gear, wearing jeans and a blazer, and his pale eyes met hers beseechingly. His bearing had changed and he glanced self-consciously at Zanah.

"I wanted to see you to er... I needed to talk to you." He looked down again for a moment before resuming. "I wanted to apologize. I have felt so bad about the other night. I'm really sorry." He stopped and sighed.

Anna had no idea what to say. He had terrified her in a brutal way and she had gone through nightmares, rage and depression. In her mind, she had killed him with her bare hands over and over again for what he had tried to do. But now that he stood there in front of her, so totally different from his usual objectionable self, she saw frailty. He looked harrowed and weakened. But she wasn't going to help him; his offence was too grievous for that. She stepped towards him but remained silent.

"I don't really know what happened. I had way too much to drink and I don't know what I was thinking," he went on, looking up into her eyes and then back at the ground. "I've never done anything like that before. I wouldn't really have done anything..."

"It felt like you were going to," said Anna quietly. Her emotions were churning. She wanted to turn away, she felt like crying, but she also wanted to grab him by the throat and tell him he should be locked up.

"I'm so sorry," he said again, and sighed. "I'm a total arsehole. I feel terrible about it. I really don't know what else to say. I hate myself, I'm an arsehole," he repeated desolately.

Anna looked at him for a long moment. Why wasn't she yelling at him? But she could feel her anger dissipating. He looked like he had been through purgatory, just as she had, but perhaps worse. His eyes were red-rimmed and tired and he appeared deflated and beaten.

"Apology accepted," she heard herself say.

There was no point in marching through reproach and reprimand. It looked and sounded like he'd done that himself, and she had heard enough of her own inner raving on the subject. She couldn't tell him it was alright; his behaviour had been appalling, and could have culminated in outright rape. But he had made the giant step of coming to face her and apologise, when it would have been easier to simply hide out and avoid her and everyone else until time smudged memories. He had surprised her.

It seemed like he was out of words but it also felt like they weren't done. Anna could feel a strange pounding sensation in her stomach, something imploring her to say something more.

He looked at her with a small smile of apology and turned to leave.

"Why aren't you this person all the time?" she burst out, the insistent force finding expression in words. He turned and looked at her questioningly.

She took another step towards him, with flaming eyes. "This person standing in front of me right now is not a hateful arsehole."

He exhaled and looked at the ground.

"But the James I have met on all other occasions, his behaviour and language *is* hateful," she continued, feeling energy pounding from her.

He seemed surprised and looked straight at her for a long moment. He spread his hands as if searching for the answer at the back of his brain.

"Male bravado, Anna. It's the way I am. Blokes, hunting blokes...you know." He laughed shortly, nervously. "We swear, we behave badly, we piss from the backs of our horses..." Anna drew her eyebrows together in momentary disapproval. "Sorry." He pressed his lips together regretfully and then turned and left.

Anna walked slowly back to Tom, not knowing quite what had possessed her to lecture him. It felt like a diatribe, though she'd actually only said a few words.

She wondered at the remarkable light and dark she was seeing in people; first David with his surprising affability, and now James. She hadn't even considered the possibility of him being affected by what he had done, and certainly not his being driven to apologise to her. Who knew he had a flip side to objectionable?

It was easy to demonise people. It was more comfortable to put them firmly in the bracket of those to be hated and despised, but life was too complicated and people, for all their horrible behaviour and tragic and abhorrent mistakes, were never all bad. She was glad she had connected with James rather than passively accepting his apology. Somehow she felt that connection would help them both. Just like she'd heard in church that Sunday when she had internally reviled him; light can't come from dark, good things couldn't come from bad. Forgiveness healed, apparently. He had come to her to apologise and she had reached back. They would never be friends, but maybe they could each start to emerge from their polar positions of turmoil and move on.

It was ten o'clock on Friday morning when Anna's phone lit up with a text message from Mateus. He had said he would be back for Christmas, but with all that had been on her mind she had given it no thought. He had landed that morning and was heading north to his family, and suggested they meet for lunch as he passed through London.

It seemed ages since they had met in New York and Anna was delighted at the thought of seeing him again. He would be a blast of welcome fresh air.

It was a very long lunch and they talked constantly. He looked slightly different and she couldn't settle on what it was.

"Have you been working out or something?" she asked him perplexedly.

"As a matter of fact I have! Hey, it's made a difference at last!" he exclaimed joyfully.

Anna laughed and looked at him with questioning eyes.

"Well, I saw myself on film a few months ago, giving a sermon, and I looked a bit like I had a coat hanger in my shirt. You know, this frame is a bit skeletal," he explained, patting his shoulders.

"Well you're on the way to becoming buff!" she said, grinning.

"What about you?" he asked with a smile.

"What about me?" she countered.

He was silent for a moment.

"You've been going to church?" he asked eventually.

"Yes. How did you guess that?"

"Something about you. You've changed," returned Mateus, looking over the rim of his glass with warm eyes.

"Don't get excited. I'm not sold on it yet," she said.

He smiled again, more broadly this time.

"What?" she said, self-conscious and flapping at him with her napkin.

"Sorry. I'm not spying on you!" said Mateus affectionately. "You seem different."

She shifted in her seat and glanced out the window. She was different to who she had been in New York. A lot had happened. Plus, her thoughts were shifting and she was more receptive to her internal feelings, and the strange synchronicities which occurred in life. But it all still seemed like fanciful wonderings of her overactive mind searching for meaning. Faith made everything so easy but there was the ever-present issue of it defying what seemed real and explainable.

"I don't know. Yes, but everyone changes all the time, don't they?" she said, uncomfortably, taking refuge in evasion. "What? You're making me self-conscious!"

"I'm just loving watching God's pursuit of you!" he said with fervour, his eyes gleaming.

Mateus had to catch the three o'clock train and Anna had to get back to work, so they reluctantly had to part, wanting to chat the whole afternoon.

"I'll see you before I leave again," promised Mateus. Then he appeared to think for a moment, and his expression grew more serious than Anna was used to seeing it. Finally he asked, "One thing; do you come across an Andrew Japson, anywhere?"

"Yes. He's around at Rosemount," said Anna, wondering what on earth Andrew was to Mateus. "He's apparently a sort of business partner to the owner there. Why do you ask?"

Mateus didn't respond immediately, and appeared to be absorbing her words.

"In fact, I saw him late one night at the church a while ago. It was very strange," added Anna, wondering if Mateus might know the connection.

Mateus frowned. "That's worrying…"

Recovering himself, he wrapped her in a hug which was brawnier hug than usual, given his new muscular physique. "We'll meet up before I leave again." Then, brightening still further, he added, "Hey, we should go to church together! Then we'll talk."

Anna's curiosity had her regretting his necessity to leave. She watched him walk away, waving over his shoulder. What was it with Andrew Japson? His effect on Mateus bothered her; Mateus was not normally grave.

She walked back to the office thoughtfully, wanting to know about his connection with Andrew. How could they know each another? He looked sombre when she mentioned the night at the church; it worried her. Of all the people she associated with, she found herself uniquely fond of Mateus. She grinned despairingly at herself; he'd be quite a catch if he weren't so impossibly religious and she weren't so hooked on Damien.

THE END OF PRETENCE

The sky was overcast and threatening on Saturday, and the hunt was in full swing. Anna, mounted on Tom, was cantering her approach to a jump tucked into a hedgerow.

"Nice easy tiger trap. Breathe deep and sit deep," said David, in an easy canter alongside her. "Keep your leg on and contact just like that. Don't get up until the last minute."

Anna and Tom paced beautifully into the jump and landed decorously the other side.

"Now sit deep, strong contact and drive," instructed David, landing behind and then advancing to pace with her again. Anna smiled at him, briefly patting Tom's neck, delighted with the feeling of control and new serenity they had achieved. It was very different from their customary charge, leap, and frantic gallop the other side, which set her nerves jangling. "Feels better, yes?" said David triumphantly.

"Much!" said Anna, as Tom continued in his steady stride.

"He's a lot of horse, and when you lose your position and driving seat, you lose that contact you need to keep him in order. He's going well. Distinctly better."

He looked authoritative and sensible as he talked, immaculate and capable astride his black hunter. She felt even better about David now he had transformed her ride, and really didn't recognise him as the character who had ravaged Chantelle in the stables. Could they have been wrong? Was it somebody else with her? The juxtaposition of the two personas didn't compute. They simply didn't belong together in the one shell.

As they reached the end of the day the route took the hunt down a familiar path.

"Uh oh! We're on course for Lofter's. That's the scary giant hedge on the hilltop!" Zanah exclaimed.

"You don't have to take it, and *you* shouldn't. He's too tired," said David, pointing at Zanah's horse.

"What? No, he can do it!" protested Zanah.

"Well, you'd better use a lot of leg," advised David, authoritatively.

Anna felt apprehensive about jumping Lofter's. She had jumped it the one time with Damien but was more relieved at having lived to tell the tale than excited at the thought of doing it again. "Are you taking him over, Anna?" David asked her.

"Yes," she said determinedly, though not sure why she was doing it.

"Ride it the same, just let him stretch," he said calmly, sticking next to her.

The hedge had been cut since the last time she jumped it and was lower and boxier but still resembled a wall as she zeroed in. Tom pulled hard against her contact, his ears pricked and tail high, exploding powerfully from the ground and clearing it beautifully. Anna shouted in triumph as she cantered from the landing and looked behind her, impressed at the size of the obstacle and her own bravery. David smiled across at her and gave her a thumbs up. Then sensing drama behind, Anna checked for Zanah, only to see Charlie off-balance and tearing through the top of the hedge, stumbling heavily as he landed. Zanah flew rag-doll-like over his shoulder, and tumbled on the muddy ground. Anna and David quickly circled back.

"Are you okay?" Anna shouted to Zanah, relieved to see her get up.

"You were lucky," remarked David, having retrieved Charlie, as he handed Zanah the reins.

"Yeah, yeah. Perhaps he was too tired," she snapped as she stretched to reach the stirrup to remount. "Overbearing bastard!" she commented to Anna under her breath as she scrambled onto Charlie's back once again.

Anna supressed a grin; David had been right but he was certainly abrasively paternal.

The rain was falling as they arrived back at Rosemount, and Zanah dismounted and looked over her shoulder down at the back of her breeches. They were brown and green from the impact she had taken on the wet ground.

"Ha! You came off at last, did you? It was only a matter of time!" laughed Olivia, rounding the corner. She wore a sweater and jeans with heeled boots which accentuated her height. She stood with her hands on her hips, surveying the damage on Zanah.

"Yes! Over Lofter's. I was just glad he didn't step on me," said Zanah, looking at Charlie.

"Lofter's? Bloody hell! Well, that's the place to do it if you're going to come off properly," said Olivia. "I'd have liked to have seen that."

"Where have you been? Not like you to miss a hunt," said Anna.

"Ugh, work. Overran a copy deadline. Nightmare, but has to be done sometimes. You two coming to the Royal Oak later?"

"That's where everyone's going?" asked Zanah. "That's a bit far out."

"Yes, someone's cousin is in the band playing there tonight so everyone's going. A lot of the hunt will be there. We're carpooling as no-one seems to know how to get there."

Anna wondered if Damien was going out that evening. She had been excited when she had seen him briefly that morning, through the crowd at the meet. A full-house venue like the pub usually proved easier for her to talk to him, unnoticed by others.

"It's a big pub. I'm sure you can avoid James if he's there," said Zanah, looking at Anna with concern.

Anna swiftly redirected her thoughts, responding with bravado as she removed Tom's saddle, "Don't worry. I've downgraded from DEFCON 1. We're now at stand-off."

James's apology and her own processing time had moved her on to a state of relative peace, and the day of hunting had given her a new energy.

"Hi."

Damien's voice came as a surprise to Anna as she walked back from Tom's field, her eyes on the grass in front of her. Her heart gave a little leap and she looked up quickly and smiled at him.

"Hi! I've missed you," she said, feeling the truth of it. She wanted to throw her arms round him.

He smiled back and his arm touched hers as they walked.

"How are you?" he asked, looking at her, and she knew he was asking if she had recovered from her ordeal.

"I'm okay. Thank you, by the way. I've realised how lucky I was that you were there," she added, looking back at him. "Why haven't I seen you?"

He sighed and looked down. "You know; work, busy." Then he looked at her again and added confidentially, "I've been lying low a bit too."

"Interrogations? Olivia grillings?" asked Anna, mimicking his staccato speech pattern.

"You know it." He was silent for a moment, seeming to be deep in thought. "I expect you heard what happened afterwards," he said eventually. "Paul took him home and I hear he's been very quiet. No-one's seen him much. He was hunting today for the first time since."

"Did you talk to him?" she asked curiously.

"No. He avoided me," he said shortly.

"He came to see me this week," said Anna, watching his expression as he turned widening eyes to her. "He seemed a completely different person. He apologised profusely."

"So he bloody well should. I'm surprised, though. That's not like him at all. He usually blunders on regardless after he's offended or damaged anyone."

Anna felt a burst of happiness to be around Damien and talking to him again. She realised she had been sombre for a long while, and reached out and brushed his hand with hers.

"Are you going to the Royal Oak this evening?"

"If you're going," he said with a confidential smile.

"I want to talk more. We'll just have to avoid Olivia," she said, whispering the last sentence.

"Yep, her and everyone else who's gossiping."

It felt like they were actually having some kind of affair, the way they were talking. Anna frowned, insisting to herself they were not. He was (to all appearances) her friend, and a friend who had stepped in to save her from a dire situation just a couple of weeks ago.

"You okay?" he asked, seeing her frown.

She sighed and gave voice to her thoughts. "Yes, it just seems crazy we can't talk without comment from others. It's not like we're Chantelle and David." He simply smiled.

"Life. See you later."

The pub was packed and pounding, with hordes of bodies apparent through the windows as they drove up. Not knowing the way to the Royal Oak, Anna had hitched a ride with Lucias, his friend Jack, Zanah and Olivia. Rain flew in the strengthening wind and the pub sign creaked on its mountings, the atmosphere swelling ominously with the approaching storm. Anna looked at the waving trees surrounding the old building. The huge rushing clouds cast moody shadows as they passed over the face of the moon.

"You've got to drink and like it this evening, Anna!" said Zanah, referring to Anna's recent teetotalism. "You must celebrate your first hunt surviving Lofter's!"

Anna decided not to remind anyone she had jumped it before, for fear of instigating talk about Damien, and said instead with a cheeky grin, "What are you celebrating, then? Your solo flight of Lofter's?"

Olivia shouted with laughter and clapped Zanah on the back.

"Ya! Let's see the bruises!" added Lucias incorrigibly, holding the door open. Zanah punched him on the arm playfully as they passed through. "What? That's what you get for larking!" he protested theatrically as he followed her in. "David told you your horse was tired!"

Anna smirked, guessing Zanah had been bad-mouthing David, and Lucias had turned it on her as a beating stick.

It took them a long time to reach the bar, filtering their way through the elbow-to-elbow crowds. It was a large pub and a popular drinking hole at the best of times, and now with the hunt swelling the ranks, it was beyond capacity. The whole effect was hot, heaving and loud. Leaning close to the person next to you was the only way to be heard over the clamour of the band and the cacophony of surrounding voices.

The crowd at the bar was three-deep and the stressed bar staff ran from person to person. Anna immediately spotted Damien, talking to Simeon, who she had met at her first hunt, as well as a couple of others.

"Where have you been? I haven't seen you for ages," Olivia asked Damien, interrupting him.

"Working," he answered shortly.

"Did you hear our Zanah fell over Lofter's today?" Olivia asked, gesturing at Zanah.

"Oi! You're not supposed to broadcast it continually!" protested Zanah, nudging at Lucias who was bending his head to inspect where she had landed.

"Obviously you're still walking," Damien said, looking amused.

"Yeah. But I could have done without David patronising me about it," she complained.

"David? He was with you?" asked Olivia.

"Yeah, though I might as well have not been there! He spent his time coaching Anna and eying her shapely butt the whole way!"

Anna was appalled and widened her eyes at Zanah. "What? You're mad. No he wasn't!" she protested. She felt Damien's eyes on her.

"He so was! Maybe you're his next target! What is it with you, Anna?" laughed Zanah exasperatedly.

"What do you mean by that?" Anna asked with a frown.

"You poor baby, you totally fail to see it, don't you?" crooned Zanah, cocking her head in mock sympathy.

"She so doesn't see it. I told her ages ago," agreed Olivia.

"I'm going to have to start drinking to survive tonight," complained Anna. Damien started to move off, but bent to Anna's ear as he passed.

"You jump Lofter's again?"

"Yes! It didn't seem quite so big this time around."

"No, you did it off-season when it was overgrown. It's about two feet shorter right now," he said. Her face must have expressed pride because he nodded, adding, "Yes, you jumped it when it was a real man's feat!" Then he was gone into the crowd.

"Oi! What did he say?" demanded Olivia.

"He just asked if I jumped Lofter's," Anna responded with practised nonchalance.

She felt flat after his departure, and didn't talk to him again over the course of the evening. But she caught his eye from time to time, which seemed to be on her with increasing frequency.

Later, as she was at the bar chatting to a girl called Bethany, one of the only other people who seemed as sober as she was, Lucias appeared in front of her and grabbed her arm.

"Hey Anna, I've got lucky. I'm going!" he said quickly.

"Er, okay," she said. "I guess we'll catch a ride with someone else."

"Good, see ya!" he said and dashed off. Thinking she had better go and find the others, Anna moved through the thinning crowd until she spotted Lucias's friend Jack, who had obviously been marooned there too.

"Hey Jack! I can't see anyone else. Have you got a ride home?" she asked.

"Oh, there you are. Olivia was looking for you; she went about twenty minutes ago with Jess. I'm going back with Simeon; he lives near me. Zanah and Lucias went off together."

"Zanah and Lucias?" exclaimed Anna.

"Yes, I've seen that coming since the hunt do," chuckled Jack. "Looks like you've been abandoned!"

"Great!" she said indignantly, annoyed at being left behind and even more irritated at not having taken responsibility and driven herself.

"I'm sure you'll find someone else to grab a ride home with," said Jack, in an uncertain tone. Anna stomped to the door, pulling out her phone to text Olivia.

Outside the wind was howling, and the storm had arrived in full force. Rain swept tempestuously in great waves, riding with the gusting wind. Anna quickly texted Olivia to see if she knew who else was left at the pub besides her, and then stood under the door's overhang for a moment taking in the violence of the storm. The moon appeared restlessly behind clouds. The huge ancient oaks surrounding the hunched old pub creaked and roared as their branches swayed and whipped in the ferocious gale.

Her phone illuminated with a response from Olivia. "Coming back," it read.

At least she had a ride home.

Unsure of how long she had to wait and unwilling to go back inside, Anna turned up the collar on her insubstantial jacket and looked doubtfully at the flickering light on the side of the pub. Despite the inhospitable conditions, she was done with the evening and preferred to be alone outside.

Wondering if there would be more shelter under the trees, she bent her head and hurried to the base of the enormous trunks hemming the pub's yard. She detected a movement and turned to see a side door to the bar open and the figure of a man step out. He appeared to see her and began to move in her direction, hunching against the squally rain. Anna stepped into the deep blackness under the trees, her back against the base of one of the thicker trunks. She could feel infinitesimal motion in its bark, almost intangibly reflecting the raging branches thrashing high above.

The shining wet leaves flapped in the blustery sheets of rain, intermittently obscuring her view. The figure continued in her direction and she felt the unmistakable alert of adrenalin, the horror of being attacked bounding again to the front of her mind. Who was it? Just as she was about to run for the pub again, a familiar voice penetrated through the wind.

"What kind of a jacket is that for a night like this?"

Her fear was instantly dismantled, replaced with a rush of feeling. It was Damien.

He ducked under a low flailing branch and stood before her. She was there alone in the dark on the wildest of nights with the very person she shouldn't be with, but who she wanted to be near more than anything. She rallied herself, put her hands in her pockets and turned her face deliberately towards him, her hair flying in the wind.

"I thought I would be running from car to pub and back to car, not standing out here in a howling gale! I didn't know you were left behind too."

"I saw you in there and I wasn't going to leave you alone. Plus I had to find some way of talking to you," he said seriously.

"You could have talked to me," she protested, feeling weary of the need to avoid being seen associating with him. He laughed shortly and shook his head.

"No I couldn't. The rumours have been flying," he said, stepping closer to her.

Anna felt a tingling sensation run through her and was glad of the dark, masking her expression as she bit her lip. It seemed the first time either of them had ever come close to outwardly acknowledging what was going on between them.

"That's the trouble with being indifferent to people," he went on. "The moment you get interested, it's a bit too damned obvious."

She dared to lift her eyes to meet his dark gaze directly, and they stood silently staring at each other. She could feel heat rising in her face and her heart accelerate. She had nothing to say. She knew she shouldn't but she wanted him, and here they were alone at last. He moved closer still, until they were almost touching. His bulky shooting jacket was open and she could feel the heat he exuded and smell the scent of him. She looked down, then up again into his eyes which held a different look now; a keen and purposeful desire that she had not seen before. She parted her lips to speak but the words didn't come. She heard him breathe out audibly and then his mouth was on hers, hot and impulsive. He drew her against him and she felt his hand, strong and very sure, drag slowly up her arm to her shoulder.

His fingers slid up her neck, his touch sending a charged thrill rushing through her. She kissed him back urgently and put her hands on his body for the first time, feeling him respond instantly.

"You drive me crazy. You know I want you," he whispered in her ear. Anna caught her breath, her heart pounding.

"I want you too," she breathed back recklessly. He stifled a groan and pushed her back a step until she felt the bark of the giant oak trunk at her back, then he held her and kissed her forcefully. Her blood hammered in her veins. The roughness of the tree behind her and the feverish heat of him pressed against her had her head spinning. She could feel his heart thundering through them both as they melded together almost out of control. Damien's voice came intense against her ear:

"My god, you feel good. I want you so much."

She gasped as she felt his mouth on her neck, wanting him to take her right there. All other reality faded into nothingness, and they blazed together in the ferocity of their own storm.

The sound of a car permeated their senses gradually, and the howling of the wind became again apparent. They both knew instinctively it had to be their ride home. Damien exhaled harshly. Anna clung to him, her head against his chest, her breath coming hard. They looked into each other's eyes and came together again hungrily. Then, silently cursing the headlights which were beaming brighter and brighter as they rounded the bend, they wrenched themselves apart.

Olivia's white Range Rover pulled up at the main door to the pub. Hidden in the dark, Damien swore. Anna looked up at him and he bent his face to hers and their lips brushed. A shiver reverberated through her. He sighed, gazing at her intensely, and then gestured with his head wordlessly towards their taxi. The headlights of the Range Rover illuminated them as they walked from the tree line. Anna was in a fuzzy half-reality. The ground beneath her didn't feel fully there, a surreal numb thud through her feet as she plodded automatically next to Damien.

Olivia slid her window down and shouted over the gale.

"It's me! What are you doing out there? Get in!"

Damien climbed in the front and Anna gratefully took the back, where she might sit quietly and collect herself. The sensation of Damien's touch was still firing through her, the scent of him on her and the image of his face leaping at her afresh, his eyes on fire as he held her against the tree. His voice echoed through her: 'You drive me crazy. You know I want you'. She bit her lip, the raw want for him rolling through her, sending her internal temperature dizzyingly high; how she wanted his solid body pressed into hers once again. They had supressed themselves so long that the first real contact had been explosive. She clenched her fists on her knees, trying to slow her heart and return herself to the reality of sitting in Olivia's back seat.

"What a night!" Olivia was exclaiming. "How long were you there? Bloody Lucias! Last time I rely on him! He went off with Zanah! I can't believe it."

Anna was silent. Obviously Damien was having trouble with his composure too because he didn't answer either.

"You alright? Been struck dumb by a lightning strike?" questioned Olivia in her usual bold way.

"You don't give a guy a moment, do you?" protested Damien as he twisted in the seat, removing his soaked jacket.

"You know it, baby!" shouted Olivia roguishly, squeezing his knee.

"Weren't you drinking earlier?" he asked, looking at her. "I called you because I had your number. I didn't necessarily mean you should be the one to come back for us."

"Yes, but not enough to impair my driving," she answered confidently. "And everyone else had gone. I couldn't very well leave you abandoned out there, could I? Try getting a taxi out here – there aren't any!"

"You're probably over the limit," he commented with a hint of criticism.

"Probably, but honestly there is no one on the roads round here at this hour at the best of times, let alone on a night like this," she answered dismissively.

"Pull over. Let me drive," he ordered.

"No-one drives this baby but me!" she said, patting the steering wheel. "Quit with the puritanical stuff. I would have been home by now if I didn't have to travel all the way back out here to fetch you. How about, 'Thank you Olivia, we're so grateful, Olivia. You're an amazing friend!'?"

"I should have driven," he muttered to himself, ignoring her facetiousness.

"You weren't exactly going to get many in that Z4!" laughed Olivia.

"Maybe not, but I'd have got Anna and me home," he retorted. "Just, drive carefully," he said in a defeated tone, gesturing out the front window.

Olivia looked sideways at him, snorting sarcastically at his ingratitude.

Damien sighed and looked at his watch. He was working early in the morning and had just a few hours of sleep before he had to leave for the airport. Left alone with Anna, he would have happily forgone the sleep, but having been interrupted he felt irritated, the need for rest before going to work nagging at him.

"Oh, come on! I know you're flying tomorrow but it's not like you pilots work hard," sneered Olivia with a grin. "Where is it tomorrow? St Lucia, San Francisco?"

He didn't answer her.

"Would you mind dropping me at my place? It's on the way," interjected Anna, sensing the atmosphere nose-diving and deciding it was the time to bail on the evening rather than have an awkward goodbye at the yard with Olivia looking on.

"Sure, but isn't your car at the yard?" Olivia asked.

"Yes, but I'll run there in the morning. I need to get a run in," said Anna, resolving on an energetic start to her day. She would need to do something to get her mind off Damien. If he was working, she wouldn't see him for a few days, and she sincerely hoped he wouldn't disappear for another two-week period, leaving her in drought and suspense.

"I was wondering how you have that sinewy figure!" exclaimed Olivia. "Running; too energetic for me! Just tell me where to drop you. Anyway, did you hear what I said? Zanah and Lucias?"

"Yes, Jack told me," said Anna. The scandal was nothing to her after what had happened between her and Damien.

"You don't sound very surprised!" exclaimed Olivia, looking for more reaction.

"They were pretty into each other at the hunt do," said Damien, looking out the window. "I'm surprised *you* didn't notice."

The country roads were dark and shiny with giant puddles which exploded over the front of the Range Rover as it thundered through. Silence had descended on them all. Anna stared out of the window, unseeing, the alluring memory of the tryst under the trees with Damien pulling her back again. How long had they been pretending? That night they had cast aside the decency to which they had clung for so long. Standing in front of one another, alone in the eye of the storm, the energy between them had ignited; and it felt amazing.

When the lights of the village came into view Anna sat forward.

"Here, just by the church," said Anna.

"My god, you live in a graveyard?" laughed Olivia.

"Just on the edge of it; it's a peaceful spot." Then she grinned, remembering Olivia's rant, and added, "Thanks for the ride. You are an amazing friend."

CHRISTMAS EVE

It being a Sunday, Anna adhered to her customary routine of going to church. Sitting in meditation each week on the hard wooden pew gave her respite from life's constant pace; a moment of pause.

That morning, however, concentration eluded her as she relived the previous night over and over again. Gazing at the lights of the Christmas tree, the vicar's words an unheard soundtrack in the background, she repeatedly zoned out, revelling in the remembered thrill. Damien had wanted her. And she had wanted him right then and there, up against that tree.

She could sit still no longer. Choosing her moment, she quietly slipped out of the service and ran home to change and collect her backpack. Then she set off fast along the high street, fuelled with the raw energy of euphoria.

Sprinting down muddy lanes, hardly noticing the puddles and broken branches that she automatically leapt or swerved, she made half-hearted efforts to be sensible. Damien was married, she reminded herself, and the impulse they had given in to the night before was taking them down a bad road; she really ought to know better.

But it was no good; she didn't know better, and she was too dizzyingly happy to care. She couldn't think about the morality of it in that moment, and any consequences seemed irrelevant and far in the future. What mattered was now. Finally she knew for certain that Damien had feelings for her, and that she hadn't been reading too much into their exchanges. She smiled to herself, feeling it spread through her like a bright ray of sunshine as she bounded up the hill to Rosemount.

Tom trotted to her as she sauntered to him across the field. It was to be a well-deserved day off for him, and she scrubbed at his forelock affectionately, holding out a large apple for him to devour, and laughing as its juice squirted from the sides of his mouth. Patting him, she gazed over at Barnabas who was happily grazing. In the absence of Damien, there was always his horse to remind her of him.

She strolled round to the bar to see if anyone else was around and popped her head in the door.

"Morning, Anna!" said Penelope from the ladder she was balanced on, hanging a star on the top of the Christmas tree. Anna was surprised to see Andrew sitting on one of the barstools, watching Penelope with concern as she leaned out dangerously. Recovering from a wobble, Penelope climbed down a couple of steps before continuing, "Obviously you were not one of the night owls last night!"

"I was out, yes, but not drinking," smiled Anna. "It makes all the difference. Want some help?"

"Yes, why not?" said Penelope. "I am abominably late with the decorations this year. I can't understand where December went."

"You and me both," agreed Anna, rootling in the box for more baubles and looking at the tree with a considering eye.

"Please don't both climb the ladder," pleaded Andrew. "I can hardly deal with the stress of watching Penelope hanging off the thing."

"Well, it wouldn't kill you to come and help too," laughed Penelope. "By the way, Annetta wanted to talk to you," she added, as she hung golden pine cones on the branches.

"Yeah, I'm sure she does," he said knowingly. "She wants to talk about the money for…"

He trailed off, apparently deciding to keep his thoughts to himself. After a moment he added meditatively, "I know what she wants."

"Why is she asking about the money anyway?" asked Penelope, balancing again, and causing him to wince.

"Ugh. She's paranoid or something," he offered inconclusively, distractedly casting his eye to the window. His gaze narrowed, and he quickly got up and walked through the back doors to the deck and out of sight. Anna and Penelope looked after him, and then at each other with puzzled faces.

"Morning, Penelope," said an agitated voice from the front entrance of the bar. Penelope turned in surprise to see Annetta standing in the doorway.

"Hello. What brings you here today?" asked Penelope, with a rush of amused understanding at the alacrity of Andrew's exit.

"Have you seen David?" asked Annetta.

"No, he's not usually here on a Sunday."

Annetta slumped against the doorframe looking exasperated.

"What's wrong?" asked Penelope, climbing down from the ladder.

"I can't find him. He went out last night; he said he was going to join the rest of them at the pub for a while. I went to bed early and it seems like he never came home!"

"What?" exclaimed Penelope. "Anna, you were at the pub last night. Did you see him?"

"No," answered Anna, thinking she knew exactly where David had been. "But it was packed to the gills. People got lost in the crowd," she added, wondering why on earth she was covering for David.

"Oh, for goodness sake!" exclaimed Annetta angrily, looking across the yard. David had just pulled up in his car.

"Where the bloody hell have you been?" she shouted, rushing out and slamming the door.

Penelope and Anna exchanged looks.

"I wouldn't want to be in trouble with her," said Anna.

"No indeed," agreed Penelope. "I think David has a bit of a trial at home sometimes," she whispered.

Anna thought how strange that was, yet at the same time so typical of many relationships; the man paternally authoritative at work and thoroughly subjugated at home. She was sure Francesca would have enormous fun telling her all about how textbook that particular dynamic was.

"Andrew?" called Penelope, looking out of the back door. "He doesn't want to encounter Annetta, clearly," she added, turning back to Anna.

"Yes, what was that about?" asked Anna, feeling the plot around Andrew become thicker by the day.

"I'm not sure," answered Penelope. "I don't think she likes him much. They do tend to rub each other up the wrong way. She has some question about the money for the polo tournament. I really don't know. I'll have to talk to Pete."

Anna couldn't think what it could be, and was preoccupied with what was going on outside, though trying not to eavesdrop too obviously.

In the yard, Annetta had launched into a heated tirade at David, who did not seem to retaliate. After a few minutes, much to Anna's amazement, he seemed to defuse Annetta's anger. They couldn't hear what was going on but the body language suggested he had given her a reason for his absence that was plausible. Annetta still looked annoyed, but presumably she would have grabbed the nearest heavy object and begun battering him if she had found out the truth. David climbed into his car again, puffing his cheeks in the manner of someone relieved to have dodged a bullet.

Anna sighed inwardly. It was surely only a matter of time before that particular drama reached its crescendo. What an idiot he was, she thought, but immediately reprimanded herself. She too was now involved in an unwise relationship which, besides being immoral, would get them both into hot water rapidly, should anyone guess what was going on.

There were just a couple of days left of work before breaking for Christmas, and Anna and Phil were making some final adjustments to their process recommendations. After Christmas they would be on the last leg of their project and it wouldn't be long before Anna left her favourite building behind and moved to the next challenge.

She had been networking for assignments but had lost focus recently, unwillingly acknowledging that she ought to be responsible and take a job which would remove her from Damien. She had scanned the international opportunities within her consultancy with an uncommitted eye. Taking herself out of the equation to save the happiness of others would be the noble, even heroic thing to do; but she felt a deep resistance. Maybe it was ridiculously martyrish? And how would she deal with Tom in her absence?

The Christmas break would have to serve as meditation time, she decided. Coercing herself into the mindset necessary to take such a big step could not be hurried. She hoped she might get to see Damien before Christmas but that seemed unlikely, and she guessed he would be as embroiled in family as everyone else for the next week or so. Of course, he may even have begun to regret what happened. Who knew?

She shook herself mentally. Whatever, she needed to see his face again; that much was undeniable. What was not so clear was how she should behave towards him after their surreal heated encounter in the gale; frankly, she had no idea. And how should she act around everybody else? She shrugged. Just the same as before, she guessed; as inconspicuously and indifferently as possible.

Along with many in London, Anna headed home early on Christmas Eve. She changed quickly and hurried to Rosemount for a last ride. Tomorrow she was driving north to her mother's house for Christmas

Day, and then there was another long journey to her father's the following day.

This is another good reason for making marriage work, she thought as she wearily considered the two days of driving she had to endure. The fragmented family proved time consuming when it came to the few precious days off over Christmas, especially living as they did miles apart. She smiled at her own uncharitable and unseasonal grumpiness. It wasn't that she didn't enjoy seeing them; they just lived too far from her life, and Tom. She simply didn't do well in the static role of idle house guest, kicking her heels and incarcerated when she could have been out riding. God, how she loved it; she was obviously a lost cause.

As Anna neared the end of the long gallop she saw a rider on the bridleway raise a hand and wave. It was Olivia, and Anna trotted over to meet her.

"I see you did what I did," said Olivia. "Rushed home for a Christmas Eve ride before all the family chaos starts!"

"You know it!" said Anna smiling. "When does chaos ensue for you?"

"This evening. I'm leaving late to drive to my folks in Norfolk just in time for eggnog, mince pies and Santa," she answered, lighting a cigarette. Anna watched her with amusement. "What?" asked Olivia, blowing smoke sideways from the edge of her mouth.

"I don't know. Smoking and riding just looks odd. It's right up there with being on the phone or listening to music while riding," said Anna, grinning.

"Gotta move with the times, Anna! You're one of those quiet old-fashioned types, aren't you?" laughed Olivia.

"A quiet old-fashioned type with healthy lungs and an awareness of what's happening around her, yes!" retorted Anna.

"Hey, how about a drink later? It's Christmas Eve after all," asked Olivia, flicking idly with her whip at a single dried leaf still hanging on an otherwise bare branch.

Anna assented. "Penelope told me she and Pete are going to the George and Dragon in the village this evening before the late carol service at the church," she remembered.

"Sounds divine and holy," said Olivia cynically, flicking her cigarette butt away. "We should join them. I'll skip the service but I'll always take the drinks!"

"Don't I know it! But you shouldn't quaff too much if you're driving!" warned Anna.

"Oh god, listen to you. You're as puritanical as Damien," complained Olivia. "I work in advertising, Anna; we consume alcohol professionally!"

"I know, you have the constitution of a concrete rhino," said Anna in mock resignation. "But they're more likely to be scouting for drunk drivers on the roads on Christmas Eve," she added.

"Yeah, yeah. Don't worry, Anna."

Snow was blowing against the windows in the side wind which had picked up and the plane bumped on the turbulence, then was weightless for a second before thumping again. Dropping finally through the thick cloud cover, Damien could see the glow of the airport through the darkness.

"This is Virgin 026, altitude 5000 feet, speed 220 knots," said Damien's first officer, Mark, as they continued their approach.

Damien focused through the driving snow. It was getting later all the time but the flight had been shorter than scheduled and he had a plan. He stared out at the glowing urban sprawl of London encroaching massively, wrapping round the luminescence of the airport itself. Praying there would be no delay in landing, he listened to the communication going on between Mark and the controller.

"Virgin 026, turn right heading 240, intercept the final approach course at 3,000 feet. Runway 27 Right. Contact tower on 118.70," said the voice of the controller.

The plane banked and Damien focussed on the runway lights through the chaotic flurrying snow. Nearly there. He deployed the landing gear and swiftly checked his watch. There had to be time.

He shook his head at the insistent snow. England may have seen more snow than usual in the last couple of years, but snow on Christmas Eve? How long had it been falling and were the roads going to be a nightmare? He had gained time during the flight but now, almost back on home turf, things seemed to be conspiring against him to eat into the lead he had built up over thousands of miles. Hearing the babble of communication in progress he redirected his attention, listening for the words he needed to hear from the tower, and felt a swell of relief at the final response.

"Virgin 026 cleared to land."

It was the perfect Christmas scene as Anna closed her front door and strolled through the peaceful churchyard, enchanting under its blanket of shimmering snow. She looked up at the illuminated church spire, stretching up into the night sky. The clouds were thick and snow fell straight down, fluffy flakes emerging from the dark above her, surrounding her and settling quickly. She searched the sky, hearing a plane overhead and saw flashing lights bouncing around in the cloud for a moment before they were swallowed up again. She wondered if Damien was flying. He could be anywhere.

She drifted down the high street, kicking the fresh snow and appreciating the cheerful Christmas lights glimmering in the windows. Wood smoke from the pub suffused the air, and looking through the window, she saw the roaring fire illuminating the faces of those inside with a romantic orange glow.

The runway was growing larger, its lights beckoning, and then the welcome sound of the plane's mechanical altitude callout resonated on the flight deck. Damien surfed a couple of gusts before raising the nose and touching down in the whirling snow storm, engines roaring. The crawl to the gate seemed interminable, waiting for other traffic as Heathrow scrambled with the Christmas Eve rush, but he was getting closer all the time.

The lights of the bustling terminal shone brightly as the passengers disembarked, all hurrying to their own versions of Christmas. The familiar thudding sounds of the ground crews setting about the plane vibrated through the hull as they worked unseen in the darkness, bent against the whipping snow.

"Right, let's get done here," said Damien, looking at his watch again as he went about the shut-down checks.

"Hey, we're really early," said Mark, grinning and handing Damien the flight log. "I might even get to that party after all!"

"Yeah, hope we're early enough," Damien answered under his breath, scribbling furiously and thrusting the paperwork for a broken anti-ice valve at Mark. "Finish that off and we can get out of here."

Soon Damien was double-timing it through the airport, breaking into a jog as he exited the terminal. He had a headlong dash ahead of him.

Olivia had already arrived and was sitting back relaxed at the table nearest the fire with Pete and Penelope.

"Merry Christmas, Anna!" Pete said, raising his glass. "Sit down and have some champagne with us."

"Why not?" she agreed, as Pete filled a glass for her from the bottle he had in an ice bucket. "No Zanah?" she asked Olivia.

"No, she's with her folks. I haven't seen her at all since the other night. I think she's been hanging out with Lucias."

"I saw them riding out together earlier today," said Penelope with a smile.

"She's been avoiding me. She knows I'll give her hell," said Olivia. Then she switched the subject and said, looking at her phone, "Hey, I messaged Damien earlier and told him we'd be here."

Anna affected casual interest, being careful to show nothing more. She was relieved when Olivia went on without looking at her:

"I doubt he'll make it, though. He was in the air at the time. I asked him where he was and he said 'over a great big boring blue bit!' He's as sulky as ever about Christmas and trying to avoid it. He said he'd rather join us than do the family party," said Olivia.

"Wouldn't we all like to side-step some of it," Anna shrugged.

"Yes, Christmas can come with a lot of baggage and crap," agreed Pete.

"Pete!" objected Penelope, appearing genuinely disturbed that he could take issue with the joyous festive period.

"I'm sorry, but it's true!" he said smiling and hugging her round the shoulders. "Every year we all put ourselves through the family gatherings which involve excessive eating and drinking and hanging out with a bunch of people all acting out their historic control dramas, ending inevitably in a fight!"

"That was only one year!" said Penelope, causing Anna and Olivia to laugh aloud.

"It's every year! The atmosphere is always trying. Anyway, what I'm attempting to express is how wonderful it is to sit here with some friends in the pub having a quiet Christmas drink! Every Christmas should be this marvellously unpressured!"

"Cheers!" agreed Anna and Olivia in unison, raising their glasses and drinking.

"How many of these have we had?" asked Penelope, pulling the bottle from the ice bucket and inspecting the level of the champagne inside. "You've become extremely loquacious!"

Pete grinned at his wife and raised his glass. "Cheers to you, Penelope. It's been a great year!"

"Hear, hear!" said Olivia enthusiastically as she got up, pulling her coat on. "Speaking of Christmas pressure, I don't want to, but I must go. If I stay any longer I'll be in trouble with the folks and also with the alcohol police here," she said, laying her hand on Anna's shoulder.

As Olivia buttoned her coat the door opened, pulling in a gust of snow and, along with it, Damien. Anna's heart jolted in her chest. She had accepted the fact that she would not see him until after Christmas, and yet there he was at the eleventh hour, an unreal vision in his snow-scattered uniform.

"And smile!" said Olivia, snapping his photo on her phone. He gave her a half smile and a questioning look.

"Come on! Two years I've known you, maybe more, and I have never once had the privilege of seeing you in your sexy uniform!"

The others laughed and Pete, who had dashed to the bar to collect another glass, swiftly filled it and handed it to Damien. "Merry Christmas, Damien!"

"That's very civilised," said Damien with a smile. Anna couldn't take her eyes off him, and there was an energetic flutter echoing through her from her stomach.

"I didn't think you'd make it," said Olivia.

"Tailwind," said Damien, sitting down and looking at Anna directly for an instant, making her heart pound faster and the glass in her hand shake.

"It looks like it's got really bad out there!" exclaimed Penelope, looking through the window.

"Yes, it's tanking down out there," said Damien. "Roads are bad. I almost lost the back end of the car at one point."

"Shit. Better go," said Olivia. "Urgh! It's going to take me ages now!" she complained.

"Drive carefully!" Anna told her.

"Don't worry. I'll drive like I'm 108 years old!" said Olivia, and opened the door with a smile. "Merry Christmas!"

"Cheers!" said Pete and they all clinked glasses. "You've obviously come straight from work," he nodded at Damien.

"Yes. I fancied a stop before the madness begins," replied Damien, looking at Anna.

"Won't you be missed on Christmas Eve?" laughed Penelope.

"Well, I landed early," he replied conspiratorially. "And my wife's at her family's place for the big annual party which I am happily not expected at."

"Sly bugger!" laughed Pete. "Don't blame you! We were just talking about that."

"Yes, you missed a full chapter and verse rant about the evils of Christmas," said Penelope.

"Hah! Plenty to be said on that subject."

"Don't encourage him! We'd be hermits if it were up to him," said Penelope, looking at her watch. "Goodness, look at the time. The carol service started ten minutes ago!"

"Okay, I hear you," said Pete draining his glass and getting up. "Sorry to rush off just as you got here, Damien. I promised Penelope we'd go to her carol service. Finish the champagne," he added, looking at the bottle which still had a couple of glasses in it.

"Thanks. Anna'll keep me company. We might catch you up," said Damien, looking over his shoulder at Pete and Penelope as they moved to the door.

They were alone again. As the door closed they turned to one another, smiles breaking onto their faces.

"Hey," said Anna shyly.

"Hey you," he replied, a glimmer of amusement in his eyes as he gazed at her.

"I didn't expect to see you."

"I'm glad I got here. I thought I was going to miss you. I drove like a hooligan," he said with a grin.

"I didn't even know you were intending to be here. I'd just about come to terms with the fact I wouldn't see you until after Christmas."

"I didn't think I'd be back in time, but then Olivia told me you'd be here when I was a third of the way across the Atlantic, and it started a crazy against-the-clock charge." He smiled, remembering his stress.

Anna laughed; having him there alone felt like an early Christmas present – the only one she wanted.

"It feels like you've been gone for weeks," she said.

"Feels that way to me too," he said, pouring the rest of the champagne into their glasses. "So, what are you doing for Christmas?"

"I'm starting the compulsory circulation tomorrow. First my Mum's place, then my Dad the next day. I'll be back on the 27th to chill. How about you?"

He looked uncomfortable. "I'm due at my in-laws' place tomorrow, for a huge family do. There's a whole troop of them. My parents the next day and I'm hoping that's it."

"Working much?" asked Anna.

"Less than I bid for. I actually tried to work for the whole holiday to get out of all of it," he said seriously.

"Olivia was right about you wanting to avoid Christmas," smirked Anna.

"Well, it would be different if I were spending it doing what I wanted, but it's always governed by others and their expectations," he said matter-of-factly. "If I could spend it riding and being with you, then I'd want to stick around."

His dark eyes rested on her. It didn't even feel like they needed to talk. A powerful energy passed between them.

"Thank God for tailwinds. I wanted to see you," he said, dropping his voice and intensifying his gaze. "I was almost out of control with you the other night."

Anna smiled and touched his hand, feeling electricity tingling between them. "You and me both."

"Seriously, if Olivia had been a second later I'd have probably dragged you into the woods."

Anna caught her breath, the heat rising in her again, instantly feeling the fiery drama of the night and how she had been willing the same thing.

"Let's get out of here," he said purposefully.

The snow had fallen fast and heavily, blanketing the village in immaculate white. Anna and Damien stepped onto the deserted street and paused. The old-fashioned street lamp illuminated the enormous snowflakes as they fell about them, seemingly in slow motion. It was almost a cliché, a surreal scene in a snow globe, but neither of them cared. Damien took both Anna's hands and turned slowly with her under the lamp.

As they moved the heat seemed to pulse between them, and they drew one another closer and closer until their bodies touched. Anna drank in every detail of his face as he moved in and kissed her.

Reluctantly coming up for air, they became aware of music from the church drifting faintly through the night.

"Come on. Let's walk," Damien said, looking around.

He put his arm round her and Anna clung to him as they strolled. It seemed like a dream as he turned his eyes to her, darkly gleaming in the dim. The words of Silent Night rang purely through the air as they approached the front door of the church and they paused for a moment, listening. The snow fell softly, faintly audible as it touched the dark clustering branches of the yew trees.

Their fingers met and intertwined, the sensation firing through Anna, making her silently draw breath and bite her lip. Damien bent his face to hers and kissed her again, more hungrily this time. Their mouths still locked together, he drew her around the corner to the darkness and shelter of the towering stone wall and slid his hands inside her coat, running them up her sides, then round her back, taking control. His touch burned through her shirt and a wave of longing rolled through her as he pressed against her. She breathed him in, abjectly craving him now. Lit with a fierce new physical honesty, she flexed her back, wantonly pushing her hips against him. He hissed softly, his lips against her neck. Anna moaned and ran her fingers up his neck and into his hair.

"Anna..?" he whispered against her, his breath coming faster.

"Yes... Oh, yess...." The words rushed recklessly from her.

He had his lips to her neck again as she unlocked the door of the cottage and they stumbled in over the threshold, and fell against the other side of the door together as it shut with a snap. The house was dark, the light on the outside of the church filtering though the small windows of the cottage just enough for them to find the stairway while dropping coats and kicking off shoes. He caught her on the stairs, laughing softly, pulling off her shirt, kissing her shoulders, as she tugged at the buttons of his. She drew him further up the narrow stairway, kicking her bedroom door open as she reached the top, pulling at his belt.

They were panting wildly as they fell on the bed together, finally feeling skin hot against skin. She revelled in the hard planes of his body, running her hands over his chest and digging her fingers into his shoulders. He bit back an exclamation, pulling away for a moment to gaze at her curves before kissing up her sides and around to her breasts, making her cry out.

"My god, I can't believe how sexy you are," he whispered.

His mouth was on hers again and she could taste him. She threw her head back and breathed in his ear, "I can't believe how hot you are. I want you so badly."

He exhaled hard and wrapped his arm about her, pulling her against him.

He drove her with a dark passion, damp with sweat, as she writhed and pressed herself to him, feeling her senses spiralling. He caught his breath, slowing their movement for a moment.

"My god, Anna, you've got me so turned on I'll explode!"

Too overcome to speak, she moaned and buried her face in his neck, kissing it and savouring the taste of his sweat. Gasping, heat pounding from his body, he abandoned all restraint and they moved as one, faster and faster, until hunger clenched and shattered and the world went up in white flames.

Anna awoke to see Damien looking at her as he stood next to the bed. She had no idea what time it was. The light from outside flickered across him, interrupted by the waving branches of trees. His shirt was open, his epaulettes glinting in the moonlight, as he slowly fastened his belt. She rolled towards him, kicking the sheet from around her feet, and knelt up in front of him on the bed, kissing his chest, the hair soft and laden with the scent of them.

"I don't think you realise how outrageously hot you look," she whispered, pressing herself against him and sliding her hands up to pull his shirt from his shoulders. She felt his hands gliding up her back, holding her to him, as he bent his face to the top of her head. He let his shirt fall to the ground and breathed against her.

"Oh fuck, I want you so much." His voice came raw in her ear.

He pulled at his belt and fell to the bed with her again, running his hands over her body and kissing her hard.

As the first light of dawn washed palely across the room, they lay together, her head on his chest as he ran his fingers through her hair.

"Anna, what do you do to me?" She looked up at him. "Damn, I'm a raging beast with you." His face seemed more supple and youthful than before, his smile lazy and knowing.

"You do the same to me."

"I can't even think about leaving right now," he said, not moving his eyes from hers. He held out his hand and she caught it in hers.

"Best Christmas present ever," she breathed. He smiled and kissed her.

"Oh yeah, definitely. Best night ever."

Looking over his shoulder to the window he sighed again and turned back to her. She kissed him and rolled back with fiery eyes, pulling him towards her, wrapping her legs around him.

"Can't do it. I just can't leave," he whispered. Duties and constraints paled to insignificance, the consequences of being late not worth a moment's thought.

Damien picked his jacket up from where it had fallen the night before and shook it.

"You want coffee or something?" Anna asked, laughing. "We've been up all night!"

He hugged her to him, answering with a smile. "I feel like I've had the best night's sleep ever."

"When will I see you again?"

"I'll come see you when you get back. What time are you home?"

"I'll make sure I'm home in time!"

"Early enough to ride out in the afternoon?" he asked. Then, with gleaming eyes, "Then we can ride some more. I'm going to be insatiable by then."

She laughed delightedly, tingling at the thought.

"Now I'm going to go, before I stay here all day." He kissed her hard.

"Can I walk you to your car?" she asked.

"No, I'll end up taking you with me and we'll just go and never be seen again."

Watching him stride down the path to the church gate, she glowed with pleasure. Oh, yes please.

CHRISTMAS PROPER (AND IMPROPER)

Anna's smile was irrepressible. She drove fast through the snow, music pulsing loud through the Land Rover. The night before played and replayed gloriously in her mind, causing her to shiver, and laugh aloud. People noticed her in traffic and smiled at her. Her bubble of joy spread far and wide that day, reflecting brightly on everything.

She arrived before lunchtime at her mother's house, striding up the garden path feeling invincible.

Her brother opened the door and grinned at her. "Well, I knew you'd arrive in time for champagne!"

She dumped her bags down and hugged him.

"So, did Santa come last night?" he asked.

She exploded with ribald laughter. He looked at her questioningly and raised an eyebrow.

"Come on, let's go get that champagne!" urged Anna, clapping him playfully on the shoulder, brimming with joy as they went to join the throng.

No amount of good food, drink and catching up with family could remove Damien's image from her mind. She felt he was standing beside her all day. At ten o'clock that evening her phone chimed, and she guessed he must be feeling the same because there on the screen was a simple text.

"Beaming all day. xxx," it read.

It wasn't until the journey home two days later that she began to wonder how long her elation would continue. Christmas had been very happy, reconnecting with her family and rediscovering how much she loved them, but behind her happiness was a breath of unease; after that delicious text, there had been no more messages from Damien.

It was probably nothing to worry about; he was just busy with family, the same as her. And since he was married he would have to be very discreet. Nevertheless, it was strange; surely he could have found a moment for her?

Red tail lights showed ahead of her and she braked sharply; hell, a tailback. Just what she didn't need. Sighing, she willed herself to be patient; there was still plenty of time to get to Rosemount. Stretching and wriggling her back against the seat, she thought about the future.

She had promised herself she would think seriously about overseas assignments during the break. The thing with Damien wasn't meant to last – it couldn't, however addicted to him she was; putting thousands of miles between them seemed the obvious way to end it. But then again, she wasn't ready to seriously entertain such a drastic idea; not now, when Christmas Eve was still vividly replaying itself in her head and the thought of seeing him again in a few hours made her catch her breath with excitement. Dammit, the future could wait.

And on that thought, the red glow in front of her subsided and the traffic started moving again. Taking her foot off the brake, she eased the Land Rover forward and started to speed up. Good sense and responsibility could go hang for a while; for now she would revel defiantly in glowing exhilaration.

Damien's car was already there when Anna drove into the yard that afternoon. She rushed to get Tom ready and was grooming him outside his stable when Damien swooped in on her, hugging her from behind and kissing her neck. She exclaimed with pleasure and twisted round in his arms, grinning. They both instinctively checked this way and that before pulling each other close and kissing furtively like school kids in a bike shelter.

"Ready in ten?" he asked as they resurfaced.

"You know it," she said with a provocative smile. He laughed wickedly, and kissed her again before turning towards his stable block.

"How was your Christmas?" she asked as they rode up the bridleway side by side.

"Well, there were some good arguments and one-upmanship to watch, plenty of drink to dull the pain," he said dryly, adding with a sidelong smile, "…and of course I had Christmas Eve night to keep me company."

"I didn't hear from you again over Christmas," remarked Anna.

"Never got the chance. Plus, I hate texting generally, so I won't be drowning you with them," he responded.

"That's fine. I'm not a big texter myself," she said, though wishing he had got in touch. She had been itching to message him, but something had stopped her. She wasn't sure what it was, exactly; maybe she just didn't want to come across as needy.

He reached for her hand and they plodded along with fingers intertwining. The electricity seemed to crackle between them and he put a hand out to her rein and pulled them both to a halt, then reached across and caressed her neck and kissed her, raising the temperature between them. Then standing in the stirrups and replanting himself on the saddle, he said, "We're going to have to stop that or I'll be dragging you into the woods." He leered at her and Anna giggled.

They galloped at the top and continued at a fast pace for the rest of the ride to stay ahead of the falling light, exuberantly leaping logs and dodging trees which encroached on the path. There was a new urgency to get back. Anna watched him as he stood in his stirrups in his customary hunting canter, and wanted him.

"Hey!" shouted Olivia as they arrived in the yard together. "You could have told me you were riding out!"

"Luck of the draw. If you're here you get lucky," grinned Damien.

"You seem perky today," said Olivia narrowing her eyes. "Good Christmas?"

"I'm in good spirits because it's over," he parried.

"Après Christmas drink at the bar?" suggested Olivia.

"No time. I'm working," said Damien, dismounting and running up his stirrups.

"Anna?" asked Olivia, as Anna dropped down at Tom's side.

"I can't right now. Catch you tomorrow instead?" she suggested. "We could ride out together? Say two o'clock?"

"Okay," agreed Olivia, following Anna as she walked with Tom. "Did Pete and Penelope drag you to the carols on Christmas Eve?"

"No, they left me and Damien to finish the champagne and went on their own."

"Did you stay long?" she probed.

"No. It was near to closing and we both had to get off," Anna lied, recalling the slow-motion scene in the falling snow. "How was your journey?" she asked, steering Olivia away from the topic of her and Damien.

"Bloody awful. The roads were a nightmare. It took the best part of six hours. I didn't arrive until the early hours!" complained Olivia. At the same moment Anna's phone chimed and she checked it quickly. "Date?" asked Olivia grinning.

"I wouldn't exactly call it that," replied Anna. "Just my friend Mateus."

Mateus was back in the south and wanted her to meet him for church. She grinned at his perseverance, thinking of what he said about God's pursuit of her. If that were truly the case, God was certainly getting His money's worth out of Mateus at the moment. Then again, He would probably be pretty disappointed in her right now.

"Mateus? You've never mentioned him," said Olivia in a tone Anna knew well.

"Olivia, you seem desperate to involve me in some clandestine liaison with someone! What is that?"

"Oh, come on, Anna! I don't get you! How can someone as gorgeous and funny as you not be involved with someone? There must be a whole dark, hidden side of you that you keep under wraps from everyone and I want to know!"

Anna laughed and took off Tom's saddle. "What can I say? Not everyone is desperate to be pair-bonded."

"I give up for now!" said Olivia, throwing her hands in the air. "I need to catch Damien about hunting."

Anna finished off her chores quickly and dashed to leave. As she passed near Damien's area she could see him untying Barnabas to turn him out, Olivia walking with him.

"Bye!" called Anna, waving at them, knowing Damien wouldn't take a moment to dismiss Olivia. He knew how to abruptly disappear.

Anna had been home for less than ten minutes when Damien knocked at the door briefly before exploding over the threshold and gathering her to him. He kicked off his yard boots and carried her bodily up the stairs, making her laugh. Raw hunger radiated from him as they fell to the bed together.

"It's going to be tricky at the yard," said Anna, her head against Damien's shoulder as they lay together in the afterglow. "Olivia is a bit like a terrier with a bone."

Damien sighed and nodded. "Yes, she won't give it up, will she?"

"When are you back?"

"Monday. And I can't believe I have to leave you again," he said, pulling her on top of him. "When are you working?"

"Not until the New Year," she answered, sinking against him.

"Good. I'm landing in the morning, around eleven. I'll come straight here."

Sunday morning was bright and cold. It felt odd to be in London after what seemed such a long time away, and moreover the city felt different. The tube was quiet and unhurried as families, up for the day to sightsee, wandered along the platform interestedly taking in their surroundings. They were a stark contrast to the weekday commuters, oblivious to everything but the need to get to work, double-timing it down the platform on auto-pilot in their collective rush for the stairs.

"Where are you?" winked the message on her phone from Mateus.

"South Ken tube," texted back Anna, as she took the stairs two at a time. In a moment she emerged into the open air and Mateus stepped to her side, wrapping her in one of his warm hugs.

"How was your Christmas?" he beamed. "Let's walk; we'll get coffee first."

They strolled along chatting. It was good to see him again, and she wondered where on earth their conversation would take them that day. Given that they were going to church together again, it was bound to be another spiritual ramble. He seemed to be converting her a little at a time, and while she didn't object, she wouldn't simply roll over. One thing she did want to ask about was the mysterious link between him and Andrew Japson, whom she hadn't seen since his rapid disappearance from the bar a couple of days before Christmas. It was a topic she would reserve for after the service, wanting time to probe a little deeper.

"What possessed you to drag me all the way into London to go to church?" she demanded. "I had to get up at work-time for this!"

"Come on, Anna! This is HTB! It's big, it's known all round the world!"

"HTB?" she queried sardonically, dragging out the syllables.

"Holy Trinity Brompton. You've got to hear the vicar there. You'll like him, he's a great speaker. He used to be a barrister."

"Well, hurrah for people who haven't been developed in the test-tube by the clergy," said Anna dryly.

"Thought you'd like that." Mateus grinned. "And also, I've got a surprise for you..!" he said, tantalisingly leaving it hanging. Anna raised her eyebrows and cocked her head at him. "Your favourite pastor is going to be there," he announced.

"Who? You?" she asked blankly.

He grinned. "Okay, your second favourite pastor."

"Who?"

"The guy we saw in New York," he said ecstatically.

The coincidence seemed odd. "What's he doing this side of the pond?" she asked in surprise.

"Dunno, maybe on holiday, but a lot of clergy the world over want to speak at HTB," he said casually.

It seemed weird; being keen to speak at a church. Being keen to play Glastonbury was fair enough, but keen to talk to a congregation in church? Were there cool venues for Christians? She smirked inwardly, then caught herself; she was being churlish.

"Speaking of pastors on holiday, I've been meaning to ask how you can leave your flock at Christmas anyway?" she asked as they sat down in the café.

"Well, it's not ideal admittedly, but it's a fair-sized church. There's an assistant pastor and other guest speakers to stand in for me. Plus I had to come back for my cousin's wedding," he shrugged.

Mateus seemed too cool to be a vicar, with his easy body language, and his newly improved physique accentuated by a close-fitting shirt and stylishly battered jeans.

"How's it going with you?" he asked her.

"My work assignment is pretty much finished. I've had Tom out hunting –"

Anna paused as he looked at her with mock impatience.

"You told me all that last time. Which means you don't want to talk about other things," he said, cocking his head to one side as he looked at her.

It seemed like everyone was constantly trying to prise information from her, but at least she could be straight with Mateus.

"No, not really," she admitted.

They sat in silence as he looked at her. Finally he took a breath and his gaze sharpened.

"Why not?"

"Because!" she said evasively, to which he raised an eyebrow. "Because maybe I just don't want your judgement," she finished.

"Why would I judge you? Does it feel like I judge you?"

"No. Never, actually. You're just so different to me. It feels like you've never put a foot wrong," she said, meeting his eye.

"Really? I'm a saint?"

"Oh, I don't know. I can't talk about it. It's a mess..." she faltered, thinking of the church's insistence on the sanctity of marriage. The altruistic constraints placed upon humanity, with all its urges and impulsions, had her doubting anew. Plainly there was something wrong with Damien's marriage, which justified their current situation, maybe? But she didn't want to talk about it with Mateus; generous and tolerant as he was, he was still a clergyman. He would never get himself embroiled in something so morally dubious.

"What do you think about the theory that everything happens for a reason?" he asked her, after a pause. She threw her head back and smiled cynically at the ceiling.

"Are you saying all my mistakes are orchestrated by God?"

"Maybe not. Your choices are your own to make with your own best conscience, and everyone makes mistakes there. But perhaps your life path has exposed you to the things you need in order to grow, leading you through events, situations and even monumental mess-ups, to where you are now. Everything serves you now and in your future."

"To what end?" she asked, frustrated and feeling disconnect.

"To return to God," he said simply. Then he added, knowing he needed to re-frame for her, "To be happy, to experience all-encompassing peace; to be whole."

Anna slumped forward, processing his thoughts. Was that really possible? Life hadn't proven to be a solidly happy experience so far.

"I doubt a person ever gets there. Life is a constant barrage of challenge," she protested.

"True. Some people never get there. And it doesn't mean that sad events won't ever happen again. It is possible though, to find peace and happiness even in the midst of all this," he said, gesturing with a sweep of his arm.

"I don't think I understand how that's achievable."

"Come on," he said getting up. "Let's go to the service."

Anna followed him out pensively.

"What if I suggested to you it was about living in the moment?" he continued as they strolled down the street. "Luckily we have hours to talk today!"

She'd been doing plenty of living in the moment recently, Anna thought, and in total disregard of the repercussions. Of course she hadn't meant to get in so deep with Damien, and she knew the inevitable end would hurt, but being with him was addictive. She remembered the last time he was with her, his breath warm against her and the sheen of sweat on his back. She shook herself. She needed to stay present. She thought of the last sermon she had attended with Mateus, in New York; she had over-ridden her own better governance. Mateus would be horrified he was hanging out with such a morally bankrupt friend.

"You're kidding me!" whispered Anna in disbelief.

Yet again the sermon was ironic in its subject and timing, fired like an arrow straight at her life. The big screen at the front shone brightly with the words; 'Soul Detox'.

The vicar smiled good-naturedly as he introduced the topic of the day, eloquently emphasising the importance of cleansing oneself of negatives, indulgences and habits which eat away at the very material of one's soul; but his words grated on Anna. She felt rebellious; she didn't want to hear about clean living again, and felt the urge to get up and leave. She had lived clean for years and frankly it was no fun. This was the first time she had been errant from virtue, and she intended to enjoy her taste of the dark side.

"Hey, it's almost January, and that means its detox time, right!" challenged the visiting pastor, his exuberant charisma bounding forth. The vast congregation stirred in their chairs.

His familiar rounded accent echoed off the vaulted stonework. "Time to get rid of all that stuff bunging up your insides from a Christmas of bad living, right? But that's not the bit I'm talking about! I'm not trying to save you from cholesterol and liver damage. There are other people who you can talk to about that, far better than I can. I'm talking about that part of you which you definitely can't live without, but so many people don't even know actually exists! A lot of people don't really believe in it. I'm talking about your soul. Did you know that you're not a body, not just a lump of meat? We're not just this crude matter," he said, grabbing at his own shoulder. "We're actually a soul. A soul, attached to, encompassing, that lump of meat! And it's time for a detox."

Anna considered as she listened; yes, she did believe in the soul. Her beliefs had shifted, and despite the lack of material evidence to suggest otherwise, a person was more than a body controlled by all its organs, with the brain as king ruling it all. There had to be more.

She thought of her beach meditations on Tresco, feeling the very energy of nature filling her full of peace. She remembered the inexplicable yet undeniable sensation in her gut, driving her to speak to James. Then there was the night in the church, where she had dashed headlong into a dangerous situation, against all logic. And of course there was the internal pull she felt to go to church which had crept up on her, and that had come about in the midst of her pointless resistance to Damien. And what about the undeniable energy which had so powerfully connected her with Damien?

Again she thought of how she didn't want it to end. But it would end, very soon. And the weight of that imminent demise and what it would do to her, to her soul, was unpleasant to contemplate. Perhaps it was all orchestrated. It did feel like a path of revelations and experiences taking her along a road she couldn't yet see.

The pastor went on energetically, talking as though he were sounding off to a friend:

"Think of the rush; that daily rush – getting out the door, the office, the meetings, the reporting, the horrible boss –" There was a murmur of laughter as the beet-red face of an overwrought man appeared on the big screen, moustache lop-sided above a toothy snarl. "There's always a horrible boss, right?" he grinned. "Then there're the expectations we lay on ourselves; all that ego-driven crap: to perform, to be the best, to win, to do our duty, to be important, to earn more and more money…" He counted them off on his fingers. "All of this, at the expense of what? At the expense of the very thing which truly nourishes us."

"Seriously, everyone, start with one thing!" He paused, holding his index finger up. "Take a moment today to identify one thing which does not contribute to your daily happiness and get rid of it." He stood silently, looking out across the sea of people, before continuing.

"If you don't truly believe in the soul, chances are you're not feeding it, you're killing it. A little at a time, the duties and demands, this crap we cram our time with in this matrix of life. Our ego tells us it's vital, but it actually means nothing except the *demise of the soul*." He emphasised the last four words, pausing between each dramatically. "Think about it, meditate on it. What makes you happy? Clear out what is sucking the life out of you, and instead feed your soul."

Anna left the church brooding. Was everyone trapped and blundering along, not seeing the big picture? Dashing around like ants, filling their days with inconsequential jobs, unimportant achievements, unfulfilling relationships and other miscellaneous stuff, missing what was actually important?

"Are we in the Matrix?" she asked Mateus, remembering the movie they had watched together at university.

"Unless you've been unplugged," he answered, immediately catching the reference.

"I mean, are we all missing something? Perhaps this all means nothing?" She shrugged, feeling demotivated, her brain overloaded and seized up. She could no longer think straight.

"Uh, oh. Apathy alert! Let's get another coffee!" said Mateus.

"Anna. You don't have to talk and I know you're independent and find your own way, but it feels like you're carrying a weight," said Mateus, as they sat in the morning sun in the window of a coffee shop.

"I got involved with the guy I told you about," said Anna, instinctively coming clean.

Mateus sat back in his seat.

"And I know it's wrong and it'll all be over soon, but it feels right at the same time," continued Anna. She stared at the table for a while and then asked, "Why is it that it's so wrong to decide you've done the wrong thing, in marrying someone, and actually there's another person who's perfect for you? Why is marriage so sacrosanct? Is it so wrong to say that this relationship has timed out?"

"Do you want me to answer?" asked Mateus.

Anna sighed, feeling the self-interest echoing in her words, and knowing where he was going to go.

After a pause Mateus said, "What happens when your second husband or wife gets boring and the real, perfect person appears on the scene? Then further along the road, you realise your third marriage was admittedly a lustful mistake, but honestly, you swear that this fourth person is definitely perfect?"

Anna looked up and smiled at him, warmed by his light-heartedness, but feeling a poignant truth. Was anyone the one and only, or did they all have their timeframe?

"So why bother? Why bother with marriage at all? I hardly ever see one work."

"Well, if you want my theory I'd say it's about life evolution," he answered thoughtfully. "Life evolves constantly, right? As a rule we all strive to personally grow. That general spiral of improvement must include everything in life and must therefore reflect on marriage." He paused briefly; then, gathering momentum, "And as a marriage travels its road, there are so many things that can happen, so many great things. It should be an amazing adventure of life and evolution or development together, knowing each other through and through. But if we get stuck on the initial thrill and insist on hitting repeat on that part, we will never have the adventure."

"That was very profound," she said, looking at him steadily, noting his lack of reference to the Bible. He seemed to have every aspect of life thoroughly thought out. "I guess that perfect version of marriage depends on having two perfect people involved?"

"Who's perfect? It does demand two people who treat each other with love and respect to allow for that growth and movement," he said, looking at her seriously.

"So if you make a mistake and choose badly, choose a piece-of-work who treats you badly or disrespects you, you're screwed?" asserted Anna, thinking somewhat bitterly of her past relationship.

"Sometimes, sure," he responded, knowing how unhappy she had been. "But there's an honourable way to do that, right? And you yourself did it that way."

Anna sighed, remembering her split from Adam. She had put up with his abuse far longer than she should before she moved out. Like most people in the situation, she had struggled on until it got unbearable. Looking back, she loathed her lack of emotional bravery.

She shifted, pushing the old memories away. Reverting to the thread Mateus had been on, she challenged;

"So you've got a great adventure with soul-filling evolution going on, but you have to suppress the urge for a thrill?"

"Hey, if you're on a great adventure with someone, that surely includes great sex!" he countered, grinning. "You were talking about sex, right?" he added with a wink.

Suddenly he seemed extremely attractive, leaning casually in his seat as he expounded his philosophy, dark blond hair stylishly messy and penetrating eyes shining into her soul. His thinking seemed light years ahead of hers. She wished she was better at taking his influence back into her regular life.

"I feel like we always talk about me," she complained, deflecting the question. "What about you? You never talk about anyone who you'd like to take on this great adventure with you."

He met her eyes and smiled. "What's the rush?"

"Please tell me you're not being wholly religious and saving yourself for her?" she grinned, wondering what he'd be like. Then she cursed herself inwardly. What was wrong with her, asking him a question like that? Was she on sexual overdrive and after everyone?

"Hey, as I said, I'm no saint," he said, smiling cryptically.

"Speaking of which, why were you asking about Andrew Japson?" she asked abruptly, feeling her opportunity arrive.

Mateus looked surprised. "Why? Does my knowing him deprive me of sainthood?"

Now he was the one deflecting.

"No," she said, meeting his gaze. "But he certainly won't be getting one anytime soon, that I can see."

He looked at her questioningly, and Anna poured out the story of the late night at the church; a story she had not shared with anyone. Hearing it come out in her own voice, it sounded far-fetched and ridiculous, even to her. What had felt like facts were now hazy and unreal, and she wondered how tired and drunk she had been. Maybe her imagination had run riot? But Mateus's eyes had grown serious, and his brow furrowed in concern.

"When was this, Anna?"

She thought for a moment. It seemed a long while ago now; she remembered that the evening had been warm, despite the wind... Then it came to her; it was the night of the polo match, the night Dom had vanished. With a sudden jolt, she wondered if the two were related, and why she had never made the connection before.

"Does the name Dominik mean anything to you?" she asked Mateus. "Dominik Laska, I think his last name was." He looked puzzled and shook his head. "It was the night he disappeared. Back at the end of summer. Pete had some high goal Argentinean players at Rosemount."

Mateus appeared to be thinking. His eyes moved as though scanning his memory, and he frowned. He pulled out his phone and scrolled the calendar as he sat forward in his seat, his face tense.

"What is it?" asked Anna. His expression scared her. His demeanour had changed completely and he seemed entirely different from the Mateus she knew.

He sighed heavily. "I'm worried. Too many things are pointing to..." He trailed off. "I can't talk about it."

"What? You can't give me a half-line like that!" she exclaimed. "Are you okay? You're surely not involved?"

"No. No, I'm not. But it's safer for you not to know anything," he clarified.

Anna was shocked. How was her pure and clean friend in the know on any criminal activity?

"Aren't you going to the police or something?" she asked with concern.

"I've nothing concrete to tell them right now." She looked at him searchingly. Anything that had Mateus looking the way he did at that moment was deadly serious. "Forget this, Anna," he advised. Then he got up and pulled his jacket on.

"You have to leave?" she asked, knowing his departure was prompted by what she had told him.

"You've set something in motion. I have to deal with it."

NEW YEAR'S EVE

It was New Year's Eve. Staring out of the window at the peaceful graveyard under its fresh coat of shimmering snow, Anna ate her breakfast and contemplated the day ahead. The weather was perfect for a morning ride, just her and Tom alone in the stillness, and they had a good three hours to enjoy themselves before Damien arrived.

Buttering another piece of toast, she shifted her thoughts to the previous day. She was still curious about Mateus's connection with Andrew, but since he had refused to be drawn all she could do was speculate. What mattered more right now was that Mateus had forced her to confront her feelings about being Damien's mistress. Despite having no intention of breaking things off then and there, she felt strength in her grim acceptance of the inevitable. There was absolutely no way she was going to be a marriage wrecker. The moral burden was far too great.

She drained the last of her coffee and stood up, eager to keep busy and prevent any more of her obsessive over-thinking.

The bridleways were mostly deserted as Tom jogged along. A robin accompanied them for a while, fluttering from branch to branch, escorting them through his territory, and a solitary walker nodded good morning, his cheeks rosy as he climbed over a stile. Everything was brightly lit by the pale sunshine which had broken through the clouds. As they emerged from the hedgerows and out on the top, the vista opened out before them, flawless and sparkling under its snowy blanket, and Tom happily bounded forth like a dog through the drifts as Anna laughed with delight.

Back in the Rosemount yard, Anna slid down from the saddle, feeling restful, and rubbed Toms head and fluffy winter fur along his neck. The moist crystals of snow glistened on his legs and underside, and she dusted absently at his coat.

"Anna, you'll never guess!" Olivia hissed, appearing suddenly and bringing haste to the tranquillity.

Anna looked at her with raised eyebrows, as she began undoing the buckles on Tom's bridle.

"Annetta caught David and Chantelle!" Olivia burst out, barely able to contain herself.

"No!" exclaimed Anna, her eyes wide.

"Yes! They apparently arranged to meet at the pub in the village to run away together!"

"What? Why on earth would he do that?" Anna gaped, marvelling at David's apparent insanity. He would not only destroy his marriage, but also the respect of his clientele. And all to run off with a girl who was surely just a quick fling.

"I have no idea, but Annetta caught him leaving their house and insisted on going with him!" Olivia was hopping on the spot now.

"No way! Can you imagine what Chantelle thought when he showed up to meet her with his bags packed and his wife sitting grimly in the passenger seat?" whispered Anna.

"I know!" shrieked Olivia. "Annetta got out and gave her a right proper telling off, apparently. I'm surprised she didn't physically assault her!"

"What was David doing?"

"Sitting in the car like a child who'd been found out," answered Olivia.

Anna was stunned. This was insane; not just weak but downright cretinous. "Honestly, where did he think it was going to go?" Anna marvelled. "Three days in a Travelodge, banging each other's brains out only to find real life is knocking at the window and he no longer has his rich wife to keep him in the style to which he's accustomed and that he can't show his face anywhere ever again! Plus, really how long is Chantelle going to find him interesting? He just ruined himself," she finished, rather sadly.

Damien's uniform was sprawled across the bedroom chair where he had flung it, and he lay propped up on one elbow on the bed.

"Are you going to the New Year's do at the yard tonight?"

"That depends. What are you doing?" asked Anna, pulling at a knot in her hair, of his making.

"Well, I'd love to tell you I'll come here and we can spend all night drinking champagne and doing what we've been doing this afternoon, but Annetta told Caroline about the Rosemount party, so…" he finished inconclusively, apology in his voice.

"Okay," said Anna with a shrug.

"Sorry," he said.

"Hey, I don't expect you to take drastic action. Your situation is more complicated than mine," said Anna, knowing she was in no position to expect anything.

"I'll sort things out soon, Anna."

"Don't make promises. We are entirely wrong in what we're doing, and I know that there's a best-before date on this." He looked surprised and concerned. "Like I said, don't worry about it right now. We've been having far too much fun to actually talk about what's going on," she said.

"Too right," he said, rolling her over.

Damien threw his coat on and put his fingertips gently to either side of Anna's face, and kissed her.

"I'll catch you this evening at some point. We will talk. Do me a favour and don't make any big decisions without me. I'm worried about you. I swear we will actually see each other and talk properly. Perhaps we'd better meet in a crowded place, somewhere there's no bed," he added, kissing her again before he closed the door behind him.

Anna's smile faded fast as the door clicked shut. What they were doing felt wrong to her, and he was in denial if he thought it could go further. Slowly she climbed the stairs to make the bed and choose an outfit for the evening.

She looked at herself in her bedroom mirror, thinking. She had spent a long time alone and miserable in the latter part of her last relationship. Right now she was with a man who lit her up, over whom she had obsessed for months, and she was determined to enjoy it while she could. She hardened herself, thinking of the evening ahead, and suddenly a mischievous smile crept over her face.

"Wow, look at you, hot chick!" said Zanah as Anna strolled to the bar that evening.

"Bloody hell, Anna!" exclaimed Olivia. "You can't fail to get lucky tonight!"

Anna looked down at her figure-hugging dress and shrugged, then gave them a triumphant grin.

"I was feeling a little wicked!"

"Well, hurrah for that! I was beginning to think you were headed for a nunnery," said Olivia.

"And what about you?" asked Anna looking up and down at Zanah, who was also sporting a tight little number.

"What about me?"

"Well, are you and Lucias an item now or was it just a one-night wonder which left some of us marooned at the pub and you with a smile on your face?" asked Anna with jaunty brutality.

"You bet she's got a smile on her face! He's what, eight years younger, isn't he!" smirked Olivia.

"Nine, but who's counting?" Zanah bounced back with a grin. "Young is good…very good!"

Olivia gave a ribald laugh and Anna grinned, thinking that Lucias would be a riot in bed, given his general physical rambunctiousness and unchecked wit.

"What will it be?" came Michael's voice from the other side of the bar.

"Get her a vodka martini, Michael! She's so Bond girl!" called Olivia. Michael looked at Anna questioningly.

"Do you know what, I will! And mix one for these two as well."

She wasn't sure why, but she felt irresponsible that evening. Perhaps it was just because she'd been with Damien all afternoon, or maybe it was the thrill of being the 'other woman', knowing he would be there with his wife and constrained to watch her across the crowded room. It was a poor motive on her part, but while she was steeped in transgression she may as well live it through.

"Cheers, ladies," said Anna as they clinked glasses.

"Oh yeah, that's what I'm talking about!" Lucias was saying to Jack, as they arrived loudly on the scene. He stood before Anna, shamelessly admiring her, and put his arm round Zanah.

"You scrubbed up well tonight, Anna! You can come home with Zanah and me!"

"Hey great idea! That'll start the new year off with a bang," said Anna with an ironic grin. The others sniggered.

"What has got into you, Anna?" demanded Olivia. "You're like this whole new person! You've either taken something or you've got a secret. Which?"

"That's for me to know and you to dot dot dot," said Anna, waving her finger playfully in front of Olivia as she drew the ellipses.

"Definitely taken something," said Zanah, staring at her.

Conversation turned to the notable absentees that evening: David, Annetta and Chantelle, and Olivia relayed the story to Zanah, who listened aghast.

"How do you know what happened, anyway?" she asked.

"Pamela saw them when she was walking her dog in the village when it all kicked off, and she was telling Penelope about it in the office when I was there. Then apparently Annetta called Penelope to excuse David from work."

"Excuse him? What's happening now? Are they staying together? Is he coming back here?" asked Anna.

"No one seems to know anything else, but David hasn't been seen since," said Olivia.

"Don't tell me, Annetta's got him locked up at home," laughed Zanah. Then, assuming an air of mock gravity, she added, "Hang on, she could actually be doing anything to him. She might have murdered him and be burying the bits."

Olivia snorted with laughter and said, "I hope he thinks it was worth it!"

Anna thought again of what a mess David had made. In spite of everything, she liked him. Zanah's fevered speculations were undoubtedly over the top, but he would certainly be suffering for his stupidity.

A few minutes later Anna saw Damien's car outside, and drifted away from her group, anxious to not be right there at the door as he arrived with his wife; the blush risk was too great.

Circumnavigating the bar, she stopped for a moment to chat to Pete and Penelope who looked as comfortable and stylish together as ever. They were two people who really were on Mateus's life adventure together. Not many seemed to achieve it. With a pang of sadness Anna knew that she wouldn't have the chance at it with Damien, yet he seemed so right for her. Maybe, she thought dolefully, she just wasn't supposed to be tied to anyone, and was destined to remain forever a lonely island.

"Wow, Caroline! Great dress!" said Olivia as Damien and his wife arrived next to her at the bar. Caroline had departed from her usual classic understated style and had donned a shamelessly short scarlet dress. "Must be night of the hot little dresses. Where's Anna? She's unusually racy tonight too," remarked Olivia, looking around for her friend.

Damien fought the urge to look too and instead leaned forward to talk to Michael over the bar, but as soon as Caroline began chatting with Olivia he furtively scanned the room and found Anna immediately. She was at the other end of the bar, jaw-droppingly stunning, sharing a joke with Lucias and Jack. Her dark hair hung in loose spiralling curls which trailed, glossy and perfect, down her back and the sleek black dress clung to her body, one long shapely leg peeking tantalisingly from a discreet split in the side. He wanted her immediately and had to tear his eyes away and suppress a wry smile, half-knowing what she was up to.

Unable to resist, he glanced over again just as she looked up and their eyes met. He saw the corners of her voluptuous mouth turn up seductively and he wrenched his gaze from her, fighting himself. He looked down at the bar then back to Anna to see her hiding a small laugh behind her fingers, and he snapped his eyes back to the bar. He could not laugh right now. But he loved it.

"Caroline looks a bit slutty tonight, don't you think?" said Zanah, as she walked up beside Anna.

"Not her normal style," agreed Anna, unconcerned.

"I wonder what she's trying to prove?" pondered Zanah.

"Maybe just that she can pull off a dress like that," suggested Anna with a shrug.

"I'm not convinced she does. It's like she's trying too hard. She told Olivia it was to keep Damien's attention!"

Anna felt a stab of anxiety. Had Caroline guessed something was up? Surely Olivia wouldn't be so brazen as to feed her suspicions? Taking a breath, she gladly followed as Zanah took her arm and marched towards the door leading onto the deck, removing her from the scene.

"Come on, I need a cigarette!" Zanah asserted boisterously.

They met eyes repeatedly during the evening, but didn't speak to each other. Damien circulated from time to time as he spotted hunting friends. The heightened suspicion they felt all around them seemed to determine that they wouldn't get a moment together, and eventually Anna forced herself to not even look in his direction; she didn't want the torture of his unattainable presence any longer.

By eleven o'clock she felt the night was done. Tiredness set in and she thought about leaving.

"You can't go!" said Zanah, seeing Anna checking the clock. "You have to see the New Year in!"

Knowing she would be hounded if she left, Anna stepped out onto the deck for a moment to wake herself up.

It was clear, crisp and still, with stars shining big and bright in the blackness of the over-arching night sky. She shivered in the cold, but felt no inclination to return to the party just yet. Leaning on the rail, she drifted into a reverie, gazing in the direction of the polo field lying anonymous in the darkness under its blanket of snow. She thought about the fun she'd had out there with Dom and the others and wondered what had become of him. The shock of his disappearance had faded away, but rather than simply not being there he'd left a definite gap – for her at least. Where had he ended up? Maybe he had even left the country...

"Hey," said a quiet voice from the darkness off the edge of the deck, startling her from her reflections. Damien stood with his collar undone and jacket open, looking up at her from the deep shadow. She quickly looked around and then hopped from the side of the deck. He grabbed her hands and pulled her to him.

"I've been looking for you for ages. You're freezing!" he said between kisses.

"I felt like a break." She looked at him quizzically. "How did you get away? I thought I wouldn't see you."

"She had a migraine so I took her home."

Anna had been trying to ignore him for so long she hadn't noticed him leave.

"What, and didn't stay with her?" She frowned.

"She told me to come back. She was just going to bed and I've been on fire watching you all night."

He pushed her against the wall and ran his hands up her body, kissing her and breathing her in. Anna felt her own fire ignite and melted wantonly against him. They resurfaced and stared into each other's eyes

"I want you right now," he insisted, scanning around and then in the direction of the stables.

"I can see how that happens," said Anna, following his gaze to the site of Chantelle and David's frenzied coupling. "But *we're* not going to be caught like that."

"Let's get out of here," he said.

"We can't just disappear. That would expose us for sure," she objected, fighting her urge to just go with him.

He sighed and buried his face in her neck. "Straight after midnight, I'm driving you home," he murmured, sliding his hands slowly down her sides to her hips, pressing against her.

She felt his hand in the split of her dress then on the inside of her thigh, making her shiver with longing. He brushed his lips against hers, his breath hot, withholding his kiss until she answered. Not caring how she would explain leaving with him at midnight, she nodded and surrendered.

As the raucous midnight cheers subsided, everyone circulated to share their alcohol-enhanced love, and Anna turned from hugging Zanah straight into Damien's arms. He had a mischievous smile in his eyes, and she felt shy and acutely self-conscious with him in such a public setting, especially one that included eagle-eyed Olivia. He stole a brief kiss, and she suppressed a giggle as she tore herself from him, moving with studied nonchalance on to the next person.

The party showed no signs of slowing, and Anna felt restless, searching the crowd for Damien. Then she spotted him; he was watching her while talking to Pete, and flicked his eyes towards the door. She saw him say good night and leave, and without hesitation she began to follow, hoping she could slip away without ceremony.

"Anna! Where are you going? You can't drive!" called Zanah, catching sight of her at the door.

Thinking fast and not stopping she looked over her shoulder and said, "I'm done. I need to go home. There're too many of us to share a taxi, and Damien said he'd drop me."

"Damien?" she heard Zanah query, but Anna was closing the door behind her, knowing that the explanation would never get any easier.

The lights of his car were on already and she leapt in next to him. He smiled at her and hit the accelerator, and they took off down the curving driveway, the headlights illuminating the encasing rhododendron hedges in a blur. Steering one-handed, he reached over and slid his hand purposefully along her leg. She leaned over and unbuttoned his shirt, running her hand inside over his chest, and kissed his neck. He set his jaw and threw his head back, catching his breath.

"Easy, Anna, you know what I'm like. I'll stop right here right now."

She laughed softly and kissed him again, feeling reckless and wild.

He took his eyes from the road for a moment and kissed her back, then refocused and changed down a gear, the engine roaring as they tore round a slower vehicle. She watched his face lit by the glow of the dashboard.

"You drive like you have sex," said Anna provocatively, seeing the fiery focus in his eyes and commanding determination as he changed gear again. He looked across at her momentarily with a charged smile.

They swooped abruptly to a halt next to the church and the engine fell quiet. He kicked his seat back and reached for her, pulling her over to him, his hand in the split of her dress again, moving swiftly upwards. Anna gasped, and kissed him longingly, undoing the rest of his shirt buttons. Then they heard voices further along the street.

"Come on," said Damien, throwing his door open. Laughing, they disentangled and fumbled their way out of the car. They crossed the churchyard almost at a run, halting suddenly as he pulled her to him, his mouth on hers with starving ferocity.

His hand was on the zip of her dress as they crossed the threshold of the cottage, and he swore against her neck as he pinned her to the inside of the door like a prisoner, holding her wrists and kissing her roughly. Anna moaned, arching her back and pressing her hips to him. There wasn't a single chance of making it up the stairs and they fell to the floor, all control gone as they made up for lost time.

"I'll be back early," promised Damien as he buttoned his shirt. "You want to hit the yard for a ride?"
"I wish you could stay," pleaded Anna.
It was three in the morning, and she wanted him again. It was as if her happiness depended on his presence.
He wrapped his arms round her and held her close, his silence answering her, reinforcing their predicament. There was no way he could stay with her.

THE INEVITABLE

The frost glittered on the gravestones outside the window in the cold bright morning light, and Anna was up early. It would be chilly but glorious out there on the Downs, a wonderful way to start the brand new year. The yard would be deserted and the bridleways serene and beautiful in the fresh of the sparkling morning, and she would be blissfully alone with Damien once again. Invigorated from a shower she felt surprisingly well, given her lack of sleep. She put on her black breeches and a thick sweater and headed downstairs to make coffee. Damien's knock came five minutes later and she answered the door, surprised.

"You did mean early," she said as she put her arms round him. "Coffee?"

He held her tight and kissed her. "Definitely; I left before breakfast."

"Won't your wife start to suspect you, constantly sneaking out?" she asked, worrying that Caroline suspected something. How was he getting away with it? It was dangerous. Their cover would be blown in no time.

"She was going to ride, anyway. Obviously the migraine was fleeting," he shrugged. "She's out a lot herself. Her horses and long hours keep her away."

"What does she do?"

"Lawyer. I hardly see her when she's on a case anyway, and there have been a lot recently."

"How very convenient," commented Anna, pouring two cups of coffee. "How long have you been married?"

He squirmed a little and looked upwards, as though trying to recall.

"About three years," he answered shortly. She smiled at him.

"It's okay. I don't expect us to last, Damien. You're married, I know that. I should have kept my distance, and not got into this with you." She looked at him imploringly. "But I just couldn't."

His eyes serious, he drew close. "There was no way I could keep away from you."

He perched himself on a stool and put a hand round his coffee, looking thoughtful. "Maybe I messed up. My marriage I mean," he added. "In retrospect, it was about the stuff that Caroline came with." Seeing Anna's look of enquiry he went on, "Her family's got money, big money, and there're cars, boats, horses, planes, whatever you want…and I have had a lot of fun with it. Sounds terrible, I know." He looked at the floor. "Not sure what she saw in me. Now we don't really talk or get on. It feels all wrong, and has been more so since the summer. I had hoped we could get through it and it would fix, but we don't spend any time together. Our lives are totally separate."

Anna guessed he had been as much a trophy for Caroline as she was a status symbol for him. He would have been an irresistible hunk wrapped in an RAF uniform when they met, and probably had her and all her hoity toity-friends salivating. But had she ever connected with him in the way Anna had? Doubtful.

But despite that, Anna had to back off. There would be no fix for his ailing marriage while she was there.

She voiced her thoughts, hardly believing she was saying the words.

Damien looked straight at her, his mouth taut. "I don't want this to end."

He pulled her to him, standing up and tilting her chin up with his fingers, and kissed her fiercely.

"And I wasn't done with last night," he whispered.

"My head!" complained Zanah.

"Tell me about it," groaned Olivia.

It was just before two in the afternoon and a watery sun illuminated the yard, its already downward trajectory casting long shadows.

"Have you heard from Anna today?" asked Zanah, checking her phone. "Her car is still where it was last night."

"No. I wonder where she is? She's usually here in the morning," mused Olivia. "There's got to be something going on between her and Damien, you know. They left pretty sharpish together last night, and I note he's not here either!"

Zanah laughed. "You think? You keep coming back to that one but I really don't think so. She wanted to leave even before midnight last night, so I'm surprised she stayed as long as she did. And he wasn't drinking. There's only so much party you can take when you're one of the only sober ones! And I guess he had to get home to Caroline," she added, looking in her grooming kit for her hoof pick. "Why do you think there's something there anyway? They don't talk much."

"I saw them kiss at midnight" said Olivia, raising her eyebrows at Zanah for effect.

"So? I kissed loads of people at midnight!"

"On the lips?" scoffed Olivia.

"Really? Are you sure? I've never seen Damien kiss *his wife* on the lips!" said Zanah, surprised. "Well, I didn't see that, and let's face it, you were totally blotto by then. She's too much of a goody-goody to mess with him."

"And then he gave her a ride home," continued Olivia, building her case. "Huh, speak of the devil; here he is." Zanah turned to see Damien's car cruising into the yard. "I wonder if we might see her soon, too?" She paused to light a cigarette.

"Well, if she hasn't ridden yet today, then it would be fair to assume she'll be here shortly," said Zanah.

"What's with you? Why so eager to make this all above board?"

"I'm just trying to ensure our friends get a fair trial!" insisted Zanah.

Olivia looked at her, blowing smoke out the side of her mouth and pointing with her cigarette, about to renew the attack; but then Anna ran into the yard.

"Well, well. Here's the other one. What interesting timing!"

For appearances' sake, Anna had hopped from Damien's car part-way to Rosemount and run the remainder of the journey; to arrive in the car of her fellow accused would conclusively seal their guilt.

She stopped, hands on hips, breathing hard. She leaned forward to relieve the cramp which was taking hold in her side. Something had possessed her as she climbed the hill to Rosemount, and she had stepped up the pace, powering along, arms pumping. Now she could feel the energy coursing through her; she was light headed and her throat was burning from the cold winter air.

She had seen Olivia and Zanah across the yard, but kept her eyes on the ground and headed for the tack room. She knew she should go over, but didn't have the will to defend herself against Olivia at that moment; thumbscrews were the least she could expect.

"Hmm. Not coming over, I see," murmured Olivia.

Zanah shook her head and smiled at her. "You sound like you're working on a stakeout!"

"Honestly! Something's going on! They've arrived within minutes of each other," Olivia insisted. "And why hasn't she come over?"

"Probably avoiding your cross-examination! I know I did!"

"Precisely! Because you were guilty, and she's behaving guilty!"

"Oh, come on! Surely she's not the type!"

"Always the quiet ones who surprise you!" asserted Olivia.

"Argh! You're making my head hurt even more than the vodka. I just don't think so of Anna. God knows where she gets her thrills, but not with a married guy. She might even be into someone at work, or maybe she's gay? Maybe she has this whole London scene going on which she doesn't share. Either way it's none of our business. Unless…" Zanah paused, grinning mischievously, "You have a thing for Damien yourself?"

Olivia made a scornful noise and walked back to where her horse was tied outside his stable. She took the reins and walked him over to Damien as he crossed the yard with Barnabas. Zanah followed, suddenly sensing she might have hit on a truth.

"Hi. Want to ride out?" Olivia called to Damien.

"Sure," he answered easily. "But it'll take me a moment. Aren't you ready to go right now?"

"Yeah, but we can school for a while," said Olivia, turning towards the arena. She added over her shoulder, "And I see Anna is here, too. Just come and get us when you're both tacked up."

Zanah trailed along behind with Charlie, laughing openly at Olivia, ready to continue hounding her as soon as they were out of Damien's earshot.

Half an hour later, the four of them were riding up the hill leading to the ridge. Anna was relieved to be riding next to a passive and hung-over Zanah.

"I think I need to adopt your minimal drinking approach," she groaned.

"Well, I did have a few last night," Anna admitted, "but I can't handle drinking much these days, so I tend to be acutely aware of the need to stop!"

"Wish I did," sighed Zanah, leaning forwards and resting her head on her horse's neck. Her feet hung free of the stirrups and she slumped, rag-doll-like, aboard a very accepting Charlie as he plodded along. "I shouldn't have come riding. I feel worse for it."

They continued in silence, Anna leaving Zanah to suffer in peace while she listened to Olivia chatting with Damien in front of them.

"How's Caroline?" Olivia was asking.

"Okay. She got up early and went riding so I can only assume it was a fleeting migraine," he said with a hint of derision in his voice.

"She looked a bit pale," commented Olivia, looking at him. "I note you confined your husbandly duties to simply taking her home, before coming back to see the New Year in!"

Damien frowned defensively. "I would have stayed home. She was going to get a cab home but I drove her, then she insisted I go back. She was only going to bed anyway."

"And did you give Anna a goodbye kiss?" asked Olivia, looking round at Anna impishly.

"Would it make you happy if I said yes?" asked Damien dryly. Then he twisted in his saddle and grinned cheerfully at Anna. "It was a good one, right, Anna?"

Anna laughed, remembering the heat flaring between them as they lay nakedly entwined on the floor of the living room.

"It was electrifying," she agreed casually, looking across the valley with a smirk and admiring his change of approach: playing with Olivia rather than suffering her jibes.

The next day seemed awkward and unnatural. Getting on the train, wedging herself among hundreds of other commuters, and clattering through Battersea and across the Thames felt distinctly wrong; discordant with all that her life had been over Christmas. Anna forced herself to re-order her mind for work; recalling where they were with the process change project, she scanned the emails on her phone.

The day was long and crammed. Her brain protested as it grated up through its gears but they made good progress and by the end of the day, she and Phil were pulling all the ends of the plan together.

"Great stuff, I'll turn you into a nerd yet, Anna," remarked Phil as he scanned the screen of his laptop. "I think we're ready to go with this. Now for the training, coaching, resistance management and all that good stuff." He grinned at her. "Want to give your brain a rest and get into this tomorrow? We can't pull an all-nighter on our first day back!"

Waiting on the concourse at Victoria for her train, Anna brought up Damien's number on her phone. She wanted to know when she would see him again.

She paused, her thumb over the call button. She had never actually called him. They were after all still clandestine. She put her phone away and resolved on going to the yard straight away, hoping she would see him there.

It was around half past eight as she arrived at Rosemount. She could see Olivia's Range Rover but no other cars. Disappointment welled in her stomach. It seemed unnaturally quiet. The arena lights were off, and she presumed Olivia had ridden earlier. Seeing a light on in the office, she stepped in to find Olivia and Penelope in situ.

"Hello, Anna. Did you work late?" asked Penelope, smiling at Anna.

"Yes, too late for the first day back," said Anna wearily. "It seems quiet here this evening."

"Yes, I think everyone has gone into shock after their first day back in routine," said Penelope.

Anna battled with herself; she wanted to ask about Damien. Had he been there? But there was no way she could enquire. To her amazement, Olivia asked for her.

"Yes, but it was strange," answered Penelope, looking up from the appointment book. "He was here but he left almost immediately, and in quite a rush."

"Really?" asked Olivia, puzzled.

"Yes, it was curious. He had Barnabas tacked up and ready to go and then he un-tacked and left."

"I wonder what's happened?" said Olivia, her customary curiosity for human drama igniting.

Anna had to admit hers was too. "Maybe he was on standby or something," she suggested casually.

"Well, I saw him on the phone just as he was walking to the mounting block and he looked like he'd just got some bad news maybe," said Penelope.

"What do you mean?" asked Olivia.

"Well, he looked sort of incredulous. He stopped dead in his tracks and..." Penelope threw her hands up and her head back, evidently re-enacting Damien's body language.

"I wonder what's happened?" Olivia exclaimed, pulling out her phone.

"You're shamelessly nosey!" scolded Anna, feeling anxious as Olivia keyed a brief text and hit the 'send' button. Had they been found out? Surely she would have heard. What else could it be? She felt worry grip her insides.

"Come on! Talk!" commanded Olivia, looking at her phone.

No. He wouldn't respond, Anna's gut told her.

She arrived home just before ten and decided to go straight to bed. She held her phone in her hand before turning the light out, wondering if she should message Damien. No, she might put him in a difficult situation. He had not responded to Olivia's message before they had left and she didn't want to reach out to him only to receive the same silence. It would add hurt and rejection to the gut-crunching anxiety she was beginning to suffer.

There was no contact the next day either. Anna was distracted and grumpy, deciding she would message him in the afternoon, but not before. She wanted him to come to her, unwilling to be the pathetic clingy girlfriend. Maybe, confronted by Caroline, he had decided to cut her off, not wanting to give up all the benefits of his marriage for the sake of a deniable fling. Maybe he wouldn't respond to any message she sent.

It was 10:32am when her phone chimed and she grabbed it instantly. It was not Damien, but Mateus. Disappointment dropped like a boulder of granite to her insides. Irritation began to form; she was annoyed at Damien for his disappearance but even more annoyed at herself for being so weak, so reliant on him for her inner calm. She told herself firmly that she was an independent, powerful woman who didn't need validation from others. She had been fine before Damien and she would be fine when he was gone! She was a lone vessel and always had been.

"So you're flying out today?" asked Anna, as they sat in Starbucks sipping lattes.

"Yes, this evening," answered Mateus.

"I'll miss you. You're the only person I really talk to, about the important stuff anyway," she said honestly. The weighty cerebral issues she and Mateus wrangled over would be taboo for most people.

"I'm honoured. I'll miss you too, but I doubt I'll be gone too long." Anna cocked her head enquiringly. "No, I think I may be back home soon. I'm going to keep my eye open for a ministry here. I love the States but I won't be there forever. I realised this visit how much I miss England and my family. And my friends," he added, touching her arm.

"You've been away three years now, right?" asked Anna.

"Yes, and you're the second renter in that cottage. I was going to sell it but it worked out well when you took it."

"It really did. It felt a bit like destiny actually," said Anna, looking into the sheen on the surface of her coffee. Then she said impulsively, "Is it anything to do with what you wouldn't talk about last time?" He looked at her, saying nothing. "Where did you go? You said I had put something in motion."

"You did. And I am concerned, but I couldn't find much out," he responded in a measured tone.

"Will you tell me?"

"Like I said before, and now I'm even more convinced; you're better off not knowing," he answered cryptically.

"You're driving me a bit mad with this," she said, touching his hand for an instant. He smiled at her, but she could see he wasn't going to share. She felt concerned again; he was unlike himself. She sighed, and changed the subject. "We should talk more. Like I said, I enjoy putting the world to rights with you."

"I thought I irritated you half the time."

"Not at all. I feel peaceful when we talk. We talk about stuff you don't normally get to talk about. I just feel calm and clear, you know? The trouble is when I get back to my real life it hits me in the face like a tidal wave and I can't think straight anymore."

"Life can be like that. That is precisely the problem. I've known so many people who have profound spiritual experiences which move them deeply, convincing them of a change in direction. Then they find 'real life' flushing away all their resolve and belief, diluting the experience away, sometimes to nothing. That's why we pray and meditate; you've got to keep in touch." Anna nodded thoughtfully. "'Real life' is such a misleading expression; a contradiction. It's a paradox! 'Real life' refers to everything which is urgently in your face, but in actual fact it's the very thing keeping us from what is important. It's the anaesthetic fog which keeps us distracted and running, ensuring we ask no critical questions."

Anna gazed at him, allowing his words to bounce around her mind. Once more she felt overloaded. "It's sounding like we're stuck in the Matrix again."

Looking at the table, sipping her coffee, Anna thought about what he had said. Mateus sat back and regarded her for a moment.

"How are you feeling?" he asked.

"Confused. I feel confused by everything at the moment, everything that's going on." She didn't want to talk about Damien, afraid that the current cliff-hanger he had left her with would send her off on a petulant, angry rant.

"Take church as one example," she started, steering her thoughts away from Damien. "I have been going pretty much every week since New York and something feels different. I have more clarity and think more about life. I'm kind of a believer; I want to be, but then I am not. It all feels like crap some days, all ridiculously unbelievable. Religious language is overbearing and so much of the stuff in the Bible is communicated in these unintelligible parables, all so sexist, threatening and violent."

She broke off for a moment, feeling her chaotic frustration, then resumed more calmly.

"It's like I feel I've been touched by something, yet am constantly repelled by what surrounds it. All the formal God-talk; the praise-be's, the amen's and the need to kill my best goat…"

Mateus looked calmly at her and said simply, "Then focus on what makes sense to you, Anna."

"Then there's all the sin and punishment stuff which keeps cropping up in any church I go in," she complained, beginning to rave once more. "It's constant at the moment! I feel like I'm being told I am a sinner, to be condemned and punished forever!"

He smiled then.

"Try and think of it as *consequence*," he said, emphasising the last word meaningfully. "It's consequence, not punishment. We alienate ourselves from the embrace of God when we think of it as punishment. If you jump off the top of Canary Wharf, you'll be dead. That's consequence, nothing more complicated. Not vengeful or vindictive, just simple consequence. If you steal my car, leaving me abandoned in Wales, you may feel guilt and will suffer my anger when I get my hands on you; that's consequence."

Anna laughed, feeling lighter. "See, why doesn't any other vicar communicate like you? Church, religion would be so much more popular!"

"I know my audience, and I like the way you challenge me," he said. "I'm glad you do. You never tended to share much in the past."

"Most people would tell you I still don't."

"If you want to talk ever, make sure you call me," he said outside as they parted, throwing his jacket on and pulling her into a big hug. "Promise me! No suffering alone. And remember to meditate."

That evening Tom was standing by the gate when she arrived at Rosemount, and Anna watched with dismay as he limped next to her toward his stable. She was running her hands over his swollen knee as Zanah appeared alongside her.

"Coming hunting tomorrow?"

"I think that's out," replied Anna. "He's going to have to have a few days off by the looks of this. How annoying. Just as I needed to get out riding," she said, grumbling the last words under her breath.

Feeling grumpy again, she headed home. What was she going to do over the weekend now? As she pulled up near the church, she saw Damien's car and felt her heart accelerate. She had become increasingly convinced that he had decided to back out, but here he was.

Damien sat in the dark shadows of the church porch, elbows on his knees, hands cupping the back of his head. He got up and stepped into the moonlight as Anna approached. Anna didn't know what to say or do, just wanting to be close again. He was wearing his uniform and looked tired and worn. She paused uncertainly, seeing no smile from him, but then stepped up to him and put her arms round him.

He pulled her close and whispered, "I know I should have called you."

She looked into his eyes, frowning slightly at the trouble she saw. His eyebrows pulled together and then he moved in and kissed her.

"What's happening? What's wrong?" She was alarmed at his expression; he looked terrible. "Were you having a conversation in there?" she asked, nodding at the church.

"More an argument," he answered. Then he looked up at the sky as if uncertain where to start.

"Come inside and let's talk," said Anna.

"No. Best not. I have to work. I should have left already but I needed to see you," he said, looking at his watch and sighing. "Plus you're not going to like this."

Horror flooded through Anna, like a cold metal hand to her innards. Seeing him there had momentarily banished her fear of the end, and she was not prepared for it if he was going to do it now. But he was going to do it. He was going to break it off with her; put it all to death violently right there in the churchyard. She swallowed and fastened her eyes on his face, feeling her heart beating painfully through her entire body.

Damien looked at the ground and back at her.

"Caroline's pregnant," he said quietly.

Anna's eyes felt hot and a giant lump filled her throat. She couldn't quite believe that she and Mateus had been talking just a few hours earlier about consequences. She had known heartbreak would come, but she wasn't ready. New Year's Eve and the day following had been so electrifying; and he had told her he didn't want it to end. Now consequence had swung around and was in her face. She felt herself physically weaken.

"Well, I guess that's it, then," she said through a grating throat.

Damien looked pained, and then angry.

"Feels like punishment." His frustration rang from him in the dim and silent churchyard.

"More of a consequence," said Anna, numbly.

"What the hell does that mean?"

Anna snapped her eyes to him in shock. He'd never had a cross word for her and his retort came like a blow. He looked furious. She felt like crying but caught herself, taking refuge in anger instead.

"Do you know what, Damien? You've been gone for two days without a word. I've been going out of my mind. And now you're here with frankly the worst news you could have! What we had is done, that's it stopped dead! And on top of all that, you're swearing at me? I don't have to put up with this shit!"

Then she walked away quickly, starting to run, stifling the inevitable sob. He was on her in a flash, catching her arm and turning her round, wrapping her in his arms.

"I'm sorry, Anna; I really am. I just can't believe this is happening!"

She buried her face against him, hot tears streaming from her eyes. He turned her face to his and wiped her tears with his thumbs. He stared into her eyes, his hunger unmistakeable. She brushed her lips against his and he pulled her against him, kissing her insatiably. Pulling away reluctantly, breathlessly, he put his forehead to Anna's for a moment.

"I can't. I can't. I have to work. I'm going to be late. I'll be back next week."

He sighed and then was gone. Anna stood, not motivated to move, hearing his car roaring away.

The weekend was agony. She wished she could sleep through it rather than suffer the long hours alone with her thoughts. With Tom out of action there were only chores to do and no option of thundering through the countryside to blast her obsessive despairing thoughts away. She knew there was no hope for them. It didn't matter what Damien said when he got back. Anna now had to take the action she had known was inevitable. Consequence had caught up with her and was forcing her to face it head on.

On Sunday she sat in uncomfortable silence throughout the entire church service, praying for the pain to pass quickly.

'If you jump off the top of Canary Wharf, you'll be dead. That's consequence,' said Mateus in her head. 'If you have a relationship with a married man, you'll end up broken hearted and alone. That's consequence.'

'Feels like punishment!' shouted Damien's voice through her mind. She jumped involuntarily. Had she fallen asleep? The service was coming to an end and she got up and left quickly. Church was not the place to be that day.

She scuffled her feet as she walked along the pathway, grumpily kicking a pebble into the graveyard. It would have been nice if Damien had actually texted something in his absence. He knew he had left her devastated. Did he actually care? Had he ever told her he loved her? She huffed at herself. Why did that matter now?

But he didn't, insisted a voice within her. It was obvious he craved the sex, but was that all it was to him? Punting another pebble, she huffed. What kind of idiot was she? She was the one who had fallen head over heels for him, obsessing about him and missing him, and all the while, he was just revelling in a highly charged affair!

Irritation having given way to subdued gloom, she resorted to working on Sunday afternoon, plodding along with the training plan she and Phil had started. Monday could not come soon enough, and when it did she was out of bed at 4:42am, determined that long hours of professional formality would numb the misery.

That afternoon Martin called Anna into head office and asked her to cover a colleague's maternity leave on another project.

"I'm sorry to pull you off," he said, anxious about Anna's feelings. "But you're the obvious choice. With you and Phil almost done, he can finish up. And this project pulls directly your skill set. We just need someone who can go in and get the thing over the line ASAP."

Anna agreed passively, too apathetic to comment. From next week she would simply transfer herself to a new place, swapping the glamour of MI6 for the tedium of covering off the final stage of a rail modernisation project. It made no difference. She felt dead inside, like nothing mattered.

"Perhaps you should take a few days out?" suggested Martin, looking concerned. "You seem a bit worn down. Just get over there on Friday and Angela can brief you."

Anna headed home with every intention of sinking into a bottle of wine. As the train passed through the suburban sprawl of outer London, she stared unseeingly out of the window. The relationship which had filled her with such reckless euphoria for the last few weeks was done. In despair she realised that for a fleeting moment she had considered the possibility that Damien might leave his marriage, and they could be together. The burden of emotional destruction would have been delegated to Caroline. After all, their marriage wasn't working; it was their fault and their issue. Anna was just on the sidelines, ready to pick up the piece she wanted.

THE JAPSON CLUB

On Tuesday, with the unexpected freedom of the day off work, Anna decided on a change of scene. Hanging about at home would render her as depressed and demotivated as the previous day, and she had to feel better. Damien had not been in contact, and she didn't expect him to be. Plainly she was right, and he didn't care for her like she cared for him. Rejection gnawed at her and the apparent one-sidedness of the relationship made her angry at him.

Standing alongside the row of coastguard cottages, absorbing the view of the Seven Sisters cliffs above the beach at Cuckmere Haven, Anna felt better, lifted above the fog of debilitating depression. The stiff breeze whipped her hair out behind her, and rosied her cheeks. The white tips of the waves raced at the beach, and the constant roar of the sea, though muffled where she was standing, filled the air with coastal energy.

Down on the beach, the rock pools shimmered, reflecting the pale blue sky in their ripples. Anna wandered along the shingle, mentally anesthetised; the tornado of obsessive thought had finally exhausted itself and fallen flat, like an impetuous raging toddler who had burnt himself out.

Persuading herself that the mental quiet was a positive thing, she continued walking over the stones, stepping over rock pools as crabs scuttled for cover under the seaweed. The tide raked at the shingle on the beach as it retreated before washing forth again, further this time, reaching pebbles which had lain dry for hours and animating them with vivid character. The swell of water at the river mouth was rising fast and soon the sea would cover the pools again, filling them afresh with drifters from the vast expanse of ocean which glittered under the hard, bright sunshine. The overhang of the cliffs offered shelter from the wind and with it a still energy which was more stagnant, more aged.

She sat on a large flat rock and stared out to the horizon, breathing the salty air deep into her lungs. Maybe this was just another of life's tests. One needed to go through experiences of pain to build the next stepping stone. She felt like an old hand at separation misery, knowing the path she would trudge for the next few months. It was her own fault; she should have known better. Was there really any point in ever letting anyone in? The ecstasy seemed all too brief and served to make the pain on the other side more poignant.

She got to her feet. Meditating under the cliff was not working for her; she was spiralling downwards again. She needed to be out in the fresh breeze of the beach, a breeze which had blown uninterrupted for endless miles over the waves, and was fresh and powerful with the dance of the sea. It would blast away her confining thoughts.

Standing on the pointed bars of rock, which stood proud from the only rock pools as yet uncovered by the sea, she tipped her head back and threw out her arms, almost hoping she could fly from there, and be carried high on the current. She would spiral away and travel for miles and miles, perhaps landing in a totally foreign place, where she could start it all again.

Evening was approaching, but she wasn't ready to head home yet. She cast her eye along the cliff line and in the distance on one of the rises she could see Belle Tout lighthouse, a brave and lonely presence standing out against the expanse of heathy grass and clear sky. She remembered walking there with her mother and father when she had been young, in happy times when the only thing to worry about was whether her little brother would try and put rabbit droppings down her tee-shirt. It would be a great place to sit and enjoy the sunset.

The sun was low as Anna parked up and wandered up the grassy path of the South Downs Way, skirting along the cliff edge, appreciating the springy feel of the wiry coastal grass beneath her feet, and the old lighthouse silhouetted against the evening sky.

It was so familiar. She stopped and stared at it, thinking of past times she had been there. She saw the wall where she and her brother used to hide, and her eyes filled with tears as she thought of that era when love and acceptance had been a given. Now that happy family was just a memory, and she could feel no love, and no support; just isolation.

Anna exhaled strongly, trying to physically quash what she knew to be wallowing in self-pity. But at the same time it felt like she needed to release what felt like old stuck energy. Turning to face the sea, the ripples reflecting the pale pink and orange in the sky, she allowed the tears to roll down her face.

She wasn't sure how long she had stood there. The appearance of two gulls riding on a current of wind from the beach below, surfaced at the cliff top, and shook her from her blank reverie. She blinked, and watched them as they rose higher and circled above her head. She wiped at her eyes, eager to remove any sign of her emotional floundering, and walked closer to the lighthouse, suddenly curious as to whether anyone still lived there.

She smiled wryly as she arrived at the entrance gate and saw an agent's board; the place was for sale. Right now the idea of living in a deserted lighthouse on a cliff top, with nothing but the ever present movement of the sea, seemed fitting. The figure of a man appeared suddenly, jogging into view then slowing his pace to an easy walk, breathing hard and circling his shoulders.

"Unbelievable," she heard herself say aloud.

It was Andrew Japson. He was wearing a wetsuit, which he had unzipped so the top section hung about his waist and his only protection from the increasing chill of the evening was a wet tee-shirt.

"How is it that you are so often in the strangest places, at precisely the same time as me?" she asked him, knowing he had not noticed her.

"Blimey. Anna! What brings you here?" he asked, visibly surprised at her presence.

"Well, I am here to enjoy the sunset at the end of a very long day," she responded honestly. "And that would seem far more normal than a person soaked through, wearing a wetsuit, on a cliff top, having apparently run some distance," she concluded, summing up what she saw.

"I went for a training swim," he answered simply.

"Of course you did," she returned, cynical humour bubbling to the surface. His random appearance had miraculously halted her suffocating melancholy. "In January?"

He smiled. "I'm doing a swim across the Solent soon. I didn't go far today though. Didn't want to push it on my first time out."

She looked him up and down quizzically. He seemed to always have something going on.

"I'm a sprint swimmer usually. But a mate challenged me, and I thought, why not?"

Shivering slightly, he pushed open the gate to Belle Tout, as Anna watched somewhat incredulously.

"Come on, I'm starting to freeze now the heat of the run has worn off," he said over his shoulder as he approached the door, pulling a key from a zip pocket. "You may as well come in, now you're here."

She followed dumbly, wondering whether there was an end to his surprises.

Inside the lighthouse, it felt warm in comparison to the chill of the descending evening. Anna looked at him. The soaking tee-shirt was stretched tightly over his well-developed torso. She was astonished. His pectorals and washboard stomach were clearly outlined, as well as large rounded biceps which stretched the arms of the tee-shirt taut. His height had surprised her on the night he had accosted her in the churchyard, but she hadn't realised how ripped he was. Suddenly conscious of her own staring, she snapped her eyes away.

"Come up to the light room," said Andrew, leading the way up the stairway to the circular glass turret which had once housed the light of the old lighthouse.

"Wow," she marvelled, turning to take in the all-surrounding view; the downland falling away to the rear, and the perfectly framed evening hovering over the calming indigo waves to the front. The scenery was captured as she had never seen it before. "So is this is your place?" she questioned.

"No," he answered shortly. "Nevertheless, I have the key."

"How? Why?"

"Why is it always 'why?' with you, Anna? So many questions. The worry will drive you crazy. Just enjoy it. You wanted to see the sunset. Enjoy the bonus of seeing it from the inside of a historic lighthouse, and also in great company!" he finished smugly. Then seeing the continued question in her eyes, he added, "I know the agent, okay. Now can you enjoy it?" He pulled the tee-shirt over his head and began peeling off the wetsuit. "You may want to look away," he remarked, raising an eyebrow. "Not that I mind you looking at me in the slightest. Though it might turn me on," he added with a smirk.

Anna hastily turned her head and took in the sunset as it settled over the sea, glinting its dramatic retreat on the waves. The sparkle on the water mesmerized her. The breadth of the cliff top, sweeping out in either direction like wings made her feel like she were riding on the breast of a gigantic seabird, soaring out over the water.

The clink of glasses behind her brought her back from her astral voyage over the waves, and she turned to see Andrew appearing at the top of the stairs with an unusual bottle and two bulbous glasses.

"What's that?" she asked.

"What does it look like?" he retorted mischievously.

"It looks like aftershave," she said, observing the bottle. It was like no bottle of spirits she'd ever seen.

"It's cognac. Just very good cognac," he said, checking the front of the bottle. "Excellent, in fact. Some of the finest in the world."

Anna looked at him doubtfully for a moment, not sure how she had gone from fearing him in the darkness of the churchyard, and suspecting him of foul play all this time, to now being isolated in a deserted lighthouse with him. No one knew where she was, and it looked like they were about to get stuck into hard liquor.

She shook her head at herself. Maybe her car would be discovered days later, in the lay-by on Beachy Head road, where she had left it. She would be assumed to be just another jumper from the clifftop made famous by all the broken-hearted souls who leapt to their deaths each year, to be dashed on the rocks below. But it didn't feel like he was a murderer that evening. Plus the acute depression of the day had left her feeling reckless; reckless enough to remain a squatter in a historic landmark, drinking with a probable criminal.

"Cheers," said Andrew, handing her a glass. "A little warmer for you."

"It's yours, right? You've not raided the cellar?" she asked, looking at the golden hues of the liquid.

"Bloody hell, Anna. No. It's mine to give. Just drink," he laughed.

It was powerful as it hit her palate and she allowed it to swirl round her tongue, creating a pleasing balanced burn.

"Hennessy Ellipse," she read from the bottle. She had never heard of it. But it looked and tasted expensive.

"Woah!" exclaimed Andrew in apparent amazement. "That's warmed me up." He refilled his empty glass, and nodded at her glass.

"Thanks, but I'm going to be working on this for longer than you!"

"Don't worry. I have wine too. I just needed to kick off right. The swim left me chilly."

"Swimming in the sea in January will do that," she remarked, raising an eyebrow.

He threw himself down on the seating which encircled the now night-time observatory, gesturing to her to join him. She acquiesced, and sank onto the cushions next to him. He had lifted her mood from the emptiness of earlier, and now, apart from the curiosity he was stirring up in her, she felt decidedly devil-may-care. Just one glass of what she was drinking would render her illegal on the road, but what the hell? There was nothing calling her home and with every sip her need to care slipped further away.

Andrew was lighting a solitary tealight, which he placed on the floor, the shadows dancing around them as the little yellow flame wavered. He looked around as though judging the effect.

"Better there," he said, to himself it seemed. "Not too obvious."

"Obvious? As in you are not supposed to be here?" she assumed aloud.

He made no response, but topped up their glasses.

"You plainly intended to spend the night here," commented Anna, thinking he seemed organized.

"Yes, but I had no idea I'd have company," he said, staring at her intently. Even in the dim light, the shocking blue of his eyes was apparent in an almost unnatural sparkle. "And I'm very glad it's you."

She looked back at him and drained her glass, the burn encompassing her throat and sending an instant bubble of warmth through her.

"I'm not convinced how safe I am with you," she admitted, truth coming freely.

He smiled and reached to touch her hand for a second. "I'm not sure what I have done to worry you so."

"Well, apart from that very odd night at the church, the veil of intrigue, the strange places you turn up in, and the connections you appear to have…"

She paused, unable to formulate a satisfactory conclusion. She found him so confusing, worrying, and fascinating all at once. Everything she had seen and heard screamed, 'keep away', but the vibe he emanated seemed straightforward and magnetic. He didn't respond, but his gaze remained on her, a half smile tilting the corners of his mouth. Eventually she came straight out with it.

"What is it you're involved in?"

He exhaled briefly through his nose in the tiniest suggestion of a laugh.

"It does you better not to know, Anna." His response sombrely echoed the words of Mateus. She looked at him, somehow trying to fathom him and draw out the reality of his situation. "And you don't want to know," he insisted.

"It sounds like you know you shouldn't be involved."

"Ah, but it's never as easy as that. A deal which sails close to the wind can have you in deeper than you think, and before you know it, you're being sucked along in the current."

Her curiosity ratcheted up a notch, and she began to feel alarmed. But before she could probe again, he got up and disappeared down the stairs, returning swiftly with a bottle of Châteauneuf-du-Pape and two wine glasses.

"I'm guessing this is another tipple for a connoisseur with a far more educated palate than mine?" she said, taking the glass he handed her.

"Pah. What sets their palates so far above anyone else's? Their own egos, presumably," he retorted.

Refusing to be deflected, Anna renewed her attack. "Seriously; what is it you are into?"

"Anna!" he exclaimed softly but insistently. "*Seriously*; it is safer for you to not know." After a long pause, he leaned in and said, "You could kiss me, though."

Anna gave an exasperated huff and looked out over the now moonlit sea for a moment before turning back to face him. He smiled and clinked his glass against hers.

"I'm not going to jump you," he reassured her with a smile. "I'm actually relatively decent one-on-one".

"Did someone die that night at the church?" she asked him suddenly. His eyes widened. "I heard them through the side door. I heard the one guy saying he wanted out, and the other guy made it pretty clear it wasn't an option. Then I'm sure I heard a scuffle or a crash or something. How did they get out of the church? You locked up behind us. Was it out that side door?"

Andrew remained silent, and looked into his glass meditatively, presumably trying to formulate a defence. Then he raised his eyes and stared at her for a moment.

"You heard a lot from an empty church," he said steadily.

Plainly she was on to something but he was not going to respond. He drained his wine glass and reached for the bottle.

"How about all this stuff, then?" asked Anna, changing tack. "Why is it you seem to be into everything, the investment, the property, the polo club, the church, and the highbrow alcohol?" she added, tipping her glass at him.

"I'm an entrepreneur, Anna. I network constantly and make money work hard, and reap the benefits. I never wanted the confines of a regular job."

"You do seem to know everyone," she agreed, gesturing around them. "I guess that's how you have the keys to a heritage landmark."

"That's what I do. I live on my wits and gather people. They're all part of the Japson Club."

"The Japson Club?" Then she laughed. It seemed to typify his way of life. Everything was his for the taking. "Am I a member?"

"Of course. Everyone I know is a member, and anyone can join. I don't care if you want to provide a business resource, a biking or drinking pal, philosophical sparring, sex, or an entity for me to beat up and loathe... Whatever you offer – and I get to decide on that – I have a use for you; you're welcomed with open arms."

It seemed fitting he had appointed himself monarch of his empire, and the decider of its members' destinies. She wondered what label he had affixed to her. She gazed into his eyes, knowing he wanted her to ask, but she wasn't going to make it easy for him. He arm-wrestled her stare with his own, and then he laughed.

"You're a smart one, Anna," he smiled, stroking the back of her hand with one finger. "You're very different to anyone I've met before. A bit of a lone ranger, aren't you? I wonder if you know how strong you are?"

"Perhaps we are alike?" she reflected. "You may surround yourself with the hordes of the Japson Club, but it feels like the inner sanctum is closed to all but you. And that's where Andrew is Andrew." She had no idea where her impressions were coming from, but she voiced them nonetheless.

"Very astute," he said with a smile. "I'd say your inner sanctum is tight shut too," he observed. "Look at the crowd who follow you. None of them know anything, really. That's why they hound you. Apart from Damien. You let him in a little further, but even then you're holding back. And so you should. He's not worthy, you know."

Anna was astounded. How did he know about Damien? Her internal reaction must have shown clearly on her face as he chuckled triumphantly.

"I'm around more than you think, and I'm very observant. Don't worry," he added, laughing again at her horror, and continued, "Apart from Olivia, the other rabble don't seem to have picked up on it."

Deciding not to deny his allegations, she picked up the thread:

"What do you mean, not worthy?"

"You know," he said matter-of-factly, as he topped up their glasses. "You've worried about it yourself. You know he's not true – to anyone. He needs his adrenal buzz. You've seen it. And it's the same when he's working; he gets his kicks from the perks of being a captain, surrounded by his adoring crew. Plenty of young impressionables there to entertain him when he's away from hunting, shooting, and any other rushes he indulges in."

Anna recoiled.

"You know I'm right. That's why you look like that. Like I said; you're smart. You just didn't want to know it."

"You're doing what everyone does," she shrugged, trying to appear casual, while her insides clenched uncomfortably. Damien's silence when he was away flooded to mind once more. "It's conjecture," she insisted.

"Maybe in their cases. But I've seen it for myself," he asserted.

"How is that possible?" she retorted, impatiently.

"You know me, Anna; I get around. I travel a lot. And so does he. I've found myself in the same place at the same time as him a couple of times."

At first she felt rage. She clenched her jaw as she looked away from Andrew, out into the blackness.

Somehow she did know it. Her early impressions had been strong, although she had gratefully rejected them when Damien had singled her out and come to her bed. But their relationship had simply smothered her gut feeling, stifling rather than disproving it. Maybe he was the player she had suspected him to be on that evening of their first ride out. Perhaps that early crushing disappointment had simply prefigured everything; an internal warning she had not heeded.

Anna sighed and pushed the anger away; she knew it was pointless. Whether Damien had been faithful to her or not, it didn't change anything. He and she were over, anyway.

Andrew was looking at his phone when she turned back to him. He stood up and looked out to the road. Then he texted briefly and sat back down. Anna watched him. Something was happening. He nonchalantly topped up their glasses again and handed Anna hers.

"You're going to have me totally insensible at this rate," she sighed, thinking of how her head would feel in the morning, but with no impulse to stop. She was on a mad road, but one which she had no intention of leaving that night.

"I'd love to have you insensible, but you're a very tough nut to crack," he said seriously.

Andrew's phone lit up again and he picked it up. Then he stood and blew out the candle, instantly robbing their night-time hide-out of its soft flickering comfort, the hard moonlight taking charge of the shadows. He was looking out at the coast road. There were lights from a vehicle moving steadily along it. As they watched, the vehicle slowed and killed its lights as it turned up the small roadway to the lighthouse.

"Stay here," he said, suddenly sober and serious. Anna was alarmed. No-one drove without lights unless they didn't want to be seen.

"What's happening?" she asked.

"Nothing to worry about. Just stay here. And best to stay quiet."

"What?!" Now she was scared.

"Don't worry. No-one's coming up here."

He disappeared down the dark stairway. She ducked down lower on the cushions as the vehicle pulled into the yard. Despite the fact there was no way she would be seen, it seemed absolutely vital that she remain undetected, and hunkering down into the cushions offered some illogical yet tangible security.

After a moment she heard snatches of brief conversation in lowered voices. Then came the sound of heavy containers being moved, and grunts of effort; apparently objects were being lifted and carried from the lighthouse out to the yard. She steeled herself and raised her head, peering out into the gloom.

Andrew was in the yard, talking with a man she didn't recognise. The harsh moonlight illuminated a dark-skinned, unshaven face, curling black hair trailing over a ridged forehead and jutting brow. The thick-lipped surly mouth was moving rapidly, allowing glimpses of large snaggled teeth; every feature radiated menace and ill temper. As she watched, a third figure moved from behind the van and walked towards them, his gait slow and heavy. He was a giant of a man; massive, powerful shoulders supported gorilla-like arms, and above them a short, thick neck led up to a square, shaven head, incongruously small on that huge body. He dwarfed Andrew and the other man, who in that moment looked up to the light tower. She reflexively dropped down beneath the level of the window, knocking her chin on the sill, and biting her lip. She squirmed into the corner of the room, and sat on the floor near the top of the stairs, listening to her own heart hammering. Surely the man hadn't seen her? Then she heard voices at the bottom of the stairs and she froze and held her breath.

"That's the last of it?" came a thick, heavily-accented voice.

"Yep. We got it all," confirmed Andrew.

Then she heard a quiet ringtone. Anna's heart jolted, and she prayed it wasn't her phone. With a swell of relief she realised it couldn't be, as she heard the same man answer.

"Yes?" He paused for a moment, clearly listening to the caller. "It's clean. We're done."

There was a grunt and the sound of receding footsteps, followed by the crunch of gravel and the banging of metal doors. The sound of the van's engine could be heard, and then it was driving away. She heard the front door shut and was thankful to hear the sound of it being locked. She breathed fully once again, and looked at her hands, which were shaking.

A shadow appeared next to her, making her insides lurch afresh. Andrew, soundlessly re-entering the room, jumped, obviously not expecting her to be hunched on the floor.

"Anna! What are you doing? You scared the crap out of me!"

He sat down next to her, laughing at himself. He suddenly looked natural and easy.

"Bloody hell!" he exclaimed. Then he looked at her face, illuminated in the moonlight, and frowned. "What have you done to yourself?" he asked, touching her lip with the tip of his thumb.

"Ugh!" she exclaimed, now feeling the sting and the iron taste of her own blood on her tongue. "I bit my damn lip, ducking out of sight of your weird friends. Who are they??" she demanded.

"You're too curious for your own good. And the huge bloke is called Clive."

"Too right; he was enormous!" interrupted Anna.

"Yeah, he used to play scrum half in professional rugby until his knee quit. Christ knows the damage he did on the pitch."

"And the other?"

"He's called The Cleaner," responded Andrew, pulling her to her feet and leading her back to where they had been sitting. His hands were warm and felt strong. He refilled their wine glasses and handed one to her. "Get that down you. It looks like you need it."

"The Cleaner? He didn't look like the kind of chap I wanted to meet," she said, taking a gulp of wine.

"No. No, you wouldn't. Not either of them," he affirmed.

"So what are you doing? Smuggling stolen goods?" she asked. That was bad enough, but his warnings had seemed dramatic if they were simply thieves. There seemed something more sinister at play.

Andrew sighed and looked out at the coast road again.

"If only that were it," he responded. Then he looked back at Anna and leaned closer, his mouth close to her ear. "I told you, I can't tell you," he whispered.

She looked sideways at him. He rested his eyes on hers and put his fingers to her chin, turning her face to inspect her lip. They were inches from one another, and she could feel the warmth of him and smell the scent of his skin. He moved slowly in increments and then put his lips to hers gently, and she felt the heat of them, and the wine swirling through her head, dizzying her. Maybe it was the surreal events of the evening, the fear, and the excess of expensive alcohol swimming through her; she hardly knew why, but suddenly she wanted him.

She leaned into him, returning his kiss, and he pulled her to him. She slid her hand up his arm, feeling his biceps and then solid pectorals which pulsed with his heartbeat, rapid and hot. Impulsively she pulled up his shirt and kissed his chest, tasting the salt of the sea on his skin. He hissed and pulled at the button on her jeans, sliding his hand underneath. Anna moaned and fell back against the cushions as he bent to her again, his mouth on hers. She ran her fingers through his hair, which was thick with salt, and touched her lips to the fine stubble on his jawline as he bit at her neck. She pressed against him, feeling his hand under her shirt; burning for him now, she reached for his belt. He moved back, as though resisting, and she stared up into his eyes, which were fiercely intense; then he closed them, sighing, before looking at her once again.

"You've no idea how much I want you," he said in a low voice. Then he sighed again. "But I can't. Not now. Not while I'm…" He faltered and stopped, then took a breath. "I know me. I can't get you involved," he concluded, as though lecturing himself.

Anna sat up, feeling like she was in a dream; none of it seemed real. She put her lips to his neck, and breathed him in.

"Oh my god," she heard him mutter.

"You don't seem the type to turn women away," she said, hearing her voice, but feeling no control.

"Not really," he groaned. "But I can't get attached to you. It's… dangerous."

She sighed and slumped against his chest, as he lay back on the cushions.

"What the hell are you into?" she heard herself say.

She had no idea what time it was, but she was awakened by a movement. The smell of the cognac came to her and she opened her eyes and looked up.

"Sorry. I tried not to wake you," said Andrew, raising a full glass to his lips. She was still lying with him, her head on his chest. She sat up, and took the glass from him as he offered it.

"Andrew, I want to know," she insisted, taking a sip and handing it back to him. "What is it that's so bad?" He blinked lazily, and his eyes were glassy. Suddenly she saw the bottle. Over half the cognac was gone. He had been drinking for some time before she had woken. "So it's not just smuggling… What else? Where is the money coming from?"

"It's smuggling," he confirmed. "But more than just booze and drugs; lately anyway." His guard had gone, and now he was talking. He looked vacant, his usual spark missing. Anna stared at him, trying to clear her head, but she couldn't. What was he saying? He took another mechanical gulp of cognac.

"What's your role?" she asked.

"I launder the money," he responded without emotion.

"How?"

"Lots of ways," he shrugged staring numbly. "Usually starts at the shop."

"What shop?" she demanded. He made no response, so she tried another question. "What are they smuggling?"

He remained silent, sipping again.

"Damn, this is good," he said absently.

"What were you moving out this evening?" she badgered.

"Some high value tech gear. And about a million quids' worth of heroin." His words came lazily, and he shrugged one shoulder nonchalantly.

"You don't seem that bothered," she pressed. "What is it that has got you bothered?" He stared blankly ahead, drinking again. She waited. "What is it?" she asked, shaking his arm.

"It's the people," he whispered. "Forget the Russian brides, and the others who are on board and willingly paying; they're easy. It's the ones that don't. The ones who are being forced, the ones who are being used, the kids…" He broke off and stared into the glass, and then drained it. "That's what fucks me up."

Anna felt the horror rattle through her. She knew it went on, but not on her plane of reality. Human trafficking was talked about on the news, by politicians and journalists. It had never been an agenda item for her, and she was happy to avoid it. Faced with it as an issue which now touched her directly, her disgust was gut-churning. Trafficking was alien and barbarous – certainly the type he was referring to – the modern form of slavery. She swallowed and looked at him. He was opening the bottle again and pouring, with unseeing eyes.

"And you can't do anything about it? You can't get them arrested?" she questioned helplessly.

"No." He drank again. She squeezed his arm, urging more response from him. To her surprise, he looked at her. "You can't, Anna. It's nearly impossible. These people can just disappear."

"And you – can't you get out?"

"Nobody leaves." His response was conclusive. He sank back on the cushions, relinquishing his glass to her.

Anna felt numb again, as she saw him pass out. Now she knew. She heard his voice again in her head; 'Nobody leaves.' That must have been what she heard in the church that night. Why the church? Who else was involved? She sighed, feeling unconsciousness creeping up on her too, and laid her head down once again on his chest.

Awoken by movement again, Anna yawned through her nose and stirred, feeling Andrew pulling upwards to look over the back of the seat and out at the dawn. Her head was thick and her breath was sour. She felt him breathe on the top of her head and kiss it, before carefully extricating himself from the cushions and disappearing down the stairs.

She opened her eyes wide and forced a few deep breaths. Sitting up, she saw the dawn emerging across the water, pale and shimmering. She checked her phone for the time, but it was dead. Groaning, she sat up. She didn't feel as bad as she had thought, but suspected she was still drunk, with the hangover yet to set in.

The welcome smell of coffee arrived in the room with Andrew, as he emerged from the stairway and put a steaming mug in front of her. She gratefully sipped at it, looking at him as he stripped off the shirt he was wearing to briefly reveal his astonishing body, before pulling a clean one over his head. She guessed they wouldn't speak of the night before.

She wondered what his game plan was. He had seemed so unhappy a few hours before; he must be planning his out. He didn't seem the type to simply accept his situation if he didn't like it.

"We need to go," he said, drinking more of his coffee as he moved across the room. "I don't want to be seen leaving here." He busied himself, packing the bottles and glasses from the preceding night into a bag. Anna got up and tidied the cushions they had slept on, feeling hazy. She gulped at her coffee, willing it to straighten her out.

Out in the driveway, the fresh sea breeze brought hope of recovery. Andrew locked the door and turned to her.

"Where are you parked?"

"Down there," she said, gesturing down to the road. Then she looked at the bags he had. There was no vehicle in the yard. Was he walking with all that he had to carry? "Do you want me to drop you somewhere?" she asked.

He thought for a moment.

"Sure," he agreed. "I left the car down at Birling Gap."

They wandered down the cliff path together in silence for a time. Anna looked across at Andrew, who, while quiet, did not appear to be suffering.

"How's your head?" she enquired.

"Not the best," he answered with a faint smile. "But I can drink like that." She supposed it was to numb the pain, now she knew the truth of his dealings.

He looked at her as they arrived at her Land Rover. "Don't talk about this, Anna."

"I suspected you'd say as much," she answered resignedly, as they climbed in.

"You won't see me for a while."

It was a definite statement, like he'd made a decision of some kind, and his face was set. She knew already that he would not elaborate, so she drove without comment.

The parking area at Birling Gap was mostly empty, early as it was, and Andrew sat forward in the passenger seat as they approached the turning.

"Shit. Anna, stop!" he commanded before she could make the turn. She obeyed quickly, alarmed at his urgency. "Just let me out and go straight away."

He grabbed his bag, swearing as it momentarily jammed under the seat. He opened the door before she had even come to a full stop and leapt out, slamming it closed and not looking back as he strode away.

Feeling shaken once again, she accelerated, not looking back.

How on earth had she got herself into this? A few months back she had arrived at Rosemount, a slightly lonely but respectable young woman who barely put a foot wrong in life. Now, aside from being involved in an illicit affair with a married man, she was driving, probably drunk, away from a criminal with whom she'd been drinking most of the night – when, that is, she wasn't crawling all over him in a frenzy of lust. It made her mind spin.

Setting her teeth, she shook her head to clear it and concentrated on the road.

Up on the grassy bank, relaxing on a wooden bench in the pale light of morning, exhaling a cloud of cigarette smoke, The Cleaner watched her go.

THE CHASE

She felt benumbed again as she trudged up the path to her cottage late that afternoon. She had got herself home early, in a daze, and had fallen into the shower before going out to ride. A day's wrestling with thoughts of Andrew and the dangerous world he was embroiled in, and her despair about her feelings for Damien, had crunched her emotional gears. Too much had happened and her mind had ceased to process; resigning its usual position as chief analyst and judge, it had opted instead to be an insensate blob in her heavy head. She was weary and needed her bed. She heard the church gate open behind her, but didn't bother to turn, unable to face faking cheerfulness with any of her friendly neighbours.

There were rapid footfalls behind her, and suddenly Damien was at her side, obviously straight from his flight as he was wearing his uniform. He put his arm round her and kissed her, permeating a glimmer of warmth into her frozen soul.

"Are you okay?" he asked.

"No," she answered flatly as she opened the door. She kicked off her boots grumpily, and went to the fridge, taking out a bottle of wine which had languished there unopened for a long while. Despite her hangover, it seemed to be what she needed. She quickly wrenched it open and poured two large glasses, putting one down in front of him on the kitchen counter.

"Probably a good idea," he said, taking a swig.

Anna took a mouthful of hers and waited for him to talk.

"Are you okay? You look like you've been up all night," he said, looking her up and down. "Don't get me wrong; whatever it is, you look hot."

"Thanks," she said with a tiny smile. He had no idea how right he was.

"What a goddam mess," he sighed, obviously picking up their conversation where it had been left on Friday.

"I gather this is unplanned?" commented Anna, jaded.

"Most definitely. We hadn't discussed having kids and frankly I wasn't up for having them, not with our relationship as it is. I told you we were distant, and starting a family wasn't on my agenda right now."

"Obviously not so distant that you evaded sleeping with her," she remarked. "When is the baby due?"

"August. August sometime," he said, looking at the floor.

Anna thought for a moment, swiftly calculating. The baby must have been conceived in November. She felt strangely gratified to know that it was before she had been with him. Ridiculous of course, because he would have slept with Caroline since, even if just to maintain appearances, for the sake of the marriage. And if Andrew was right about him, he was sleeping with any number of others anyhow. She sighed and took another sip of wine.

Damien knitted his brows together, obviously struggling with his thoughts. Anna slumped forwards, her elbows on the counter top and her hands to the back of her head, and groaned.

"This is shit."

"I'm sorry. This is my fault," he sighed.

Anna shook her head, knowing she was equally to blame. She had known better than to get involved with him, but as the days of indiscretion slipped by, her own enjoyment had become the priority, diluting any guilt she had felt. And despite her doubts about him, being close to him once more persuaded her that she was still impossibly hooked.

"How on earth am I going to stop being with you?" she asked, emotion wavering in her voice.

"I don't want to stop seeing you."

She shook her head again and affirmed for herself as much as him: "No. You know you have to make it work, now. What kind of man ditches his pregnant wife and leaves her as a single parent and the child fatherless?"

It all seemed so tragically stereotypical, everyone involved now forced into a corner, consequence in their faces like a loaded gun. All because of the same passive procrastination which had caused Anna's past relationship to fail so spectacularly; it had been easier to drift unconsciously in unhappiness rather step up and face the truth. It was almost as if pain was a constant, an obligatory element; you could choose to have it early, or it would be mandatory later, presented as a final bill with tax.

Damien groaned and chugged his wine.

"Want to drown your sorrows some more?" asked Anna, downing the last of her own.

He looked at her with the faintest of smiles. "Definitely. But you know this can only go one way?"

"Won't your wife be at home waiting for you?"

"No way. She's been working on a case and told me she hasn't even bothered going home the last night or so. It's a wonder she even took a few hours out when she found she was pregnant," he said bitterly, drawing Anna close.

"How convenient," she murmured, abandoning the moral fight, unable to resist him. She was in so deep, how much worse could the pain get?

Damien was up early for the midweek hunt.

"You want to ride in the hunt today?" he asked.

"Tom has been lame, so I'm sticking with schooling him today. Maybe we can hack out tomorrow if you're here," she suggested.

It seemed almost as if they were back to where they were before; she felt happy and replete for the first time in days. Obviously she had to sever their relationship at some point, but it could wait; for now it was enough that they had at last spent a whole night together.

She thought back to her night with Andrew, the discomfort of guilt now sweeping over her. What had she been thinking? Firmly reminding herself that she had been recklessly drunk and emotional, she pushed remorse away.

Anna had been in the arena with Tom for over half an hour, pleased to find him pacing well and back to normal, though excited after his days off.

"He's going well," said a voice Anna hadn't heard for a while; she turned in surprise. David was leaning casually against the wall near the entrance.

"David, I haven't seen you for ages!" she exclaimed. She realised immediately she probably shouldn't have commented on his absence, in case he felt under pressure to explain himself, but he simply shrugged.

"I took some time out."

"Have you got a lesson?" asked Anna, walking Tom to the gate and sliding from the saddle.

"Yes. Pamela, now her leg has mended," he said gesturing over his shoulder. "How's the hunting?"

"Tom's been lame so I haven't hunted since I rode with you. Thank you for that; you had an impact on my ride that day."

"My pleasure. We should ride together again," said David as he opened the gate for her.

They chatted for a while, him rubbing Tom's head from time to time.

Hooves crossed the yard and they both looked over to see Damien and Annetta riding towards them. To her amusement, Anna noted hard stares on both of them; Damien's projected at David and Annetta's pointed at herself. She thought she saw the most fleeting of satisfied grins flash across David's face.

"Good hunting?" he asked them.

"Yes thank you, darling," said Annetta with an edge to her voice. "Have you had a lesson, Anna?"

"I was just watching her school Tom," said David mildly.

"Well, I'm going to un-tack," said Anna, her own agony of the last few days leaving her wryly amused at the politics. Wretchedness had left her seasoned and experienced, qualified to laugh cynically at misery.

"What's David up to?" asked Damien, walking beside Anna as she led Tom to the field to turn him out.

"What do you mean?" she asked.

"You're so innocent, Anna," he said with a smile. "He has a way of looking at you."

"I don't think so. And if he does he's probably just trying to annoy Annetta in the only way he can."

"He certainly did that!" laughed Damien. "I hear he's a bit whipped at home."

"Well, you don't need to worry about me. I've learnt my lesson. No more messing around with people at the yard, especially married ones, they're off the menu."

Damien gave her a playful nudge.

She marvelled at how quickly and powerfully emotions ebbed and flowed. One minute depression was at high tide, surrounding her with the threat of drowning, and the next levity returned, sun umbrellas were up on the beach, and she was enjoying paddling in calm shallow waters again. Maybe she was becoming mentally unbalanced?

Thursday was cold and bright. Everything in the churchyard was washed with a pale light, and the pathway and gravestones sparkled with frost. A chill breeze freshened the air and Anna looked up at the glimmering weather vane at the top of the church spire as it turned, reflecting the sunshine. She had slept well and felt more refreshed than she had in days. With Tom sound again, she was looking forward to hacking out with Damien.

The midweek crowd wandered the yard that morning, taking their time as they chatted and groomed their horses. Penelope and Annetta were riding towards the gate as Anna and Damien were leaving, mounted on Tom and Barney. They all plodded down the driveway together, Anna hoping that they were going to be riding off in different directions once they reached the road.

"I meant to ask you yesterday, Annetta," said Damien, sounding as if he begrudged having to make conversation, "When did you move your boy here?" gesturing at her hunter.

"Just after Christmas. I did have him at home, but I wanted to keep an eye on David," she said blatantly, in a hard tone.

There wasn't much anyone could say in response so they rode on in silence. Anna assumed she was under suspicion too, given the look Annetta had fired at her the previous day.

"We'll join you", announced Annetta, as they all reached the road and she saw Damien turn for the bridleway. Anna bristled inwardly; she really wanted to be alone with Damien, especially if their days were numbered. "Congratulations, by the way," Annetta went on, turning to look meaningfully at Damien. "I bumped into Caroline yesterday."

Obviously surprised, Damien widened his eyes.

"She *told* you? It's rather early to be telling people," he said uncomfortably. He looked to the sky momentarily and Anna could tell he was annoyed.

"Caroline's pregnant?" asked Penelope in a rapturous voice, putting two and two together. Damien nodded. "That's marvellous! But don't worry, I won't say anything" she added.

Anna rode along in silence. She guessed she should have played along with the charade and congratulated him herself for the sake of the others but the thought of being so false repulsed her. Gloom began to descend on her once again.

Conversation was driven by Penelope and Annetta as they ambled along the bridleway, and turned to babies and pregnancy. Anna felt stroppy with Annetta. She got an unpleasant vibe from her and felt drawn to understanding David's recent mutiny. It seemed wrong and insensitive that she had said anything to Damien, particularly in front of others; moreover, in doing so she had effortlessly brought about a return of Anna's depression. Damien too had sunk into a sulky silence, only partially participating in conversation, responding only when he had no option but to do so. Their afternoon was destroyed and the momentary rays of happiness she had felt were again obscured by the depressing shadow of the ticking clock which loomed over them.

She glowered unseeingly at the hedgerow, as Penelope gushed.

"It's going to be so exciting for you! Honestly, you can't know until you actually have them there in your life. I find my niece and nephew are such an amazing delight to be around."

Her words grated on Anna and pulled her dour mood around her like a blanket. This was just the beginning. It was only going to get more and more painful. If she stayed at Rosemount she would be the pathetic heart-torn has-been, witness to the unfolding domestic bliss, lying like a doormat unnoticed and dirtied by the unconscious passage of others' celebratory feet. He would become wrapped in it, washed away from her, until one day he would wonder what he ever saw in her. This was it; tomorrow she would go to the office and ask Martin about the most far-flung assignments. Gibraltar, Hong Kong, New York, the North Pole, she didn't care.

She fixed her eyes on the pommel of her saddle and pulled Tom to a halt. He tossed his head and skipped sideways, unwilling to leave the group.

"Are you okay, Anna?" asked Penelope, noticing her having fallen back. The rest of the group halted and turned to look at her.

Anna felt a familiar lump in her throat and gulped angrily. She willed herself to talk but didn't have the words. It felt like she was in a vacuum. Finally she managed to work her mouth and let any thought come.

"I'm done here," she said shortly, to surprised eyes. "I'll... I'm going back." With that she turned and kicked Tom up to trot, then canter. She could see the path which led to the top of the ridge, curving up through the woods, and she urged Tom faster.

Damien stared at the empty space she left on the path. Everything inside willed him to give chase, but how would that look to Penelope and Annetta? Suddenly he didn't care; they didn't matter and he had to talk to Anna. He kicked Barnabas and turned him swiftly.

"Damien!" called Penelope in alarm, starting to turn too.

"Don't follow me!" he shouted over his shoulder and spurred Barnabas on up the hill, pounding after the departing Tom.

"What on earth...? Something's wrong," said Penelope, completely confused.

"I knew it. Something's going on there. That girl has them all going," said Annetta with grim certainty, watching the waving branches pushed aside by Barnabas as he had spun on the path, the only sign left of him or Damien.

Free of the group, Tom was getting into his stride and cantered powerfully up the hill, leaping tree roots with agility. Anna, tears now streaming from her eyes, thought she heard a shout and glanced quickly behind her down the hill. She spotted Damien at the bottom, up in his stirrups as he charged Barnabas at a frightening pace. Shocked at his following her, she urged Tom on. There was nothing to talk about and maybe it would be better to never see him again; let this maniacal charge be the end of it all. She could disappear in the small hours, just the way Dom had. She saw the bridleway open out to the beginning of the flat and called to Tom to fly, and he did. Her breath left her as he flattened, faster than ever, his lightning speed carrying her away.

Reaching the top of the bridleway Damien fixed his eye on the fleeing forms, already hopelessly distant. He looked around desperately, knowing he couldn't match their pace, trying to think of a way to cut her off. Deciding fast, he swerved off the gallop, taking a gamble on Anna's direction. He would have to play to his own strengths if he was going to catch her.

Tensing his jaw, he steered Barnabas across the bridle path and headlong into the woods. There was no path and the ground was uneven. He felt time slipping away as he wound and ducked under branches to where the trees ceased and a sheer hillside dived downhill into open land.

"Easy, Barney," he said, slowing Barnabas, who checked his stride and bent his neck to look at the challenge plunging away before him. Not pausing at the head of the drop, Damien put his leg to Barnabas's side and they slid and slithered downwards. With his weight balanced above the haphazard movement of Barnabas beneath him on the steep uneven hillside, Damien rose in his stirrups, trying to track Anna from the high vantage point. Then he saw her, a swift form flashing between breaks of hedgerow further down the valley.

"Come on Barney, we can get them!" he said, urging him on.

Anna slowed as she turned from the gallop, taking a narrow path which led down into the valley. Tom was breathing strongly from their blistering bolt. He needed to cool. Hell, no-one could catch them anyway, and they were off the beaten path.

They walked for a time, coming to a gateway which led to a large field, curving away over a hill with woods and a hedge along the top side of it. As the gate swung shut behind her Anna stopped, listening. Had she heard something? Feeling pursued once again, she kicked Tom to canter, and then gallop. The grass blurred beneath them and the wind blew in her face.

Damien joined a footpath and followed it for a time, searching the vista for Anna. He knew she was further down the valley and couldn't lose her for long or the trail would go cold. Looking ahead he saw a narrow stile blocking his way and beyond it the path began curving away uphill.

Swiftly he threw a glance around for a way out. To his right a five-barred gate in the hedge led to a field, but it was chained and padlocked to a post. Cursing, he swung Barnabas around and urged him back up the track a little way before turning him again and kicking him hard. There was hardly any run-up and his heart was in his mouth as he drove with his legs and collected Barnabas up, willing him upwards as they exploded from the ground. The horse's massive form propelled athletically, hind legs flexing and then tucking. Damien looked along Barney's neck at his tall pricked ears as he stretched forward, hearing the light clang of a hoof clipping the top bar of the gate, but they cleared it and landed powerfully on the other side.

"Good lad!" he murmured to Barnabas, as they immediately surged forward again towards a copse which banked the fields further down.

Anna guided Tom up the shoulder of the field near to the hedge, trying to see a route down. In her turmoil, she had taken a wrong turn and was now in unchartered territory, and feeling lost. She had to get back to the yard and get out of there. At that moment there was a crashing of undergrowth and branches, and just ahead of her Barnabas exploded over the top of the hedge from the woods, causing both her and Tom to leap in horror. Tom veered sharply away from the hedge and stopped dead to stare at whatever had just arrived on the scene, then he threw his head and bucked, as he took off again. Anna felt herself coming loose and falling sideways, grabbing Tom's mane to pull herself back into the saddle.

"Anna!" shouted Damien, leaning backwards on his long descent from the top of the hedge. Barnabas landed on the soft ground and regained the chase with the force of a hurricane. Tom was off-balance as Anna righted herself, and seeing his opportunity Damien leaned out, reaching for her rein.

"No!" screamed Anna.

"Stop now! Anna!" he pleaded, grasping her wrist. Anna felt her determination to escape lessen at his touch, and she took a breath as they slowed.

"Why didn't you just let me go?" she shouted. "There's no point! None of this is going to work! I'm going! I'm taking Tom, I'm getting a project overseas and I'm going!"

"Hold on, calm down!" urged Damien as their horses turned in a circle together.

"No, what's the point? If I stay here I live in pain, a pathetic depressed loser! I used to be cool and carefree and now I'm an obsessed wreck," Anna raged. "You're not going to be interested in me. You think you are but once your baby comes along that'll be it, and that's fair enough, but I have to go!"

Damien, holding her rein forcefully now, brought them both to a stop and put his hand to her shoulder, grasping it firmly. Both horses were soaked and breathing hard.

"Anna!" he implored her. "Listen! It's not mine!" he shouted.

She stopped, taking a sharp intake of breath; did she hear right? She was shaking, her heart pounded and new tears sprung to her eyes.

"What?" she stuttered in confusion and shock. She was utterly spent and felt faintness sweep over her. He looked at her insistently and keeping his eyes on hers and his hand on her rein, he dismounted and reached up to her, urging her from her saddle. She slithered down from the back of Tom with no fight, collapsing against him in exhaustion.

Seeing a log close by, he guided Anna and the two steaming horses towards it. He pulled Anna down to sit on the log with him.

"I'm sorry I didn't tell you earlier," he said. "I was trying to get out of the yard quickly, just the two of us, to tell you then."

"Not yours," repeated Anna mechanically, her hands still shaking. He swung his leg over the log to sit astride it, facing her, and took her hands in his.

"I sat there for ages last night with my old rosters and the calendar. I even used one of those online conception date things. There's no way it's mine!" Anna looked at him with uncertain eyes. "I can't believe

I missed it before. I guess I didn't even think about it in the shock of hearing about becoming a father."

"Doctors' dates aren't exact," said Anna doubtfully.

"Even allowing for a margin of error, it can't be mine." He looked into her eyes.

"You seem so sure," said Anna, searching his face.

"I am. It was allegedly around the time of your first hunt; you remember?"

Anna nodded, recalling the adrenalin-fuelled day and the unfortunate and horrific grand finale to the evening, with James.

"I was away a lot in the two weeks before and Caroline was at the stables all the time, training for whatever competition it was. We simply weren't home together, not awake anyway."

"So you're saying, she's having an affair?" faltered Anna. He exhaled briefly through his nose.

"Ironic, isn't it," he said flatly.

"I feel kind of ecstatic and sorry at the same time but I can't move," Anna said faintly, as she watched their horses snuffling through the dead leaves searching out the uninspiring winter grass.

"I'm just glad we're all still alive," he said with a small laugh, shaking his head as he recalled the hair-raising obstacles he had tackled to reach her. "That was quite a dash, Anna. I've never hunted anything so hard!"

"Where did you come from?" she asked, looking back up the field.

"Up there," he gestured. "From the steepest face, through the woods and over the biggest things I could find!" He rose to his feet and took her hands, pulling her up too. "Let's get these chaps home."

Mounted once again, Anna looked up at the hedge over which Damien had erupted into the field.

"There's no earthly way that hedge should be jumped," she said, as they ambled back the way she had come.

He looked up at it and agreed, remembering his alarm as he had crested it and seen the drop yawning beneath him.

The stable yard was quiet. A solitary rider was tacking up a rounded bay cob down the far end of the nearest stable block, but thankfully there was no sign of Annetta or Penelope.

"Looks like we're alone. Let's get un-tacked and out of here," said Damien in a low voice.

Anna nodded and rode Tom to his stable.

"Your place," commanded Damien, pointing at her as they walked across the yard to leave.

Back in the village, her legs felt weak as she climbed from her Land Rover.

"Pub," said Damien, appearing next to her and putting his arm about her. Hugging him, she obediently fell in step alongside in the afternoon sunshine. "We both definitely need a beer," he added.

"Definitely," agreed Anna, feeling the glimmerings of muscle pain beginning. The prolonged dash had been hugely physical, and coupled with the emotional tsunami she felt weary through and through. "How are your muscles?" she asked.

He smiled. "Yeah, I can tell I'll be feeling it tomorrow. I can't actually believe some of the things I made Barney do."

"Certainly testament to his fitness," she said.

"And bravery," he added, nodding. "He's a good man."

The landlord greeted them as they both gratefully took a seat at the bar.

"You look like people in need of refreshment," he said cheerfully. "What's it to be? I've got January Jack Frost on tap, if you want the ale of the moment."

"Sounds good," said Damien. "Anna?"

"Make that two," she answered.

"You been riding?" asked Jack, holding a glass to the beer tap.

"Yes. Bit of a high-speed cross-country pursuit," said Damien grinning.

"Yeah? Who won?"

"Kind of a dead heat," said Anna, looking at Damien. "I trump him on speed."

"And I trump her on stamina and balls of steel," added Damien, to which Jack chuckled.

"I still can't believe you jumped that hedge!" laughed Anna as Jack put their beers on the bar and took the money from Damien.

"Yes, that and the vertical hillside and the five-bar gate with a ten foot run-up; they all had me a tad concerned," said Damien with a grin, clinking her glass with his. Anna gaped.

"What? You didn't?!"

She paused for a mouthful of beer before prompting him to recount his adventure, listening dumbfounded. He was the boldest rider she had ever met and she couldn't believe he had chased her so determinedly. She looked down, feeling bad for putting him through it all, just as he had discovered his wife's unfaithfulness. She thought of her evening in the lighthouse with Andrew and felt another pang of guilt.

Damien was watching her, head cocked to one side.

"I'm sorry about Caroline." The pathetic irony made her words feel meaningless.

"I can't be devastated. I'd be a hypocrite if I was. I should have realised. There have been an unrealistic number of cases, working late and horse duties. I guess it worked out conveniently for me and I didn't give it much thought," he reflected.

He was silent for a moment, and then said in a harder tone, "I could have done without thinking I was going to be a father. Why did she do that?"

Anna couldn't answer. Maybe Caroline was covering for a while, making her mind up about who she wanted to be with. Maybe the baby was the result of a fling.

Silence hung in the air until Damien looked at her and said, "I don't really feel like being in that house right now. Do you mind if I stay with you for a couple of days?"

"Absolutely you can stay with me," she agreed, taking his hand. "I wonder how long it's been going on?" she pondered, suddenly concerned about him.

"Hmm. Don't know. I'm sure to find out soon enough. Right now I'm worried about you," he said, fixing his gaze on her.

"Why?"

"You've proven to be a flight risk. I'm worried you're going to go off on your own, do more thinking, and disappear again."

"I won't. I have no idea what Penelope and Annetta thought, though."

"Yes," said Damien, grimacing and scratching his head. "I'm pretty sure rumours will be flying now."

"Sorry," she said, feeling terrible for her outburst. He shrugged and checked his watch.

"Right, I need to fetch some things, and you're coming with me."

NEW BEGINNINGS

Anna was stunned as they turned in through the towering gateposts of Damien's driveway. The house was enormous; a rambling square-edged pile of opulent Edwardiana. Creeper climbed up one side, skirting an acre of rich red brickwork and reaching up to one of the innumerable dormer windows, giving it the look of a property contentedly rooted in its spot. She hadn't thought much about where he lived, neglecting to consider the wealth to which he had alluded.

Plainly money – and obviously there was plenty of it – didn't buy happiness in marriage, she thought as she stared at the house in disbelief. Looking to the side, she saw perfect stripes mown into the immaculate lawn, and a straight path lined neatly with low box hedges that lent a classic formality as it guided the visitor to the large imposing front door. Brick pillars divided the gravel driveway from the edge of the gardens, the winter stalks of aged roses clambering leggily around them.

Damien pulled up and jumped out. Anna followed him along the edge of the house to a back door which opened off a large stone patio overlooking a kitchen garden, where herbs and lavender lay twiggy and dormant until spring.

The back door opened onto an enormous kitchen which would have sat comfortably on the pages of any glossy lifestyle magazine, its shiny granite counter tops perfect and spotless, and the obviously bespoke cabinetry mellow and dignified, with ornate handles.

Damien headed off through the kitchen door and out into an expansive double-height hallway, where a broad and solid staircase rose to the next floor, passing through a right angle, to meet a gallery hemming the upper level. Anna stood, turning in the centre of the space, taking in her surroundings. Artwork hung on the walls; various classic scenes of riders in hunting pink leaping hedges after packs of hounds across the unmistakable roll of the English countryside under leaden skies. There were also old portraits of bemedalled military figures with swords at their sides.

"You must feel positively cramped at my place," said Anna, in wonder. She had had no idea of the grandeur to which he was accustomed.

He was part way up the staircase and threw his eye swiftly about the hallway without emotion.

"Family money, like I told you."

Anna felt awkward about following him but nervous standing where she was; what if Caroline suddenly walked through the door? She didn't have long to fret as Damien soon reappeared at the head of the stairs carrying a large overnight holdall and a flight bag on wheels. He took the stairs in the manner of someone accustomed to rushing down them on a daily basis, unconscious of the splendour.

He looked at Anna, who was still gazing around. Then he dropped his bags and put his arms round her, kissing her passionately. Her awkwardness at being there melted away in an instant and she relaxed into his embrace, feeling the temperature rise. They parted and grinned at each other.

"Let's pick this up later. Best not here." He picked up his bags once again as she watched him.

"Not while you may yet come out of this almost squeaky clean," she remarked, winking and kissing him again, provoking him to drop his bags for a second time.

"No, no. We need to go. This is getting way too hot as usual!" he breathed, squeezing her.

A chocolate Labrador bounded at Damien as he closed the back door, and he bent to greet it affectionately.

"Hello, Dylan!" he said, rubbing the dog's head. Then he looked up as a wiry, resilient-looking old man wearing a flat cap and carrying tools stepped up onto the patio. "Hello, Bob. I see you've been keeping Dylan entertained."

"Yes, he enjoys padding with me. I didn't know you were around. It's been quiet here lately. Is your good lady working?" answered Bob, stopping and smiling at Damien, then bending to pat Dylan.

"Apparently so," said Damien, looking quickly at Anna. "I'm just making a flying visit. I'll be working again for a few days."

"Right ho. When you're back, I'll talk to you about the work you wanted done in the outhouse."

"Yes, sure," said Damien quickly. "Listen, I've got to dash now."

"Alright. See you anon," said Bob, touching the peak of his cap to acknowledge Anna, before moving off.

"Gardener?" asked Anna.

"Gardener, handyman, dog walker – well, Dylan practically lives with him, rather than us," said Damien. "Gotta have a guy like that at a place like this. It's full-time. It'd fall apart without the likes of him."

"Maybe you're more accustomed to your lifestyle than you think. You sound like a landowner, a lord of the manor if you will," laughed Anna, assessing him with a fond yet satirical eye. "What work was he talking about?"

"Just a couple of things I was doing to the party pad," he responded briefly, appearing uninterested in the subject.

Anna left it. It didn't matter. The revelations of the day seemed to have decriminalised their relationship, and it felt like he was all hers; a status she had never really bargained for.

Anna was up early for work, keen to get her day done and be back home with Damien as soon as she could. It was dark outside and she was rushing to get out of the house for the 6:20am train.

"I don't know if you're going to get out the door this morning," said Damien, hugging Anna from behind as she reached for her coat.

"Why?" asked Anna, turning and kissing him.

"Look at you!" he said, running his hands down her sides and taking her in, head to toe.

"You seem to have a thing for business attire," she laughed.

"*You* in business attire maybe. I'm not the sort of chap to pursue big-bottomed businessmen down Regent Street, though."

Anna laughed, raising her eyebrows.

"This coming from a man who works in the profession that owns sexy-at-work uniforms!" she protested. "I wish I'd seen you in your military flight suit, or whatever you call the Top Gun look!"

"Ah yes, used many a time to great effect in the target-rich environment of an overseas bar. I'm sure I can dig it out," he grinned, pouring coffee.

"It's statements like that which give people the impression you're a cad!" laughed Anna. "What are you up to today, anyway?"

"I'm going to see if Barney is sound after all you put him through yesterday," he said with a smile. "I'll check Tom, too."

"I can't believe that was just yesterday. A lot seems to have happened. When are you working next?" she asked him.

"Sunday. You want to hunt Saturday?"

"Why not," agreed Anna, hugging him.

"Well, if David's after you, that would be a good reason not to."

"Ride with me then," Anna suggested, shaking her head.

"I would but in George's absence I said I'd whip-in."

"What is this obsession people seem to have about David being after me anyway? You should have seen the look Annetta gave me yesterday."

"You just don't see it, do you?" he said, kissing her. "Anyway, Annetta can be a vindictive bitch. Don't take it personally."

"Yes, I'm not mad about facing anyone at the yard at the moment, given what she's probably been saying about me after yesterday."

"Just enjoy the game and keep them guessing."

"Is that what you do?" Anna challenged, thinking of his detached manner at Rosemount. Then seeing the time, she pulled on her coat. "Gotta go."

He drew her to him by her scarf and kissed her with deliberation.

"You know, chasing you yesterday was quite a buzz now I think about it," he said looking at her with sultry eyes, moving in on her with more fire.

"Now I really have to go," she said, reluctantly pulling away, wanting to stay and be carried off in the raw heat of his storm. He grinned and released her.

Anna's smile stayed with her. She felt a warm glow surrounding her, detaching her from the gravity of her fellow passengers, all reading newspapers or scrolling through emails on their phones, frowning and fretting about bad news or the workload of the day. Anna was dancing above it all, unable to focus on her book or hold a solid thought, as the train carried her on its single-minded charge into London. She thought of Damien over the months she had known him: the detached and mysterious stranger she had first met; his eyes in the candlelight; racing him at gallop over the downs; their first kiss on the raging night of the storm; the unforgettable heat of Christmas Eve; and the fiery lover she had left at her door. It had been a crazy rollercoaster plunging through every extreme emotion she could think of.

Reality seeped back as the train clattered metallically over the bridge crossing the Thames, and she looked down at the grey waves jostling a group of Canada geese dabbling on its surface. A large herring gull sat preening on a post, bringing her thoughts back to the cliff edge at Belle Tout.

The night with Andrew in the lighthouse was a bizarre and fuzzy memory. What had happened to him afterwards, and why he had sent her off so abruptly? She thought of what he had said about Damien; he must have been wrong, or at least, even if it were true in the past, it could not be true now. Damien was free, and he wanted to be with her, a thought which made her tingle. For a moment she felt guilty about her wantonness with Andrew, but dismissed it; not only had she believed she was single, but depression and almost senseless drunkenness had had her out of control that night.

Damien had Barnabas and Tom tied side by side outside his stable and was running his hands down Tom's right foreleg when Penelope crossed the yard.

"Damien! I didn't see you or Anna again yesterday. Was everything okay?" she asked as she approached, concern in her voice. Damien looked up momentarily as he lifted Tom's hoof.

"Yes. She just had a bit on her mind," he said casually.

"Is he okay?" asked Penelope, looking at Tom. She was curious to know more, hearing Annetta's suspicions ringing through her thoughts. She knew Damien caught the eye of most women on the yard but he was always so reserved. And Anna certainly didn't seem the type; in fact they were similar in a way, she thought; maybe they got on well because of it.

"He's alright. Probably a bit stiff; he had quite a run," Damien answered, straightening up and patting Tom, who put his nose to Damien's head and sniffed him.

"You caught her, then?" asked Penelope.

"After a while – and a few obstacles," added Damien with a wistful grin.

"We were wondering what on earth was wrong," said Annetta pointedly, who had drifted up to them unnoticed. "She looked almost unhinged."

Damien said nothing but just leant against the stable door, stroking Barnabas's nose. If he was rattled he didn't show it.

"I'd better get on," said Penelope, sensing Damien shutting down. Annetta had a way of irritating people, and she didn't wish to be party to it.

As Penelope walked away towards the office, Annetta watched her go and then stepped closer to Damien, looking at him keenly.

"Is there something going on?" she asked.

Damien's face hardened and he met her stare.

"What do you mean?" His voice was stony. She might have her husband whipped but she wasn't going to come close to thinking she could push him around.

"There's obviously something between you. She seems to have a few of the men round here in a tailspin," she said contemptuously.

Swallowing his anger, he said nothing and took a step back towards Tom to continue checking his legs. He was not going to rise to her bait. What a bitch!

"I was worried, Damien," she went on sternly.

Her abrasive tone nagged at him. How did she have the nerve to keep on at him? No wonder her husband wanted out. He felt like knocking her down himself. And she wasn't finished; there was more to come! The woman was relentless.

"Caroline's a friend and she's pregnant, and I don't want to see her hurt," finished Annetta accusingly.

Damien stopped and smiled at the ground. It was time to shut this woman up. Seriously, who the hell did she think she was?

He straightened up and stepped close to her, close enough to detect the faint hint of Chanel and see the heightened flush spread over her cheeks at the physical confrontation. He looked down into her eyes from his commanding height, and said softly, "I know you're on scoundrel alert right now because of David, but I don't think you know Caroline or her situation very well. And you need to back off," he concluded, emphasising the last words with a flicker of menace.

Surprise and anger flitted across Annetta's features as she gazed up at him. Damien turned back to Tom, deliberately and dismissively.

Annetta moved away, glancing back at him, perturbed. Obviously, given the gossipmongers on the yard, everyone knew about David's indiscretion, but Damien's shoving it under her nose was unnerving. She couldn't believe she had allowed him to get away with talking to her like that. There was obviously something going on and she wasn't going to let him intimidate her into silence. Was there any man who could be trusted?

Returning from putting the horses out, Damien saw Pete and strolled over to him.

"Ridden today, Damien?" asked Pete, watching as Chantelle's horse was loaded into a trailer behind her father's Land Rover.

"No, I'm giving him the day off," said Damien, turning to watch too.

"Poor Chantelle," said Penelope, joining them. Pete sniggered.

"She's leaving us?" asked Damien, knowing very well the reason why.

"Yes. Hasn't shown her face here since…well, all the stuff that happened," said Pete. "That's her cousin apparently," he said, nodding at the girl who was now closing up the trailer.

"I heard about it," said Damien.

"I think everyone has," answered Pete.

"I haven't said anything," said Penelope, mortified.

"Yes, but Olivia overheard Pamela telling you and you know how discreet she is," said Damien diplomatically.

"Her father was none too happy with David," Pete said. "And I'm not surprised."

"I don't think it helped that he found incriminating evidence of illicit activity in the middle of his mahogany dining table," laughed Damien, feeling a little rowdy and triumphant after shutting Annetta down, and exuberant at the thought of seeing Anna again in a few hours.

Pete did a double-take at Damien and guffawed. "What?" he exclaimed.

"Damien! Pete!" cried Penelope in horror.

"It's true. I was hunting with her father on Wednesday and he was banging on about his disgust at finding a damning impression on his highly polished table," Damien explained, grinning mischievously at Penelope's consternation.

Pete doubled over, laughing raucously.

"Pete, honestly!" exclaimed Penelope, batting at his arm. Pete regained some modicum of composure and grinned at his wife.

"Honestly Penel, you're so sweet and innocent. You look like you're about to make the sign of the cross in front of you!"

Damien snorted with laughter, setting Pete off again. Penelope gaped at them.

"You hunting men are all the same! I dread to think of some of the conversations you have!" she exclaimed, appalled.

"You've got to be kidding me!" Anna said to herself, stopping dead in her tracks as she crossed the office with Angela, whose maternity leave she would be covering.

There was no mistaking the man ambling towards her, wearing the same horrible grey rumpled suit he always wore; it was Greg, her bête noir from last year's job.

"You're taking over from what's-her-face here?" he exclaimed as he reached them.

Anna shook her head and smiled wearily. She had felt secure that he was consigned to history, but here he was again like a very bad penny.

"'What's-her-face'?" repeated Angela. "Honestly, Greg, you are unutterably rude!"

"I see nothing changes," said Anna dryly, regarding Greg. "Yes, to answer your question, and I'm praying we won't be working closely."

He gave her a watery smile. "Good, let's use this meeting room." Then he turned and wandered through the door of the closest room.

"I'm so happy to be leaving him!" said Angela ecstatically, following Greg to the meeting room nevertheless.

"Don't over-celebrate," urged Anna. "I honestly thought I would never see him again. The guy just gets continually recycled."

"Oh good, there's coffee!" Greg exclaimed, pouring himself one and gulping from the cup even before he'd replaced the coffee pot on the table. He grabbed a handful of cookies and, cramming one in his mouth, threw himself down on one of the chairs and crossed his ankle over his knee.

"Right, this is what's going on..." He broke off. "Aren't you going to sit down?" he demanded indignantly, spraying crumbs.

Anna looked at him, fighting the smile which was spilling onto her face. However unenthused she was at being thrust back into his orbit, she could at least see the funny side. He was bizarre and ridiculous; it was as though he'd been written for a comedy.

"Alright then, Greg, for old times' sake," said Anna, consciously joining in the farce and plonking herself down on a chair. He opened his mouth to continue, and she held up a restraining hand.

"Wait, wait! I should get my laptop out and make a file on this."

"Don't worry about that, you can use this," he said, tossing a notepad and pen at her across the table. Anna gave a disbelieving chuckle at the persistent arrogance of the man.

"What's funny?" Greg asked, beginning to smile a little himself. Angela took a seat and looked on, amused.

"Well, let's start with the basics. I came here for a briefing with my colleague so I can adequately cover her for the remainder of this project. What are you here for?" Anna asked him serenely.

"I'm here to see that the briefing is actually effective," said Greg, to which Angela made an indignant noise.

"I think you may *hamper* the effectiveness of the briefing," she said.

"Okay, well if you insist," he said heaving himself up out of the seat. "I'll be here on Monday to cover off the bits she misses."

He sauntered out, pausing to take another cookie and slide it into his mouth whole, unhinging his jaw in reptilian fashion.

"Wow," said Anna, closing her eyes as she tried to clear the mental image.

"I wish I was staying for a few more days. Watching you handle Greg is hilarious!" laughed Angela.

"Yes, we've worked together... well, I correct myself; I have worked in the same office where he wasted space and government money before," said Anna, feeling buoyant.

"He seemed to enjoy it," said Angela. "I'd watch out or you may have an undesirable admirer."

Anna shuddered at the thought, and quickly suggested they resume their briefing back at Angela's desk. She wanted to be out of London before the commuter rush began.

Pacing in the small kitchen in the cottage, Damien was on his phone.

"Hi, Sarah. It's Damien." He paused as Caroline's secretary greeted him. It seemed he had spoken more to her over the last couple of weeks than he had Caroline. He continued, "Listen, I'm trying to reach Caroline but I can't get her. I understand it's going to be a working weekend for her..."

As he was speaking Anna opened the front door and stepped in, wearing a broad smile. Damien moved across the room and put his arm round her and kissed her silently, still holding the phone to his ear. "Oh, she's not? Huh...that's interesting. No, no, don't worry. Thanks. Bye."

He hung up with a thoughtful look on his face.

"Who was that?" Anna asked.

"Caroline's PA. Caroline texted earlier to say she's working the weekend and I thought I'd do a background check. Her PA says she's not working on a case and hadn't said anything about weekend work."

Anna frowned. "Which means that she's presumably with whoever it is she's been seeing."

"Yes, and she's not been home in over a week as far as I know," he said.

"So the two of you have done with avoiding each other and you've *both* moved out?"

It seemed such a travesty; two supposedly mature professional people evading the truth about their situation to such an extent that they had left their house unoccupied. And it wasn't as if it was a small house either; they could probably both live in it without ever having to meet.

Damien was evidently thinking along the same lines.

"Yes, stupid, isn't it?" he said. "Ironic to the point of being ridiculous."

"So I wonder where she is?" pondered Anna.

"That's the million dollar question. Presumably in London somewhere, and totally untraceable."

STORM

Saturday was a hunt day as usual and Anna was mounted up on Tom in good time before the crowd left the yard. She met Damien's eye for a moment as he sat on Barnabas, hunting whip coiled in his hand, talking to Paul.

Feeling watched, she noticed Annetta's piercing stare on her, which a second later was turned on David as he gave Anna an acknowledging wave. Anna smiled despairingly at the politics. Things had been easier when she was an island. Now she was an outcast, either unwelcome or unable to join anyone else there.

She felt a hand touch her shoulder briefly and turned to see Olivia mounted up and smiling next to her.

"I haven't seen you for a while," she said.

Anna felt relieved at the presence of a friend, and relaxed a little.

"Looks like there's a storm brewing. I think we'll be wet by the end of the day. Look at that," Olivia said, pointing with her whip. Standing ominously on the horizon was a massive threatening thunderhead.

Sure enough, some spots of rain were falling as they rode out. The meet was outside the George and Dragon in the village and the puddles were alive with falling rain by the time they got there. Over the cacophony of horseshoes clacking on the street, Olivia was full of conversation about the removal of Chantelle's horse from the yard, which Anna had already heard about from Damien the day before.

"Yes, I was glad to get her thrown out," said Annetta as she appeared next to Olivia.

Olivia looked mortified, not realising Annetta had been in earshot.

"We certainly don't need stray predatory females sniffing round the place like that," Annetta added in a hard tone.

"Sorry, Annetta," said Olivia. "Are you okay?"

"Yes. I know what he's like," she said gesturing balefully in David's direction. "But he's never actually gone through with it before. We'll get through this but he will be suffering for quite some time."

"Well, I admire you. I think you've come out of it with dignity," added Olivia, treading water.

"Yes, well. It's a marriage and sometimes it's hard," said Annetta, leaning forward a little and looking round Olivia at Anna. Anna pretended not to be listening and stared into the distance down the high street.

"Whoops. That was a bit weird. What was the stink-eye at you for?" asked Olivia as the hunt moved off and she watched Annetta ride ahead. "I guess David likes you too much and she's pissed off with anyone he associates with at the moment."

Damien had warned Anna of Annetta's suspicions, but she was resentful nonetheless. There had been such contempt in Annetta's voice. She wondered why women were often so hard on each other, when the men involved were at least half the issue. Maybe it was a primal competitive urge; better to fight your own sex and win the men yourself. Or maybe women expected better morals from one another? Annetta, certainly, seemed to come from a position of grim acceptance that the general sexual nature of men was akin to the pack of hounds they were following.

"I reckon she's in the dark," said Anna in a low voice, glowering at Annetta's back. "David has probably had it away with loads of his clients but unfortunately for him this time he chose badly. Chantelle was too young and indiscreet to realize what it was. Rather than just enjoying the illicitness, she wanted the whole deal and wound up exposing the entire thing."

Olivia looked at her, impressed.

"Anna! I've not heard this sort of thing from you before! Fancy you coming out with the parameters for a covert affair! Bravo! I like it!" she marvelled, making Anna grin self-consciously.

"You're probably right," Olivia went on. "David should have avoided Chantelle. She was too obvious and too stupid for it. It's almost like she was a lure. He could have been bedding his ladies for years but this time, rather than grabbing an inconspicuous chocolate, he went for the bright pink candy in the box, and got caught with the sticky pink stuff all over him."

Anna smirked at the analogy. David's karma did appear to have caught up with him. It seemed everyone's consequences constantly pursued them, hunted them, unfailingly taking them down at some point.

As if aware of her thoughts, the prevailing breeze shifted up a gear and it began to blow in earnest. She bent her head down, trying to use the peak of her riding hat to shelter her eyes from the rain which was now whipping at them in the strengthening wind.

"I don't think this is going to be fun today," she remarked, feeling a cold drop of rain run down her neck. She rubbed at it with the collar of her jacket, which was already soaked.

"Yes. I'm not doing the full six hours if this keeps up!" agreed Olivia.

The weather did not let up, and in fact got worse. The wind began gusting and the rain drops increased in size, lashing mercilessly at them as they cantered over the already saturated ground. The thunderhead was gigantic and Anna saw lightning flickering under it, followed by the far-off rumble of thunder rolling around the sky.

She loved storms; the pitiless majesty of nature or God proclaiming its undeniable sovereignty over the insignificant ants below. Anna imagined the hunt looked like a tiny pack of specks from up there, moving infinitesimally across the darkened landscape, so full of purpose and fire down on the ground, yet silent, negligible and inconsequential from the viewpoint of the mighty swirl of angry power above.

"I've had enough of this!" Anna called to Olivia.

The rain was coming in sheets now and the wind pummelled at them. Tom's neck was bent over as he attempted to shield his face from the onslaught. Anna shivered, completely saturated. The wind whipped any heat from her and she was suddenly aware of how far they were from home.

"It seems the huntsman agrees with you. We're done here," said Olivia, looking ahead at the retreating field. "Let's go!"

They turned as the hounds passed them and followed the field. Damien rode past, pausing for a moment to pace next to Anna.

"Extreme!" shouted Anna.

"Yeah, about time we quit! There were horses slipping and going down. Lucky no-one got hurt!" Then he held his hand out and she reached back to touch it for a moment before he urged Barnabas faster to catch the front field. "Ride safe!" he called.

"What was that?" asked Olivia as she caught Anna.

"He was just saying there were horses falling up at the front," said Anna, focussing ahead.

"No not that, the quick hand hold!" shouted Olivia.

"Oh, that," said Anna smiling, realising there was no obvious easy answer to explain it away. "Nothing. Just camaraderie."

"Not buying it!" Olivia insisted. "You're so damned secretive. There's something going on. He's into you! And don't tell me you don't see it! In fact, you know it! I was right!" she shouted over the wind, her eyes widening as she latched onto the scent. "Tell me what's happened!"

In the next moment lightning flooded the entire field with an erratic electric glare for a prolonged instant before plunging them back into moody darkness, and an apocalyptic crash of thunder surrounded them. Tom's ears flattened for a second and he bolted forwards. Anna sat deep and swerved around the group ahead, focusing on steadying him through the field of frightened horses, their heads thrown high and whites of eyes showing. She just wanted to get back as fast as possible and without incident. She called reassuringly to him over the wind, bringing him back to her. Thursday's extreme dash seemed to have bolstered his stamina and he pounded along steadily, bravely, deep chest working and ears alert to her every word.

Anna's relief at getting back to the yard was immense; she felt like a bedraggled mariner finally finding his way home.

She rode round to Tom's stable and leapt to the ground, peeling his saturated tack from him and checking his legs. The horizontal rain and the water running down the paths had washed his coat clean of mud. He grunted and held his head low before launching into a full body shake, then stood licking his lips and snorting. She threw his fleece blanket over him and left him in his stable with a pile of hay, as she gathered her soaked tack and went to put it away, feeling her clothes cold and wet against her skin.

The tack room was warm and reminiscent of a steam room with the moisture in the air from all the bodies jammed in, everyone dripping and talking animatedly. Anna pulled a towel from her locker and wiped her saddle down. Then she spotted Damien sitting on the bench with one boot off, talking on his phone. At first she couldn't hear him over the hubbub of other voices, but then, fixing her attention on him, she could just make it out.

"Oh, is she?" he was saying. "Right now?" He listened for a moment. "But there's no sign of her? Okay, thanks...No, don't worry, I won't mention you. Bye."

He put the phone down and swiftly pulled his boot back on. He looked up straight into Anna's eyes. "Anna! Quick, come!"

"What is it?" she asked alarmed, stepping to his side.

"I'll explain on the way," he said.

"Where?" demanded Olivia, who had arrived just in time to overhear them. Damien ignored her, hanging up Barnabas's bridle hurriedly and grabbing his sodden hunt coat.

"Well?" persisted Olivia, turning her eyes to Anna, who shrugged and spread her hands expressively.

"Where are you taking Anna?" she said, blocking Damien.

"She's moral support," said Damien shortly, not bothering to meet her eye and physically moving her aside.

Anna sensed she shouldn't ask any questions so she simply followed Damien, back out into the storm which was still raging. He ran to his car and leapt in, starting the engine as he hit the seat, and Anna hurriedly jumped in next to him. He reversed out of the space with his normal deftness and in one fluid movement turned his eyes to front, changed gear and accelerated. Anna reached for her seatbelt and settled herself as they sped down the driveway. He dabbed the brakes at the end, not stopping, and turned onto the road to the village.

"Okay," he began, "so I was talking to a girl who was new to our hunt at the meet. Turned out she's boarding at Caroline's yard and said she had seen her there this morning. I asked her to give me a shout if her car was still there when she got back."

Damien paused at a junction and then accelerated again. Anna watched him, noting his focussed determination.

"Why are we rushing so?" she asked calmly, not wishing to antagonise him. He was evidently more than a little worked up.

"I want this done. It's been on my mind. I've got this feeling she's been seeing whoever it is for a while now," he said tensely.

Anna sat quiet, waiting for him to speak again.

He took a breath and let it out aggressively. Anna felt her heart beating harder, more insistently. Why was he suddenly so furious?

"Remember that first ride we went on? That fantastic ride? She ruined that for me. She couldn't leave me a message; oh no, she had to call the yard in a tizz and insist that I get home that instant to go to some shit fake double date she'd organised." He drummed angrily on the steering wheel. "Why? Things were crappy at home anyway. Couldn't leave me to a moment of pleasure, damn her! No, she was having an affair and decided to drag me along in her charade!" He took a breath, building to the clincher. "I have spent the last however many months it's been resisting you, even avoiding you, for the sake of my bloody so-called marriage. And all the while she's been seeing him!"

"Do you know that?"

"No. But I've got a strong feeling I'm right. I've been thinking about the work patterns and the extra-long hours spent at her yard. She's been messing me around all this time!"

Anna had never seen him rant like this; it unnerved her. She tentatively put out her hand, catching his and squeezing it. He bit his lip and shot her a quick glance.

"Sorry. She's made me mad," he said more quietly. Then he sighed and threw his head back on the headrest, accelerating harder, and added with an edge to his voice, "I just need to have it out with her. She's been constantly absent and unobtainable. Now I've tracked her down I want to have the fight."

Anna wasn't sure why she was there. What had she to do with any of this? She decided to make herself scarce when they arrived. This was his battle, not hers.

They drove for another fifteen minutes on a road that was rapidly becoming a fast-flowing river. He braked and swung into a driveway. Carved horses' heads mounted on twin stone pillars stared impassively at the BMW as they passed between them. Anna couldn't see much through the blur of rain on the windows except for paddocks and a large barn which she supposed housed an arena. Damien stopped the car and took a grim breath.

"Come with me. Don't sit and wait. I've no idea how long this will take."

"Okay, but I'll back off when you find her."

They ran to the entrance of the barn through the sweeping sheets of rain, which doused them afresh. There were a few cars parked nearby and Damien pointed wordlessly at a silver Jaguar sitting sleek and silent in the deluge. Anna assumed it belonged to Caroline.

The hammering of the rain was loud on the roof of the barn as they entered and looked along its length. The wide well-swept walkway lined by stables on both sides was deserted. Anna could see into the arena at the end of the row, but it too was quiet and there were no lights on. The whole place held an ominous hush.

"Where are her horses?" asked Anna in a low voice.

"No idea. I never come here."

He scanned the horses in the stables as they moved along the row. There was a side door leading out to another open area and Anna peered out. It too was deserted and the rain pounded the concrete surface relentlessly. There were trailers stored to the far end of the yard; one large one protruding slightly looked familiar, but her attention was pulled away as Damien beckoned.

"Anna, this way," he said, moving off along a second stable wing.

She turned to follow, feeling uncertain and bothered at being there. It felt like they were trespassing and that no good could come of it. He had stopped at a stable halfway down the row, looking at an enormous high headed chestnut mare. She had tiny white specks on her shoulder and rump and was immaculately groomed.

"Quite some horse," commented Anna, guessing this was Caroline's horse, and feeling unsurprised that it bore a resemblance to the famous royal favourite, Toytown.

Damien grunted, looking around. "But where is *she*?" Then he looked past Anna and, touching her shoulder, moved back along the aisle.

"Hi, Bethany," he said, approaching a girl Anna recognised after a moment as the one she had met at the bar of The Royal Oak on the night of her epic first kiss with Damien. Bethany obviously recognised Anna too, smiling briefly as she approached. It was strange how threads came together so coincidentally, like a trail of breadcrumbs.

"Any idea where she could be?" asked Damien. "I don't know this place at all."

"Well, I've just come from the feed store and there's no-one down there, or in the club room," she said. "Maybe she left and I didn't see her?"

Damien shook his head. "Her car's still there."

Bethany twisted her mouth and looked down. Anna cocked her head and looked at her; there was something she didn't want to say.

"Listen, I don't want to get involved," said Bethany awkwardly. She lowered her voice. "But did you know that there's an apartment here?"

"She's moved in here?" asked Damien incredulously.

Bethany looked uncomfortable and shrugged her shoulders, backing away.

"Where is it?" called Damien after her.

Walking swiftly now, Bethany looked briefly back over her shoulder and gestured silently at a small flight of wooden stairs leading up.

Damien immediately headed off and charged up the stairs two at a time, Anna hastening to follow, catching up as he paused at the top in front of a door. He took a deep breath as he put his hand out and opened it.

Beyond was a small communal area which overlooked the arena. There was no-one there and the room was dim and unlit. Just a single red light glowed on a coffee maker standing on a side table. Anna felt nervous and stretched out her hand to Damien, grasping his firmly. They stood motionless, listening.

Anna spotted a door to the left and gestured at it, squeezing Damien's hand. They moved forward quietly together, listening. There was nothing but the howl of the wind and the hammer of rain on the roof above them.

Damien stepped up to the door, put his hand on the handle and turned it slowly. The door opened with a soft creak.

Beyond was a cramped entrance area where a collection of yard boots and riding boots lay in an untidy sprawl. Passing silently through the door Damien took a few steps forward to reach the edge of the main room. It was the typical den of a horse rider camped out at a barn; functional and little attention to tidiness. Hay and other debris lay on the floor round the entrance, creeping over the carpet into the rest of the apartment. A copy of 'Horse & Hound' lay open on the large rumpled sofa which sat along one wall, and there was a small dining table with two mismatched chairs in the corner where a tiny kitchen could be glimpsed. The hum of a fridge in the kitchen was the only sound.

Maybe there was no-one there? Anna felt conscious of her breath and heartbeat. They had broken into someone's private abode. Abruptly a door on the right of the main room opened and there was a quick laugh from inside. Anna felt her heart pound harder.

Caroline crossed the room, walking towards the kitchen with a smile on her face. She was wearing a large tee-shirt, too big to be hers, and apparently not much else. As she drew level with them she stopped dead, suddenly catching sight of Damien. Anna silently retreated a few steps to the front door, willing herself invisible. Damien's face was set, hard and focussed. He had the dangerous look she'd seen once before directed at James.

Caroline, plainly lost for words, stood rooted to the spot, pale, staring at him. Tilting his head, he looked at her silently.

"Hey!" called a man's voice from the unseen room, seeming to imply that Caroline had been absent too long. Damien moved his head again, raising his eyebrows. Watching from her corner, Anna realised with a stab of pain that they needed no words to communicate. Finally Caroline managed to summon up words.

"Damien? What...?" she faltered.

"What...?" repeated Damien, leaving the word hanging, slinging it back to her.

"What are you doing here?" she managed, stonily. There was the sound of activity from the adjacent room. Damien kept his eyes on Caroline.

"Well, on discovering that you were not in fact working, and being unable to get anything more than a text message from you, I thought it was time for a chat."

"You checked up on me!" she exclaimed, her voice rising indignantly.

"There're only so many cases a lawyer can work on before they burn out," he said meaningfully.

"Don't condescend to me! There's only so much a person can take of your bloody tiresome manner!" she shouted, her temper fraying immediately.

"Oh really? *My* manner?" he answered, his voice steady but emphatic.

Anna closed her eyes, not daring to move. Why was she here? This was not her fight. She was an unwilling audience whose presence was unjustified.

As if reading her mind, Caroline pointed aggressively at her. "And what the hell is she doing here?" she barked. Anna quaked inwardly.

"Don't bring her into it!" he warned her.

"Well, what *is* she doing here?" demanded Caroline.

"She's being a friend to me," answered Damien coldly. "Who's that in there? A friend? Presumably a *good* friend, given your state of undress?"

Anna knew she should leave right then. She should just turn, open the door and run, but she found herself unable to move, rooted to her spot behind Damien.

There was another movement from the next room, and she flicked her eyes to the door, then back to Caroline. She looked younger without her normal finery, and her pale face was frighteningly angry. She stood straight in the tee-shirt which hung to her thighs. Suddenly Anna realised the shirt was familiar; 'IPC,' it read, under the logo of a palm tree crossed with two polo mallets.

The figure of another person appeared silently at the door of the unseen room. Anna's insides leapt violently. Standing on quiet alert, hands at his sides, wearing only his jeans, was Dom. She couldn't move her eyes from him. How was it him? She felt unable to speak or even blink. She simply stared, her lips parted in astonishment. She had thought she would never see him again, that he'd vanished forever, yet all the while...

Damien evidently had it more together than any of them and turned towards Dom.

"Huh! Look who we found, after all this time. You certainly lay low under the radar for a while."

Dom didn't speak.

"Bit old for you, don't you think?" Damien challenged Caroline.

"What the hell do you care, anyway?" she snapped. Dom walked up to Caroline and put his hands on her shoulders.

"You're okay," he urged her in a quiet voice, revealing a side Anna had never seen in him.

"Mind giving us a moment?" Damien said in a steely voice. Dom looked at him for a second then evaded his eyes.

"Sure," he answered shortly. Then he leaned towards Caroline and said softly, "You okay if I step out?"

"Yes," she said, looking shaken.

Dom walked carefully round Damien, who didn't move. As he neared the door he met Anna's eyes, grabbed boots and a jacket and gestured to the door with his head. Anna, still stunned, dumbly turned and opened it.

In the small room outside Dom paused to pull on his boots and throw his coat on, zipping it up as he moved towards the door to the stairs. Anna followed, her eyes rooted to the back of him.

At the bottom of the stairs Dom paused and, plainly deciding there was nowhere to go, he leant against one of the stables and put his hands in his pockets and looked at the floor. Anna positioned herself opposite him, taking in his familiar ruggedness and wavy hair, but wondering who he really was.

Dom eventually looked up at Anna with his clear blue eyes.

"Hey," he said simply, in a quiet bashful tone.

Anna met his gaze, reacquainting herself with him silently. She had no idea what to say. There were so many questions which she didn't know if she had the right to ask, but after a second she surrendered to them.

"Is this where you've been all this time?"

He moved his head apologetically.

He'd been so close! How did no-one know? Suddenly she was sure it had been him she had seen on the street outside her office.

"I missed you!" she exclaimed bitterly, surprised at her own intensity. "You just disappeared! You were my friend and you just vanished!" she continued fiercely, clicking her fingers emphatically. "I got to the yard early and you'd already gone with everything!" Her emotions were rolling through her and she was angry at him. "What about Karen? Did you ever let *your wife* know what happened to you?" she asked incredulously.

Dom sighed and said, "She tracked me down at work in the end."

"I can't believe you just vanished on her! Please tell me she's okay and you've sorted stuff out?"

"Of course," he said defensively. Then seeming to relax a little, he sighed and looked at the floor. "I gave her the house. I gave her everything, basically."

Anna shook her head, trying to understand him. He had simply vacated his life without bothering to set anybody straight beforehand; it was that evasion of the unpleasant confrontation again, in the extreme. It seemed incredible the lengths a person would go to, to avoid pain. But all it did was create more!

"I don't get it! If you're leaving anyway, you've made up your mind, it's make or break; everything's going to kick off or fall apart, but you think you can just skip that bit and run off?"

Dom sighed. Obviously tired of the topic, he pleaded, "Just leave it, Anna." Anna glared at him. "I'm sorry," he amended. "You were my friend and I was really sorry to leave that."

"You didn't have to. You could have talked to me," she insisted.

"No, I couldn't. I couldn't talk to anyone. I did the unthinkable; I was leaving my wife for a younger, also-married woman, and wife of another friend of yours. No-one would have supported what I did, and you would have been between a rock and a hard place."

Reluctantly, Anna realised he was right. Being party to his secret would have thrown her into a terrible situation with Damien and she would have been forced to betray one of them. She supposed she should be grateful for the fact he had shown some presence of mind and consideration, however appallingly he was behaving otherwise.

"When did this start anyway? When did you meet her? Polo player, a man who never bothers with any other horse activity apart from the odd six-horse hack on the Downs, meets staunch eventer? I don't get it."

Dom hesitated, then sighed and gave a one-shoulder shrug.

"I met her through work, quite a while ago now."

"Back in summer, when you arrived?" questioned Anna. She hadn't thought of the work angle at all.

"No, before that," he admitted shortly, but not expanding.

"Why go to Rosemount? The same yard as her husband!" she exclaimed disbelievingly as more occurred to her, wondering at his thought processes.

Dom smiled at that.

"Not ideal, but I didn't want to commit to one of the big polo clubs. It was nearly the end of season and I wasn't down here for the polo really. I actually played more than I intended. I just wanted a place to have some fun and I figured I wouldn't see him much; he's not a polo player."

Anna shook her head, recalling Caroline's derision at the riding ability of polo players. What a tangled web of subterfuge and deceit. She guessed that seeing Caroline at the yard on the evening before he left, hanging out with her husband, must have toppled Dom over the edge. Thinking back, his agitation had been obvious, though a mystery at the time.

It seemed outrageously irresponsible of Caroline to force the issue so, impelling him to desert everybody and create so much drama and upset. What drew them together? Their characters seemed so different.

Upstairs in the apartment over the barn Damien was pacing.

"And how long have you had this place?" he demanded, looking round the room. "Or is this his place? Where he's been hiding out since he dumped his wife and disappeared without a word? What an *honourable* character!"

Caroline, stinging from the sarcasm, looked up at him with angry tears welling in her eyes.

"It's his place, okay. Anyway, what have you been up to? What about Anna? I've seen you together at Rosemount! You always seek her out!"

"What; the same way I *seek out* my other friends there?"

"Oh, please! You know you do! You've always hung out with the men; you never normally bothered with the women unless they came simpering up to you," spat Caroline. "And now here you are with her! Annetta was plainly right!"

"Of course; she's been playing secret agent! Let's not forget that she's fresh from finding her husband screwing a teenager, and in the mind of Annetta that puts *all* men into the same bastard category, and she's out to kill as many as possible!" he discharged. "And what if I do like Anna? What if I am seeing her? How long have you been seeing him? Why is it my impression it's been for a good long time? Your workload certainly increased back in summer, incidentally as soon as he arrived at Rosemount!"

"You've never cared about my working hours. You never gave a shit!" Caroline yelled back.

They glowered at one another in silence for a moment.

Damien turned and paced a few steps, rolling his head on his shoulders, before launching into the attack again.

"And I can't believe you're pregnant by him! What a bloody mess!"

"What are you talking about? *You're* the bloody father!" she snapped back.

Damien stopped in his tracks and looked straight at her, shock mingled with disbelief on his face.

"What? No. Don't give me that! I worked it out."

"And obviously got it wrong! Of course it's yours!"

"How would you even know, if you've been fucking the pair of us?" he snarled.

Caroline recoiled and then she stepped up close, her eyes boring into him. "I know, okay, Damien. It was that night we did in Paris… Up against the window in the Shangri-La? You don't remember?"

Downstairs the atmosphere had eased and everyday conversation prevailed.

"Stick and balled over the winter?" asked Dom.

"I played a couple of times with Lucias and Pete. It's not the same inside in the winter and it's not the same without you," Anna responded honestly. "What about you?"

"No. I put all my horses out as soon as I got here. They're on winter turn out and I'll bring them in and start working them up again in March." Dom grimaced, remembering the urge to lie low when he arrived which had divorced him even from the last lingering warm days on the polo scene.

"So what does a guy like you do over the winter? I know you don't hunt or anything," asked Anna.

Dom met her eye with a bit of the old play in his expression, and suppressed a smile. Suddenly realising that he was thinking of Caroline, she gasped, "You're terrible!"

"Sorry. That was cheap," he admitted.

They regarded each other with a smile. It was like they were friends again. Anna felt a glimmer of the easy, high spirits which he had always inspired, but beneath it was a thread of anxiety. They might have begun to regain their friendship, but upstairs there was a storm raging.

"So what else has been going on over there at Rosemount?" asked Dom with a grin.

Putting aside her unease, Anna told him about Chantelle and David, her usual distaste for gossip evaporating in the pleasure of talking to him again.

"That's one helluva scandal!" he exclaimed, jaw dropping. "What a terrible bunch of folk we all are in this crazy horse world!"

Anna grinned and nodded.

"You should know!" she joked, feeling slightly hypocritical.

"Yeah? Well, what are you doing here? He was never one to talk much," he said jerking his head upwards. "And she complains about how insular he is."

"Meaning?" asked Anna, playing for time.

"What's with you two?" he asked, smiling mischievously. "You look good together!"

She shrugged, looking away. Despite her ease with him she wouldn't be completely open.

Dom grinned and left it.

"It must be a bit of a change of scene for you," remarked Anna, changing the subject. "Living in an apartment over a horse barn."

"Ya, it certainly beats having property to look after," he agreed with a smirk. "Speaking of which, have you seen their house?"

"You've been there? As in *been with her* there?" Anna emphasised, taken aback.

"Yeah. Bit naughty I know," he said, with a gleam in his eye.

"Yes! Very naughty, and risky. That would be the cockroach on top of your depravity pie!" said Anna sternly, torn between enjoying his company and disgust. Dom sniggered. "It's not funny! It's bad enough without adding insult to injury and doing the deed in his house!"

"Huh, like that's going to make a difference! They'll bury me face down as it is. Anyway, it only happened once, on New Year's!" he objected, still grinning.

"On New Year's Eve?" hissed Anna in disbelief. "The night Caroline claimed to have a migraine?

So that's why she sent Damien back to the party," she added to herself, thinking of the lurid red dress Caroline had worn that night. She had set it up and lied to Damien!

"Was that premeditated?" she asked, giving voice to her question.

He didn't say anything but his face gave affirmation enough.

"That's bad. That's really bad."

She knew she was an outrageous fraud, given how she and Damien had ended the evening, but at least they were opportunists and not conspirators.

Dom still smiled, but with less amusement. He could see Anna was rattled but the entire episode had hardened him, and by the looks of it she wasn't so lily-white herself. Anyway, what did it matter? Breaches, transgressions, wrongdoings, he'd done them all. They were stacked up with no obvious repayment terms, and he was past caring.

In spite of herself Anna still felt affection for Dom. They had enjoyed a buoyant, upbeat friendship, and besides giving her a new hobby he had distracted her from some of the pain she'd gone through with Damien. Dom's extroverted uncompromising fun had been a highlight of her summer. She sighed and shook her head slightly, unsure of her feelings, and then determinedly focussed on the future.

"And now you're going to be a father," she said matter-of-factly.

"What? What do you mean?" he responded with genuine bewilderment.

"She hasn't told you?!" She choked on her words, stunned.

Up in the apartment, combat had subsided and Damien stood close to Caroline, looking at her seriously.

"What are we doing, then?" he asked quietly.

"I think we both know. There's no way in hell this baby will be born into scandal," insisted Caroline. Damien sighed.

"You're being honest with me, now? If I find it's not mine…"

"The baby is yours, okay!" she interrupted. Then, conspiratorially, "We mention nothing to anyone about this. Definitely not my parents, no friends… I've already been asked if we are alright."

Damien sighed again.

PANDEMONIUM, FATE AND DEATH

Anna sat in the dark, staring at the wall in her living room. She had no idea how long she had been there. The emotional horror of the drive home had left her almost catatonic.

Damien had said very little. When he had finally trudged downstairs and Dom, tense and white, all his insouciance flattened, had mumbled a hurried goodbye and stumbled up to the apartment to join Caroline, he had been unable to meet her eye. Right then she knew. She had known, of course, the instant Dom gaped at her in bewilderment, but in the midst of her shock she had clung on to a glimmer of hope. Now there could be no hiding from the truth. It was over. The baby was his, and she was history.

Sitting beside Damien as he drove steadily back to the village, the only sound the rhythmic click of the windscreen wipers lashing back and forth, she had fought her emotions and lost. She stared out of the window at the pounding rain, the tears streaming down her face as she gulped for breath, her stomach roiling. She could glimpse him glancing at her in concern – once he stretched a tentative hand towards her – but there was no comfort he could offer, and he knew it.

The journey had seemed interminable; and far too short. When they arrived at the cottage she flung herself out of the car and hurried up the path, desperate for privacy. She heard him say something but she ignored it, fumbling for her keys. Then she was inside, the door closed behind her, the red lights of Damien's car pulling away, and she was alone.

A square of washy blue light glowed faintly in the darkness. Anna stirred. Looking sideways, she could see the caller's name on the screen; it was Olivia, obviously chasing response to her repeated texts, hustling for news. She reached out mechanically to switch it off and slumped back against the cushions. There would be no talking to anyone that night.

When she awoke, still in the same position, her body aching and her brain clogged, the rain had stopped and it was quiet. A quick tap on her phone showed that it was 1.30am. She lay unmoving, listening to the steady plop of water dripping from the guttering onto the path outside. It seemed unnaturally dark, and then she realised that the spire light of the church was switched off. She sat up slowly and looked out across the graveyard with numb eyes.

A figure could be dimly seen moving along the main path to the front porch. Something nagged at her, but it took a few moments for her mind to register the connection. Then she remembered; Andrew. She hadn't seen him since the night in the lighthouse, and in the emotional tumult of the last week she had given him little thought. When she had thought of him, it was with a spasm of guilt at her wanton betrayal of Damien; the smuggling, the drugs, and Andrew's haunted eyes as he spoke of the forced trafficking of youngsters had all receded from her memory, swept aside by her own relationship traumas. But now she did remember, and with it, the sounds she had heard from within the church that night so long ago. And right this very minute something was happening again, in the dark, at the church. She had spent too much time on what did not matter and now she must focus on what did.

    She leaned forward, forcing herself to overcome the shellshock that slurred her thoughts, and pulled on her jacket from where it lay around her. It was still damp, but she didn't care. Whoever was heading to the church in the early hours of the morning was connected with the horror that had Andrew so scared. Stepping into her running shoes, she opened the door.

Keeping to the bushes at the edge of the path, she moved swiftly and silently to the massive wall which abutted the solid stone porchway of the church. Then she heard the voices, and froze. Stepping between the shrubs crowding against the wall, she was well concealed. The scent of cigarette smoke wafted on the breeze.

"What about the money from that?" asked a man's voice she didn't recognize.

"It's clean. Gone. Andrew put it through the shop and then through some do up at that posh equestrian place on the hill."

The second voice was familiar, though Anna couldn't place it. And the flicker of memory vanished as she took in the significance of those few casual words. So Andrew was using Rosemount for money-laundering. Of course he was; why hadn't she seen it before? That would explain Annetta's suspicions about the accounts, and Andrew's precipitous exit when they were decorating the Christmas tree. It was all falling into place now. Hurriedly she brought her mind back to the present, and focused on the conversation taking place in the porch.

"I'm worried about him, though," continued the voice. "He's been different these last few days."

"Have we been monitoring?" queried the first man.

"Yes." There was something in the crisp enunciation of that response which nagged at Anna. Then with a jolt of recognition, she realised that the voice was that of the vicar. Her mind reeled. How could that be? He was a man of the cloth, for heaven's sake; they didn't involve themselves in drug-running and dealing in human misery. It was unthinkable; blasphemous. Besides, he came across as such a kind, paternal man; it seemed impossible that the studious, scholarly dressed figure who addressed her so eloquently from the pulpit every Sunday could be standing here talking of criminal matters with such callous unconcern.

"There's more here than we expected," stated the first voice.

"What can I say? Apparently the job was more lucrative than we had hitherto supposed," came the response, colder now. There was a grunt from a third presence under the porch.

"You could say," confirmed the heavy voice Anna immediately identified as The Cleaner.

"Ah, of course. Our departed colleague can no longer collect his share. How very convenient." Anna felt nauseous, suspecting that the 'colleague' was the desperate voice she had heard behind the side door of the church, that summer's night. There was a scuffle of feet and the voice resumed: "We should go."

With a surge of alarm, Anna swiftly crouched to the ground amongst the bushes, hugging her knees to her chest, praying they would leave along the main pathway to the street. If they passed by her, there was every chance they would see her, and by now she knew beyond all doubt that they were killers. They left silently, one slinging his cigarette butt to the ground; it rolled along the path, coming to rest within a pace of Anna. She held her breath and stared as its scarlet ember died and turned black.

Fat grey clouds blew across the sky the next morning, and the sun showed itself intermittently. Anna blinked, and squirmed from her awkward position on the sofa, feeling a wrench in her neck and stiffness in her back. She limped up the stairs to the shower. She would go to church that morning, not for the message – which would no doubt lacerate her recent unwise decisions afresh – but to watch, or rather listen to, the vicar.

There was an earthy scent on the strong wind, and the sunlight shifting through the moving clouds flickered on the gravestones. The church bells pealed, and would have lent an old-fashioned romance to the scene that morning if the bombshell of the previous day had not rendered the very idea of romance grimly ironic; Anna was almost glad of the distraction of the sinister night-time meeting. She gazed at the ancient lichen-covered graves, wondering what the occupants, restful under their stones, could tell of the secrets of the church.

Pounding along the country roads to Rosemount after the service, Anna wrestled with what she actually knew. Watching the vicar intently throughout the service, she had seen nothing of the hard callousness she had heard in the voice of the previous night; in fact he had convinced her that she was wrong, his smiling face and cheery greeting seeming warmer than ever. The kindness he exuded as he delicately enunciated his message was tangible, and his appearance in his patterned cardigan was so homely… No, his involvement was impossible; he would be shocked at the use of his church over the last few months, and should begin locking it like so many of the other parishes.

So, her vicar was innocent, and moreover she knew she had nothing to tell the police; anything she had overheard would sound like conjecture, or even fantasy. She had no names, and events at the lighthouse would only incriminate Andrew, who now sounded like he was in danger himself. She wondered where he was and what he was doing. It seemed certain that things were coming to an ominous head.

Monday morning brought gloomy weather, and with the intrigue of Saturday night fading to the background, Anna's feelings turned black, dwelling once again on the severance of her relationship with Damien. But it was different now; there was a hard edge to her mood, which niggled at her insistently. This time there was anger, and self-reproach.

Giving up on her efforts to focus on work, she marched into the office kitchen for coffee and a break. The relentless bombardment of evidence presented that morning by her infallible mind was exhausting; proving with every surfacing memory what a sham her relationship had been and how little she had meant to Damien. She had been the drama to punctuate his stagnant marriage. And sometime in the future another woman would go through the same; feeling singled out and like she had met her soul mate, only find herself discarded and recounting the facts, cursing herself for a fool.

He had not once told her he loved her. There were no texts when he was away, and he never asked what was going on in her life. It had just been sex, and the excitement of someone new, the thrill of a new relationship. She sighed as she stirred her coffee and then flung the spoon into the sink. She was furious at herself; what an idiot she was, mourning the dissolution of the relationship for the second time!

"Fool me once…" she grunted dourly.

She had known it was over as soon as he told her about the baby, but in her haste to escape heartbreak, had too easily believed him when he said the baby wasn't his. But he had seemed so certain! She tensed her jaw determinedly; this was the end, and the last time Damien would be the source of her unhappiness. She sipped at her coffee, staring out of the window at the heavy clouds. Her phone binged with an incoming message, and she looked at the screen listlessly.

"Meet tomorrow night?"

She did a double-take. Unbelievably, it was Damien.

"?" she typed and sent. Why was he in contact after the crushing pain of the news he had delivered to her on Saturday? He needed to go.

"Flying from NY. Landing at 4. Want to see you," came the response.

"Why?"

"Why do you think?"

What did that mean? Did he think they were going to continue their affair, while Caroline carried his baby to term? And when the baby was born, presumably he planned to have Anna as his bit on the side? She could hear Andrew's words ringing through her head: 'You know he's not true – to anyone. He needs his adrenal buzz.'

Not this time, she thought. She would no longer be his toy; she had finally learnt her lesson, and he had made his decision to retreat to an insipid marriage and his wife's money. She thought of their giant Edwardian mansion and growled. Her opinion of him, which had once soared so high, was nose-diving.

"Go spend time in your party pad!" she spat at her phone, thinking of the time she had been there with him. Of course he didn't want to elaborate on the renovations his handyman had hinted at; he had no real intention of giving up his grandiose playground. She stifled an audible exclamation of disgust. "And this is the first time you text me! Bastard!" she exclaimed aloud in the empty kitchen. Apparently she was now a target to be reclaimed, rather than a reliable distraction. She glowered at her phone and threw it aside.

"OMG. Looks like you need to talk."

Francesca stood in the doorway, regarding her with wide eyes. Anna could barely see through her own fog of self-rage.

"I've been so fucking stupid!" she vented, incredulity mingling with anger and regret, her voice cracking with emotion. "He never gave a damn about me! All he thought about was sex, while I was head over heels like a love-sick dummy!"

"Did you ever tell him how you felt?" asked Francesca quietly.

"Yes!" protested Anna reflexively. Then she thought for a second, and admitted, "No. No, I guess I didn't. But he should have known! It was obvious!" But perhaps it wasn't; she had no idea now. Her head and heart were jammed.

"Come on, honey. Let's get out of here for a bit," coaxed Francesca.

Anna looked at her gratefully; she felt she had woefully abandoned her friend, shutting her out of late, and yet there she was, just when she needed her most.

It was nearly 7pm when Anna got off the train at the end of the day. She sat in the Land Rover, wondering what to do. Her mood was flat, but Francesca's good sense had been soothing. She had helped halt the fiery downward spiral, and Anna felt some closure. She didn't want to go straight home, though, and Rosemount seemed a bad idea; she was too sullen for pleasantries and too volatile for questions.

Suddenly inspiration struck: food. She wasn't especially hungry, but she certainly didn't feel like cooking, and there was a decent Thai place a short drive away. It would serve as a distraction. She pulled off her work shoes and reached for her boots.

She was picking up the second boot from the passenger footwell when she saw a business card lying just under the seat. She frowned and reached for it.

'Fontwell Flooring,' read the card.

"Weird," she remarked under her breath.

There was no name, but the only other person who had been in her vehicle recently was Andrew, and she remembered his panic as he left; his bag had been wedged beneath the seat, so the card must have fallen from a side pocket.

Then another thought struck her; he had mentioned a shop where the laundering process began, and she had heard it alluded to again by one of the men at the church on Saturday. It was a long shot, but maybe this was the shop.

The address was in a town about half an hour away. Making a snap decision, she started the engine. Andrew had disappeared and there was a remote possibility he could be there. And if her idea came to nothing, at least she'd get Thai food on the way back.

There was no sign of Fontwell Flooring on the quaint high street. At the address on the card there was merely an antique shop with a faded burgundy frontage. Leaning sideways to look out of the passenger window, she saw there were a couple of storeys above it with small windows, but no side door. Anna scanned the street again. The next building along was The Angel Inn and at the far end of it was a sign indicating parking at the rear.

The gravel driveway of the pub led to an area hemmed with lighted posts, where five other vehicles were parked. Anna reversed into a space near the exit, feeling it prudent should she need to get away quickly. Smiling grimly at her own dramatics, she climbed from the Land Rover. Fontwell Flooring would probably be locked up, even if she could find the place.

To the left of the parking area, a narrow path led her to the back of the high street buildings. Furtively, she hurried to the gate leading to the building she assumed she needed; it stood ajar, and with a quick check over her shoulder she stepped through.

She found herself in a small dark yard overhung by tall mature trees. In the far corner was a metal fire escape leading to the building's upper floors, and without pausing long enough for her nerves to get the better of her, she ran quietly up the steps.

Oddly, the fire door at the top was slightly ajar, and she opened it a little further to look inside. A musty hallway with brown carpet led to a room which, if her sense of direction served her, must overlook the high street. There was no sign of life, and nothing to suggest Andrew was there. Feeling jittery at trespassing, she turned to leave, but then stopped. Had she really driven so far out of her way and got herself into the building, only to leave having not investigated fully? Wasn't Andrew her friend?

Dismissing the internal voice that insisted she hardly knew him, and that she was taking an outrageous risk for no good reason, she turned back and pulled the door open.

Inside she listened for a moment and then padded along the hallway to the room beyond. No lamp was on but the yellow haze of the street light flooded through the window, revealing the few objects inhabiting the space. There was a shabby desk with an old wooden chair, and a small stack of elderly carpet samples and ceramic tiles under a layer of dust. She frowned; some flooring outfit.

She walked gingerly across the uneven floor and peered out the window, down onto the high street, wondering when Andrew had last been there. Judging by the sloping ceiling, she was in the attic; therefore there was a storey between this room and the antique shop. As she turned from the window she saw a filing cabinet behind the open door. She crossed back to it, wondering if there were anything inside which might serve as evidence.

She pulled open the top drawer, knowing immediately she was being childishly hopeful; if they killed people to keep them quiet, they wouldn't be leaving evidence of their illicit activities handily stashed in a filing cabinet. With a grimace she pushed the drawer shut and turned to leave, as she did so brushing against a jacket hanging on the back of the door. Even before she registered that it looked familiar, she caught the scent of the wearer: a particular essence and maybe a hint of Armani. With a flash of recognition she realised the jacket belonged to Andrew. Quickly rifling through it, she found a small object in the inside breast pocket. It was a memory stick.

Footsteps sounded on the stairs. Feeling a lurch through her insides, she squeezed behind the door and stood stock still, out of sight of anyone looking from the hallway.

Whoever it was had plainly stopped by the fire escape door through which she had entered. Voices came from the hallway. She held her breath, willing them to leave, and not come her way. Then she heard more feet climbing the stairs from the level below.

"It's clean. Nothing here," came the unmistakeable thick accent of The Cleaner.

Anna turned cold. What had she been thinking? Now she was trapped in a room, its only exit blocked by a man she knew was lethal.

The response came in the same hard tone she had heard on Saturday night: "Good. We won't come back here, just in case. Get it put on the market tomorrow."

"Yes. I check outside."

Anna peered through the crack between the door and the frame. She could see two men: one of them The Cleaner, as he headed out to the fire escape, and the second with his back to her, silhouetted against the pale light above the door. A ringtone sounded, and he quickly answered, turning so that the glow caught his face.

Shock rattled through Anna.

It was the vicar.

She saw the familiar receding curly hair, the long nose, the glasses, but gone was the scholarly cleric with his scruffy cords, dog collar and warm smile; in his place stood a cold-eyed man leaning against the wall in a black leather jacket, foot tapping impatiently, one talon-like hand clenched around his phone. The contrast between this cruel-looking stranger and the man she thought she knew made him almost more terrifying than The Cleaner.

"Andrew," he announced, "I was wondering when I'd hear from you."

There was a pause. Anna waited, her eyes wide and sore from not having blinked.

"You're at the church? Well, I'm at the shop, looking for the data from the last deal. Where is it?"

Anna heard him shift against the wall, and she peeped through the crack again. The vicar's brow was puckered in mild concern, as if he'd mislaid a library book. His face was a palimpsest, the kindly cleric flickeringly overlaying the killer beneath; only the hard, dead eyes remained unchanged. She shivered inwardly and refocused, listening.

"Why have you got it? Oh, I see." He sighed. "It sounds like you're trying to blackmail me, and you of all people know that won't wash." He tutted and confirmed, "I'm on my way."

Anna heard the sound of the fire door being pulled open. The vicar was talking again into his phone: "Clive? Mr Japson is at the church and he has something I need. You're closest, so I want you go there and secure him."

Anna swallowed, feeling her throat contract painfully. She was pressed against the wall, still gripping the memory stick. What was Andrew doing? And what did 'secure' mean? For god's sake, were they going to kill him?

There was the faint ring of footsteps receding on the fire escape and then all was quiet. Ann waited for what seemed an eternity, then silently eased herself from behind the door, and peered round it. The feeble light of the fire exit sign showed that the hall was empty.

Taking a deep breath, she pulled out her phone and scrolled through her contacts. Damn; she had never got Andrew's number.

She had to get to him. She was the only person who had some clue as to what was going on, who was on his side.

She checked the hallway again, then stole along to the fire exit door and pushed gently on it. Rain had begun to fall, pattering in the trees and pinging softly on the metal of the fire escape, disguising the sound of her steps as she descended.

Stepping through the gateway, she scanned the path ahead. It was clear, and she followed it to the corner. The lighting of the parking area revealed no movement, and she ran like a hare for her Land Rover, reaching for her keys as she rounded the back of the van parked next to her.

She stopped dead.

The Cleaner was leaning against the driver's door of her Land Rover. He looked at her impassively, and straightened up. Anna stared at him in horror.

"Your expression says you know me," he remarked. The flick of humour in his voice was paradoxically terrifying. "I wondered when I might come across you."

"What? ...I..I don't know what you mean," Anna stuttered.

"I clocked your plate the morning you dropped Japson off. And got a good look at your beautiful face too." His mouth curled reminiscently. "And I saw you arrive tonight," he added, his black eyes boring into her from the shadow of his pronounced brow.

Anna stepped backwards, but he was on her in a flash. Before she could even cry out, he twisted her round and held her fast, one hand over her mouth and the other holding her wrist, bending her arm up behind her back. His skin was warm, fingers reeking of stale tobacco.

His phone buzzed, and he quickly forced her to the gravel, hand still clamped to her mouth, knee cruelly pinning her down. Trapped in his iron grip, she scanned around desperately, seeing only the night sky and the dirty underside of the van, the faint smell of oil mingling with earthy tang of rain-soaked gravel.

"I was right," he said shortly into his phone, shifting his weight more securely.

"Search for the file." The voice on the other end was peremptory.

"And?" he enquired.

This time she didn't hear the response, but she could guess it from the eyes of her assailant as he looked down at her; her murder had just been ordered.

She felt sick. Of course they wouldn't leave her alive. They killed anyone in their path, and her blundering innocence meant nothing; she was there, so she was involved.

The Cleaner grunted and pulled her up, dragging her back towards the shop. In terror and disbelief she battled against him, knowing her life depended on escaping him immediately. Once inside he could do whatever he wanted with her.

She tried to scream, but his heavy hand was clamped over her mouth and jaw; all that escaped was a terrified whimper. Hot tears streamed from her eyes, and she fought for air, but his fingers were partially blocking her nose was. She choked, and struggled, but his grip was unrelenting.

Throwing herself backwards, she pressed against him, feet out in front of her, bracing against his movement, but he pulled her arm higher, and she yelped silently as searing pain tore through her shoulder blade. It was no good; he simply changed position, and dragged her along with him.

They were approaching the dark pathway leading to the back of the high street buildings. Desperately she changed tack, letting her legs go limp so that she fell to her knees on the wet ground. The Cleaner swore and kicked her in the ribs, hard. Anna heard her own cry, like a howl from somewhere else, as he stooped to gather her up.

There was a shout from behind, and she saw two men hurrying towards them. If they were reinforcements she knew there was no hope; all she could do was wreak as much noise and damage as possible. Gasping in pain as The Cleaner hauled her up, she kicked out at him and then, finding his arm with her teeth, bit down as viciously as she could, tasting blood as he ripped it away.

Another shout: "Oi! What the hell?! Are you alright, love?"

With a sudden surge of hope she realised the two men were looking out for her. Not more killers, then; just regular blokes who had been in the pub. She kicked again and screamed.

The Cleaner dropped her and swung at the first man, knocking him to the ground. The second man yelled over his shoulder and launched himself at The Cleaner as three others ran over.

She scrambled to her feet and staggered a few steps. As the second man hit the ground, Anna's head snapped back as she was yanked back by her hair, and she fell backwards, feeling gravel grazing her back and her head bouncing on impact. The air was full of frenzied voices and feet scuffled around her. Rolling sideways she saw The Cleaner in rapid retreat, followed by two of the men. She heard the gruff voice of one of her rescuers as he checked on one of his friends, while another pulled her to her feet.

"No!" croaked Anna, spluttering through her constricted throat, gagging and gasping for air.

"Are you okay?" asked her helper, as he wiped blood from his nose.

"They mustn't chase him," she gasped, her voice grating, head swimming as he steadied her. "He's dangerous."

"No shit! I'm calling the police."

"I've got to go!" Anna insisted. Her world was spinning and everyone was in slow motion, but she reached again for her keys, starting back to the Land Rover.

There were protests behind her but she ignored them. She lurched, stumbling on legs of jelly, and pulled open her door. Shaking uncontrollably, she fumbled at the ignition, growling in relief when the engine fired. She fought to control her breathing, and commanded herself to focus. She didn't have time for shock; she had to get to the church.

The vicar stared in disbelief at Clive's lifeless body sprawled face down on the floor of the vestry. Blood was spattered across the floor, and oozed in a deep red puddle around the shattered head, rapidly soaking into a pile of crumpled vestments. Next to them, Andrew lay on his back, breathing rapidly.

"The fucking great bastard got more fight than he expected," he gasped, spluttering blood.

"Still cocky, even now," mused the vicar, frowning as he pressed his foot to the wound in the side of Andrew's stomach, causing him to roar in pain. Abruptly the vicar bent over him and searched his coat pockets. Finding nothing, he straightened up.

"I'm not sure what you intended to achieve here tonight, Japson. Where is the data?"

"Hidden."

The vicar pulled out his phone, dialled, and put it to his ear.

"Clive has made a mess. Where are you?" His expression grew darker. "I see. This evening is rapidly becoming a complete misadventure. I sense the files are in the wrong hands. We're going to have to clear out, so follow procedure. The priority is here, now. You've got your work cut out," he added, looking around at the carnage. "Use the usual place. Seal it well. I'm leaving now. How long?"

Zipping the phone back in his jacket, he stared impassively down at Andrew.

"What? You're just going to stand there and watch me die?" Andrew choked, his breath coming faster.

"Why did you do this?" The tone was one of polite enquiry.

"I had to stop it," gasped Andrew. "You're dealing in slavery, and murder."

The vicar's lip lifted in a sneer. "You thought we were in the business of improving lives?"

Andrew muttered and spat blood.

"Think about it, Andrew, as you lie here. You've made a mistake."

The vicar shook his head, and strode towards the door. He paused on the threshold, looked over his shoulder, and said with a tinge of regret, "You shouldn't have got anyone else involved. That girl you sent to the shop is with our friend now, and you know his ways; when he searches her for the file, he'll do it very, very thoroughly."

The room was silent again. Andrew closed his eyes, shuddering as pain wracked his body. It had all gone horribly wrong. The plan which had been so watertight had failed catastrophically, and now his own death stared him in the face.

Gripping at his stomach he raised his head from the floor, groaning as the pain tore through him in strands. Who had been at the shop? It must have been Anna, but why? What was she doing there? If it was her, it was his fault for getting her involved. She could be dead by now, and if he couldn't get up, he was shortly to follow. He gave a hard sob, and closed his eyes.

It was the feminine exclamation of horror which shook him alert. She was ghostly white as she appeared above him, her blue eyes wide with horror.

"Anna," he whispered.

She was too late.

"Oh my god! Andrew!"

Crouching at his side, Anna gazed in terror at the blood oozing from his wound, adding to the impossible amounts of it around him. She swayed, giddily reaching for the ground, feeling her hands wet with the gore on the stones.

There was a noise from outside the room.

"Go!" hissed Andrew. "Now!"

Anna didn't move, her eyes like saucers and her teeth chattering.

"Now, Anna! Go! It's The Cleaner, and he will kill you!"

She looked dazedly at the door she had come through.

"Side door," he whispered, looking towards it.

"I can't leave you!"

"Go! Go now!" Andrew commanded huskily, pushing weakly at Anna with a blood-soaked hand.

There were footsteps approaching the passage. Anna staggered to her feet and stumbled across the floor. She twisted the big key in the lock and pulled at the heavy door, then fled blindly into the night.

FALLOUT

The twitter of the birds signalled the arrival of dawn, its faint light shimmering on the floor tiles. Blinking, willing her eyes to focus, Anna realised she was staring at the ceramic column of her bathroom sink. Her body felt battered, and her throat was sour and raw.

Whimpering, she eased herself up on her elbows to her knees, and then grasped the sink and hauled her stiff and aching frame up from the floor, moaning at the sharp stabbing pain in her ribs. Staring into the mirror, she registered that she looked dreadful; there was a red bruise and a bump on the side of her forehead, her hair was tangled and dark circles cut deep under her eyes. Her skin was pale and puffy, her eyelids swollen. She let her breath out, craning closer to the glass, examining the damage.

"What a mess," she muttered, bending to drink from the cold tap. She could only assume she had got home, thrown up and then passed out right there on the bathroom floor. Suddenly remembering the night before, she turned and staggered through the bathroom door, grasping at the frame to steady herself, and crossed the landing to her bedroom.

Out of the window, she could see two police cars parked on the road outside the church. As she watched, a police van arrived and officers in overalls climbed out.

She tried to make sense of what she was seeing. What had happened after she left? Who had called the police? Had someone walked in on the scene of carnage in the vestry; some poor unsuspecting elderly volunteer? Good God, please no! Feeling nausea sweep over her, she lurched back to the bathroom.

By lunchtime, the village street was crowded with vehicles; media vans with TV crews, reporters, locals and the swelling ranks of police officers. A cordon had been stretched around the church, and Anna watched the proceedings, crouched on her sofa.

Too disorientated to face a conversation, she had emailed Martin, telling him she was too ill to go to work. Greg would be sneering sardonically at her failure to appear on her very first day, but she couldn't bring herself to care. She had been through hell – beaten up, twice escaping death by the skin of her teeth, witness to unimaginable horrors – and she could no more tackle a work day than she could fly to the moon.

She had forced herself into the shower, and was in front of her bedroom mirror, examining the bruises which throbbed on her legs and torso, when her phone lit up with another call from Olivia.

Anna looked at it indecisively. Perhaps she should answer – she couldn't hide forever – but what on earth could she say? Abruptly she silenced the call, wincing as a sharp twinge shot through her ribs.

The pain was getting worse; the damage her body had taken the night before had set in, and it felt like someone had clubbed her with a baseball bat. She was stiff and sore and feverish, and her stomach was rebelling.

A knock at the door made her jump, and she crossed the room to peep out of the window down to the porch. Her view was partly obscured by the angled roof, but the back and shoulder she could see were obviously those of a police officer. Swallowing, she quickly pulled on leggings and a sweater and then hurried for the stairs, sweeping her hair over to cover the lump on her forehead.

To her relief, it turned out to be a courtesy call; the police were checking on the residents whose homes surrounded the church, explaining that access to the church was blocked. When asked if she had seen anything last night Anna feigned ignorance, pretending to be merely surprised and somewhat rattled at the disturbance on her doorstep.

She wasn't sure why she was lying, but it seemed essential to keep quiet. What if The Cleaner was still out there looking for her? He and the rest of them would stop at nothing to cover their tracks, and she was most definitely a dangerous loose end. If she went out, she would be accosted the moment she reached the bank of reporters, and then there was every chance she would be photographed… No, she had to lie low.

On the television BBC News was talking politics and she looked out of the window again, puzzled. She could see TV crews setting up lights; presumably they were preparing to film, but it had yet to hit the national news. Her phone lit up again.

"Ugh! You really don't quit," croaked Anna, looking at Olivia's name on the screen. Then making a snap decision, she answered.

"Olivia."

"Anna! Finally! What the hell is happening? I drove through the village earlier and there's shedloads of reporters and police outside the church! Where are you?"

"At home," sighed Anna.

"Are you okay? What's happening there?"

"Apparently there's been a murder in the church." In her mind's eye she saw Andrew, face plastered with blood, lying on the vestry floor.

"A *murder*?! In the church? Bloody hell, it's like something from The Da Vinci Code! Who?"

"They haven't said. I'm watching the news now but there's nothing," answered Anna mechanically, her eyes on the television screen.

"You're not working today? Can't you leave?" asked Olivia.

"No, I'm taking the day off sick."

"Is this to do with yesterday? What happened? I was worried about you! I texted you about ten times!"

"I saw," Anna answered wearily.

"Well, why didn't you get back to me? What happened? There's something going on with you and Damien, isn't there?" Olivia insisted.

Anna's eyes glazed as she stared unseeingly at the television.

"It's not my tale to tell. You'll have to ask Damien," she responded flatly. He could deal with this, she thought tiredly; not her responsibility.

"Fuck off! You know he doesn't talk! I haven't heard a peep from him and I've left him even more messages than I left you," protested Olivia.

"Well, I can't. It's his thing and I can't talk about it," responded Anna, woodenly. "It would be wrong."

"Are you sure you're okay? You sound weird, like you've been up all night. You *are* alright?"

"I'm sick. I told you. Do me a favour and check on Tom today, will you? I don't think I'll get there. I've got to go – I don't feel good."

Overwhelming fatigue hit her as she hung up and she sank back onto the sofa, curling up in a ball.

When she finally opened her eyes it was to the disorientating sight of her own street appearing on the television screen. The view she knew so intimately illuminated the room, while a news reporter she had seen a hundred times before stood next to the front gate of the church, speaking earnestly into a microphone.

"Well, all we know at this point, Sophie, is that four bodies were discovered inside the church. Police have stated that a crypt was found open, a crypt which was apparently not known about until now, and forensic teams have been working for some hours already."

The picture changed to the television studio, 'Breaking News – Sussex Church Murder' running across the bottom of the screen, Sophie Raworth enquiring gravely, "Do we know the identities of the bodies removed from the church?"

"Not at present. However, five minutes before we came on air, some human remains were taken away for examination by members of the forensic team."

"And are we to understand, Reeta, that these bodies are related to the activities of an established gang of human traffickers that the police have been after for some time?"

"Yes, that's right. But the location is quite extraordinary. A parish church in a sleepy village in deepest Sussex? Enquiries must be made."

Anna zoned out again as they discussed the village and the history of the church, but her attention was caught when the familiar face of one of her elderly neighbours appeared on the screen.

"Well, yes, we can't believe it. We've lived by this churchyard for years and it's a lovely tranquil spot, and it's very difficult to believe this sort of thing has gone on, very difficult indeed…"

Anna turned her eyes to the window, looking out at the church, and wondered queasily about Andrew. He was presumably one of the bodies. Had the Cleaner finished him off?

She slumped back on the cushions; it was all too much to take in.

Shaken from sleep by her phone again, she groggily answered her mother's overwrought enquiries, aware of the subdued ping of incoming texts in her ear; now it had hit the news, she would be drowning in questions from well-meaning, inquisitorial friends and family.

She couldn't deal with them; she had been through enough, and was still in shock. She needed to decompress, she needed peace. And as her mother's voice continued, an unheard soundtrack in the background, she decided; she needed Tresco. Soon.

No arrests were broadcast on the news the next day, the absence of the vicar being one of the news sensations of the morning. Questions as to whether he had been involved or had been kidnapped were bandied about. Knowing the truth, Anna became increasingly concerned that she was in danger of being tracked down by anyone still at large; they had wanted to kill her, after all. There was every chance, if they knew where to find her, that they would be back.

She tried to catch up on sleep but it was impossible; the second she nodded off, images of the blood in the church and being held to the ground by The Cleaner jerked her awake. She had to get out for a bit, even if just to visit Tom.

She looked out at the street and the quantities of people milling about. Another corpse had been removed that morning, again the identity not disclosed, and media attention was at fever pitch. She had to go and ride; she couldn't remain a prisoner in her own house.

She climbed the stairs determinedly and pulled on her breeches, gasping as the tightness of them aggravated her swollen bruises. She looked out at her Land Rover, which was boxed in by the surrounding media vehicles, and sighed.

Anna chose her moment. As the hordes congregated round a police spokesman, clamouring for more information on the body removed that morning, she nipped out of the cottage, a baseball cap pulled low, and wheeled her bike down the path. Swiftly hopping on, she cycled away along the back road to Rosemount.

It had been a gentle ride which took her to the top of the Downs above the chaos of the village, and into the freshness of clean air. It seemed as if she hadn't ridden for weeks, and she and Tom had ambled along happily in the chill breeze, enjoying the clear view for miles over the undulating countryside.

Taking her feet from the stirrups, she rubbed at Tom's neck affectionately, appreciating the fluffiness of his winter fur. Penelope called out to her as she slid carefully from the saddle, feeling her bruises complaining as they passed over the lumps and bumps of Tom's tack.

"Anna! I feel like I haven't seen you in an age," exclaimed Penelope. "You must be living with pandemonium on your doorstep, from what I saw on the television just now!"

Anna agreed as she undid the girth straps.

"How awful it is," Penelope tutted. "They said that one of the bodies was a Nigerian girl, only seventeen, one of the victims of trafficking. Poor, poor girl!"

"That's horrible," agreed Anna quietly. "Did they identify any more of the victims?"

"Only one other; a London lawyer who had apparently been missing since last summer."

Anna felt sick, figuring this was the man she had heard through the side door the night Dom disappeared. She had been so close to it all – it was frightening.

"The media is going mad with that one as they believe he was involved, and some link has been drawn between him and the Foreign Secretary," Penelope continued.

"I bet they're hysterical," agreed Anna. "Possible human trafficker conveniently associated with the British government's foreign affairs! Next they'll be dredging up the historical atrocities of the Empire and slavery…"

Penelope sighed and nodded. "Yes, and what with the vicar missing as well…" She shook her head. "This thing will go on for ever."

Penelope was right; it was going to drag on and on. Making a snap decision, Anna decided to go home, pack and leave that very evening.

The tack room was empty as she stowed her saddle, and she sat down on a bench and pulled out her phone. A quick internet search showed a sleeper service for Newquay, leaving from Paddington that night at quarter to midnight. She stood and closed her locker, thinking of what she needed to do.

"Hi," said a quiet voice.

Anna jumped involuntarily, looking up to see Damien standing at the doorway.

He sighed, seeing the hurt and resentment in her eyes. "I'm so sorry, Anna. I really am."

She bit her lip as she zipped up her backpack, saying nothing.

"But you yourself said it would come to this," he continued.

She gasped; how dare he! Suddenly furious, she rounded on him.

"Yes, but that was before I had been persuaded that in fact my boyfriend's wife was leaving him, pregnant with another man's baby, and my boyfriend was *moving in with me!*" She spat the words out. "It's a bit rich, coming from the stupid bloody idiot who couldn't accept the truth and didn't want to split up! And as for the asinine text messages–" She paused, her chest heaving, then flung at him: "What kind of fool do you think I am?!"

Damien slumped against the door frame and gazed at the ceiling. He groaned. After a beat he looked at her again and opened his mouth, seeming to search for an explanation. Eventually he muttered, "I did…I do care for you, Anna. I wish it wasn't like this."

Setting her jaw determinedly, Anna threw her backpack on her shoulder.

"You know what, Damien, maybe I'll accept that at some point, but right now I'm so boiling bloody mad with you that I can't talk to you."

He looked like he was about to respond, and she shut him down, holding up her hand.

"No. Just don't. And apart from all that, you haven't the first clue of the hell I'm going through right now. I'm out of here for a while."

He caught at her arm as she pushed past him, stopping her in the doorway and turning her face with his hand. Then she realised that, without her hat, and her hair tied back for riding, the now black bruise on her head was obvious.

"What the hell?" he asked in alarm. "Anna?" She felt the prickle of hot tears as she looked back at him. "What happened?"

There was concern in his deep eyes, and he tilted his head, searching her face. His hand was still on her arm, warm, making her heart beat faster.

The familiar scent of him made her head swim and she swallowed hard. "Do me a favour and look out for Tom while I'm away?" she asked.

"Answer me. Where are you going? What's happened? Why do you look like you've been beaten up?" he pressed insistently, blocking her way. "Can I help?"

She gazed at his solid chest and then up into his face, wishing she could be close to him again, wanting to feel his arms around her once more. How had they gone from such intimacy to this?

"I wish you could. But that's done now."

TRESCO

It was after dark when Anna looked out of the window onto the street. The revelations of the day, with the identities of the bodies and the government connection now being excitedly bandied about, ensured that activity continued into the night.

The bright spotlights, reporters and cameras made leaving via the front door most unappealing. Maybe she was being stupidly paranoid, but she did not want to risk being caught on TV.

She checked her phone. She had to leave for the station right away if she was to catch her connection to the overnight train. She dialled a local taxi firm and ordered one to meet her on a back street behind the graveyard, and then left through the back door, locking up as she went.

Heaving her case up over the tall garden wall, she allowed it to drop the other side, hearing it crunch onto the dead brambles. Then she put her hands on top of the wall and hauled herself upwards, scrabbling with her feet, griping at the shooting pain in her ribs as she pulled herself up to sit astride the brickwork.

She peered into the darkness of the copse behind, trying to see what she'd be landing on. Taking a breath, she swung her leg over and pushed off from the top of the wall, missing the brambles and landing on the dead leaves beyond. Stifling a yelp at the jarring impact, she righted herself, collected her case and tugged it behind her as she beat her way through the scrub and under the twiggy branches. She emerged furtively the other side of the wood and checked the street, then seeing a taxi approaching, slithered down the bank and stepped into the yellow puddle of light beneath the street lamp, hand upraised.

Anna felt marginally safer once the door to her sleeper cabin was closed and the train was slowly pulling away from the station. Luckily there was no-one sharing with her, and she crawled gratefully into the bottom bunk and pulled the cover up to her chin, listening to the screech of the wheels on the rails and the passage of feet outside the cabin. Finally she was on her way to a place she wouldn't be found. There she could sleep, and think, and most importantly, be safe.

In the gold of the early morning sky a thin ribbon travelled slowly; it wavered, fractured and then re-formed. Anna blinked, trying to focus, then she heard them; migratory geese were calling on the wind to each other, bent on their mission, high up in formation. She pulled her coat around her and hitched her scarf up as she sat protected in the lee of the dune.

She had slept like the dead the previous night and woken early with a hankering to start her day on the beach. She sipped at the coffee in her travel mug, warm and comforting, and gazed at the immaculate sand, deserted but for the small scuttling waders as they scurried for drifters brought in by the surf. The ever-present roar of the sea wrapped her reassuringly, and the soft breeze ruffling at the marram grass around her was fresh and soothing.

It had been two days since she landed on Tresco, and as ever the timelessness and tranquillity of the island had dislodged from her mind things which were best forgotten. The anxiety of the days in her cottage had receded from her thoughts, as though caught on the current of the ocean, and the horror of the night in the church was becoming an indistinct blur. She felt she could breathe again, surrounded only by wildlife and those who studied it avidly. No one was interested in her here.

Later that day Anna wandered along to the village store in the late afternoon sun. A stiff breeze blew across the coastal path and seagulls wheeled overhead, their harsh cries resonating in the salty air.

She looked over at the quay to where a couple of boats were moored and bobbing on the tide, and wondered if any fishermen had come in with anything fresh she could buy. Life was so simple on the island, and she wondered how long it would be before she tired of being there. Maybe never. Did she really need more?

She had called Martin the day after she landed on Tresco, painfully telling him she had endured a break-up and needed to take some time out. He had been kind and understanding, but she knew she didn't have long. Nevertheless, a week or so on Tresco would be enough to settle her sanity, and by the time she returned the media swarm outside her cottage would be over. Then she would have to knuckle back down to real life once again, and put behind her the events of the past year.

Moodily she scuffed at the dirt as she pondered what that would mean. She would probably have to leave Rosemount, judging by the effect Damien had had on her in those moments in the tack room. Perhaps a new work assignment which took her away from London would help answer that. Then there was the threat posed by the vicar and The Cleaner, both still on the run; how could she ensure she was safe from them?

She stopped and breathed deep, tilting her head back and appreciating the watery winter sun. Her obsessing could go on hold for now; she just needed to feel better.

The light sparkled on the water as she stepped onto the uneven stonework of the jetty, listening to the slosh of the waves at the wall. She saw the first boat was a fishing boat; lobster pots were stacked on the deck, and faded pink buoys hung from its sides, but it was empty, so she continued along to look at the second; a shabby affair with peeling woodwork. Then she slowed, hearing a laugh and a familiar voice raised in protest.

"Put a sock in it, will you? Get over yourself! We're here now, so let's grab a pint; there's a pub right there! C'mon!"

As Anna drew level, she stopped dead, staring in utter disbelief, convinced her eyes were playing tricks.

There were two men on the deck. Andrew Japson lazed on the seat in the bows, his feet up, wearing a sling on his left arm. As she watched, he removed the baseball cap he was wearing and slung it playfully at Mateus, who was grinning as he wound a coil of rope round his forearm.

Rubbing her eyes, Anna looked again. This was no mirage; Andrew, large as life and cocky as ever, was right in front of her, along with Mateus, who was more relaxed than she had ever seen him.

She stepped to the edge of the harbour wall. Catching her movement, they both looked up at the same moment, Mateus immediately dropping the rope and climbing from the boat.

"I told you she'd be here!" exclaimed Mateus triumphantly, pushing at Andrew.

"Easy on the arm, mate!" Andrew protested, holding out a defensive hand. "And yes, you did. I can't quite believe you were right, but plainly you know her better than I do."

Anna caught his meaningful glance at her as he sipped at his beer, its golden tones illuminated by the sun flooding through the window of The New Inn, where they all sat huddled round a small table.

"I still can't believe you're brothers," she insisted.

"Half-brothers, Anna, half-brothers; get it right. Hell, if I'd grown up in the same household as him I might have got religion too – ugh; mind the ribs!" he added, as Mateus pushed him again.

"Enough, pipsqueak! A little piety would have done you the world of good," announced Mateus with a smug smile.

Calling them to order, Anna focussed on Mateus.

"You never went back to the US, did you?"

"I didn't," he admitted.

"He didn't tell *anyone* he stayed put in the UK, including me!" added Andrew.

"What?" she yelped. "You, of all people, abandoned your family and your flock?!"

Mateus looked serious, and sighed. "A long while ago, when I was curate at the church, I became suspicious something was going on there, but I dismissed it. And with the New York ministry, I forgot about it, and it seemed insignificant." He took a breath. "Until I saw you at Christmas. You stirred up all those thoughts again and I figured something was really happening there. And when you implied Andrew was involved, I hunted him down and got him to talk."

"Yeah," exhaled Andrew. "In the most efficient way you know how."

Anna thought of how Andrew had talked in the lighthouse. "You got him drunk?" she gasped.

"More than that! Ugh; I was wasted…," Andrew said, shaking his head.

Mateus threw his hand up. "Whatever. He survived. And it got me a vague outline of his idiotic scheme; obviously there was no way it would work, but he was so set on it I knew there'd be no talking him out of it."

Andrew rolled his eyes and slurped his pint.

"So you followed him?" Anna asked uncertainly.

"Yes. Everywhere. I had to watch out for him, and find my own way to expose Josh and whoever else was involved."

"And what was the plan?" she asked Andrew.

"It was a terrible plan," interjected Mateus.

"No, it wasn't!" Andrew protested.

"Oh really?" challenged Mateus. "So how were you going to get out of the crypt?"

Andrew looked away and sighed. Anna looked from one to the other, wide-eyed.

"He was going to stage his own death, which everyone knows is virtually impossible," gloated Mateus.

"Not in this case it wouldn't have been!" protested Andrew. "I suffered a catalogue of a worst-case scenarios."

"So he planned to be at the church, luring Josh there by having stolen their latest financial records," Mateus elaborated. "And he had it all set up; all the fake blood, fake wound etcetera etcetera…"

"Which were impressive, you have to admit," interjected Andrew.

"Yes, actually they were moderately convincing," acknowledged Mateus. Turning back to Anna, he continued: "But then Josh set Clive on him – six foot five and all muscle."

"That's the first worst-case scenario!" interrupted Andrew. "It wasn't supposed to happen; I'd already called Clive and sent him to London, so he'd be out of the picture. Or at least I thought I had."

"But?" prompted Anna.

"But it turns out Josh had told them all to run my orders past him before acting on them."

"Of course; he said he didn't trust you," Anna commented, thinking of what she had heard as she crouched outside the church porch.

"How did you know that?" they both asked at once.

"Never mind. We can come back to that," she stated firmly. "I want to know what happened that night. So that's the huge guy I saw that night at the lighthouse with you? He was the one the vicar sent for you?" Andrew nodded. "How the hell did you survive that?"

"I'm not entirely sure, to be honest. I knew he'd send someone up front; he always does. So there was always going to be a struggle – there had to be for me to plausibly have been stabbed. But I hadn't planned for Clive…"

Mateus exhaled and shook his head, while Anna stared at them both.

"So you're telling me the wound I saw was fake?"

"That one was. But he got me in the back. Luckily it turned out he just missed my liver." He nodded as she gaped at him. "You wouldn't believe the pain. I still can't move that well."

"And you broke your arm?" she asked, looking at the sling.

"No, I tore the tendon trying to take him down. Not sure how I actually managed that in the end."

"I finished him off for you, that's how!" Mateus finished, exasperated.

There was a pause. Both Andrew and Anna stared at Mateus. It seemed to Anna that this must be the first time Andrew and Mateus had talked of what happened, and she watched as they glared at each other. They seemed exhausted, and she guessed they had been on the run ever since, up until the point they turned up on Tresco in a boat which looked like it had been scrapped long ago.

Mateus continued wearily. "Yes, after you got the knife from him and stabbed him, he went down at the same time as you passed out. I clobbered him over the head, or he'd have got up and finished the job."

"You killed him?!" Andrew's voice rose on the words, and Anna looked around, suddenly remembering their surroundings. Nobody was listening so she turned back, to see Mateus nodding slightly, looking grim.

"Why didn't you help before then?" Andrew exclaimed indignantly.

"I'd only just arrived! And lucky I did. He was bellowing like a wounded bull, but he had more fight left than you."

They sat in silence, Anna hardly able to process what she was hearing. She imagined the scene: Andrew out cold, Clive writhing on the floor, and Mateus... It beggared belief; she couldn't picture him pounding a man over the head until it killed him. She stared at him, wondering how on earth he was dealing with it. How could he reconcile it with his faith?

Mateus shrugged and looked down at the table.

"I saw on the news they found a crypt where they were hiding bodies," said Anna, determinedly changing the subject. "Did you know about that?"

"I knew there was a crypt," sighed Mateus. "I didn't know how to get into it – I thought it was blocked off."

Andrew turned to Anna. "And I only found out about it after that summer night you were at the church. After you left, I hung around and saw The Cleaner leave without the body of the guy they ended. He took a breath. "Then when the girl from Nigeria showed up dead back before Christmas, I followed him. He took her into the church and left empty-handed. I knew they were hiding the bodies somewhere, and I had to find where, so I could link them to Josh." His gaze sharpened. "Anyway, what happened to you? They told me they caught you at the shop so I thought you were history! What were you doing there? How did you even know about it?"

Anna recounted finding the business card, and her hiding in the building, only to walk into The Cleaner as she tried to leave.

"He actually got his hands on you?!" exclaimed Andrew, aghast. "Fuck! Anna, you're beyond lucky to be sitting here now! No one gets away from that guy."

"I figured," she said, recalling the deadly black eyes staring down at her as he pinned her to the ground. "If those blokes hadn't shown up..." She shivered.

Andrew sat back and looked thoughtfully at her, then raised his eyebrows. "Sounds like everyone's evening went horribly wrong," he remarked wryly.

"It was the only reason I left the church in the end," shuddered Anna. "I knew he'd kill me."

Mateus had been staring at her, wide-eyed, but at this he shook himself. "Thankfully it was wasn't him you heard; it was me. I knew whoever Josh had sent to deal with Andrew was minutes away, and you'd be in the crypt with him if I didn't frighten you off."

"Not that my bloody brother told me that!" scoffed Andrew, bitterly. "Just left me there wondering what I heard and when the last of my blood would drain away! Yeah, yeah," he added as Mateus looked at him quizzically, "I get that you couldn't have waltzed in and whispered in my shell-like, but even so...."

"But why stage your own death?" insisted Anna, unable to fathom why he had gone to such lengths. "Why not just give the information to the police and then disappear?"

"I had to give them bodies," he explained. "The only way to do that was to find the entrance to the crypt. And if I apparently died right in the church, Josh and co would of course dump my body down there, plus they'd think I was dead so I could slip away and take up another life."

"You almost did!" remarked Anna dryly. "A life on the other side of the Styx! You didn't look good, you know. You were choking on blood, for god's sake!"

"That was fake." At Anna's twitch of annoyance, he added hastily, "But the hole in my back was real, and I really thought I was going to croak."

"And assuming you survived that far, how on earth were you going to get out of the crypt?" added Anna, horrified at the thought of him abandoned alive, unable to escape.

"I was confident I could get out," Andrew assured her.

Mateus huffed and rolled his eyes. "It was a terrible plan. Come on, face it; you were desperate and you miscalculated. And if it weren't for me, you'd have rotted in the crypt! As it was, by the time I got you out you'd lost so much blood you were delirious. Idiot!"

"Agh! The pair of you!" barked Andrew in exasperation. "I had it sorted!"

Counting off on his fingers, he explained: "I sent Clive off so he wouldn't be the one sent to kill me; I knew The Cleaner would be with Josh at the shop at the time; and I knew I could overpower any of the others he might send. Then I'd have made it look like I got stabbed in the fight and be found dead there. They'd dump me in the crypt and I'd put the financial records of the last deal with the other bodies down there, let myself out and go to Tahiti and live happily ever after. I'd alert the police from a phone which wasn't mine and then I'd watch the news unfold, and the gang would be blown wide open! It would have worked!"

Ignoring Mateus's patent disbelief, Anna pondered the logic of it, sipping at her beer. She winced at the thought of actually being stabbed, thinking of the pain she endured from her own ordeal.

"And then what happened? You went to hospital?" she asked.

"I drove him as far away as I could and he was admitted as a drunken dim-wit who didn't know what had happened to him, and he got patched up there," said Mateus, frowning. "And then once he'd had enough blood and fluids to resurrect, he checked himself out, and we left."

Anna leant back in her chair, trying to remember the scene in the vestry. She had been in her own fog of shock before she even saw all the blood.

"What did you do? Google 'fake your own death'?" she asked.

"Something like that," said Andrew with a grin.

"You do realise, don't you, that if the wounds you were faking were real, you'd have bled out before you started chatting with Josh? You're lucky he didn't smell a rat," accused Mateus.

"He always did call me a resilient bastard," grinned Andrew.

Mateus grunted. "I wish you'd been resilient enough not to get yourself stabbed in the first place, so I didn't have to step in and…do what I had to do."

"So you hit Clive over the head?" Andrew asked, leaning forward. "What did you use?"

"Look, it doesn't matter!" protested Mateus. He was more anxious than Anna had ever seen him. "His head…it cracked…" Mateus rose to his feet abruptly, his face pale. "Need air," he said shortly, moving swiftly for the door.

Andrew and Anna were silent for a moment.

"If he knew half the stuff that guy did, he wouldn't feel as guilty," sighed Andrew.

"I'm sure he's never even had a fight before," said Anna.

Andrew looked at her and smirked, shaking his head. "How little you know of him."

Anna stared at him, wondering what he was saying. Did Mateus have some alter-ego? Forcing herself to drop the thought, she continued:

"So you played dead?"

"Yup. In fact, that bit went like clockwork." Andrew nonchalantly swigged the last of his beer. "The Cleaner knew by then that they were clearing out, so he just wrapped me in plastic and put me in the crypt, which turned out to be under a stone near the altar. My biggest problem was not squealing in pain." He winced at the memory. "And then he dumped Clive on top of me in a casket. Weighed a ton; it took me ages to squirm out from underneath. Given the state I was in, I'm not sure how I did it."

Anna thought of going to the bar for more beer, but decided she had to hear the rest first. "And you found the other bodies?"

"Yeah; well, I found one. I was passing out again by then. You wouldn't believe the stench!"

Anna grimaced. "And you left these files you were talking about in the crypt?"

Andrew pulled a face and looked embarrassed. "That was another hiccup; turns out I didn't have them. I realised after Mateus found me and got me out of there that they were in the jacket I left at the shop. Luckily it seems the police made some links without the files– " He broke off as Anna's eyes widened.

"On a memory stick in the inside pocket?" she exclaimed. "I've got them!"

"No way!" He sat back and puffed his cheeks. "I'd say you're best off hiding that stick and never speaking of it."

"Great; thanks for that," retorted Anna. "I can't believe how far I've been sucked into this without even knowing what was going on!" she went on resentfully. "And wouldn't it just have been better to go to the police in the first place? There's the witness protection programme."

"You know me better than that, Anna. There's no freedom there. Anyway, that wouldn't have kept me safe."

"What about me? Am I safe from them?"

"Oh, you won't matter to them now," he answered dismissively. "They'll have left the country anyway. Me, though – nah, not so much. There's a vendetta there – if they discover I'm alive." He sighed resignedly, and then looked at her again. "You can go back to your cottage and your life."

Anna stared at him, wondering what he would do. Was he going to take up where he had left off, brokering dodgy deals, always skipping one step ahead of the law? She was just about to ask when Mateus reappeared.

"I need another beer," he said, walking past them.

"I haven't seen him drink beer in years," said Anna, watching as he approached the bar.

"He's more complicated than you think," remarked Andrew, gesturing after Mateus with his head. "He's the reason we are here, you know. When he couldn't reach you, he thought you might be here."

Anna felt guilty. She had begun ignoring messages, and hadn't charged her phone in the last 24 hours.

"Lord knows how he guessed you were on Tresco," continued Andrew, looking at her steadily. "He's another reason I didn't unleash myself on you that night in the lighthouse."

"You knew we were friends, even then?"

"If that's what you call it," he responded, grinning cryptically. "You've plainly done that thing you do, and have no idea what you do to him." He got up to join Mateus at the bar.

Anna shook her head, stunned. Was he saying that Mateus had a crush on her? Surely he couldn't have, given everything that he knew about her – and if he had, why had he never said anything? She felt weird, thinking of the stuff she had admitted to him over the last few months.

But perhaps it was just Andrew doing his usual thing of provocatively stirring reaction in any way he could. She caught his eye and waved her empty glass at him, smiling in relief as he gave her a thumbs up – at this point she needed another drink. Damn Andrew; no sooner had she started to find some kind of peace then he shook her up again!

Looking at them both as they stood at the bar chatting, Anna felt her irritation subside. Whatever Mateus's feelings were, he'd always been there for her, and she couldn't help liking Andrew, however annoying he was. She wanted to tell them how grateful she was that they had come to find her; she felt different, relieved, and like it was going to be alright.

She leaned back in her chair and sighed. So much had changed, even in the short time since she had sat on the beach that morning. Only a year ago she'd wanted space to breathe, to get over Adam. Well, she'd certainly accomplished the second of those, but as for the first? Whatever space she'd found had filled up all too quickly with new threats to her self-security, and it seemed she'd spent less time breathing fresh air than she had choking on trauma. Perhaps, after all, equilibrium was an illusion?

Inwardly shaking her head, she pushed the thought away. That sort of soul-searching could wait. For now she was on Tresco, with two staunch friends, and the horror of the past few days was beginning to fade. She would take a few more days, and then report to Martin at HQ and ask for an assignment away from London. Finally the time for that procrastinated move had come. She and Tom would go find another place to explore.

She thought of Damien, wondering how he would take to fatherhood; not well, she judged, with a wry smile. Probably he would continue as normal, punctuating his marital boredom with affairs on the side. She waited for a twinge of unhappiness at the thought, but there was none; the horror of the past few days had thrust him to the back of her mind, and their break-up now seemed insignificant. Perhaps he did care for her, like he said, but in the end it made no difference; he was back with Caroline, and she had to move on.

She remembered how she had once supposed he and Caroline were people users, crashing through the lives of others, set on their own agenda and indifferent to the damage left in their wake. One thing she had learnt with certainty was that people and life were unpredictable, and neither could be controlled in any way. All she could control were her own actions and reactions; whatever changes came her way, she must accept them, adapt, and survive.

And on that thought Anna pushed her chair back and stood up, then strolled over to join Andrew and Mateus.

As she reached them, her attention was caught by the assortment of bottles behind the bar.

"Are you after something stronger?" asked Andrew, suddenly noticing her, and following her eyes.

"Just wondering if they have Hennessy Ellipse," said Anna with a roguish smile.

To her surprise, the man pulling her pint laughed out loud. "We make a pretty good living here, but we're not that lucrative an establishment yet!" he chuckled.

Anna looked at Andrew questioningly, and nudged him as he evaded her eyes.

"Okay, okay," he conceded, continuing in a low voice, "That was about ten thousand pounds worth of stolen cognac."

"What?!" she shrieked. "So you lied! It wasn't yours!"

"I prefer to say I gave the truth a bit of scope for the purposes of that evening." He grinned reminiscently. "C'mon! You were initiated properly!" She snorted, marvelling at his irrepressible attitude. He winked at her. "Onwards, Anna, onwards; this is just the beginning, right?"

He raised his pint. "The Japson Club!" he proclaimed, and clinked her glass.

END

CPSIA information can be obtained
at www.ICGtesting.com
Printed in the USA
LVHW08s1056230718
584604LV00001BA/101/P